THE HARVEST OF DESIRE

He exclaimed, "I swear I would rather do battle with the British than endure this torture again!"

Caro's eyes widened, but she did not speak. Reaching out, Alec pulled her roughly to him, his expression softening somewhat at the touch of her body against his.

"This is all your fault, you know!" he told her in a dangerous voice. "You have tampered with me in ways that should be outlawed! I vow that I would have done myself a favor if I had left you beneath that tree, you vixen! I am no fool, madame! I knew you were dangerous stuff . . . but by then it was too late!"

CAROLINE

SET IN THE POST-REVOLUTIONARY AMERICA OF THE 1780's—A STORMY NOVEL OF WILD INNOCENCE AND RAGING PASSIONS!

Caroline

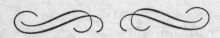

Cynthia Challed Wright

BALLANTINE BOOKS • NEW YORK

To Rick—who never doubted

Library of Congress Catalog Card Number: 77-6200

ISBN 0-345-27323-0

Manufactured in the United States of America

First Edition: December 1977

Chapter One

ONE COULD HARDLY IMAGINE A MORE PERFECT October day, for the autumn of 1783 had painted the
Connecticut landscape in her most glorious colors. The
low mountains were a riot of flaming oranges, reds,
and yellows which contrasted sharply with the clear
azure of the sky. The air had a clean chill to it, and
Alexandre Beauvisage, winding his way between the
trees astride a handsome stallion, felt very good indeed. He had been brimming with a rich euphoria for
over a month now—ever since the final Peace Treaty
had been signed in Paris. The last eight years of war
had been long—at times unbearably so—but victory
made all the bloodshed and tragedy seem worthwhile.
The cost of freedom had been high, but that shining
prize belonged to America at last.

Granted, it had been two years since the British had
laid down their arms to General Washington at Yorktown. Only the most sporadic fighting had occurred
since then, and the majority of the American soldiers
had been able to go home to their families long ago.

Alec grimaced when he thought back over his own
life during the past two years. All through the Revolution he had only occasionally played the part of
soldier; his had been a unique role tailored especially
to his talents and background. He had been a mixture
of spy and scout, given the trickiest and usually the

1

most dangerous assignments. After Yorktown, Alec had been able to return to his home and business at intervals, but just as he would settle back into a normal pattern of life his services would be needed again.

"We simply can't trust anyone else to carry off this plan without being detected, Beauvisage. You are a master!" the officer in charge would declare. Alec had to admit that despite the terrible aspects of war, there was a certain thrill in the role he played. He had roamed the swamps of South Carolina with Frances Marion, captained a sleek privateer, and drunk cognac with Washington and Lafayette on the banks of the Hudson. He had been required to put his ingenuity and intelligence to full use, and the constant danger had been stimulating. Perhaps the return to full-time everyday life would prove boring?

A bright patch of color beneath a tree at the side of the trail caught Alec's attention, rousing him from his reverie. Gently he brought his horse, Ivan, to a stop and dismounted, walking back to pick up the bundle. It appeared to be a packet of garments drawn hastily together inside a piece of bottle-green silk. Alec was puzzled by the good condition of the material; it was clean and new-looking. He squatted down among the masses of crisp, dry leaves, preparing to open the bundle, when a low, soft moan came from the trees to his left. Alec's head jerked up, every feature on his handsome face instantly becoming alert. Springing to his feet, he dropped the bundle and was off as lightly as a cat in the direction of the noise. In a moment he had spotted its source—a small form lying at the foot of an oak tree about twenty-five feet away. Cautiously, Alec drew a pistol from his belt and moved forward. From a distance, he perceived the figure to be that of a young boy, clad in ill-fitting gray breeches, a loose white work smock, and a green tricorn hat that seemed to cover his entire head. Alec drew alongside the boy and, seeing that both hands were lying limp at his sides, he replaced his pistol and knelt down beside the still form. His dark brows came together over puzzled eyes as he peered closer at two suspicious shapes outlined against the loose shirt. Tentatively, Alec placed a hand over one of the bulges, which proved beyond a doubt to be a beautifully formed, uncorseted breast.

"What the hell?" he muttered in bewilderment while pulling the green hat away. Nearly three feet of lustrous honey-colored hair spilled out over the rusty leaves and Alec let out a low whistle as he bent over the girl's face. She looked little more than eighteen, and for a moment he felt that he must be dreaming. The girl had the face of a winsome angel. Her eyes appeared large, even while closed, and were fringed by long, silky lashes which brushed her creamy skin. Alec's gaze took in her tiny nose, and came to rest on the most appealing lips he had ever seen. Almost inaudibly, he murmured, "Sweet . . ." as he gently raised her head and cradled it in his arms. Alec ran a brown finger over her cheek and through one silky curl, then, almost instinctively, he tipped her little chin up with his forefinger and covered her mouth with his own. As he slipped his tongue between her lips, tasting their sweetness, he felt them move gently in response. With a start he drew back, thinking, Who do you think you are, Beauvisage—a damned Prince Charming? Involuntarily, his mouth twisted in a smile of cynical amusement. What do you suppose I've got myself into this time? he wondered, and grinned in spite of himself.

The girl felt as if she was gliding down to earth from a great height, and seemed to touch ground with only the smallest jolt. She opened her eyes slowly and looked up into a most remarkable face. It was brown and lean, framed by shining raven-black hair that was drawn casually back and tied at the neck with a piece

3

of leather. He was bearded, but it failed to disguise his charming half-smile or the contrast of his flashing white teeth with tanned skin. Above a straight nose sparkled eyes of an amazing, intense turquoise color which held her own almost against her will. As she became more fully conscious she realized that she felt no fear, although he held her in his arms and his muscles were hard against her cheek.

Alec, for his part, found himself looking into warm caramel-brown eyes flecked with gold. The girl was simply exquisite!

"M'lady, I would be extremely gratified if you could attempt to explain your presence here. I must confess to a curiosity that grows stronger by the minute!"

As the girl struggled to sit up, Alec braced her with his arm. Suddenly, a throbbing pain spread across the right side of her head; she raised her hand gingerly to touch what proved to be a large lump. Alec gently parted her glossy hair and looked closely at the swollen area. His forehead creased at the sight of the nasty bump and several patches of dried blood.

"Tell me now, what has happened here? What is your name, child, and where do you come from?" His deep voice had grown sharp with concern.

The girl covered her eyes as though collecting her thoughts. Then, slowly, she drew her hand away and looked at Alec, her eyes brimming with sudden tears.

"Oh, sir—I don't seem to be able to remember! I cannot recall a thing—not even my own name!"

Several minutes of questioning brought Alec no closer to the truth. He surmised that the girl had probably been riding and caught her head on a low-hanging branch. Perhaps something had frightened the horse, causing her to lose control. At any rate, the steed was gone, and Alec was left with a memoryless injured woman-child dressed in boy's clothing.

He had propped her up against a tree trunk and

4

was pacing back and forth through the dry leaves. The girl was alternately investigating the clothes in the green silk bundle and watching Alec stride to and fro. He moved with a natural grace and suppressed strength that were easy to admire. His fawn-colored breeches were close-fitting and showed the play of muscles in his lean thighs with each step he took. Umber leather boots, softly shining, rose to his knees, and a linen shirt split down the front to reveal a well-muscled chest, covered with softly curling black hair.

Suddenly the girl's soft voice broke the rhythm of Alec's rustling stride through the leaves.

"Sir, you wouldn't be a pirate by any chance, would you? Perhaps you're ashore to bury your treasure . . . ?"

One black brow shot up, then he threw back his head and laughed with pure delight.

"Why do you ask that, pray tell?"

"Well . . . you look the way I suppose pirates must look. Quite swashbuckling and adventurous, really. Rather unscrupulous, too." She found him grinning at her and blushed furiously. "I'm sorry about that last. It certainly wasn't a very nice thing to say, was it?"

Alec strolled over to drop down beside her and clasped one soft hand between his strong brown ones.

"Think nothing of it, *chérie*. I admire your candor, and, to be honest, I must confess that I laugh in part because you hit quite near the truth. Actually, my father was indeed a pirate—a French buccaneer of the first water. If the war had not intervened, perhaps I would have followed in his footsteps!" Alec's smile held a hint of mockery, but there was warmth in his turquoise eyes. They darkened, however, as the problem at hand returned to his thoughts. Gesturing at the clothes which lay on the piece of green silk, he asked:

"You don't see anything there that sparks your memory?" He had already been through the bundle himself, but found little that looked informative. There was another simple white smock, one of the loose shirts worn by Colonial men as part of their working attire. It was split a good way down the front to allow for easy doffing, and Alec was having some difficulty keeping his eyes away from the front of the smock the girl was presently wearing. Also inside the bundle were a few items of well-made underclothing, a lacy fichu, and some dainty shoes. Lastly, there was a lovely dress, simple but pretty, the color of buttercups and trimmed in pure white eyelet lace. Inside of it were wrapped a fine china hairbrush, two satin ribbons, and a bar of jasmine-scented soap.

The girl looked up at Alec and shook her head in bewilderment.

"I cannot place a thing. This is all so confusing— and frightening! Sir, what will you do with me?" Her brown eyes were wide and her tiny chin trembled. Alec reached out and gathered her into his arms. Although he was uncomfortably conscious of two ripe breasts pressing firmly against his chest, he managed to restrain himself so that he only stroked her hair in a brotherly fashion.

"Listen, *chérie,* what did you imagine I would do —leave you here alone in the woods? I may look unscrupulous, but I believe that you will find I have a definite streak of decency! You shall come with me back to my home and we'll find out who you are. In the meantime, perhaps you'll recover your memory."

Impulsively, she hugged him, and Alec could smell the sweetness of clover in her rich hair. Her voice was warm with excitement in his ear:

"You would do that for me? How shall I ever thank you?"

Alec could think of a few ways, but feared that none of them would meet with her approval. He could not resist smiling to himself as the girl loosened her grasp on him to look up and ask:

6

"Sir, could you tell me your name? And what shall *mine* be?"

"Ah, yes! Pray forgive me for neglecting to introduce myself. I am known as Alexandre Beauvisage, but you must call me Alec. As for your own name, I think it should be your choice."

A smile lit her face, revealing deep dimples, and she clapped her hands together with delight.

"What fun—being able to choose one's own name! And yours, sir, is wonderful and most fitting. 'Handsome face'!"

Alec colored beneath his beard and bit his lip.

"Yes, unfortunately, that is the meaning. A constant source of embarrassment to me, I assure you."

"But why? Certainly it is perfect for you! It would only prove embarrassing if you were a homely man, I should think!"

Alec relaxed and was chuckling softly when a sudden realization struck him.

"*Chérie*, you must have some education in the French language. You know, that's no small accomplishment for a female, especially one who has grown up during a time of war in a relatively undeveloped country. You must have come from a good family . . ." His voice trailed off and he drew his black brows together in a frown. "Why, I wonder, were you running away?"

"Do you think that is what I was doing?"

"My dear, that is the only reasonable conclusion I can draw from this rather inexpert disguise. Also, you were more than a little off the main road. To be precise, you were miles from the nearest house. I can't imagine what you were planning to do before you had this accident, and I feel certain that you were well on your way to being hopelessly lost." He paused, stroking his beard thoughtfully. "*Chérie,* I can't but think that you were running away in great haste from someone or something. Your belongings were quickly assem-

7

bled . . . and you were taking an escape route to which you could not have given much thought. As a matter of fact, you must have deliberately crossed over the Boston Post Road some miles back."

Alec glanced over at the girl next to him only to find her in perfect profile, staring dreamily into space. He lifted one honey-colored curl from her shoulder and teasingly flicked it across her tilted nose. His voice held a note of ironic amusement.

"Ma petite, you do wonders for a man's ego. I can see that you hold my brilliant conversation in high esteem!"

"Oh—sir—Alec, please to not be offended!" Relief spread across her face at the sight of his flickering smile and twinkling turquoise eyes. "Oh! You are teasing me! I am glad you are not angry, because I was daydreaming for a good reason. My name! To me it is so important, and I hope you'll approve of my choice." She moved closer to him and paused dramatically. "It is . . . Caroline. Don't you think that is the loveliest-sounding name?"

She spoke the syllables with such warmth that to Alec the name Caroline did indeed sound beautiful. His face softened as he regarded this girl who was smiling at him so radiantly in the midst of what should have been a terrible crisis for her. It occurred to him that most young ladies of his acquaintance would probably be carrying on quite hysterically (between fainting spells) if they were in Caroline's position. She was lost, unable to remember anything, and perhaps worst of all, left in the woods with only a hot-blooded rogue to rely on. Alec was just beginning to realize how truly different from other females this one was. Gently, he touched her soft cheek with one suntanned hand and smiled most appealingly.

"I believe that you have chosen the most beautiful name in existence, little Caro."

8

Twilight gathered quickly, and Caroline did not notice the approaching darkness until she felt a chill in the air. She and Alec were both astride the black horse, Ivan, who was patiently making his way through the trees. Caroline sat in front of Alec, who held her securely around her petite waist. His nearness unnerved her, and during all the hours they had been riding she had found it difficult to think—and heaven knew she had plenty to think about! Caroline realized that the discomfort she felt wasn't because Alec repulsed her; instead, it seemed that all her senses were full of him. His arm was strong and her skin seemed to tingle beneath it. She would watch his brown hand holding the reins, and find herself fascinated by its deft movements. She was leaning into his broad chest and his chin brushed the top of her head. She thought he smelled wonderful.

Riding into a clearing, Alec brought Ivan to a standstill and Caroline came back down to earth.

"Well, *chérie,*" he inquired lightly, "how does this strike you as an inn? Ceilings of tree branches and carpets of leaves are the latest fashion, I'm told."

Caroline smiled up at him. "These look like very comfortable accommodations, sir!"

Indeed it was a lovely spot. The trees joined overhead to form a perfect canopy and the blanket of leaves on the ground looked almost plush. Alec swung down from the horse's back and reached up to grasp Caroline around her waist. He lifted her off Ivan and suddenly they were face to face, Alec's hands still resting on her hips. He looked down into her brown-and-gold eyes and saw in them something he could not read. Moving his palms up her back slowly, Alec could feel the hot blood rising in him, and then Ivan pushed his nose against them and whinnied gustily.

Nervously, Caroline laughed and turned to pet the horse's neck.

"Well, Ivan, I suppose you'd like to have the rest of those things off your back, too!"

Alec watched her, taking in with interest the rosey stain which spread up her face and the small pulse beating at the base of her neck.

It was not yet dark when the three of them set off through the trees to find a stream. They didn't have far to go, and while Ivan drank and Caroline washed, Alec went in search of food and firewood. He had good luck, and before long he and Caroline were seated by a cozy fire feasting on dried beef and johnnycake from Alec's saddlebags, nuts, berries, and sweet water. They drank from a small wooden cup which Alec produced, explaining that he had carved it in camp early in the war and still carried it with him in his pack. After they finished eating, Alec leaned back against a tree to smoke a thin brown cheroot. Caroline sat nearer the fire, and as they talked he watched her face, which was framed by molten-gold firelight. Her hair spilling over her shoulders, she looked poignantly young and vulnerable in her voluminous shirt.

"Will you tell me about my future?" she asked. "Where are we going? And what will you do with me after we get there?"

Alec smiled behind the thin curls of smoke which drifted up and dissolved into the darkness.

"Ah, yes, infant. I imagine your head must be full of questions! To begin with, we are going to Philadelphia, where I live. I believe that after we arrive I shall install you at my parents' home. It wouldn't help you at all socially to be living at my house! As it is, if I were any sort of gentleman at all I'd marry you as soon as we encounter a parson."

Caroline's eyes were wide with astonishment.

"Marry me! Whatever for?"

"Why, to make an honest woman out of you, my dear. Moral codes these days don't have clauses allowing men and women to spend the night together

10

unchaperoned—no matter how innocent the circumstances may be. And in our case, I have a feeling we'll be alone together several nights." He was smiling at her as if the prospect delighted him, and Caroline shifted uneasily. "However, no one needs to know what our circumstances have been before we arrived in Philadelphia. I will find you a maid in New York, if possible, and no one should know that she has not accompanied you on our entire journey—down the Post Road from Hartford. Besides," and he grinned again, looking to Caroline like Satan himself, "I am not a particularly honorable man, especially where women are concerned. Take that as fair warning, *chérie!* Also, I have no intention of ruining both our lives by trapping us into a marriage neither of us wants—just for the sake of propriety. You are young and very beautiful, Caro, and I'm certain that there will be scores of young swains in Philadelphia who will be eager to win your affections. Besides, we must make sure that you are not already married!"

Caroline's eyes had been growing larger with each sentence Alec spoke, but with his last words her mouth dropped open.

"Married! Me? But—but—"

"It is entirely possible, Caro, that you were running away from a husband."

Alec had no doubt that she was old enough, for he had become quite familiar with the curves beneath her smock during their ride on Ivan that day. Her breasts were firm, swelling gently against her shirtfront, and her hips curved in a most attractive way. Alec knew a great deal about women, and there was no doubt in his mind that this Caro was indeed a delightfully fully-grown woman.

Caro—how she liked the way Alec pronounced her new nickname!—sat quietly for a few minutes, her profile pensive in the firelight. Finally, Alec broke the silence.

11

"You look like you're trying to remember something, *chérie*."

"I am." She paused. "You know, I feel as if I know all about myself, but for the moment it all eludes me. It's as though it's there, in my head, but I cannot reach it."

"Or perhaps you don't want to," he offered gently.

"What do you mean?"

"Only that whatever is in your past may be so painful to you that you've buried it—blocked it out—without even realizing it."

Their eyes met, and though she did not speak, Alec knew that she understood what he was saying. Her face was so lovely, and in it he could see bewilderment and fear. In that moment, Alec promised himself that if he should discover her past and her family and find them in some way unsuitable, he would not tell Caro. After all, he reasoned, she must have had good cause to take such risks to get away.

The air was growing colder and Alec moved forward from the shadows to add more wood to the fire. Caro observed him with interest, uneasily aware of his nearness. He turned to look at her, reaching out to grasp one of her hands.

"Are you warm enough? Here, put this on." He wrapped his own heavy blue wool coat around her shoulders. It was a handsome garment with a rich satin lining, wide lapels, and gold buttons. Then Caro found herself leaning back against the tree next to him, his arm around her, her cheek against his chest. A sudden feeling of well-being flooded her, and she began to ask him more questions. At length, the conversation turned to his family, which Alec described with relish.

"My father was really a pirate—I wasn't lying about that. He did a great deal of illegal trading with the colonies during the days when trade with England was so expensive and troublesome. Actually, it was all quite respectable then. Father tells wonderful stories

12

about the rounds of entertainment from the merchants of New York when he would put into port with his cargo. He really led a wild, adventurous life, but I believe he met my mother just in time."

"Where did they meet?" asked Caro, by now completely fascinated. Alec threw back his head and laughed with delight.

"Quite classic circumstances, I assure you! My father captured her ship."

"Her ship!?"

"Yes, she was on board one of the few luxurious passenger vessels of that time, bound from Russia for the colonies to visit her brother and his wife. Father confiscated all the valuables from her ship, foremost among which was my mother!"

"Alec!" Caro exclaimed. He was chuckling in amusement.

"Yes, my dear, I'm afraid the worst happened—for after all, my father was no gentleman. Seems to be a family trait. At any rate, my mother appears to have enjoyed herself immensely, and soon my father had not only returned all the stolen goods, but also married my mother there at sea. She accompanied him on his pirate ship's last voyage to America and they settled down in Philadelphia to live happily ever after. I stand with my four brothers and sisters as proof of that."

Caro looked up to see white teeth flash against his black beard.

"Your father gave up his pirating?"

"Oh, yes—the only voyages he makes now are with my mother to visit their respective families in Russia and France and to inspect some family vineyards they own in the Loire Valley. After my parents married, Father began ship-building, and as the business grew he branched out into several other interests. These days, when I am home, I am his partner in the ships."

"When you are home?"

"I have been quite occupied these last years in the war for independence."

"Oh—of course!" Caro felt something click in her brain, but even though she squeezed her eyes closed, she could not catch it in time.

"Do you remember anything about the war?" Alec queried, looking down at her face.

"Yes, I seem to, though I hadn't thought of it until you said the words. Suddenly now, I can remember it all but rather indistinctly—the deaths, and women all alone, and living with hardships. But I simply cannot see faces in my mind, or recall names."

They were silent for a moment, then Caro, eyes wide with frustration, blurted:

"Alec, I don't even know where we are!"

"That is easily enough answered, infant. We are in Connecticut, nearing its western border and the Hudson River. We will follow that to New York City, and then journey on farther south to Philadelphia."

"But, if you are a man of means, why are you here in the woods with only a horse? Isn't the war over now?"

"Yes, it's over. And, Caro, you mustn't let Ivan hear you speak of him as though he were of no consequence!" He had lowered his voice conspiratorially. "You see, he believes he is absolutely the finest horse ever born—the superior of any man." He paused. "Except me, of course."

"Of course!" Caro giggled, and Ivan peered at them suspiciously from the other side of the fire. Alec squeezed her shoulder and continued:

"To answer your question, I was inspecting a farm I recently acquired in northern Connecticut. As a matter of fact, it was left to me by one of my comrades who died at Yorktown. I am used these days to traveling light. I like to be responsible to only myself; to go at my own pace and to enjoy the woods in autumn

14

before returning to city life. Besides, I have some friends in this area that I enjoy visiting. We'll be staying with some in a few days, and I'm hoping to borrow a horse for you."

"Will we go on horseback all the way to Philadelphia?"

"No, no, *chérie*. My coach will be meeting us in New York."

"I have only one more question. Who will you say I am?"

Alec smiled with satisfaction.

"Actually, it all fits together brilliantly. You, Caro, are the poor orphaned daughter of my friend from the war. Much to my surprise, you came with the farm! You'll be my ward, and it will all be cozy and respectable."

Caro felt her eyelids drooping and she smiled to herself contentedly, snuggling against Alec's broad chest.

"Well," she murmured drowsily, "I suppose I shall have to trust you. . . ."

Chapter Two

THE MORNING WAS DELIGHTFUL, AND TO CARO EVERY breath was redolent of autumn. As she and Alec rode astride the patient Ivan, she could not resist a smile as she remembered the events of the morning. Her mood had been so capricious that Alec seemed constantly to be watching her with one eyebrow cocked. He had smiled at her though, that small charming half-smile that let her know it was all right. And, beneath the cynically raised brow, his eyes twinkled.

It had begun before the sun was fully risen. Caro awoke, feeling completely refreshed, her face against Alec's chest. There was a coarse, heavy blanket covering them both and Caro felt oddly stirred by the warmth of his lean, sinewy body. She could hear his heart beating steadily through his shirt; it was a comforting sound which made her feel instinctively safe and secure. Gingerly, she slipped from under the blanket and sat up. Alec was sound asleep, his left arm thrown across the top of his head. In repose his face and the combination of golden-brown skin and shining raven-black hair were even more handsome than Caro remembered. She was surprised and somehow touched to notice how long his eyelashes were. When he was awake, they were totally obscured by the turquoise eyes.

Caro forced her gaze from Alec's face and stood up. Ivan whinnied softly from across the clearing and tossed his mane. She went to him and stroked the beautiful black head as he nuzzled her neck. Feeling unreasonably happy, Caro giggled in spite of herself,

16

and put her arms around Ivan's neck to hug him. Suddenly, she felt a strong desire for a bath. The air was unusually mild and she remembered the bar of soap inside her green silk bundle. Impulsively, she got it, moving quietly, and also pulled out clean underclothes and the fresh smock. With Ivan by her side, she scampered off toward the stream. Barely concealing herself behind a bush, Caro shed her clothes and plunged into the water, soap in hand. She only had to wade a short distance to find water deep enough to cover her breasts. It was cold, but she felt deliciously invigorated as she began soaping herself briskly. Ivan watched from the bank and she laughed out loud at him.

"Ivan, do I shock you?"

A deep, cynical voice answered her: "My dear, I cannot believe that Ivan is feeling anything but pure pleasure!"

Alec stepped out of the trees, looking sleepy and bemused. Under his bold scrutiny, Caro crossed her hands over her breasts, blushing deeply. She tried to speak, without success.

"Please, *chérie,*" Alec admonished mockingly, "do not let me interrupt you! Actually, I am quite relieved to find you here. When I awoke to discover you and Ivan missing I feared you were both off for parts unknown! It is reassuring to know I did not misjudge you."

He smiled at her warmly and Caro relaxed. Before she knew what she was doing she had sent a splash of water at him and laughingly inquired:

"So, sir, you thought me a thief?"

It was then that the eyebrow cocked for the first time that day.

"*Ma petite,* your modesty is certainly short-lived!" His eyes seemed to penetrate the water, taking in every detail of her body. Caro surprised them both by smiling brightly.

"I am feeling too wonderful today to be bothered

17

with modesty! And now, if you don't mind, I would like to wash my hair. This water is growing uncomfortably chilly."

Alec's eyebrow rose even higher. Tempted though he was to join her, he moved farther downstream. Then he pulled off his own shirt and leaned over the bank to splash his face and chest, and fill his canteen. As he returned to the woods, Caro was bent over, her back to him, scrubbing her sudsy head.

Soon, as she was rinsing the last of the soap away, Ivan appeared on the bank holding a clean towel in his mouth. Caro took it gratefully, laughing softly to herself. After dressing, she wrapped the towel around her long hair and ran barefoot through the leaves back to their camp. As they breakfasted on berries, cornbread, and hot coffee Alec had brewed, Caro brushed her honey hair, letting it dry in the sunlight. Falling in soft curls, it nearly reached her waist. Leaning back on his forearm in the brittle leaves, Alec watched her over his coffee.

"Do you have any idea how beautiful your hair is?"

She looked up in surprise, feeling herself blush again. "Is it?"

"For God's sake, don't be embarrassed! You should be proud of it. Caro, do you know what women do nowadays to their hair? It's hideous—a crime against everything female. They wire it into nests a foot high and smother it in powder. Lord knows how many rodents and birds make their homes in women's coiffures these days." He sat up and leaned toward her, his black brows drawn together in a frown. "Let me tell you right now that I shall never allow you to ruin your hair that way. You may be out of fashion, but you will be the most beautiful woman in Philadelphia."

Something in his serious tone brought out the new-found devil in Caro. She tickled his nose with a lock of her hair and laughed.

"I suppose, Mr. Beauvisage, that you intend to run

my life from now on?" Her eyes were sparkling with mischief as she jumped to her feet. Alec's eyebrow was raised again and he rose leisurely to stand before her. One side of his mouth curved up; Caro stared back at him boldly.

"My dear," Alec said slowly, "I am not at all sure that a spanking might not be in order here. However, I fear you are past the age for that. Besides, the alternative seems much more appealing."

And then she was crushed in his arms and he tipped her chin up, his turquoise eyes piercing. "Yes, Caro, I intend to run your life from now on. And I flatter myself that you shall enjoy it." His mouth was on hers then, firm, compelling, and searching. As his tongue parted her lips, Caro felt a shivering sensation that spread over her entire body. Her heart was pounding wildly and she was shocked to find herself kissing him back, her lips warm and moist and slowly demanding. Then his mouth was on her neck, his beard soft yet ticklish, and her skin burned beneath his lips. His face was in her hair as he inhaled its heady scent, and kissed the base of her silky neck and the soft, sweet, first curve of her breast. Gasping, Caro could not imagine what had happened to her body, for every nerve was exploding under his ardent touch.

Alec reached to the neckline of her smock, intending to tear the entire garment away. His lips found the fragrant valley between her breasts and then he felt her heart, racing more quickly than he would have believed possible.

Suddenly he was aware of what he was doing, and his hardness and insistence subsided along with the tide of his passion. Grasping Caro's arms, he pushed himself away from her and looked into her face. In it, Alec saw open desire: drooping eyelids barely concealing her dilated pupils, cheeks flushed deep rose, and soft lips looking well kissed and luscious. Yet, he also saw an innocence so obvious that it jolted him. Caro

19

was clearly a girl who had discovered the sensuous feelings in her body for the first time. In that moment, Alec knew she was not married to anyone, and had probably never even been kissed before now, let alone by a rake like himself.

He put his hand up, running it through his hair and letting out a low whistle. Caro sat down hard in the leaves and put her hands up to her burning cheeks.

"Oh dear," she murmured, and Alec was amazed to see her eyes pool with luminous tears. Quickly he squatted down next to her and touched her hot cheek with his brown hand. When he spoke, it was with a gentleness she had never heard before.

"Little Caro, please forgive me. I told you I was no gentleman—you should have slapped me at once!" As her blush deepened, Alec realized how shocked she must have been by her own body's response. He sensed that if she had been able to slap him, she would have. "Look," he smiled, "I promise to *try* to behave properly. I really am not in the habit of raping young virgins." Caro looked up at this, but said nothing. "Can we be friends again, *chérie?* Would you like to slap me?"

He was grinning now, and could see the tenseness go out of her face. She raised her chin, laughing in spite of herself, and slapped him right across the cheek as hard as she could. Ruefully, Alec put his hand up to his beard and the eyebrow went back up as he watched her stand up and begin gathering her things together. Ivan slowly walked over to nuzzle his nose against Alec's head.

"Ivan," he murmured thoughtfully, "I have a feeling that life from now on will be extremely interesting. What do you think?"

Ivan threw back his head and whinnied happily, a gesture that reminded Caro of his master.

Now, as they rode along in the October sunshine, Caro felt marvelously happy. She pondered only briefly the physical encounter between her and Alec, for the memory of it made her uncomfortable. She was a little bothered, too, about the changeableness of her feelings. All day she had fluctuated between embarrassed shyness and impulsive mischievousness. Somehow she sensed that Alec was to blame, but wasn't sure why or how. He had been quiet during the morning's ride, but was still charming and congenial when he spoke. Caro decided that to a man of the world like Alec, one little kiss would mean nothing. She only wished she could dismiss it from her mind as easily and completely.

Luckily, the October scenery offered temporary diversion. The mountains surrounding them were actually irregular, mounded hills which seemed to run on into infinity. Chestnut, red and white oak, rock maple, black cherry, ash, and yellow birch trees mingled closely, offering a beautiful variety of colors. Through the morning, Caro had glimpsed dozens of different animals and birds, including a huge moose, a mink, and a flock of heron. The pigeons overhead flew so close together that they virtually blocked out the sun that shone through the trees, and Alec laughingly assured her that there was always an ample supply of food available to them.

Presently, Ivan trotted out of the woods into a sprawling open field, covered with late wild flowers and tall grasses. Immediately, Caro noticed the honey-colored, well-built horse, wearing a bridle and saddle, that stood grazing in the middle of the meadow. Alec whistled softly and murmured:

"What have we here? Am I to believe that God really does answer prayers?"

Ivan lost no time in letting out a joyful whinny of greeting while closing the distance between them and the other horse. The mare looked up from her meal as they approached and neighed with pure delight. Obviously, she only had eyes for Caro, and it was readily

21

apparent to Alec that this was the missing horse. Her expressive brown eyes were full of recognition, and she nuzzled against Caro affectionately.

"Alec, I am certain that I know this horse!"

"Yes, and I am certain that this horse knows you, *chérie*," he smiled ironically, swinging himself down from Ivan's back to check the other animal for injury.

"She seems fine. Something must have spooked her at the time of your fall and she probably lost her way."

Caro decided to call the mare Molly and Alec privately wondered how close that was to her actual name. Meanwhile, Ivan seemed smitten and was openly attempting to woo Molly. However she, womanlike, played hard to get and Alec and Caro could not resist laughing at the black stallion's antics.

They ate lunch there in the meadow while the horses frolicked in the grass. Alec secured Caro's things to Molly's saddle, then helped her up.

That afternoon they covered a great distance, but Caro missed Alec's arms around her. She missed his familiar, masculine scent, and she missed watching the play of his strong, lean hand on the reins. At the same time, being in control of her own horse made her more mischievous than ever. Every time they reached a straight length of trail she gave Molly her head and the two of them would disappear from Alec's view. More than once, Caro circled Molly back through the trees to surprise him. At first, Alec was tolerant and amused by these antics, then he grew irritated. But, by the end of the afternoon he found himself letting Ivan charge along with Molly. Caro's eyes would flash with excitement and her cheeks colored as they raced side by side.

The sun was low behind the trees, shading the woods with pink and orange, when Alec caught up to Molly and signaled for Caro to stop. She followed him into a clearing, watching as he dismounted.

"What are you doing?"

Alec was smiling like an affectionate father dealing with a wayward child.

"I hate to put an end to your playtime, infant, but it's nearly dark and I am hungry. And I daresay that your horse is the most tired of us all. I don't wonder that she tried to elude you yesterday!"

Caro hopped down beside him, her face burning. In her outrage, the teasing note in Alec's voice was lost on her. Suddenly she felt wretched—like a spoiled brat—and she was horrified to hear the words that spilled from her mouth:

"That is an abominable thing to say! Just because I have been trying to enjoy myself and have some fun with Molly there is no reason for you to scold me! All day long you have been raising that horrid eyebrow at me and giving me disapproving looks. Well, I truly resent your attitude, sir, and I am beginning to believe that you are nothing but a stodgy, boring, ill-tempered *old* man!"

By this time, Caro was breathing hard, her eyes sparkling first with anger and then with tears. She had her little hands clenched as if to strike him, and Alec offered helpfully:

"Would you care to hit me again? I can take it, you know. I'm in wonderful shape for a man my age." He smiled at her so winningly that Caro felt all her anger melt away. The tears stung her eyes and she blinked them back furiously. Alec was making a determined effort not to show his amusement, which he knew would only humiliate her further. Indeed, all during her heated speech, it had taken great self-control for him to keep from laughing out loud. Now, to save Caro from the embarrassment of showing him her tears, Alec reached out and folded her into his arms. She wept quietly against his warm chest, loving the texture of the muslin shirt he wore, and immediately felt better. Alec tipped her chin up to smile into her shining eyes.

23

"It's all right, you know. I think I understand you better than you believe, Caro."

"You do?"

"I have an idea that you have been doing and saying things today that you've longed to do and say for years. And, although I hate to admit it, your antics have proven to be a refreshing change."

"Change from what?"

Alec loosened himself from her grasp and casually began to unsaddle Ivan as he talked: "You have no idea what the women are like that I know. Spontaneity and naturalness are dead—now replaced by all the proper virtues. Females have become laughably predictable, for each lives in mortal fear of doing something different!" He grinned at her, showing white teeth, and shrugged his shoulders. "Believe me, society is exceedingly tedious. I suppose that's why I spend so little time in it."

Caro smiled back at him, and relaxed now, began to unsaddle Molly, humming under her breath.

Alec shot four plump pigeons for dinner and Caro gathered blueberries and cranberries in her tricorn hat. They roasted the pigeons on a spit and Caro thought food had never smelled so appetizing. Darkness had fallen quickly, and except for her acute hunger, Caro felt strangely at peace. She watched Alec turn the spit, which he had built skillfully out of fallen tree branches. When the pigeons were done, Caro ate her portion greedily with her hands, trying to ignore Alec's amused gaze. Finally she burst out:

"Do you always have to look at me as though I were some hugely funny joke?" She tried to sound stern, but her brown eyes were twinkling. Alec put his head back and laughed out loud.

"*Chérie,* I wouldn't say you are a joke to me, but rather an enjoyment. It has been a long time since I've seen a girl with your looks behave just as she pleases. That is, outside of my own family."

Caro waited until she had finished her meat before asking Alec what he meant. Stretching full out in the leaves, he crossed his arms behind his head and chuckled softly to himself.

"Of course, you'll meet them all soon enough, but I suppose it's only fair to warn you. Not that they're bad people, or mean, but just a trifle crazy!"

"Like you?" Caro inquired innocently.

"Ha! *Touché, ma petite!* Yes, like me. Perhaps it's all that French and Russian blood mixed together, but I can't help feeling it's all mainly due to the combination of Maman and Father. I guess that when I told you the story of my parents I neglected to describe their four other offspring. I have one older sister, Danielle, who seems to be the only sane person in the family—a quality which has served to rather set her apart, I'm afraid. Then there is Nicholai, who is twenty-two and full of the devil. He has been cutting a wide swath through Philadelphia since the war ended, breaking hearts at every turn." Alec grinned with affection. "Natalya is only seventeen, and just returned from two years of schooling in France. I have a room for her at my house that she uses when my parents are away. She seems to prefer staying with me to Danielle's house, and I can hardly blame her! You'll like her, Caro, she's a lot like you—guileless, emotional, and in love with life.

"Katya is the baby. I believe she was eight her last birthday. She was quite a surprise for everyone, for Maman was well past forty at the time of her birth. She's a delightful child, though, and quite precocious due to her extensive travels. Usually she accompanies my parents wherever they go, and speaks fluent Russian and French."

"All of you have Russian names except for Danielle!"

"Yes—she is named for my father's mother who is still alive. Believe it or not, she is eighty and just this year came over from France with Natalya to live in Philadelphia. She has her own little house and is completely independent. A remarkable woman!

"It was Maman's idea to name Danielle for her, but after that she felt it was only fair to use Russian first names since our surname is so obviously French. And believe me, we grew up strongly influenced by both cultures. I can't help feeling that only in America could a family like ours live so happily."

Caro smiled dreamily. "Oh, Alec, it all sounds so wonderful. I only hope they'll like me. Are you certain your parents won't mind my living with them? We really must find my own family soon, for I hate to impose on yours this way. And I wonder . . . I wonder where I came from, and if my home was as happy as yours is?"

Alec propped himself up on his forearm and studied her intently, his black brows drawn together.

"Caro, you mustn't be concerned about imposing on my family. My mother could have invented both maternal instinct and hospitality, she is so well endowed with both. I know my family will love you and in no time at all you will be one of them. I want you to leave your past and the people in it to me. Don't doubt that I shall discover where you came from, nor that I shall take care of you in the meantime. Do we understand one another?"

Caro's golden-brown eyes were wide and serious.

"All right, Alec. Anyhow, I don't seem to have much choice, for my fate appears already to be in your hands." She ventured a small smile, unaware of how seductive her innocence was. "Didn't you inform me earlier that you intend to run my life from now on?"

Chapter Three

ANGRY GRAY CLOUDS SCUDDED ACROSS THE SKY AS
Alec broke camp the next morning. The wind was bitterly cold, whipping brown leaves up into his face, and
the woods looked dark and desolate.

"For God's sake, Caro, hurry up!"

Her cheeks bright in the cold air, Caro was hastily
braiding her hair. "You needn't bark at me! I'm going
as fast as I can!"

She scrambled up, tucking her braids beneath her
tricorn hat. Alec was saddling Molly, and Caro
wrapped up her green bundle to tie on the side. Then,
just as she was about to hop onto Molly's back, Alec
grasped her arm and she turned to find him holding
out his coat.

"Here," he said curtly, "put this on. It's going to be
colder than hell today."

Caro let him help her into it, and couldn't repress a
giggle when she saw that it reached her ankles, and
her hands were lost under the gold-braided cuffs.
Alec's face softened, and Caro perceived a tiny twitch
of his lips behind the black beard. Seizing the opportunity, she laid her hand on his arm.

"Please, Alec, don't be angry with me today. It already looks like it will be a long, cold ride and I shall
be miserable if you are scowling at me all day."

Alec looked down at the little face gazing up at him

27

so earnestly. Damned if she didn't look ridiculous, her forehead covered by the large hat, her body swimming in his heavy blue coat. Without thinking, he reached inside the coat and put his hands on the warm curves of her hips, as if to reassure himself they were still there.

"All right, infant, you win." He smiled ironically. "And I wasn't really mad at you, but at this weather. We've got to try like hell to beat the storm; thank God we'll have a roof over our heads tonight."

His brown fingers were fastening the heavy buttons now, and then he lifted her effortlessly onto Molly's back. Caro hitched the coat up so she could sit astride, then looked down into Alec's gleaming turquoise eyes.

"One more thing, Caro," he admonished. "No games today! The first time you and that horse start cavorting around you'll be off her back and across my knee so fast your head will spin. Understood?"

Caro beamed as she gave him a mock salute. "Understood, sir!"

They were riding into the biting wind when Alec thought to himself that he'd be lucky to make it through the day without contracting pneumonia—especially if the storm broke before they reached the Wallingham farm. He was wearing his buckskins, thanking God that he had had the foresight to bring them along. Alec frowned again to himself as he remembered the way he had spoken to Caro that morning and the bewildered look on her face. Damn the chit—was it possible that she was so innocent at her age that she was unaware of the effect she was having on him? Where had she come from? A convent? He could feel his blood rising all over again when he remembered last night.

She had flirted with him so artlessly that he was perplexed by it all. And, if that wasn't bad enough, she had given him the most beguiling smile when she announced she was sleepy, and brought the blanket roll over to him as if it were the most natural thing in the world. Her skin had a beautiful apricot tint in the firelight, and had looked just as soft. She had arranged the blanket cozily to cover them both, then had snuggled on her side against the length of his body, her back against his chest. To his further horror, Caro had then reached over to pull his arm around her waist, murmuring:

"That's much better. I'm quite warm now. Good night, Alec . . . sweet dreams."

Her eyes had closed contentedly, and there was a faint smile on her lips—those lips which Alec had decided had surely been created just for kissing. He couldn't remember ever seeing a more tastefully sensuous mouth; tantalizing without being vulgarly full. Her long eyelashes swept across her cheeks and Alec had instinctively bent his face down against her rich, glossy hair. Its clover scent mingled with the heady jasmine fragrance of her soap, intoxicating him. He saw the lovely curve of her neck, and longing to press his lips against it, realized that Caro had placed his hand so that his thumb was barely an inch from her breast. She was asleep, he knew it, and slowly he moved his fingers up to softly touch the curve that swelled beneath her muslin shirt. He found her rosy nipple and felt it stiffen as he caressed her. Caro smiled and cuddled closer to Alec in her sleep. He had been shocked to feel the almost unbearable pressure and heat in his loins, to realize that every nerve in his body actually ached for this girl. Suddenly the total irony and absurdity of his situation struck home and Alec had pulled his hand away from her breast as though it were aflame. He got up, covering her with his half of the blanket, and hunkered down next to the smoldering fire to light a cheroot.

"Fool!" he had chided himself. "To think of the women I have bedded without blinking an eye—the greatest beauties in the colonies swoon at my smile!"

A bitterly mocking smile twisted his mouth. "Here I am, a hardened rogue with nerves of steel, thirty-one years of age, acting like a virgin schoolboy as I try to work up the courage to touch a sleeping girl's breast—through her clothes, no less! Next I'll be breaking out in sweat whenever the chit comes near!"

He had paced through the leaves, swearing to himself while casting poisonous glances at the sleeping Caro. Alec had vowed then that no virgin would be his undoing, deciding that all he needed was to return to Philadelphia where he knew at least two beautiful women who anxiously awaited his return to their beds. "I've just been without a woman too long," he decided angrily. But still he had been unable to sleep, spending the better part of the night smoking and staring broodingly into the dying fire.

Now, as he and Caro rode through the slate-gray morning, Alec glanced worriedly at the threatening clouds overhead. God knew the weather hadn't improved his mood any, and to top things off, his head was pounding from so little sleep and such a great deal of tormented frustration.

Since they hadn't taken time for breakfast, when he spotted a grove of apple trees Alec decided that a quick lunch might be in order. Signaling to Caro to stop, he swung himself off Ivan's back. Caro was only slightly surprised that he didn't come to help her down as she watched him load his gun before she dismounted. Alec went off to look for game while Caro made herself comfortable on the ground, ravenously devouring two juicy apples and half the remaining johnnycake, washing it down with cold water from Alec's canteen. She was feeding Ivan and Molly apples when Alec appeared looking slightly more cheerful, two plump rabbits in hand. Caro couldn't help admiring the way he looked in his buckskins. The leather was soft and supple, clinging to his lithe, well-muscled body, and she thought he looked like a true

30

mountain man. His teeth were white against his beard as he smiled at her.

"Well, at least one problem is solved. We can count on a hearty meal tonight."

Caro watched Alec tie the rabbits across the back of his saddle, then stroll over to pick a few apples from a nearby tree. She came over to give him the remaining johnnycake and water, sitting down beside him as he ate.

"Alec, I just wanted to ask you what you meant when you said that we would have a roof over our heads tonight. My curiosity has been killing me!"

Alec lounged against a tree trunk, talking while he ate, but never seeming to have his mouth full.

"Well, infant, we're going to a farm that belongs to some very old friends of mine. The story is damned sad. The Wallinghams own a fine farm not far from here, close to the Hudson River. We're back on the brink of civilization now! At any rate, they had cattle and sheep and James sweated to make things grow there. How we met is too long a story to go into now —let us just say that the war brought me to their home when I needed help. Elizabeth Wallingham took me in, gave me a bed and food until I was well— even though James was a loyalist, fighting for the British. Years went by that she didn't hear from him, and since I was pretty much a loner during the war and on the move, I checked on her and the children from time to time. I was worried about the consequences for them when the war ended. James finally made it home, just in time for the outcry from all the neighbors that the Tories be banished. Even now it's at a fever pitch and the loyalist families are still moving out—thousands of them. The persecution from us so-called fair-minded Americans has been merciless and totally narrow-minded."

Caro had never seen Alec so serious, or heard such bitterness in his voice.

"The Wallinghams deeded their farm to me before the patriots could take it away from them. All the other loyalists in the Hudson River Valley have lost their farms and all their possessions, as if they were less than human. Of course, I am keeping Wallinghams' farm for him against the day they may be able to return. In the meantime, I look after it when I can, and I plan to install a friend of mine in it soon. We'll stay there tonight and I have an idea we may find some clothes there, too—hopefully a second coat! After tonight we'll be among people again all the way home, for I have a long string of friends between here and Philadelphia."

"Alec, I'm so sorry for the Wallinghams. How did they get away, and where did they go?"

"Well, most of the Tories are going up to Nova Scotia. I hear they're shouting 'Hell or Halifax' from the transports. However, I managed to pull a few strings and get the Wallingham family on board one of our ships bound for France. They can cross the Channel to England after they arrive, where they at least will have some friends and family. If it looks like they'll be staying on indefinitely I will sell their property and send them the money."

"It was wonderful of you to do so much for them!" Caro exclaimed, impressed by his courage and honesty.

Alec shrugged, his eyes opaque. Rising to his feet, he brushed off his pants and held out a hand to her.

"Come on. I don't like the looks of that sky or the idea of riding in a storm."

They rode all afternoon without speaking. Thunder rumbled ominously, echoing through the hills around them, and every now and then a silver branch of lightning would split the black sky. Mercifully, the rain did not come, but the clouds overhead were roiling with their burdens.

The land around them was undergoing subtle changes the closer they got to the Hudson River. The forests of Connecticut altered into the rolling hills and lush woodlands of New York. Caro had still not seen a single house when suddenly they reached the crest of a hill and she found herself gazing down at a quaint stone dwelling nestled in the valley below. There were fields of Indian corn, rye, and buckwheat sloping up the sides of the hills, and near the house was a small apple orchard. Caro saw a stone barn, and next to it was one field covered with pumpkins and other vegetables. Everything was ripe for harvest; the farm, though small, looked cozy and prosperous.

Alec had stopped beside her, his hand shielding his eyes in the cold wind as he gazed at the scene below them. He turned to Caro to speak when suddenly there was a deafening explosion of thunder and lightning all at once, and the clouds burst open. Without a second's hesitation, Alec rode straight into the icy sheets of rain toward the farmhouse. Somehow, Caro followed him, though she couldn't see a thing through the torrent. Minutes later, they were outside the stone barn, the door of which was open several feet, space enough for the horses to pass inside. To Caro, it was heaven, and she was so grateful for the refuge that it was several seconds before she noticed a cow and horse already occupied the barn.

Alec was already off Ivan's back and he came over to help her down. Caro realized then that the heavy wool coat she wore was soaked through. Alec helped her out of the sodden garment, staring openly at her breasts swelling boldly against the clinging wet shirt. With an effort, he dragged his eyes away and put an arm around Caro's shoulders.

"Well, *chérie,* this is the Wallingham farm. Luckily it's the one furthest east at this point in the Hudson River Valley—I doubt we could have gone much farther in that storm."

33

"That's the truth! But Alec, if they are gone why is the barn door open, and why are there animals here?"

He smiled without amusement.

"They came to Philadelphia only a month ago—this is the first time I have been here since then. You see, a large part of my reason for taking that circuitous route through Connecticut was my desire to check on this property. James told me that he had no means of disposing of these animals, and decided to merely leave the barn door ajar so that they might go out to the pasture. Lord only knows what we shall do with them when we leave here. Perhaps Van DerPat will buy them."

Caro was shivering by this time, and Alec hurriedly began to unsaddle their horses and supply them with feed. Soon he and Caro were dashing through the rain to the house; the key was already in Alec's hand and with one deft movement he had the door unlocked and open.

The room they entered was large and sparsely furnished. The floor consisted of huge wooden planks and the ceiling was sturdily beamed. The dominant feature of the room was a magnificent stone hearth laden with fresh logs and rimmed by cast-iron kettles and pots of every size. The mantel, which ran close to the ceiling, was lined with pieces of china and several small porcelain figurines. Caro walked slowly around the room, running her hand over the dusty furniture. There was a worn high-back settle before the fireplace, which was flanked by a tiny cradle and a ladderback armchair with a beautifully embroidered crewel seat. A sturdy gateleg table stood in the middle of the room, surrounded by four brace-back Windsor chairs, while near the large front window there was a graceful spinning wheel, still threaded with flax. There were two hooked rugs on the floor, one patterned with pieces of fruit, the other with autumn flowers. The windows were without curtains except for a short eyelet ruffle across the top. They were deep windows with wide sills which obviously served as seats. The rain pelted the tiny glass panes relentlessly.

"Well, it was thoughtful of James to lay this fire for us," Alec said as he kindled the logs with a tinderbox. Before long they were burning cheerfully and Alec gathered some coals in a tin fire scoop and moved to tend the other hearths in the adjacent rooms. Meanwhile, Caro had positioned herself on the pine settle before the fire and was peeling off her wet boots. The warmth of the blaze felt delicious, and she stretched her legs out, wiggling her toes contentedly. Alec chuckled softly from the doorway.

"You make that simple act look very enjoyable, *chérie!* Wouldn't you like to put on some dry clothes? I see that Elizabeth left behind quite a few things, and I'm certain you're nearly the same size."

Caro hopped up and ran barefoot across the wooden floor, curiously following Alec into the first large bed-chamber. It was dominated by a huge canopy bed, hung with blue and orange crewel drapes. However, Caro ran straight to the wall, giving a cry of delight at the sight of a little alcove bed. It was built right into the wall like a cupboard, and even had little doors to seal it off. Impulsively, Caro climbed the three-step ladder into the bed. Peeping out at Alec, she exclaimed:

"I've never seen anything so cozy! Couldn't we sleep in here?"

One of Alec's black eyebrows shot up.

"*We?* Infant, if I were to share that bed with you there would be little sleeping done! Besides, I'm sure you would be much more comfortable in this big bed. Allow me to play the gentleman and occupy that —ah—closet."

Stung by his sarcasm, Caro raised her chin stubbornly. She could tell by the sudden hardness in Alec's eyes and voice that she had said the wrong thing, but his attitude confused her.

"No! I want this bed! Anyhow, that other one is more your size."

Alec stared at her for only a moment before replying evenly, "Very well. Now won't you come out of there and put on some dry clothes like a good girl? The last thing I need on my hands now is a sick child."

Caro felt tears welling up in her eyes and there was a lump in her throat that made it impossible to swallow. She knew it was not so much what Alec had said, but the tone of his voice that hurt. Why did he keep referring to her as a child, making her feel so stupid and inadequate? She blinked back her tears and climbed out of the bed, suddenly clumsy. There was no doubt that Alec had seen her tears, but he turned away abruptly to show her the wardrobe full of clothes. After he left the room, Caro sank into a wing-back chair next to the window and began to sob wretchedly. The rain drummed ceaselessly against the glass and the room seemed dark, cold, and cheerless. Her bare feet were like ice. She realized now that all the events of the last two days had been made bearable because of Alec. His charm and warmth had chased away her fears, and his stability had given her security. It was obvious that he was a rogue, but that fact had only served to make all that was happening seem an exciting adventure. Yet today he had been different; cool, withdrawn, frowning, and this unfathomable change in him was making her miserable.

Caro cried until she felt better. Finally, she wiped her eyes with her sleeve. Telling herself that tears would solve nothing, she got up halfheartedly to look through the dresses in the wardrobe. Handmade, they were mostly fashioned of wool or muslin in plain colors. However, one dress caught Caro's eye, and she immediately felt sure that its owner must have overlooked it in her haste to pack. It was a lovely gown of sprigged muslin in green and yellow. The neckline was scooped low, trimmed with a narrow frill, and the waist was encircled by a wide sash. Hastily, Caro shed her wet boy's clothing, pulling off the hat as well. She found a plainly made chemise in the bureau, along with other undergarments and some clean white stockings.

As she dressed she felt her mood lighten and by the time she fastened the little hooks down the front of the dress, she was positively ebullient. The mirror over the bureau was hazy, but Caro could see that she looked lovely. Alec had brought her green bundle into the bedroom, and she pulled out the brush and ribbons. There was little she could do with her coif without pins, but she brushed it near the fire until it was dry and glossy, then pulled the hair back from her temples and tied it with the ribbon over the crown of her head. Her cheeks were flushed from her crying, and Caro knew the color made her more attractive. She only regretted that the shoes she'd carried in the packet were damp, forcing her to walk around in the stockings, and that Mrs. Wallingham had not been as amply endowed as she was. The neckline on the gown was cut low, and allowed little room for her breasts. They swelled up behind the ruffled trim, making Caro feel self-conscious. Still, she knew she looked pretty, and was determined to bring Alec out of his black mood.

Chapter Four

THE TANTALIZING AROMA OF ROASTING MEAT FILLED
the room, and there were carrots cooking in a pot over
the fire as well. Alec had discovered them along with
a few other staples, including a full bottle of brandy.
He felt he had never needed a drink so much and
was beginning a second glassful when the bedroom
door opened and Caro hesitantly stepped out.

Alec felt the hot blood pulse in his loins almost immediately. He couldn't believe that she could look so
beautiful. Her honey-gold hair shone bright in the firelight; drawn back from her forehead, it threw her delicate features into sharp relief. The golden sparks in
her brown eyes seemed to challenge him, and her chin
with its tiny cleft was raised. The indistinct lighting
made it impossible to tell if it was defensiveness or
defiance that Alec saw in Caro's face. His eyes raked
her boldly then, lingering on the tempting bare curve
of her bosom, which seemed to be begging for his lips.
Her waist was tiny, set off by the wide sash, and her
ankles and stockinged feet looked ridiculously small.
Swallowing hard, he heard himself say:

"You have no shoes?"

"No. Mine are wet."

"Oh," with an absent nod. He had just made a
decision.

Caro thought she had never seen Alec look so attractive. He also had changed his clothes and now wore a fine white shirt with a cravat knotted expertly at his neck. His bearded face was shadowy in the firelight, but the turquoise eyes seemed to sparkle more than ever. Caro noticed his cheekbones for the first time, and wondered if the chin behind his beard was as finely chiseled as the rest of his face.

They ate dinner quietly, hungrily, but Caro could sense that Alec's mood had mellowed. Although he no longer seemed angry, it was as though he were guarding against softening toward her. His eyes seemed to be on her constantly, but Caro could not read their enigmatic expression.

When they had finished eating Caro went over to sit by the fire and Alec came up behind her with two glasses of brandy.

"Sip this slowly," he told her. "It will keep you warm tonight."

Caro watched as he bent over the fire to light a small square-cut cheroot. The aroma of the cigar filled the room, and she loved it. Alec sat down beside her on the settle, crossing his right ankle over his left knee, and regarded her through half-closed eyes. Caro felt nervous and turned her attention to the glass of brandy. Sipping it warily, she was surprised to feel it burn her mouth then slide down her throat, spreading a delicious glow through her entire body. She beamed at Alec with delight.

"This is wonderful! What is it?"

Alec allowed himself a small smile. "Come now, *ma petite*. Don't tell me you've never tasted brandy?"

Offended by the mocking note in his voice, Caro replied, "Why, I'm sure I haven't! That is, unless I've forgotten."

"Oh, certainly," he drawled, "that must be the answer."

Caro was shocked to see the cynical twist to Alec's mouth. Flustered, she looked away.

"Go on," Alec said curtly. "Drink the brandy."

She obeyed, taking larger sips as she grew used to the delicious fiery sensation. They sat in silence for several minutes, and when Caro finally looked up into Alec's eyes she saw a glow in them much different from the twinkling she had grown used to. His face was shadowed and lawless-looking; his eyes were darker, like glittering sapphires. Caro was feeling flushed and light-headed and she heard herself laugh nervously.

"Alec! Why are you looking at me that way?"

She felt his fingers grasp her arm abruptly, his touch sending a shiver through her that went straight to the place between her legs. Caro was shocked by her instant response and felt a twinge of instinctive panic. Alec did not move, but one brown finger traced a slow trail up the soft inside of her arm, stifling her efforts to breathe.

"Come on, *chérie,*" he said in a low, even voice. "Why don't you drop that façade of innocence? Believe me, you have accomplished your purpose, for at this moment I desire you more than I have desired any female in years. It was a good act, but I am afraid it couldn't last. No woman on earth could be so ridiculously naïve and yet purposely seductive at the same time—and I am no fool. I don't know what your game is, my dear, but for my part, I am ready to surrender —though not unconditionally. You will never win marriage from me, but I shall take care of you and enjoy you for a long time to come. I believe you'll make an exquisite mistress."

The combination of the brandy and Alec's caressing hand had rendered Caro insensible. His words came to her through a fog, making no sense at all. She tried to think as she watched him grind out his cheroot, but then he reached out, grasping her hands, and pulled her to her feet.

"Alec, I—" She felt his mouth come down against

hers, driving all coherent thought from her mind. His arms held her against the length of his body like bands of steel, while his tongue found its way inside her mouth and explored. Then his lips brushed her neck and he murmured, "God, your hair is glorious!" Caro was flooded with hot waves of desire, conscious of nothing except Alec's mouth searing her skin and the warm tingling between her thighs. She barely felt him pick her up and carry her to the bedroom; the brandy had done well its work of destroying her inhibitions, and the hungry way she responded to him dispelled any lingering doubts Alec might have held about Caro's true nature. She gave him no resistance at all when he quickly unhooked her dress.

"This gown was an excellent choice, my love. It told me all I needed to know about you!" Alec didn't see the confusion in Caro's eyes, which lasted only until he began kissing the soft curve of her shoulder. His mouth never left her body as he undressed her. She felt his beard against her breasts and then his tongue, and the new sensations it evoked made her shudder. She hesitantly ran her hands through his shining raven hair as his lips traced a fiery pattern along the satiny surface of her abdomen until they reached her navel, then Caro felt him on top of her, his hard chest covered with crisp black hair brushing her flaming taut nipples. When she opened her eyes, Alec saw a desire in them to match his, and he kissed her demandingly, bruising her tender mouth.

Parting her slim legs with his knee, Alec slid his hands down to caress her softly, then more insistently until Caro moaned aloud and Alec could wait no longer to possess her. He shifted and thrust his hardness deep inside her, surprised by the resistance he felt. Caro's eyes were suddenly wide, blazing with fear and confusion. She opened her mouth as if to scream, but Alec silenced her with his own lips and gentle movement. Then he felt her arms go eagerly around

41

his neck as her body arched to meet his, her resistance torn away with a firm thrust. Their motions were rhythmically united as they rocked faster and faster with their building pleasure. She began to shudder at the same moment of his own release, and their cries echoed as one in the softly lit room. The violence of Alec's climax surprised him, as did the deep feeling of well-being that flooded him afterward as he nibbled softly on Caro's earlobe. For a moment he couldn't move, then slowly he lifted himself off Caro. She lay totally still for a full minute before opening her eyes. They were filled with an unmistakable terror. Alec propped himself on an elbow to touch her cheek with his free hand. The flashing grin Caro had grown to love was back, but at such cost!

"Ah, love, there's nothing to be afraid of! You were wonderful. As a matter of fact, I'm tempted to believe you're a witch and have cast a spell over me, for I am at a loss to recall an experience in my past quite so remarkable."

Caro began to tremble, dry-eyed, covering her breasts with her hands. Her face was white, all her passion replaced by fear and shock. Alec's grin faded and he sat up, thrusting aside the drapes around the bed to let in more firelight. He turned back to look at Caro, and then he saw the dark stain spreading beneath her thighs. Black brows met over his eyes as he stared in disbelief.

"Oh my God, Caro."

She began to move at last, shrinking back into the corner of the bed, still dry-eyed, cowering like a wounded animal. Her hair fell all around her in a golden cloud, veiling her nakedness.

Muttering "Oh, *Jesus*," Alec quickly pulled on his breeches and strode to the bureau. He found a long bedgown almost immediately, and went to Caro, lifting her arms and pulling it over her head. He swept her hair out gently, smoothing it back from her face and buttoning up the high ruffled neck of the garment. Caro only stared at him, expressionlessly. Alec bent and lifted her in his arms, carrying her out to the parlor to place her before the fire. He quickly produced a plump quilt and tucked it around her legs, then poured a small amount of brandy in a glass and held it to her lips.

"I know you must hate this stuff now, but maybe it will bring you out of that trance. Please try and drink a little, Caro."

She obeyed him mechanically, and the liquor had the desired effect. Caro sank back against the settle, covering her face with her hands.

"Oh, Alec," she choked, "what did I do?"

It was a great relief for him to hear her speak, and he sat down beside her, gathering her into his arms.

"Not you, infant. It was all my fault. What a fool I have been! God, I could beat myself for being so pigheaded! I promise you, Caro, when you feel better I will let you wear my boot with a brick in the toe and you may kick me as hard as you like."

Her head was against his bare chest and she giggled softly.

"It is a tempting suggestion, Alec, but I fear it would do no more good than that slap yesterday."

Encouraged, he tipped her chin up with his forefinger and stared into her eyes.

"Caro, I was very wrong tonight. Nothing can change what I did to you, and I'll not ask you to forgive me. But, I think if we are going to travel together it is time we laid our cards on the table. I'll let you inside my mind now and I expect you to do the same. My mistake with you, little one, was allowing myself to judge you tonight by the same standards I've used to judge every other female I've known. I had slowly come to realize how different you were, but my desire to have you gave me an excuse to fall into the old trap. Actually," he smiled ruefully, "I suppose you were the one who got trapped."

Caro sat up, moving away from his chest. The warmth of his bare skin and the mat of black hair coupled with the aroma of cigar smoke and brandy that clung to him to stir her senses. She couldn't think clearly and was ashamed of her feelings now that she knew what they had led her to. The memory of what had happened between her and Alec had a dreamlike quality; only the vague burning pain between her thighs reminded her that it had been all too real. Now Caro curled into the opposite corner of the settle, wrapping the quilt more tightly against her body as if for protection. She managed a small smile, for the expression on Alec's face made her feel sorry for him.

"Please don't look at me like that, Alec!"

"Christ, Caro, I can't help it! Do you know that you are the first virgin I have ever bedded? And my tactics—I feel like I've molested a child or some other such reprehensible thing. There is just no excuse for my behavior. I'll be damned if I haven't been acting like a dolt since I first saw you. If only I could figure out why you have this power to bring out the worst in me!" Alec brought his fist down hard on the arm of the settle. "I've known scores of women in my life and have always prided myself on my great self-control. Believe me, Caro, there's good reason why I've never made love to a virgin—that sort of involvement can get very sticky. I—" Then he stopped, closing his mouth and scowling as though sorry he had shown her so much of himself. Caro leaned forward, laying her hand on his brown arm, then withdrawing it as if she'd been burned.

"Please, Alec, don't blame yourself. It's much my own fault. But you must believe me when I tell you that I didn't know"—she blushed—"I didn't know what could happen. The cards I have to show are these: I am what I seem, no more and no less. I may not remember my past, but some things I am sure of. I know I never drank brandy, or learned to play these games you spoke of earlier. And . . ." her voice grew soft and she dropped her eyes, "I'm sure I've never known what a man and woman do together."

Alec looked pained, but then his eyes began to twinkle and he turned a smile on her that melted her heart.

"Caro, you'll probably hate me for this, but I must say it. I can't imagine where you came from, but if you grew up in a convent it is fortunate that you ran away, for you certainly do not have the makings of a nun!"

Caro's face burned so that she was sure she must be crimson. Alec only laughed, his white teeth flashing in the shadows.

"You know, you're especially lovely when you blush that way. And don't worry that I think badly of you, *ma petite,* for I believe that you must be quite the most remarkable female I have ever known. I only wish the circumstances were different. As it is, I think it's probably best—for you anyway—and who knows? maybe for me, too—if we try to forget tonight ever happened. You have a wonderful future ahead of you in Philadelphia and I shan't attempt to tarnish your perfection any more than I already have. You're certain to meet some nice boy who will never know you're not a virgin. Lord knows I envy him!"

Alec reached out to touch her hot cheek with one brown hand. Slowly he leaned forward and kissed her gently, tasting the sweetness of her lips. He drew back slightly then, raising one black brow regretfully.

"So, Caro, I'll make you a vow, because only for you could I attempt to be so honorable." Alec's voice mocked the seriousness of his words. "I'll not touch you or kiss you again. I'll do my damnedest to become a model of propriety until we reach Philadelphia and

I deliver you into the protection of my mother. She'll keep you safe from cads like me."

Disappointment involuntarily welled up in Caro, though she tried to fight it down. Alec moved away, the laughter dying out in his eyes as he leaned back and stared into the dwindling flames. Neither of them could have realized at that moment how much they would each come to regret that honorable vow of Alec's.

He helped her up then and took her into bed. Caro crawled inside her little alcove and Alec tucked the quilts around her. Turning her golden-brown eyes on him, she murmured:

"Alec, I just want to tell you—you haven't been a dolt at all. If I have seen only your worst side the last two days, I am certainly anxious to see you at your best!"

Amused, he replied drily, "Well, that's very generous of you, my dear. I should tell you, though, that you can aid me in my monkish cause by wearing a fichu or modesty piece with Elizabeth's dresses if they all—ah—enhance your charms the way the one tonight did. I must confess that my task was much easier when you were dressed as a boy!"

He grinned at her then, looking like a devil in the darkness.

"You have a beautiful body, Caro. Really magnificent!"

"Alec!"

"Good night, *chérie*."

It was a strange night, and Caro drifted in and out of sleep. Tossing and turning, she dreamed of people who had no faces, as the wind drove the rain relentlessly against the little house. At one point it began to hail and Caro sat up straight in bed, her heart pounding in terror. Peeping out of her alcove, she could see that the big bed was empty, its drapes still pulled back.

Her feeling of isolation was unreasoning and frightening, and she climbed down the little ladder, knowing only that she had to be certain that Alec was there somewhere. Hailstones clattered against the windowpanes and the floor was cold against her bare feet as Caro crept across the dark room and pushed the door open to peer into the parlor. The fire there was much brighter and Alec was standing in front of it, wide awake, smoking, and staring into the flames. He was wearing his shirt again, though it was unbuttoned, and his soft high boots. Caro had come to recognize that looking into fires with fathomless eyes was a habit of Alec's. He seemed to lose himself in the flames, as though he saw answers or reasons there. She watched him for a long time, and if he was aware of her presence he never gave a sign. Caro wondered what was in his mind, and was surprised at the strength of her desire to know him. She could sense, though, that it was his intention to keep himself closed off, revealing only a fraction of the whole. Although she was unsure in her conscious mind what they had done together that night, Caro remembered meeting his eyes at one point, and she was certain that they had been completely open, mirroring Alec's soul. Now, as she looked at him, tall and broad and hard, Caro felt a rush of warm contentment. Quietly, she crept back to her bed and fell instantly into a deep, dreamless sleep.

Chapter Five

"ROUSE YOURSELF, SLEEPYHEAD! IF YOU BELIEVE THAT I will do all the woman's work here while you lie abed all day, you are sadly mistaken!"

Caro's face was buried deep in her feather pillow, and her body was drawn up into a ball so that her bottom was high in the air beneath the quilts. Alec's voice barely impinged on her blissful slumber, but when he tore back the covers and brought the palm of his hand down on her round derrière she came back to earth with a squeal. Irritably opening one oval eye, she could see him sideways, his turquoise eyes sparkling with amusement. One black brow moved in a now familiar quirk as he said drily:

"M'lady, will you rouse yourself willingly, or must I carry you from that bed like a sack of potatoes? I imagine the sight of you upside down in that bedgown would be extremely—ah—interesting!"

Caro lifted the corner of her mouth to mutter darkly, "Beast," then turned her face from her pillow with a sigh. "Are you always in the habit of getting up in the middle of the night?"

"My dear, I'm afraid the darkness outside is rather misleading. Actually, it's nearly noon and you are showing yourself to be a regular dormouse."

Caro's head came up with a jerk.

"Noon! You must be joking!"

When she sat up, Alec could see the soft round outline of her breasts against her flannel gown, and he thought how warm her skin would be after sleep. He suddenly turned away toward the door.

"On the contrary, Caro, I couldn't be more serious. Hurry and dress before your breakfast goes cold."

She stared after him in puzzlement as the door closed, then scrambled down the ladder to look outside. The wind had subsided, but the rain still fell steadily and the sky was a dark, steely gray behind the black clouds. Shivering, Caro washed hastily with the cold water Alec had apparently put in the pitcher on the bureau. She dressed in a heavy chocolate-colored gown, wrapping the fichu from her bundle around her shoulders and fastening it at her bodice with a gold pin from Elizabeth's drawer. Her shoes were dry now, thankfully, and she slipped them on over borrowed brown stockings. She was standing in front of the mirror, brushing out her burnished curls when the door opened and Alec appeared.

"Well," he commented, "I'm glad to see you are up and about. I wouldn't want to catch you in a compromising situation!" There was laughter dancing in his eyes as he paused to rub his bearded jaw thoughtfully. "However, on the other hand . . ."

Caro felt herself flush and pressed the back of her brush against his lips.

"Please—don't go on!"

She began to braid her hair, watching Alec move about the room as he shed a damp-looking shirt and replaced it with a roughly woven, biscuit colored one with open cuffs. The garment was a shade lighter than his tanned face, and curling black hair showed inside the open collar, covering the base of his neck. His breeches were a darker beige, skimming his slim hips and long, well-muscled thighs. The boots he wore were soft, cuffed at the tops, and only slightly more bronze than his skin. In Caro's eyes, Alec moved with a combination of grace and power that seemed more animal-like than human. He reminded her of a great wild cat, a panther perhaps. Coming up beside her at the mirror, Alec raked lean fingers through his raven hair, then fastened it at his neck with a thin length of leather. Caro was wrestling with her braids, wishing for three hands, when Alec reached out to take the pieces of white satin from her. Wordlessly, Caro held the ends of her braids up against her ears so that they formed circlets which brushed her shoulders, while Alec swiftly fastened the ribbons around them into neat bows. His eyes met hers then, looking up at him so earnestly, and he felt a painful jolt of remorse for what he had robbed her of the night before. Christ, he thought, I must be deranged, developing a conscience at my age.

Caro saw Alec's eyes go opaque, then he grasped her elbow, roughly propelling her around and out of the room. The parlor was warm, and a tantalizing blend of aromas filled the air. Plates and silver were on the table, along with a brightly painted toleware coffeepot sitting on a trivet. Caro couldn't believe her eyes when they fell on a plate of steaming biscuits.

"Alec! Are those really biscuits? Where did they come from?"

"Of course they're real. I baked them," he replied coolly.

"*You*—" she turned incredulous eyes on him.

"My dear child, you will soon find that I can do anything. Now kindly cease your chatter until after breakfast. I prefer my food hot."

Caro saw that his eyes were full of laughter, but she believed his claim when she tasted the biscuits. Spread with honey, they melted in her mouth like pure ambrosia. The coffee was rich and strong, and Caro soon felt fortified. She poured herself a second cup and relaxed a little in her chair, gazing around the room.

A huge, dead turkey lay next to the door.

"Where did *that* come from?"

Alec glanced at her over his coffee mug.

"I shot it. Did you imagine that it fell from the rafters or blew in with the rain?"

"*Shot* it! Today?"

"Of course today." His voice was bored. "We have to eat, don't we?"

Caro could see that Alec's patience was wearing thin, so she kept silent. She had never seen such a large turkey, though, and was glad that she was fond of the meat for she guessed it would serve as the main course for several meals.

After breakfast, Caro began to explore the rest of the house. The floor plan was classically Dutch Colonial, one room deep and three rooms long. There was a smaller bedchamber for the children on the other side of the parlor. It was furnished with a trundle bed, neatly made up, and Caro felt her eyes prick with tears at the sight of a worn wooden top lying abandoned on the floor.

Behind the parlor was a loom room which Alec told her he had helped to build the year before.

"They refused to believe they'd have to go. They had it all rationalized—kept telling me if they became totally self-sufficient and stayed away from the neighbors, they'd be left alone. James was convinced that this remote location would save them, and Elizabeth clung to that cliché about America being a cradle of free thought. Fools."

Hoping to distract him, Caro turned to the pots of dye.

"Where did they get these?"

"Some of them I brought last spring, particularly the indigo for the blue, but most of these they made themselves. The orange comes from bittersweet, and the green is derived from pressed goldenrod blossoms. Elizabeth might have made the red from sumac or pokeberry or even dogwood. Onionskins are used for yellow; blueberries or poison ivy for purple. And—I believe the black comes from alder bark."

Caro wanted to ask him how he knew, but kept silent. The loom filled nearly the entire room, leaving only enough space for a large cupboard containing dishes, wooden bowls, and staple foods—molasses, salt, flour, apples, carrots, and jam for the most part.

Back in the main room, Alec began to prepare the turkey for roasting while Caro cleaned up the breakfast dishes. That task accomplished, she pulled a chair up to the small bookcase to investigate its contents. The books were well cared for, and Caro found that she recognized most of the names printed on the bindings: Richardson, Steele, Boswell, Addison, Johnson, Marlowe, and Shakespeare. Pulling out a volume of Shakespeare's sonnets, she spied yellowed paper against the back of the bookcase. After lifting out several more books she could see that there were newspapers, carefully folded and obviously hidden for a reason. Caro put her head up and looked around at Alec, who was working on the giant turkey with his back to her.

"Alec?"

"Hmm?" He did not look up. "Christ, but this is awful work to be doing indoors."

"Alec, could you come over here for a moment?"

He straightened, wiping his hands on a bloodstained towel, and walked over to her.

"Caro, what are you doing with all those books out? I certainly hope we won't be here that long!" Alec's voice was dry, and Caro flashed him an impulsive grin, showing her dimples.

"Don't be silly! I just wondered what those are." She pointed to the newspapers still wedged against the back of the shelf, and Alec settled back on his heels to look inside. The top of his head was only a few inches from her face, and she stared at his thick, shin-

52

ing black hair. It lay against the sides of his head like two raven's wings, and Caro fought a strong impulse to touch it. Vaguely, she recalled having had her hands in that hair the night before, and her face grew hot. All of it seemed like it had been some strange dream—she was uneasily aware that there had been no quality of a nightmare about it for her. Alec's voice startled her, bringing her back to earth with a jolt. He had pulled the newspapers from their hiding place and thumbed through them casually, a rueful smile tugging at the corners of his mouth.

"Ah, Caro, believe me, these constitute no treasure or mystery. I suppose James hid them in case of a search—especially for Elizabeth's sake while she was here alone." Alec sauntered over to the hearth where he tossed the papers into the flames. "Those were copies of the *Royal Gazette*. James Rivington published it in New York during the war, and it was well known for expressing pro-Tory sentiments. I've heard recently that Rivington has been giving secret information to Washington all along, though. I suppose that makes Wallingham rather a fool, *n'est-ce pas?* He admired Rivington greatly for his courage of conviction—well, let's hope James doesn't hear the truth."

Caro got up and walked over near him.

"Alec, do you think Mr. Wallingham was a fool all around? About the war, and England, I mean?"

Alec propped an expensive boot against the hearth and leaned forward, looking into the fire and rubbing his bearded jaw.

"Well, I liked the man, and I certainly would not deny his courage or intelligence. But, let us say I feel he was a bit out of touch with reality when it came to Britain and King George . . . and all the other issues involved in the fight for independence. He had all these notions built up in him over a lifetime, and they were part of his principles—he saw his loyalty to the King in the same light as his fidelity to Elizabeth

53

. . . or God. Actually, James should probably have never come to America in the first place. Or, perhaps if he had lived in a city, nearer the action and events, he would have developed a different perspective." Alec pulled his eyes from the fire and looked at Caro. Their turquoise depths were warm with a mixture of compassion and realism. "I doubt it, though. Let's just be glad the Wallinghams lost nothing more valuable than their home here. I have a feeling that in the long run they'll be happier in England. I hope so, at any rate."

"You don't think they'll be back?"

"Frankly, no."

Alec returned to the turkey and said nothing more for the next hour. However, after the bird was cleaned and plucked and on the spit over the fire, he sought Caro out in the bedroom where she was mending a torn shirt of his. She noticed that he had scrubbed away all traces of blood from his hands and forearms, and he was smiling. Watching him drop down beside her on the bed, Caro froze for a moment, somehow feeling that Alec was about to kiss her. His eyes were gleaming recklessly, but then he lay back against the spread, watching her in amusement.

"You looked like a cornered fawn for a moment there, Caro. Were you afraid I might force myself on you? It must be quite a revolting thought to strike such terror into your heart!"

Caro bent her head over her sewing, trying to think of a cutting reply, when she felt his hand touch her back. Her heart began to pound, and she heard herself say in an unnaturally loud voice: "Believe me, even though you are certainly no gentleman, I am not terrified of you in the least!"

Alec's fingers closed over the back of her gown and she was pulled back against the bed. Propping himself on an elbow, he looked down at her and Caro could see sheer devilment in his eyes. Yet, he did not touch her.

"You're right; I am certainly no gentleman! I'm glad you've learned that at last and if you're as bright as you appear, you won't be forgetting it, my dear. Not for a moment." Beneath the cynical overtones, Caro could sense the warning in his voice. "And, I'm also happy to hear you aren't terrified of me. Actually, I suppose that's the last emotion I want to inspire in you!"

He was looking down at her with open desire. The velvet soft curve of her neck was only inches away, and the fragrance of clover rose from her hair and skin. Her cinnamon eyes were wide with poorly concealed anxiety mingled with desire, and the braided circlets of honey hair made her look adorably young. It took every ounce of restraint he possessed to pull himself away and get to his feet. Caro sat up, clutching at the bosom-concealing fichu fastened so securely at her bodice. Turning away to flick an imaginary piece of lint from his sleeve, he commented with studied casualness:

"Well, infant, I originally came in here to see if you would care to brave the rain to pay a visit to Molly in the barn. She was looking rather forlorn this morning, despite Ivan's constant attentions."

Caro's face was transformed with delight. "Oh yes! That's a wonderful idea!"

"I'm so glad you think so!" he rejoined mockingly.

Wearing an old pair of James Wallingham's boots, Alec half carried Caro through the boglike mud in the yard. The coat she held over her head offered little protection from the driving rain, and once inside the barn, Alec muttered: "Christ, I should have known better than to bring you out in this."

She didn't care, though. Molly almost lunged at her with joy, and Caro was oblivious to all else. Alec watched them momentarily, struck by the obviously deep bond of affection existing between them. It was hard to realize that Caro had no real memory of Molly beyond the two previous days.

Ivan was prancing and strutting around the barn and Alec grinned at him.

"I suppose you've been in here taking advantage of the rain, old boy. Poor Molly hasn't a chance against your charm."

Ivan whinnied in gay agreement and Alec set about his tasks while Caro chattered to Molly, brushing the mare until her coat gleamed. Alec was in the far corner of the barn when he called to her: "How does the idea of a real bath strike you, *chérie?*"

Caro giggled, not even looking up.

"Why, I'd love one. While you're at it, why don't you order me a coach with six white horses?"

"Perhaps you'd care to step this way, infant? I can hardly credit that you still doubt my abilities!" Alec replied drily, arching one black eyebrow. Caro eyed him warily as she made her way across the barn only to peer inside an empty stall and be faced with a giant black kettle.

"Alec, what has that monstrosity got to do with a bath?" She was sure that behind his beard she could see his cheeks crease with dimples.

"Why everything, my dear! *This* will be our bathtub!"

"Our bathtub! But, it's horrid-looking, and completely the wrong shape! Why, it looks like it was designed for a—a—"

"Hog?" he supplied helpfully.

Caro's eyes narrowed suspiciously.

"All right, sir, please tell me what this kettle is supposed to be. I know it is too big to cook in, and I'm *sure* it's not a bathtub!"

Alec threw back his raven head then and laughed deeply. "Ah, Caro, you're too sharp for me. And it's unfair of me to tease you this way. Actually, this kettle is used on the day of hog-killing to boil the poor unfortunates in before the hair is scraped off. Don't worry!—they're already dead. The hog-killing usually would be taking place about now, but James sold all the pigs and the kettle has stayed in storage this year."

Caro was staring at the huge iron pot with undisguised distaste.

"Are you really serious about *bathing* in this?"

"As a matter of fact, I am. A little scrubbing and it will be as good as new. The only drawback is that it will have to stay here in the barn, and it could tend to get chilly in here! I can build a fire though, and bring in water to heat from the pump. Frankly, the thought of a hot bath is hugely appealing to me!" He watched Caro's face soften as his words sank in.

"Well, a bath would be lovely! Do you suppose I could wash my hair?"

"Undoubtedly! I'll be glad to help." Alec's eyes were flashing with devilish amusement. "Certainly you must realize that you'll need me on hand to pour the water!"

Caro's chin tilted indignantly.

"You'll do no such thing, Mr. Beauvisage. I'd sooner bathe in cold water."

In the end, they decided to put off their baths until the next day. The afternoon was on the wane, and Caro was predicting with great assurance that the rain would end that night. Alec told her that even if the storm stopped they would be staying put for at least another day in order to give the roads a chance to dry somewhat.

Upon returning to the house that afternoon, Caro challenged Alec to a game of piquet, which he accepted rather skeptically. She beat him, however, and his competitive instinct was roused. Caro's dimples showed in a smile of pure delight as Alec scratched his head, frowning.

"I can't recall losing to a woman at cards since my childhood—except, perhaps, for a few isolated instances when I let the female win in order to gain a very different sort of advantage for myself."

"Well, Mr. Know-it-all," sang Caro, "you have met your match. I know in my heart that I am an expert at this!"

Alec's brow was furrowed with concentration for the next two hours, and Caro was averaging a victory in one out of four games. It was the aroma of the turkey that finally caused them to quit, and Alec leaned back in his chair, studying Caro with mingled respect and bewilderment.

"Do you play chess, *chérie?*"

She smiled benignly. "Of course."

"Fine. After supper we'll have a game. Or two." He paused, rubbing his jaw. "I can hardly wait to find out where you've come from. You are the most unique female I have ever known!"

"Is that a compliment?"

"Well, I hate to admit it, but I suppose it is."

Caro stood up and gazed down at Alec's handsome face for a moment.

"You don't like to be beaten, do you?" she inquired mischievously. Alec rose and then he was the one looking down; his nearness made her throat constrict.

"Let's just say I am not used to losing to beautiful women. However, it's an experience that I am not averse to trying out."

That night, Caro lay in her deep goose-down bed, listening to the dimming patter of the rain. She had retired over an hour before, but Alec was still in the parlor. Remembering his earlier words about losing to women, she couldn't help feeling that any female who attempted to win a victory over him would be disappointed. Although she had put up a good fight in their two chess games, he had still defeated her easily. And afterwards, when they said goodnight, Alec held her elbows and absently ran his brown hands up her arms. That simple gesture had made her so weak in her knee that she was sure he could see it in her flushed face. Now she thought, There must be some men who are made to be victorious in everything they do. Certainly no one could ever hope to dominate Alec in any way. She fell asleep as the image of his handsome face, concentrating over the chess board, drifted across her mind.

Chapter Six

THE NEXT MORNING, CARO WOKE EARLY, WHILE THE sky was barely rinsing gray. She sat up in her cozy alcove and tried to see outside through the parted window curtains. True to her prediction, the rain had stopped except for a stubborn drizzle. Caro's first impulse was to snuggle back into the warm quilts, but she felt surprisingly alert.

I'll beat Alec out of bed this day, she told herself as she climbed down the ladder. Somehow, it didn't occur to her that he would be sleeping in the big bed, for she had never seen him there. Yet, as she padded barefoot across the floor to the wardrobe she passed the parted drapes of the bed and saw Alec lying on it. His hair was startlingly black against the white pillow, and his sooty lashes looked uncommonly long. He was breathing deeply through his nose, and Caro could see that he was sleeping very soundly. Impulsively, she reached out to touch his bare chest, covered with its mat of black hair. The warmth of his skin startled her, and a wave of emotion swept over her. In his sleep, Alec somehow seemed so much more open and accessible, and Caro felt both moved and disturbed by this. Hastily, she turned away to the wardrobe and quietly drew out a clean spice-colored gown and the necessary accessories. After dressing in the children's bedchamber, she located a tiny comb and ran it through her hair, tying it back with the same brown ribbon she had worn all night. The shade of the dress set off her peach-toned complexion and gold hair, and she looked fresh and young with her scrubbed face and glossy curls down to her waist.

Going into the living room, Caro poked at the glowing fire, adding a couple of logs in hope that they would come to life. Then she made a pot of coffee, somehow sure of the procedure involved. "My past must not have included servants!" she smiled to herself. As the coffee brewed, Caro puttered around the room, straightening things up and feeling strangely contented. Deciding that she would have to produce some breakfast for Alec, she went back to the cupboards to investigate. In the top drawer was a folder of loosely bound recipes written in long hand, and Caro was intrigued by one for "Apple Cornbread." After checking to be certain that she had all the ingredients, she set to work, peeling and slicing apples. Then she mixed cornmeal, milk, and the remaining dry ingredients in a bowl, trying to imagine the look on Alec's face when he discovered her accomplishment. Finally, she turned the batter into a pan, covering it with the apple slices and cinnamon. There was a roasting kitchen in front of the fire, and she put the bread into it to bake. The coffee was done by this time and Caro sat down on the settle to sip from her mug, feeling very proud of herself. Her thoughts drifted for a while, then she remembered the giant kettle in the barn and Alec's promise of a bath today. She could hardly wait—the mere thought of hot water and a bar of soap was glorious. Deciding to speed things along, Caro heated a pan of water, found a bar of lye soap, and went out to the barn. She fed Ivan and Molly, who continually gave each other long soulful looks.

"Molly, what about me? Am I no longer first in your heart?" Caro queried teasingly. She let them outside then, for the rain had now stopped completely and the sun was struggling to break through the clouds. Caro stood on the threshold of the barn, watching the horses prance up the hillside. Then, leaving the door open to let in the light, she took a stiff brush from a hook on the wall and approached the ugly black kettle. It wasn't as filthy as she had feared. When Alec had explained its purpose, Caro had envisioned old blood and lard inside the pot, but most of the dirt was simply dust and cobwebs.

She worked hard, pouring the water inside and scrubbing vigorously with the brush and strong soap. She was leaning all the way inside, trying to reach the bottom of the kettle with one arm while holding her hair and bracing herself with the other when she heard the barn door swing closed with a rusty groan. Caro's first thought was that it must be Alec, and she blushed, realizing what a comical picture she must have made. She was struggling to get up when a hand grasped her by the hair and pulled her roughly to her feet. Caro found herself looking across the kettle into narrow yellow eyes that struck an eerie chord in her memory, while another, unseen man who held her hair pulled upward so forcefully that Caro bit her lip to keep from wincing.

The two men stood looking at her as she lifted her chin in instinctive defiance, then they began to converse in German. The man with the yellow eyes was very thin with a hooked nose and a cruel-looking red mouth. His companion, who held her hair, was shorter and much heavier. He had thick lips which he licked nervously, and bulging eyes which showed the whites all around. They were dressed almost identically, in shabby black coats and tricorn hats over dark yellow breeches. Both wore swords, and the fat man's coat was open to reveal some red cloth.

Caro realized that they had to be Hessians, German mercenary soldiers that Alec had already told her about. They were talking about her, and the suggestive tone of their voices was unmistakable. The fat man pulled her hair up even higher and pressed his wet lips against her neck. Caro shuddered and gave him a look which she hoped was withering, but both men only laughed obscenely, and suddenly the thin one produced a long, evil-looking knife and held it to her throat. He grinned then, showing brown teeth, and gestured to his companion, who released his hold on Caro's hair, tearing the ribbon out of it at the same time. He put his thick fingers in her curls, exclaiming at their softness, and Caro could hear him begin to pant. Somehow, that sound frightened her more than the knife, for then she was sure about what they were going to do. Momentarily, she considered refusing to cooperate, or even fighting them, but the yellow eyes of the thin man were so inhuman-looking that Caro knew he would not hesitate to kill her. Her only thought was that she wanted to live, no matter what.

During the nightmare of degradation that followed, Caro stared straight ahead, her chin raised in silent defiance. The thin man never took his eyes from her face, or moved the knife from her throat as his companion pulled off Caro's coat and unfastened all the tiny buttons down her bodice with fat trembling fingers. She felt her dress being torn from her shoulders, then he was ripping her chemise, and the sound of his hot, rasping breath seemed to fill the entire barn. Caro's eyes filled with tears as he began pawing her naked breasts and pinching her nipples cruelly. As he licked her breasts voraciously the blade of the knife was pushed just a fraction harder against her throat. The fat man began to touch her everywhere, and pulled her buttocks toward him, rubbing himself excitedly against her. While he breathed as though he were having an asthma attack, Caro began to feel her stomach turn, for in spite of this revolting man, she felt herself begin to respond.

Then, just as he was clumsily pulling at the waistband of her pantalets, there was a sudden crash as the door of the barn flew open against the wall.

"That will be all, gentlemen. Kindly drop that knife," Alec's deep voice rang out, and the yellow-eyed man was startled enough to turn slightly, moving the knife down just enough for Caro to grab it. Her mind was crowded with crazy, incoherent thoughts as she plunged the blade into the fat man's stomach with all the strength she possessed. Then, she stood up, exposed breasts heaving, and stared down at him with total horror in her eyes, not even reacting when the shot rang out which killed the other man.

Alec was beside her in an instant, wrapping her in his coat, then looking down at the man he had shot with eyes that had gone from turquoise to stormy sapphire-blue. When he spoke, his voice was like steel: "I should have tortured you first."

The man with the yellow eyes stared up at Alec in disbelief.

"Beauvisage!" he choked in a heavy accent, and then his head fell to one side. Caro began to scream convulsively and Alec bent down, picking her up in his arms to carry her back to the house.

Caro remembered very little with any clarity after that. Two days had passed when she woke up in a sun-washed bedroom in Van DerPat Manor, feeling like her old self for the first time. Her first thought was how wonderful it was to feel warm sunlight again, and then she lay back on her pillow and tried to piece together the events since the assault. Very vaguely, she remembered that Alec had dressed her and given her some brandy, and she knew that his arms had held her through it all, his voice firmly reassuring her that everything would be all right. It seemed that they had left the farm almost immediately, and Caro was sure she had ridden with Alec, for she could recall very little of the journey, and nothing at all of their arrival. She was certain that she must be at Van DerPat Manor, for that was where he had told her they would stop next.

To keep herself from thinking about what had happened in the barn, Caro got out of bed and went to the window. Its panoramic view of the Hudson River in autumn was more beautiful than she had ever imagined. The lawn beneath her window was perfectly groomed, dotted with beds of late-fall flowers in shades of rust and gold. Beyond the lawn lay a road which wound perilously close to the sheer edges of the hills rising above the mighty Hudson. Chestnut, oak, spruce, and walnut trees covered the hillsides in an impossibly brilliant tapestry, contrasting strikingly with the clear, vivid blue of the river. Across on the west bank, Caro could see that the tops of the hills were actually cliffs which plummeted straight down halfway to the water before they softened into tree-covered hillsides. As for the Hudson itself, "It seems so alive," Caro mused aloud, "like a huge vein, giving life and vitality to all the land around it."

Her reverie was broken by a quiet click as the door opened, and Caro spun around to see Alec at the threshold. Without thinking, she ran to meet him, eager to feel his arms about her, and he welcomed her with a strong hug.

"What are you doing out of bed, infant? Have you lost your senses? You'll give me gray hair while I'm still in my youth!"

Caro could hear the teasing note in his voice, and she drew back her head to look into his dancing eyes.

"Oh, Alec, it feels so wonderful to see the sun out —I simply had to get a look at that view!" Dimples showed deep in her cheeks as she added, "Besides, you are long past your first bloom of youth, and probably long overdue for gray hair!"

Alec's turquoise eyes opened wide in mock horror. "Madame, I am deeply wounded by your implication!

And now—back into bed. I'll not have you fainting on me again. My poor arms are still weak from carrying you everywhere the past two days."

"Are you suggesting that I am overweight?"

Suddenly she was close to him again, and his hands were resting on her hips. He put his face down near hers, breathing in the clover scent of her hair as he murmured in her ear:

"On the contrary, *chérie*. Your body is still magnificent. Must you force me to repeat my compliments?"

Caro was acutely conscious of the fact that she wore nothing but a thin batiste bedgown which did little to conceal her curves. Looking up at Alec, her throat constricted in a way that made speech impossible, and she couldn't have been more surprised when she felt his arms encircle her back, pulling her close so that her body was pressed against the length of his.

"Ah, Caro, you'll never know how happy I am to see you up and feeling so well. Believe it or not, you had me worried." Alec paused, the serious look in his eyes softening. "You look absolutely enchanting, *chérie*. All soft and sleepy . . ." His voice trailed off, and then he was kissing her.

Caro melted in his arms, overcome by a desire so strong it frightened her. The warmth of Alec's skin, the appealing masculine scent that clung to him, and the lazy expertise of his kiss all combined to assail her senses with amazing intensity. Suddenly she found herself pushing him away and turning her face from his, her heart pounding so loudly she was sure Alec could hear it.

"Oh, please," she gasped, her eyes like saucers. "Alec, you *must* stop. I—I feel so confused."

He tipped her chin up and smiled down into her worried eyes.

"Little one, I just wanted you to remember that

lovemaking is usually enjoyable. You won't deny that you like to be kissed by me, will you?"

Caro shook her head.

"Well, then, try to keep that kiss imprinted on your mind and think of it whenever you find your thoughts straying toward your experience the other day. Now, come on—let's get you into bed."

Impulsively, Caro gave Alec a hug, mainly to feel the comforting strength of his arms around her when he returned her embrace. Then he led her to bed, pulled up the heavy counterpane, and perched casually on the edge of the bed. His next question was blunt:

"Caro, how much of the last two days do you remember?"

"Well," she replied frankly, "I remember the men— and what they did. I shall never forget, Alec. You know, there was something about that awful man with the yellow eyes that jolted my memory. He seemed to remind me of someone I knew—that's a gruesome thought, isn't it!

"I killed the fat man, I remember that, too, though it is all a red blur in my mind. It hurts to think of it. And . . . you shot the other one, didn't you?"

Alec didn't answer for a long moment as he mulled over her words about the yellow-eyed man. His expression was distant and he rubbed a brown knuckle against his bearded jaw before refocusing on Caro and her question.

"Yes, but that's of no consequence," he repeated brusquely. "By the way, I probably would have slept through it all if not for your burning bread! At any rate, I want you to know that I'm very proud of you for what you did, Caro. You've got an uncommon amount of courage for a female. Furthermore, I want to urge you now not to dwell on what happened. You are a lovely girl in every way, and you've been mistreated lately by a variety of villainous types—

myself among them. You must not let what's happened spoil you, though, for the majority of men in this world are well behaved and respectful."

The impish gleam was back in Caro's eyes.

"That certainly sounds boring! I believe I would prefer a villainous type like you over some simpering milksop. Also, I am not used to such sobriety from you, Alec. Don't worry so. I shall do my best to forget the entire incident—as soon as I have thanked you for that daring rescue!"

White teeth showed in a flashing grin as Alec raised one eyebrow and bowed slightly.

"It was my pleasure, *chérie*. Damsels in distress are my specialty."

"Now tell me about what we've been up to lately. And, where are we? Van DerPat Manor?"

"Yes—you remembered that? We left just as soon as I got you quieted down, which amounted to your lapsing into a sort of trance. We arrived here that same evening, and you've been asleep in this bed ever since."

"What did you do with the men?"

"I brought the bodies along—Molly had to carry them, poor thing. I couldn't risk leaving them there, though, in case someone should try to involve James Wallingham. There's no question of blame in our case, though, because there's been no love lost between the Americans and the Hessians. During the war they earned quite a reputation for rape as well as other unsavory pastimes. I've heard that nearly five thousand of them are remaining here now that the war is over, so no one will be sorry to see two of the worst ones dead."

"I imagine the Van DerPats will be happy to hear I'm up and around so they can get us out of here. It certainly has been nice of them to take care of me this way."

"Well, they're good people. Stephen Van DerPat

has been a shipowner and trader for years, and he and my father are old friends. I've known them all since I was a child."

Caro dimpled. "I find it hard to believe that you were ever a child!"

She was interrupted by a knock at the door and a voice calling, "Sacha, is everything all right?"

Alec did not move from his place on the bed, but replied, "Come in, Gretchen."

The door opened to admit a vision of pure loveliness, and suddenly Caro understood why Alec hadn't been bored at Van DerPat Manor. The girl who was approaching the bed was tall and slenderly fragile with a beautiful pink and ivory complexion. Her silver-blond hair was arranged elegantly, falling over one bare shoulder in three long ringlets. Large chinablue eyes dominated her perfect oval face, their color accentuated by a fashionable gown of blue silk cut low to reveal a long neck and most of her small white breasts. Above all, however, Caro noticed the way the girl was looking at Alec. There could be no mistaking the fact that she loved him and obviously felt possessive toward him, for as she smiled at Caro her eyes were relaying a very different message.

Alec, however, was grinning lazily as he offered: "Gretchen Van DerPat, may I present Caroline—ah—Bergman, my ward. Caroline, this is Gretchen."

They smiled at one another most charmingly.

"Miss Van DerPat, you must allow me to thank you for your hospitality these past two days. You have been very kind."

Gretchen showed perfect white teeth in a dazzling smile that she turned directly on Alec. "Miss Bergman, my parents deserve all your gratitude. I was only glad to help in my own small way—hmm, Sacha?"

Alec grinned with such unconcealed amusement that Caro longed to slap him. "You've been wonderful, *mon amour*," he told Gretchen.

"There is a friend of yours who has arrived down-stairs and Papa sent me up to get you. Don't forget that you promised to take me riding this afternoon, though. Friend or no friend!" Gretchen turned her clear blue eyes directly on Caro. "Miss Bergman, I'm sure you're anxious to get some rest, so I'll shoo Sacha out of here. I know how tiring he can be!"

Alec made no move to get up, only gesturing to Gretchen to leave the room.

"You go on, *ma petite*. Tell your father and my mystery guest that I shall join them directly."

Gretchen barely managed to repress a pout before making her exit, and Caro watched with relief as her rustling silk skirts disappeared out the door. When she turned back to Alec she felt curiously on the brink of tears. It was impossible to disguise the sarcasm in her voice as she inquired:

"Sacha?"

Alec looked completely unperturbed, but his eyes were alert as he answered, "Yes, that's my family name. Maman has called me that since the day I was born. I imagine you'll be hearing it a great deal from now on."

"I suppose that only your inner circle of friends is permitted to call you that?"

Alec's eyebrow lifted as he replied drily, "On the contrary, *chérie*. You are free to call me anything you like. It seems to me to be a matter of negligible importance."

"Well, I choose to call you Alec!"

"Fine!" There was a sharp note in his voice as he stood up and continued: "Jealousy does not become you, Caro. I know many women well, and I make it a rule not to cultivate shrews. You and I are no longer alone in the woods, my dear, and you had better be-gin adjusting to that fact."

From far away, Caro heard herself answer hotly, "In that case, Mr. Beauvisage, may I suggest that you begin treating me more like your ward and less like your whore!"

Every muscle in Alec's face was rigid, his eyes were angry blue flames, and when he spoke his caustic voice cut Caro like a knife.

"It will give me the greatest pleasure to stop treating you like a whore, my dear, just as soon as you stop behaving like one."

Then, after bowing mockingly, he was gone, closing the door sharply behind him. Caro thought she heard Gretchen's voice in the hallway, and hot tears of anger and humiliation pricked her eyes. Her stomach cramped up as waves of nausea swept over her and she put her head back on the pillow, letting the tears spill out of her eyes. Even the sunshine pouring generously into the room could not cheer Caro as she realized that from that moment on nothing would be the same between her and Alec.

"Gretchen is the first person from the outside world I've seen since Alec and I met," she mused sadly, unwilling to count the two men in the barn. "And already he's forgotten me and our friendship. What will become of me after we reach Philadelphia?"

Chapter Seven

CARO WAS SITTING UP IN BED, POKING AROUND AT A light lunch when there was a knock at the door. Thinking it was a maid returning for her tray, she called:

"I'm not quite finished yet. Could you come back a little later?"

The door cracked open and a plump, cheerful face appeared.

"My dear girl, it is I: Katrina Van DerPat. May I visit with you for a short while?"

"Oh, certainly! Please pardon my manners!"

Mrs. Van DerPat was inside in a twinkling. Caro was immediately charmed by her hostess, a small, round, flaxen-haired Dutchwoman with twinkling blue eyes as friendly as her daughter's had been cool. She settled herself on the edge of the bed and clasped Caro's hand.

"Dear Caroline, I want to welcome you to Van DerPat Manor. We are so pleased to have you here, for we adore Sacha. As his ward, our love for you is automatic!"

Caro found herself smiling back, some of her gloom dispelled by her hostess's infectious good cheer.

"But I should be thanking you. It has been so good of you to take me in—a stranger to you. I can never express the depth of my gratitude, Mrs. Van DerPat."

"You must call me Katrina, and never consider yourself a stranger here, for we have known Sacha since he was born, and he has always been a part of our family. He tells us you are all alone in the world, so we must step in to remedy that situation!"

"Well, thank you! You are very kind!"

"Sacha tells me that he had planned to give you some additional details on our family but was interrupted by the arrival of Colonel Kosciuszko. So, he has asked me to answer any questions you might have."

Caro opened her mouth to speak, but Mrs. Van DerPat went right on.

"We live here on the east bank of the Hudson just above Tarrytown, so you are not a great distance from New York. There are only four of us in the family—myself, my husband Stephen, our son Peter, who is fourteen, and our daughter Gretchen, who is eighteen." She paused then, eyeing Caro with concern. "I understand you have already met Gretchen, and I wish you hadn't—at least not before I could speak to you. I do hope she wasn't rude! You must realize, my dear, that Gretchen has been infatuated with Sacha since she was a child. He is thirteen years her senior and has always been an uncommonly handsome man with that unique charm which has no name—you've recognized it, I'm sure. Well, Sacha has always loved to travel, and he and Jean-Philippe, his father, would come up here from time to time to visit us and engage in all the sporting activities which are so popular in these parts. And, I would take Gretchen on shopping excursions down to Philadelphia to visit Antonia, Sacha's mother, and his sister Natalya, who is Gretchen's age. Gretchen has always been older; perhaps because we have been so secluded here and she has associated primarily with adults. And, I believe that the fact of our seclusion contributed greatly to her infatuation with Sacha, for she has had few prolonged

73

acquaintances with other men. Not that I am at all certain it would help, for what average man can measure up to Sacha's extraordinary standard? After the war broke out, Stephen took pains to maintain his neutrality and we saw fewer people than ever. Sacha was in and out of the Hudson River Valley all during those eight years, and he befriends whomever he pleases, regardless of what people say. So, he always visited us, and Gretchen's attachment to him deepened with each passing year.

"Last spring," Mrs. Van DerPat continued, "he came to see us after a long absence, and upon finding Gretchen all grown up he proceeded to stay a full week. I know he gave her the same warnings he gives all women about his lack of scruples, but she actually believes she can win him!" Katrina paused momentarily, patting Caro's hand. "It will take a far more extraordinary female than Gretchen though, to truly win Sacha's heart. As a matter of fact, I am beginning to doubt the existence of such a woman! Gretchen may be beautiful and clever, but Sacha has a score of ladies with those qualities at his beck and call. She is sadly lacking in humor, unselfishness, warmth, as well as many other important virtues. She has been very unhappy and on edge since Sacha brought you here. I don't like having to say that, but I feel certain you could sense it when you met her. My daughter dislikes having to share Sacha with anyone, even a girl who is for all intents, his daughter! Gretchen cannot see, or will not admit, that he has only the most casual interest in her—she provides him with female diversion while he is here, and nothing more. Someday she will be deeply hurt, but until then I must try not to interfere *too* much, for children must learn these lessons on their own. At any rate, you must make allowances for her rudeness. You look like a very perceptive young woman to me, Caroline, and I'm sure you must understand that love can do strange things to a person under its spell."

Katrina continued to chatter on about their life at the manor, but Caro was still thinking about what she had been told about Gretchen—and Alec. Mrs. Van DerPat's conversation seemed to be very innocent, but Caro couldn't help wondering if a subtle warning was intended for her as well. What remained of her lunch lay cold on her plate when Katrina stood up to go. Her blue eyes were twinkling as she exclaimed:

"How could I forget my main reason for visiting you? Sacha has asked me to arrange for you to have a bath, then he would like you to join us downstairs if you feel strong enough. Would you enjoy that?"

"Oh, yes, Mrs.—Katrina. I have felt so isolated for so long that I would love to be around other people at last. The only problem is that I have just one dress." Impulsively, Caro jumped out of bed and pulled on the too-long robe which had been set out for her. Opening the heavy wardrobe doors, she saw her yellow gown, neatly pressed and hanging inside. She withdrew it and held it up against herself.

"I know this dress must be very unfashionable. I do not have a farthingale or bum roll to wear like Gretchen—nor do I think that this dress would accommodate one. The sleeves are all wrong, and the bodice—"

"My dear child, it is a lovely dress! You will look charming in it."

"But Gretchen has such beautiful gowns—at least the one she had on this morning was. I feel so drab next to her; her eyes are blue and her hair has such a dazzling blond color. She has a fabulous complexion—"

"And you do also, Caroline. I know it is fashionable to have pure-white skin, but just between you and me, I am sure that in reality your peach-toned complexion is much more attractive and appealing. As for your hair and eyes, would it make you feel better if I related the flattering way Sacha described you to us the night he brought you here? He said that you had honey hair and caramel eyes with a personality equally as sweet and delicious. No one could ever use those words to describe Gretchen!"

Caro was clutching the gown against her, fighting a strong impulse to cry. Katrina merely took the dress and hung it up, then gave Caro a reassuring hug.

"You rest now, and I'll have a maid prepare a bath for you and let you know when dinner will be. Perhaps I'll send up a glass of wine to quiet your nerves, although I must assure you that you have nothing to be frightened of. You are among friends here!"

Caro napped the rest of the afternoon, awakening to find that a beautifully crafted bathtub had been brought into her room. The maid asked her for her choice of fragrance, after which a procession of girls arrived with containers of steaming water. Caro soon found herself soaking in shoulder-deep jasmine-scented water.

If only I had not quarreled with Alec this morning, she thought. I would be in heaven now if he had not left me in such a dismal mood.

A plump maid named Mary dried and dressed Caro's hair after her bath, exclaiming over its unusual color and luster. Caro refused to let her insert pads into her coiffure, insisting on a simple, elegant style with no powder. Mary was doubtful, but in the end she was so enthusiastic about the results that she slipped fresh yellow and white flowers into some random curls.

Her simple gown was the color of creamy butter, its only trimming being handmade eyelet lace. Caro donned white stockings and shoes, then stood before the mirror to appraise her appearance.

The two days in bed had not paled her gold-toned complexion, and Caro privately thought that the roses in her cheeks were probably caused by nerves. Her dress was very simple, but she couldn't help believing that it flattered her. It fit closely at her tiny waist and accentuated her breasts to perfection, the lace trim screening their first curve demurely. She gazed back into her golden-brown eyes, which were shining with anticipation.

I'm not so nervous about all those others, she thought, as I am about seeing Alec. The memory of his parting words returned hurtfully and the angry image of his cold, handsome face appeared in her mind.

"If I may say so, miss, you look just beautiful. Like one o' those fairies you hear tales of as a child!" Mary's face appeared behind her, pink-cheeked with pleasure in her accomplishment.

"Thank you, Mary. What time did Mrs. Van DerPat say I should go to the parlor?"

"Seven o' clock, miss. It's five after the hour now."

Caro was somehow surprised that Alec had not come to escort her to meet his friends.

"Well, I suppose I'd better be going then. Thank you for all your help, Mary."

"Oh, it was my pleasure, miss. You just enjoy yourself! You'll find the front parlor on the left at the end of the entry hall."

Caro made her way down the wide hallway slowly, gazing around her in admiration. She peered into the first open door she encountered out of idle curiosity, and was surprised to see Alec sitting alone in a corner of what appeared to be a library, staring into the fire and smoking. The room was shadowy, but Caro was certain it was Alec, for there was no mistaking his broad shoulders and dark unpowdered hair. On an impulse, she went in. Her approach was quiet, and Alec was apparently so deep in thought that he did not hear her footsteps. She stood almost beside him before he looked up in surprise, and Caro saw for a moment an unguarded expression of open admiration cross his face.

"My God, Caro, for a moment I thought I was having a dream! You look absolutely lovely—like the first daffodil in springtime."

Impulsively, Caro smiled back and sat down beside him. She noticed his attire then, but tried not to betray the impression his appearance made on her. His suit was well-cut from a soft black fabric with silver buttons, beneath which he wore an elegant slate-gray silk vest. The glow of the firelight accentuated his snowy cravat and finely chiseled clean-shaven face.

"Alec, your beard is gone!"

His chin was just as square as she had expected, his jawline and cheekbones making his tanned face more appealing than ever. His lips turned up a fraction on one side in response to Caro's exclamation.

"Yes. You'll find that beards are not at all the vogue in polite society these days. I happen to enjoy mine, though, so I cultivate one whenever I am away."

There was a long, awkward pause then, during which Alec smoked slowly, staring back into the fire with narrowed eyes. Finally he looked up and their eyes met.

"Alec, I—"

He expelled a cloud of smoke, and raised his hand. "No, let me. I behaved despicably this morning, not for the first time where you're concerned. I'm an unfeeling cad, as I'm sure you've realized on your own. It will be a blessing for you to get to Philadelphia where you can meet men who will treat you with the respect you deserve. Let me just add that the things I said today were unnecessarily cruel and wholly untrue —and I beg you to accept my apologies."

Caro longed to reach out and touch him, to pour out her own feelings, but there was something in Alec's voice and expression that held her in check. He seemed withdrawn and unusually serious, and the wall which he had erected between them once before was back.

He is undoubtedly the most unpredictable, confounding man in the world, Caro thought in exasperation. There must be a method to his madness, so far be it from me to try to tamper with his moods again!

She raised her chin and managed a stiff smile. "Certainly you're forgiven. I behaved very childishly myself this morning, and I assure you it won't happen again."

Standing up, Caro looked down at the dark, handsome face with its piercing turquoise eyes that had come to mean so many bewildering things to her.

"I really must go," she blurted out suddenly, and darted out of the room like a golden sunbeam in the darkness. Alec rose, looking after her, his cheroot clenched between white teeth.

Caro easily found the parlor next to the front door, and somehow cleared her head sufficiently to make her appearance. Katrina Van DerPat, dressed in over-ruffled powder-blue silk, rushed to Caro's side.

"My dear child, you look absolutely entrancing! Everyone has been so anxious to meet you. By the by, you didn't happen to encounter Sacha on your way out did you?"

"Uh—yes, I did. He's in the library."

"Dearest girl, your voice sounds so hoarse. Do have a glass of wine!"

A goblet filled with crimson liquid was produced, and Caro eyed it dubiously, remembering the brandy. Then, on an impulse she accepted it and sampled it immediately.

"This is delicious, Mrs. Van DerPat!"

"Katrina. And of course it is; it's from France!"

Then she grasped Caro's arm and guided her around the room, making exuberant introductions. Peter Van DerPat had gone to bed, so Stephen, the head of the house, was the first person Caro met. He was tall, pencil-thin, yet somehow imposing with his long, narrow nose and sharp blue eyes. The white, neatly curled wig he wore accentuated his pale skin, but Caro still felt a vitality emanating from him.

"Miss Bergman, I am honored to make your acquaintance. I have heard nothing but compliments about you, and now I can see why!"

Stephen Van DerPat smiled warmly, revealing more teeth than Caro had ever seen in one person's mouth.

"Mr. Van DerPat, the pleasure is mine, for you have been a most kind and generous host to me!"

As Caro chatted with Van DerPat she watched Gretchen out of the corner of her eye. She wore a fashionable white wig and her dress was spectacular, consisting of a rich ivory satin petticoat with a carnation-pink satin overskirt edged in lace and drawn up into an elaborate, jewel-studded bustle. The bodice of the gown was cut to accentuate her narrow waist and creamy white shoulders, and when Katrina brought Caro face to face with Gretchen she could see diamonds in her ears. Neither girl had spoken when suddenly a tall, extraordinary-looking man appeared between them. He was slender and elegant with wavy brown hair and large, liquid brown eyes topped by slashing dark brows. His face was not handsome, yet there was a fascination about it with its high cheekbones, dominant nose, and magnetic white smile. Caro guessed he was even taller than Alec, but it was easy to see he was not proportioned nearly as well. When he spoke, his accent was pronounced, yet his English grammar was flawless.

"I am certain I have died and gone to heaven, for it would be impossible to find two such perfect angels on this earth!"

Gretchen blushed behind her French fan while Caro smiled at him with pleasure. Katrina spoke up: "Gretchen and Caroline, I would like you to meet Colonel Thaddeus Kosciuszko, General Green's famous Polish engineer. He has become quite a colorful hero these days! Colonel, this is my daughter, Gretchen, and Sacha's ward, Miss Caroline Bergman."

Kosciuszko kissed Gretchen's hand courteously, but pressed his lips against Caro's fingers for an embarrassingly long time.

"You must pardon me for staring, mademoiselle, but the sight of your glorious hair is too much for a mere mortal like me."

Now it was Caro's turn to blush, and she wished she too had a fan to hide behind. Gretchen was watching enviously, and her chance to escape gracefully came when Alec appeared in the doorway. Caro watched her hurry to his side, noticing that Alec looked more distant and aloof than ever. Gretchen took his arm possessively, smiling openly at Caro.

Thaddeus Kosciuszko watched both girls with his expressive brown eyes, then turned to look at his old friend, Sacha Beauvisage. They had met in Moscow as wild young men, and again in France while both were in school, and their paths had crossed many times during the Revolution. Kosciuszko had only stopped over at Van DerPat Manor because word had reached Washington's camp at Newburgh that Beauvisage was visiting here. He had thought at the time that Gretchen Van DerPat might have been what was keeping Sacha from getting up to Newburgh, but now he knew better. Kosciuszko had seldom encountered a female with a beauty and aura of attraction to match Caroline Bergman's, and he had never seen his usually devil-may-care friend look so disagreeable. Obviously there was more than a guardian-ward relationship in progress here, and knowing Sacha, it did not surprise him in the least. The only question was, what had gone wrong? Now, Alec smiled slightly, lifting one black brow in silent greeting, and Kosciuszko returned it by raising his hand in a half-mocking salute, then proceeded to turn all his attention and considerable charm on Caro.

By the time they went in to dinner, Kosciuszko was calling the girl on his arm Caro, and she was calling him Kosci. After her second glass of wine, her depression lifted and she felt like they were very old friends. Thaddeus took care to seat Caro at the opposite end of the table from Alec and his dark looks.

Dinner began with steaming bowls of clam and mushroom bisque, and it tasted so good to Caro she almost forgot her manners. Kosciuszko was a charming, witty conversationalist who was careful never to mention Alec's name, though the sight of the latter's grim watchful countenance pleased Caro.

The main course and side dishes arrived before the conversation began to fan out to include everyone. At the sight of the goose with sauerkraut stuffing, baked acorn squash, young greens with bacon dressing, and hot biscuits, Caro felt like a person who had never eaten before. She was so wrapped up in eating that she was perfectly content to sit and listen to the men talk. Most of the conversation was directed at Kosciuszko, concerning his visit to Newburgh.

"How is our good general faring these days?" Stephen Van DerPat inquired.

"Not well at all, sir. You would be insulted to hear the adjectives he uses to describe these mountains. As you well know, General Washington has been lodged at Newburgh over two years, and he sorely misses his plantation life in Virginia. Also, he was complaining to me of the lack of amusements in his life these days."

Alec looked up irritably. "What a baseless charge! I have spent many months at Newburgh in the general's company, and I know that the people of the Hudson have made every effort to keep him entertained. I, for one, was seldom bored there, and my only complaint was that soldier's old refrain of desire for female companionship! In fact, some of my most

82

pleasant memories of the war years are of Newburgh. We had great fun skating on the river in the winter months, and riding in parties along the banks during the summer." He smiled then in spite of himself. "I shall never forget Baron von Steuben's fishing expedition! He returned to tell us he had caught a whale, and we all rushed down to the bank to see it for ourselves. There lay a Hudson River eel—which the good baron's German accent had transformed into 'whale.' No amount of kidding from us could diminish his pride, though!"

Everyone was laughing, Caro included, and Alec's mood lightened somewhat as they discussed the famous "birthday party" Washington had given in honor of the French Dauphin in May 1782. The soldiers had built a green canopy to sit beneath as five hundred of them feasted on roast oxen and drank toasts to the French.

"I believe that the general himself was feeling those toasts when our musicians began to play 'Soldier's Joy,' " laughed Alec. "I shall never forget the sight of our revered commander stepping off with one of the soldiers, doing no less than the gander hop!"

He went on to recall the fire that had been ignited at the end of the party. Men had strewn saplings all the way down the west bank, and when they were lit, the flames leaped brilliantly into the blue-black sky, traveling northward until the fire seemed to jump the river and move south along the east bank.

"Those beautiful Hudson hills became the most startling silhouettes, and the river itself seemed to change to fire," Alec recalled. "I'm not a man given to emotion, but that sight has stayed lodged in my memory ever since. It was all so unreal—like an act of God."

Everyone was watching Alec, and then Kosciuszko broke the silence by lifting his glass. "For my own part, I say here's to the Hudson, a magnificent river, and to the land called America. May freedom reign here forever." Everyone joined feelingly in the toast, and then he added, "I happened to meet Count de Ségur at Newburgh. He was visiting there for the first time, and became totally enchanted with the Hudson River Valley. He called the river a 'vast sea flowing between forests centuries old,' and I found it an apt description."

Dessert arrived then, a concord grape tart accompanying the added delicacy of ice cream. Caro made everyone laugh in disbelief when she insisted that she had never eaten, or even heard of, ice cream. Every spoonful she took elicited a new exclamation from her on its flavor and texture. Even Alec found himself smiling, unable to resist her artless, gamine charm. Gretchen was not pleased by all the attention Caro was attracting, and proceeded to turn her pretty face up to Alec, attempting to draw him into conversation.

Hot buttered rum was served last, and when Alec next glanced down the table at Caro he found her sipping hers with flushed, dimpled cheeks, giggling at some remark of Kosciuszko's. As Alec watched, he remembered their night together in the farmhouse after he had plied Caro with brandy. Her warm-blooded sensuous response to his advances was all too clear now in his mind. as he watched her conversing so intimately with his so-called friend.

"Sacha, why do you spend so much time watching your ward?" Gretchen asked petulantly. "Surely you are not that conscientious a guardian! I feel certain that she is quite adult and can take care of herself with Colonel Kosciuszko. Besides, she seems to be enjoying herself immensely, which is more than I can say for you!"

Gretchen's words did not produce the desired effect on Alec. To her frustration, he seemed to watch Caro even more grimly.

Finally the party was adjourned to the parlor, where

Alec virtually ignored Gretchen. She had been hoping to persuade him to take her outside for a stroll, for she was anxious to wear her new mink-trimmed pelisse. However, Alec became engaged in a political discussion with her father which ended abruptly when he saw Kosciuszko pour another glass of wine for Caro. Turning from Van DerPat in mid-sentence, he strode across the room and grasped Caro by the arm. She looked up into his flashing eyes and angry face in surprise.

"Alec, whatever is the matter with you?"

"Give me that wine. You've had enough." He removed the glass and handed it to Kosciuszko. "Go and drink this yourself. As far away as possible."

Thaddeus, far from seeming angry, smiled cheerfully at Alec. "Now, Sacha, my old friend, I feel sure you do not mean what you say. And I cannot believe that you would consider treating this charming young woman as a child. Why, you have taken girls a good deal younger—"

"That's enough. The manner in which I treat my ward is entirely my own business. Let me just add that I am acting in her own best interests. Now, if you'll excuse us, I will return to speak to you shortly."

"But, Sacha!"

Alec was propelling Caro across the room to Stephen Van DerPat, who had been watching the drama in bewilderment.

"Stephen, Miss Bergman wishes to bid you goodnight. Since we will be leaving early tomorrow she feels in need of her beauty sleep. Isn't that so, Caroline?"

Caro nodded and managed a small smile, and then they were out of the room. Alec shifted his grip from her arm to her hand then, and Caro rubbed the flesh above her elbow as she ran along beside him down the hall to her bedchamber. Her natural impulse to argue and yell at him in indignation was squelched by an even more instinctive fear. She had never seen Alec look like this and had no idea what to make of it.

When they reached Caro's room, Alec flung open the door and thrust her inside. She was surprised to see him follow, closing the door behind them with a bang, but his first words were even more startling.

"Just what did you think you were doing out there tonight? How many glasses of wine would it have taken for Kosci to get you into bed?"

Caro stood just inches away from him, staring up into his blazing eyes, and felt her outrage conquer fear. She slapped him with all her strength, delighting in the surprise that showed on his face for a split second.

"You are undoubtedly the *most* odious, insufferable, self-serving, confused man alive! What kind of twisted brain do you have?" Her eyes flashed dangerously.

"Believe me, sweetheart, my brain is not too twisted to see when a female is encouraging a man's advances, which is exactly what you were doing tonight! And I know Kosci well enough to be certain that he would not have hesitated to accept your invitation. I would have thought, if you are really the kind of nice girl you keep insisting you are, that you would have learned your lesson the night you lost your virginity after too much brandy. Or perhaps I've been wrong again and you really are just a clever actress?"

"Mr. Beauvisage, I do not have to stand here and listen to these insults from you! You repeatedly tell me to meet other men, and so I do, and I was only trying to have a good time! Which, by the way, was hardly easy with you glowering at me all evening like an overprotective grandfather! Are you saying now that I should not talk to other men? I do wish you would make up your mind!"

Caro's voice was getting stronger by the minute; her face was flushed, her eyes shooting angry golden sparks. Alec was suddenly struck anew by her beauty and found his own rage dissolving, replaced by his usual cool composure. Caro was astonished to see him smile at her ironically, raising one eyebrow in a now familiar gesture.

"Infant, for such a lovely, sweet girl you have developed the tongue of a viper."

"Mr. Beauvisage, you have been an excellent teacher," she returned frostily, clenching her little fists in an effort to regain control. Alec was regarding her in silent amusement when she suddenly raised her chin and exclaimed:

"I simply wish to make a point to you, sir, and then my argument will be done. All night long you have been behaving as though you really were my guardian —and one of little cheer at that! I would be better off with a sour-faced parson to look after me! The detail that truly irks me, though, is the fact that you are *not* my guardian, and sir, if you tell me you were acting for the benefit of the others, I shall not believe it! I had thought, until today, that you were a light-hearted rogue and we were partners in some gay masquerade. I do not attempt anymore to understand the complexities of your mind, but I would like to be told the reason for your behavior this evening!"

She was looking him straight in the eye, patches of bright color on her cheeks.

"Have I really been so despicable?" he inquired gently.

"A toad! A tiresome toad, intent on ruining my first opportunity for a good time!"

Alec gripped her elbows, pulling her closer. "You say I may not behave toward you as a guardian, but I can recall a time not so long ago when you were only too happy to agree to my running your life! If I were not taking care of you, my dear, you should be lying long dead beneath a tree in Connecticut, or worse yet, raped and abused and probably killed in

Wallinghams' barn. Do you not think that the responsibility I have undertaken entitles me to a few rights in overseeing your life?" He could feel Caro's heart beating against his, and her lips parted a little as though to receive his kiss.

"But Alec," she said huskily, "why should you care so much that you turn into an oppressive parent? Can't you see that I am not a person to be controlled— at least not by coldness or harshness! Even your protection would not be worth my freedom to me."

Alec's head came down then, his lips crushing Caro's as their mutual desire began to build and Caro's arms went around Alec's waist, pulling him closer. Abruptly, feeling that he was drowning in her soft lips, Alec released her arms and started to walk away, frowning. When he reached the door he turned back, looking at Caro's stunned expression.

"I'm sorry, Caro—again, for the thousandth time it seems. Even I do not know what demon has taken possession of me, but I shall take pains not to interfere anymore. I can't promise total neutrality," he smiled bleakly, "but I'll do what I can. I'll see you at breakfast."

"Are we still leaving tomorrow?" she inquired softly, not permitting her voice to betray her pounding senses.

"God, yes!"

Chapter Eight

KOSCIUSZKO WAS WAITING IN THE HALLWAY WHEN Alec emerged from Caro's room.

"Well, Kosci, I hope you have not been eavesdropping?"

"If I have, then the entire household is also guilty! Everyone in the parlor could hear the shouts of 'odious,' and 'insufferable,' and 'toad,' to mention only a few. To be honest, I only came up when things got quiet—I was afraid you might have killed her!" Spying the darkening stain on Alec's cheek, he smiled. "I can see now that my worries were unfounded—the girl can obviously take care of herself!"

Alec recognized the twinkle in his friend's eye and felt himself relax.

"I'll admit that she has a streak of hellcat in her. Quite the colorful vocabulary, *n'est-ce pas?*"

"Quite!"

"My friend, let us repair to the library for a glass of brandy. I have been in constant need of a drink ever since I first laid eyes on Caro!"

The two handsome young men headed down the hall together and soon were settled in matching wing chairs before the fire, brandy and cigars in hand. Kosciuszko looked for all the familiar signs of relaxation in his friend before he inquired:

"Sacha, wherever did you find that treasure?"

"Ha! You have never encountered a more troublesome treasure than that one! That chit is like a perfect rose with innumerable hidden thorns—each one more surprising and painful than the last!"

"Perhaps, but I have never known you to waste time and energy on troublesome females. Are you getting soft in your old age?"

"I am beginning to believe it, my friend! Ever since Caro has come into my life everything has been topsy-turvy, and the game which I have always played with such finesse suddenly has a new set of rules in some foreign language I cannot translate!"

"Sacha, you are speaking in riddles. Are you in love with the girl?" He searched awkwardly for his next words. "You know, since Emily, I have wondered if you would ever . . ."

Alec cut him off, ignoring the last, and threw up his hands in mock horror. "God forbid! If this is love, then give me my gun and put it to my head! Listen, Kosci, I am really very weary of this entire subject. Let us just say that my actions tonight were prompted by Caro's uncommon innocence and naïveté. She is too damn trusting for her own good, particularly after a little wine, and I know you very well, my friend."

"Come now, Beauvisage, do not tell me that you have gotten mixed up with a virgin! What would be even more improbable is the notion that she has remained one after what appears to be a reasonably long acquaintance with *you!*"

"Let us pursue another topic. What have you been doing other than visiting General Washington? What do you hear from Gates?"

"All right, Sacha, I shall drop the subject—regretfully. Let me just add one last remark. If you could have heard yourself and Caroline arguing tonight—and don't worry, we did not hear enough words to make sense of it, though your tones were clear enough!—you would have been convinced, as I am, that you two were quarreling as only lovers can. If you are not, which I doubt, then you should be. Your young ward has a body which looks like a delicious piece of fruit, ripe for the picking, to be devoured and enjoyed by someone who could appreciate—"

"*Enough!* That, my friend, is exactly the reason why I removed her from your sight! And I cannot believe what a Slavic meddler you've become! Now, let us speak of other matters; I am beginning to feel smothered by that vixen even when she is not present!"

Kosciuszko grinned devilishly. "That sounds to me like an enviable predicament!"

In her room, Caro was just leaning over to blow out her candle when there was a knock at the door.

"Who is it?" she called, pulling up the covers.

Katrina Van DerPat peeped in, wearing a distracted smile. "Are you all right, my dear? It sounded as though you and Sacha were having a royal row! Whatever was he so perturbed about?"

Caro frowned grumpily. "Your dear Sacha was playing the role of the grouchy, straitlaced, puritanical guardian to the hilt. He was warning me about the evils of wine and male companionship!" Her voice was sharp with sarcasm and Katrina came closer to the bed, peering at her in perplexity.

"Sacha—straitlaced and puritanical? My dear child, I can hardly credit—"

"Neither could I! I can see that my life is going to be as dull as a Sunday sermon from now on. He is determined that I shall never have a moment's fun. He expects me to behave like a withered-up old maid!"

Katrina hardly knew what to make of someone fast-talking and even interrupting her, not to mention the accusations Caro was leveling on Alec.

"Well, now, my dear, I can't help feeling a tiny bit relieved about these disclosures of yours. It does my heart good to hear that Sacha is taking his responsibilities seriously, for I won't deny that I had my doubts when he told me you were his ward."

"Your . . . doubts?" Caro's voice was barely audible.

"Well, I hate to say this, but Sacha is not my idea of the perfect guardian for a beautiful young girl. Truth to tell, I could hardly imagine what your papa was thinking of when he decided on Sacha to raise you! He's always been such a dashing, devil-may-care sort of fellow that I was half afraid he might neglect his duties completely, leaving you to the mercy of all those men in Philadelphia . . . or—I shouldn't say this, but—well, when I first saw you I was even afraid that Sacha might look on you—well, not as a ward. So, my dear, although I can understand your irritation, I must be frank and admit that it's a weight off my mind. Sacha must be feeling very fatherly toward you!"

Caro's face had been turning from white to red and back again, but Katrina's last words elicited a miserable, "Yes, I know" from her.

"Now, now, you must cheer up," advised Katrina. "I feel certain that Sacha's little sister will take him in hand and see to it that you are able to meet all sorts of young men and women your own age. Besides, Sacha's own social life is so—er—active that he probably won't be able to keep much of an eagle eye on you. No doubt you and he will see very little of each other once you reach Philadelphia, for he tells me he plans to install you at his parents' house. His attitude will count for a lot, though, and now I feel more certain that he will carefully screen all your young men. Don't be downhearted, dear child, for you may almost count on an early marriage to some fine, respectable boy. I only wish my Gretchen had your opportunities; Sacha is practically the only man she sees, and he is far from the ideal son-in-law, for all we love him. I feel nothing but sympathy for the woman he marries,

92

for trying to tame Sacha would be tantamount to leashing a panther—and just as impossible."

"Yes, he is rather like a panther," Caro murmured disconsolately.

"My dear, I don't believe I have succeeded in cheering you up at all! However, where words fail, material objects often succeed." Katrina clapped her dimpled hands in excitement. "I have a surprise for you!"

With that, she darted out of the room and returned holding aloft a hanger which displayed a perfectly tailored pine-green velvet riding habit. It included a hip-length jacket and short waistcoat, both with wide, turned-back collars. There was a frilled shirt, complete with a cravat, and the skirt was hoopless and bell-shaped. In her right hand Katrina carried a small green tricorn hat which sported a pure-white plume. Caro couldn't resist Katrina's infectious beaming smile and she hopped out of bed to get a closer look at the garment.

"Mrs.—Katrina, what is this?"

"It is yours, my dear! When Sacha said you were leaving tomorrow I remembered him telling us that during your journey here you had ridden astride, wearing boy's breeches. Well, since Sacha will not provide you with a carriage (as well he should), I want to see to it that you are able to at least ride like the lady you are."

"But, where did it come from?"

"Well, I must confess that I did not pull it out of a hat! Actually, it has all come about through a convenient coincidence. Gretchen's aunt in Holland had sent this across the Atlantic for Gretchen's eighteenth birthday in March of last year. It just broke our hearts when we saw it, for it was obvious that my sister still had Gretchen's measurements from three years ago, and the girl has grown more than four inches since then! I'm certain, however, that you will be perfect for it!" Surveying the outline of Caro's bosom beneath her bedgown, Katrina frowned slightly. "The only problem might be the bustline. Why don't you try it on now, and then if it needs altering, I can have it done before tomorrow."

Caro woke early the next morning, as the first pink streaks creased the dark sky. Although it had been very late when she and Katrina had said goodnight, she had slept lightly, an edge of excitement keeping her half awake. Rolling over in bed, she saw the beautiful green riding habit hanging inside the open wardrobe. How could Katrina have sneaked that in here without my knowing it? she asked herself as she lit the lamp on her nightstand.

Springing out of bed, she splashed her face with cool water, then rubbed her cheeks briskly with a thick towel. Clean underclothes had been laid out and she slipped them on quickly, anxious to try on the habit. With the alterations that Katrina had made during the night, it fit like a glove, perfectly accentuating her generous curves. Impulsively, Caro attempted to tie the cravat herself, trying to remember how Alec's looked. The finished product seemed passable, and she turned her attention to her hair. The thought of riding with it pinned up elaborately distressed her. "I should be forced to trot along at a sweetly sedate pace in order to keep my hair in place," she thought disgustedly. "I refuse!"

Picking up her brush, Caro applied it vigorously to the long, shining curls until her hair crackled and gleamed. There was an assortment of ribbons, headpieces, and combs in the dresser drawer and she found a wide satin ribbon which she tied around her hair at the base of her neck, throwing her features into sharper relief. In the rosy glow of dawn, Caro looked lovely as she surveyed herself in the mirror. The pine green of her habit suited her peach, gold, and brown coloring and the garment looked elegant and smart on her petite body. The curls which fell down her back like a golden waterfall added the perfect finishing touch to her ensemble as she tried on the little tricorn hat. Silently Caro clasped her hands together and grinned happily at her reflection.

Moments later she was on her way down the hallway carrying the hat. She could hear clattering in the kitchens on the lower level of the house, accompanied by hushed servants' voices. No one else appeared to be awake, and Caro decided to watch the last moments of sunrise from the veranda. Her jacket was quite heavy, and the morning air was unusually mild for October. There was a divided stairway that led down to the vast lawn, and Caro arbitrarily descended the left side.

The view of the Hudson beyond the velvety expanse of grass was breathtaking, for the mountains stood out in deep shades of purple against the muted orange and pink sky. Caro was so engrossed in the sight that she did not hear Stephen Van DerPat until he spoke:

"Beautiful, isn't it?"

Caro looked up in surprise, but managed to answer him quite naturally. "It really takes my breath away. I've never seen anything so lovely!"

Van DerPat was garbed in plain brown breeches and a thick black coat which revealed only a hint of his loosely tied cravat. His face looked starker than ever in the early-morning light.

"What brings you out at this hour, Miss Bergman?"

"I simply woke up for some odd reason and then I was eager to try on this lovely riding habit your wife was kind enough to give me. Once dressed, I couldn't resist the lure of that sunrise!"

He smiled. "For my part, I am just an early riser by habit. My office is there"—he gestured to a small stone building east of the house—"and I like to work while it's quiet. We have so many visitors that it's often difficult to find any other chance."

"What sort of work do you do, Mr. Van DerPat?"

"Well, they call me lieutenant governor of New York, which sounds a lot more important than it really is. Most of my responsibilities lie right here with the people in this valley."

"How interesting! I had no idea that you were involved in life outside your manor."

"Well, I keep busy," he replied shyly.

"Mr. Van DerPat, would it be presumptuous of me to ask you to show me around the grounds a bit and tell me about your manor? You know, I've been cooped up in my bedroom for so long—"

"Miss Bergman, I am flattered by your interest. I would be very pleased to give you a brief tour. If I begin to bore you, though, please let me know!"

Caro laughed. "Do not worry, for I shall enjoy every word!"

They strolled slowly around the grounds as Stephen Van DerPat told her the story of his manor house in his quiet voice.

"Actually, the house is in quite bad repair at the moment, for during the war it received no small amount of damage. Next year, though, I hope to have it restored to its previous good looks."

"I think it's simply magnificent!" Caro exclaimed as they stood on the sloping lawn gazing back up at the house. The high red roof seemed to glow in the early dawn, and the veranda circled all the way around in perfect proportions. The structure itself was solidly and simply constructed of stone with many large, shuttered windows. There were vines of every description climbing the pillars which ringed the house in support of the veranda, while the trees along the walkways blazed with fiery leaves.

"Have you lived here long, Mr. Van DerPat?"

"Over twenty years. I brought Katrina here as a

child bride of seventeen and we've stayed ever since. That house was built nearly one hundred years ago by my grandfather; it has a proud family heritage and I pray that we never lose it. That is why I had to retain neutrality during the war—for the sake of the manor. There was too much action nearby and I do not believe that this house would be standing now if I had declared myself. Many, many families in this valley depend on me in one way or another; there were numerous reasons why I felt I had to put my lands before my politics."

"I am sure you did the right thing," Caro agreed.

They continued their walking conversation until Stephen suddenly realized that the sun had fully risen. The sky was deep blue, the breeze only slightly chilly, and it promised to be a glorious day.

When Caro and Stephen entered the dining room Alec looked up from his coffee with a frown.

"I see you're up!"

"Yes, I am up! As a matter of fact, I have been outside for nearly an hour. Mr. Van DerPat has been kind enough to show me around the grounds."

"That's fine. Just don't fall alseep on Molly in mid-afternoon."

Caro sat down, glaring openly at him, hurt and angry that he had not noticed her riding habit. There were steaming platters of eggs, ham, sausage, biscuits, and muffins on the table, so Caro began to fill her plate, eating with angry vigor. She did not lift her eyes from her food until she heard Katrina's cheerful voice exclaiming:

"Good morning, Sacha! Don't you think Caroline looks simply ravishing in her riding habit? We were certain that it couldn't fail to lighten that black mood of yours!"

Caro felt her cheeks redden, then heard herself blurt out: "Nothing could lighten Alec's black mood! I was right about him from the beginning; he is nothing but a stodgy, boring, ill-tempered *old* man!"

Stephen Van DerPat spluttered in his coffee, then exclaimed: "My dear girl, if Sacha is an *old* man, I shudder to think what that makes me!"

It was still early when they said their good-byes to the Van DerPat family. Gretchen was looking hopeful in spite of her sadness, for she had overheard Caro's breakfast outburst.

Katrina wore a worried smile as she kissed Caro and Alec each with affection, whispering in the latter's ear, "Be gentle on the girl, Sacha."

He smiled back grimly. "Believe me, I've been trying, but the imp refuses to cooperate and allow me to behave like a gentleman. Sometimes I'd like to—"

Katrina interrupted, unsure of what he might say, and not wanting to find out. "Well, she may be impulsive and a trifle too outspoken—"

"A *trifle?*"

"—but you must remember she is a lady and you are her guardian. Her father entrusted you with a grave responsibility and I'm sure you are man enough to live up to that, my dear."

Alec's expression was as petulant as a little boy's as he mounted his horse, calling to Caro, "Come on, and let's get moving."

Thaddeus Kosciuszko had drawn her off under a tree to say good-bye and Alec found the earnest expression on his friend's face rather sickening. Kosci helped Caro onto her horse with much flair, then proceeded to kiss her gloved hand lingeringly as he looked up at her face. When he came over to bid Alec good-bye he was met with a caustic:

"I hope I won't be seeing you for a while, comrade, if you take my meaning . . . ?"

"Dear friend, you will be pleased to learn that I am soon departing for my mother country. So, you see, all this fuss you have been making has been totally unnecessary!"

Alec reached out then to grip his hand. "Take care, Kosci."

"You too, Sacha. I will be sure to give your regards to Sonya, and—"

"Yes, yes. Have a safe journey."

They were off then, bound for New York and a world which was fresh from a long war, still exulting over the sweetest victory ever.

As Ivan and Molly carried them out of sight of the house, Alec looked over at Caro with a reluctant grin.

"By the way, *chérie,* you look lovely in that habit."

Caro's face lit up with a smile that dimpled her cheeks and warmed Alec's heart. She almost imagined she detected a faint blush in his cheeks before he turned his face away. The wind ruffled his shining black hair, and Caro thought his cheekbones looked more pronounced than ever in profile. Although she had no idea what was in store for her once they reached bustling Philadelphia, as she gazed down at the great Hudson River below them, then back at Alec's handsome face, Caro felt contented to leave her fate in Alec's hands.

Chapter Nine

NEW YORK WAS VERY DISAPPOINTING TO CARO, FOR
Alec had neglected to tell her that the long years of
war had transformed it into a shambles. The British
were still in residence even now, and nothing had
been done to restore all the ruined buildings. There
had been two massive fires in 1776 and 1778 which
had destroyed at least a quarter of the city. Lamps
were broken, garbage lay all around, and even the
streets were torn up. The general atmosphere was one
of silence, inactivity, and even defeat. Caro, expecting
to find a city alive with triumph and jubilation, was
sadly disappointed.

Alec, however, seemed to have a talent for dis-
covering hidden treasures, and during their two days
in New York Caro would have forgotten the state of
the city if she had not looked outside the windows of
the inn where they were staying. Alec was greeted at
the Bull's Head with an effusiveness and respect that
startled his young companion. The burly innkeeper, a
Mr. Horace Shillingsworth, seemed to Caro to be on
the verge of kissing Alec's feet as he rushed out to
help them dismount. His total lack of curiosity and
surprise at the sight of Caro made her wonder all the
more about Alec's life-style—and about what sort of
future awaited her in Philadelphia. In fact, the only
time she saw Mr. Shillingsworth raise his bushy eye-

brows in surprise was when Alec ordered separate rooms for them.

The inn was a haven of comfort, good cheer, and constant service. The fact that Caro was with Alec seemed to make her extremely worthy in the eyes of Mr. Shillingsworth, for soon after she reached her chamber and began to remove her dusty plumed hat a serving girl appeared with a basin of fresh water. She curtseyed four or five times as she inquired repeatedly if there was anything she could bring her "ladyship." Caro finally had to lead the poor girl to the door in order to persuade her to leave the room, and when her footsteps died away Caro slipped outside and crossed the passageway to knock on Alec's door. He opened it to find her standing there in her stockinged feet, her hair unbound and falling over her shoulders, and wearing only the velvet skirt and lacy blouse of her riding habit. Two bright patches of color stood out on her cheeks, and Alec couldn't resist a smile as he waved her in.

"Missing me already, eh? My dear, this is most unconventional, but I suppose it is a bit late for us to begin observing the dictates of propriety, *n'est-ce pas?*"

Caro glanced distractedly at Alec's mocking grin, barely noticing the fact that he wore only a muslin shirt above the waist, open down the front to reveal his brown chest. She strode across the room, turning around to exclaim:

"Alec, everyone here seems to be under the mistaken impression that you are some sort of royalty! I thought that the war was fought to rid this country of a king!"

He threw back his head and laughed with immense delight. *"Chérie,* what has led you to the conclusion that I am considered to be a king? And why are you so put out by it?"

"I did not mean a king! Perhaps a duke—or what-

101

ever rank is necessary to earn me the title of 'your ladyship'! I find all this bowing and scraping extremely unsettling, especially considering the fact that you are only a—a scoundrel of the first water!"

Alec's renewed laughter only served to increase Caro's frustration. She strode over to him, pushing at his chest to gain his attention.

"I am pleased that you find my vexation such a good joke, sir!"

He looked down at her, his bright turquoise eyes twinkling with enjoyment. "Ah, Caro, you are adorable when you are angry. Please, tell me now who has been calling you 'your ladyship'?"

"Some poor, sniveling little maid who obviously thinks you are God!"

Alec suppressed a fresh burst of laughter with an effort and Caro raised her chin even higher as she added: "You may find all this very amusing, but I do not enjoy the prospect of spending the rest of my time here with that fawning serving girl curtseying at me every time I turn around. It's just not right, Alec! I feel very dishonest somehow!"

"My dear, please do not upset yourself so. I shall simply tell Shillingsworth that you do not require a maid. I am perfectly capable of hooking up your gowns," he finished with an irrepressible grin. Caro tried to look stern, but the dancing light in his eyes was impossible to resist, and she soon found herself laughing along with him.

"Alec, you are a devil! However, I would be so pleased if you could manage to rid me of that maid. Servants make me nervous—even Mary at the Van DerPats'. I feel uncomfortable when someone acts inferior to me."

"Well, that's all very well, but you may as well get used to the idea of having a maid, for you shall have one all your own after we arrive in Philadelphia. Let me assure you, though, that my parents' employees

102

are friendly and quite informal. No one will be calling you 'your ladyship'!"

"Will you kindly tell me why everyone in this place is in such awe of you," Caro demanded. "It's positively indecent!"

Alec quirked an amused eyebrow. "That bad, eh? Actually, *chérie,* you needn't think that I have been courting this extravagant treatment. My father has been coming to this inn for many years, so that is part of it. As for the rest—well, let us just say that I have acquired something of a reputation over the years. You may as well know it now, for you will discover repeatedly that those people who are close to me are quite loyal. I have told you I do not crave the social spotlight, so do not expect to find me well known. There is a certain vein of people, however . . ."

"Who know you to be an infamous villain who will go to any lengths to avoid being classified as a gentleman!" Caro interrupted with a rueful smile.

Alec's white teeth flashed in a sudden grin. *"Touché, chérie!* And enough said on this matter. I find it singularly distasteful to discuss myself. I suggest that you take comfort in the fact that you are being well cared for, and be grateful that I have not torn your clothes from your body and proceeded to ravish you with great enjoyment. Now, my dear, I suggest that you return to your room and put some clothes on before—"

There was a short knock on the door, and then it opened halfway.

"Monsieur? It is I, Pierre!"

The man who appeared in the doorway was smiling broadly, trying to look nonchalant at the sight of Alec and Caro, both in various stages of undress.

"Ah!" he exclaimed cheerfully, "I see that you are engaged, monsieur. Kindly excuse me, and accept my apology for the intrusion." His bright dark eyes twinkled knowingly. "I should have expected—"

Alec sighed in mock exasperation.

"Will you come in here and stop that babbling, Pierre? Close the door! Where have you been the past hour?"

"I am very sorry that I was not present to greet you, monsieur," Pierre replied humbly as he closed the door. "However, I hope that you will endeavor to understand my predicament when I explain that Maurice and I repaired to Fraunces Tavern in Pearl Street earlier this afternoon, where we became involved in a game of faro. A sum of money changed hands, and—"

"Come to the point, man!" Alec demanded, barely repressing a smile at Pierre's long-winded speech.

"Maurice was obliged to play two more games than we had planned in order to win back my losses, monsieur." Pierre was beaming with all the charm of an errant child who is confident of forgiveness.

"Which I trust he managed to do?"

"Bien sûr, monsieur!"

"Fine. I am happy to hear that the episode is ended, for I was growing excessively bored by your account of it!"

Pierre smiled back imperturbably. "It is good to see you, monsieur! I trust that you have had a pleasant journey?"

"Pleasant is hardly the adjective that comes to mind, but I suppose that in a queer sort of way it fits. Now, Pierre, permit me to present to you Mademoiselle Caroline Bergman. She will be with us from now on."

"Congratulations, monsieur!" Pierre ejaculated. "Ah, *mon Dieu!* If you will permit me to say so, I was beginning to doubt that this happy day would ever occur!"

Alec cast his eyes heavenward, raising his hand to silence his valet.

"Enough! I am sorry to dash your hopes, but I am afraid that you must retain those doubts a while longer, Pierre. Miss Bergman is my ward. She is Josef Bergman's daughter."

Pierre rushed over to Caro, bowing before her as he attempted to conceal his disappointment.

"Mademoiselle, please pardon my outburst. How could I have been so impetuous? May I say now that I am very pleased to make your acquaintance—and allow me to add that you have a great man as your guardian."

"Will you shut your mouth, Pierre?"

Alec's tone was affectionately brusque, and Caro found herself charmed by the tiny man who was bowing before her. The white, curled wig he wore made him look very old, and Caro was still certain that Pierre was at least many years Alec's senior. He was barely as tall as she and only slightly heavier, and there was such extravagant warmth and cheerfulness in his impish face that she felt irresistibly drawn to him.

"Please stop bowing!" Alec exclaimed. "Miss Bergman feels that everyone is her equal, so you must not act so subservient toward her. Now then, Caro, this is Pierre DuBois, my valet and self-appointed guardian angel. He seems to feel that I cannot exist without his services and constant advice."

Caro's face was alight with the smile she turned on Pierre, and her dimples showed deeply on either side of her pretty mouth.

"Mr. DuBois, I am so happy to meet you! Alec never mentioned you before, so your existence is a pleasant surprise for me. I have a feeling we are going to be good friends!"

Before Pierre could respond, Alec interjected dismally, "That is what I am afraid of!"

It was nearly time for Caro to dress for supper when there was an unexpected tapping at her door. She was in the process of bathing as best she could from the shallow basin, and bristled at the interruption which obliged her to don her robe and go to the door. Certain that it was the little serving girl again, she was surprised to see Alec standing on the threshold with a woman. His companion was as tall as Gretchen had been, but much more voluptuous, with brilliant red hair arranged in an intricate style that drew Caro's eyes irresistibly.

Alec chuckled. "Don't tell me you are at a loss for words for once, infant? Please stop gaping—it is uncommonly rude even though Madame Vontaine's beauty is obviously fascinating. Colette, allow me to present Caroline Bergman."

Madame Vontaine's catlike green eyes seemed to slant even more dramatically as she smiled down at Caro.

"Alec, what a child! She appears so . . . so . . . virginal!"

Caro stared even harder, totally unable to speak.

"Are you saying that you cannot do it?" Alec inquired sharply.

"Au contraire, mon brave. Dressing her will be a rare treat; I shall feel like a sculptor with fresh clay, or an artist with a clean canvas."

"Yes, well, that's all perfectly fine, but I just want it understood that you aren't to get too carried away by your creative instincts! Caro has no need of artifice to make her beautiful. I want you to see to it that everything I buy for her only enhances her natural attributes and does not obscure them."

Madame Vontaine narrowed her eyes as though insulted. "Monsieur, I wish that you would trust me. I am an artist, and I have an inborn feeling for these matters. Now! Leave us, *s'il vous plaît."*

Alec was turning away when Caro found her voice.

"Wait! Will you kindly tell me what is going on here?"

"You're getting some proper clothes, *chérie*," Alec grinned. "You seemed so proud in that riding habit that I decided to get you a few more things so your wardrobe won't be suspiciously scanty when we arrive in Philadelphia. We wouldn't want my family to think you only own two gowns! Madame Vontaine is an—er, old friend of mine. She runs one of the last remaining women's clothing shops in New York City, which has become quite exclusive because of all the mysteriously imported French fabric she sews with!"

Madame tilted up her nose with dignity and sniffed. "As an artist, I have become accustomed to the best."

"But," interrupted Caro, "how can you make dresses for me when we will only be here another day?"

"Happily," Alec responded, "Colette keeps a large number of sample dresses for her models. It is our hope that some of them may be altered to fit you."

Suddenly he reached out and put his hands around her tiny waist, which had been hidden in the loose folds of her robe. "How does this look, Colette?"

"Exquisite!"

Two hours later, Caro descended to join Alec in the dining room of the inn. Madame Vontaine had kept her well occupied as she measured, then produced a large reticule filled with dozens of fabrics in every color. She had held them against Caro's skin, eyes, and hair, one by one.

"You have difficult coloring, *ma petite*," Madame had exclaimed more than once. "Your skin tone is *très*—ah, unique. It is lovely, but it restricts the colors you can wear."

She had seemed hopeful, though, when she left, and Caro could not help feeling a trifle excited at the thought of new gowns. She donned her wilted-looking yellow dress for supper, acutely conscious of her hunger.

Downstairs, Caro met Pierre immediately. It appeared that he was waiting for her.

"Hello, Pierre! I am simply ravenous. Alec must force them to feed me, for it is all his fault that I have been closeted in my chamber all this time. Where is the tyrant?"

Pierre squirmed uncomfortably. "I regret to say that he is not here, mademoiselle. He had—ah, another engagement this evening. He waited until a short while ago to tell you himself, but he could tarry no longer." The expression of undisguised disappointment on Caro's face was heartrending to Pierre. "Please do not look so sad, mademoiselle! After all, I am here to keep you company. I am a sorry replacement, I know—"

"Oh, no, Pierre. Do not say so. As a matter of fact, I have been spending entirely too many hours in Alec's company. You may have noticed that we do not deal very well together, and lately I seem to be a constant source of irritation to him. I am certain that it is the best thing that he has gone out on his own tonight."

Pierre, though relieved, was unconvinced. He had not yet decided exactly what the connection was between his master and this young girl, but he was sure there was more to the situation than met the eye. The look on Caro's face when she learned of Alec's absence was far more eloquent to Pierre than her earnest speech.

He sat with her while she ate, and noticed that her appetite was not as great as she had earlier proclaimed. Afterward, they adjourned to the taproom where they engaged in several lively games of whist and backgammon. By the end of the evening, Caro felt very close to the little Frenchman, and before retiring they sat before the hearth and talked. Pierre told her of his early life in France. He had been a cabin boy on Jean-Philippe Beauvisage's pirate ship and came to live in the colonies out of necessity, for he had been on Beauvisage's last voyage, when he had abducted Alec's mother.

"It was five years before M. Beauvisage sailed again to France," Pierre explained. "Of course, he offered all his crew free passage home, but I was very young then and overly impressed by the dashing *capitaine*. I begged him to find me a position in his new household, and he managed to do so. I have grown more devoted to the family with each passing year. Now, of course, I am the personal valet to M. Alexandre." He smiled brightly. "I feel young all over again, for each day in his service is an adventure."

Caro grinned in spite of herself. "Yes, I have that same feeling! Tell me, though, Pierre, do you think that Alec's parents will not mind having me come to live with them?"

"Ah! So that is Monsieur's plan! But, *non*, mademoiselle, do not be troubled. Monsieur and Madame Beauvisage are magnificent people. *Très extraordinaire*. You are sure to love them, and I know that they will welcome you with open arms if their son says that you are to be part of the family."

At that moment the clock in the entry hall struck twelve and Pierre yawned with studied nonchalance. Caro cast one last despairing glance at the door before sighing:

"Well, I suppose I've kept you up quite late enough, Pierre."

"Mademoiselle must be very tired after such a long journey." He paused then, before plunging on: "Besides, I feel certain that Monsieur will not be coming back anytime soon. And, if you will permit me to suggest it, he would not appreciate finding you here waiting for him."

Caro opened her mouth as if to protest her innocence, then seemed to think better of it. "I suppose I would be wise to listen to you, for certainly you must be closer to understanding the workings of Alec's brain than I am. I was that obvious, then?"

Pierre's smile was warm and compassionate. "Mademoiselle, I have known M. Alexandre for many years, and have witnessed the devastating effect that he has on females more times than I can count. Besides, I would be a fool to believe that a charming girl like yourself would spend so many hours with an old man like me out of choice!"

Caro retorted, "I must insist to you that I am not in love with Alec or anything like that. I'll admit that I do seem to have some sort of jumbled feeling for him, which half the time seems to be anger or hatred! Anyway, I will soon be meeting all manner of handsome young men in Philadelphia. Katrina Van DerPat is certain that I shall make an excellent marriage very soon. And even if I weren't going to meet other men, I would never let myself get all tangled up emotionally with Alec, for I am no fool, Pierre! I saw the way Gretchen Van DerPat kept making calf-eyes at him last night and it nauseated me! You are very much mistaken if you think I shall fall in line behind all the females you just mentioned, for I do not intend to let Alec or anyone else break my heart!"

Caro's voice was growing stronger by the moment as her chin rose higher in her determination. Pierre was looking at her with such bewildered concern that she leaned forward to lay a tiny hand on his arm.

"You must excuse my outburst, Pierre. Ever since I met Alec I seem to feel all stirred up and I guess I needed to let out some of those pent-up frustrations. I simply refuse to sacrifice myself on an altar as though he were some god. Other girls may do it, but I cannot allow myself to be ordinary. Can you understand the way I feel?"

He nodded, staring at her in fascination, his dark

eyes twinkling. Caro's voice grew softer as she continued with a smile:

"And Pierre, you must not underestimate your own charm and personality. I have truly enjoyed our evening together. It was very relaxing, which is a welcome change from the way I feel with Alec. We don't seem to be able to spend an hour together without ending it in a shouting match."

Pierre escorted Caro upstairs to her room and bade her a warm goodnight. She was happy to know that she had a friend, especially one who showed promise of acting as a buffer between her and the volatile person of Alexandre Beauvisage.

Once in bed, Caro found that in spite of her extreme weariness she was unable to fall asleep. Her ears were tuned to the sound of Alec's footsteps, and she alternated between imagining where he was and trying not to think about him at all. Finally she drifted off into a fitful slumber, only to awaken hours later to the far-off sound of Alec's deep, muffled laughter. Caro was on the verge of getting out of bed to investigate further when a soft, feminine voice reached her ears. She could not make out the words, but the sound of Alec's answering chuckle told her all she needed to know. Huddling under the deep quilts, she was suddenly very cold, and was surprised to feel bitter tears stinging her eyes and spilling onto her cheeks. Clenching her hands into little fists, as Caro recalled the wonderful, shameful night *she* had spent in his arms, she whispered defiantly:

"You devil! I hate you!"

Chapter Ten

THE FOLLOWING MORNING, CARO WAS DETERMINED TO
be as cold to Alec as possible, for she was angry at
herself for feeling hurt, and angrier still at him for
inflicting it. She was feeling extremely disconsolate as
well as tired, for her night's sleep had left her more
worn out than she was before she retired. The day
started off well despite her anger, for Madame
Vontaine had a new dress sent over before Caro had
even finished drinking her chocolate. When one of
Madame Vontaine's shopgirls entered the room displaying her new gown, she felt like a child receiving
a long-desired birthday gift.

The dress itself was lovely beyond words, made
very simply of a rich cream-colored fabric overlaid
with transparent pale-green gauze. There was a
wide dark-green velvet sash at the waist, tied to
one side, and Caro saw that the girl was holding a thin
band of matching material to be fastened around her
neck. She had brought shoes, too, as well as underclothes, stockings, and even a hat, which was dark
green with a cluster of frothy cream-colored feathers
emerging from a wide brim. Caro was enchanted, and
even allowed the girl to help her dress and arrange her
hair. The gown was perfect for her, and she knew it
as she surveyed herself happily in the mirror. The girl
from Madame Vontaine's slipped away then, assured

that her errand was successfully completed, and Caro decided to go downstairs.

When she reached the entrance to the dining hall she stopped short, for she was startled to see Alec seated within. He was talking to a man she had never seen, leaning back in his chair with a cool elegance that made her heart pound maddeningly. Wearing no vest or coat, the soft lines of his linen shirt revealed the outline of his broad shoulders and chest. His expertly tied cravat was startlingly white against his tanned, finely chiseled face and the sweep of raven black hair caught neatly at his neck. Even from a distance Caro could see the cynical gleam in his turquoise eyes. He did not see her at first, and she used the moment to calm herself and summon up her best manner of cold disdain. Then, as she stepped forward, Alec glanced up and flashed an irresistible grin that instantly melted her frosty resolve. He rose, slim-hipped and agile, to surprise Caro by raising her hand to his mouth and kissing it with lips that scorched her skin.

"*Chérie,* you look superb! Absolutely perfect. You know I am not a man given to idle compliments, so you must believe me when I flatter you!"

Caro hardly knew what to make of his open good humor. He looked completely rested, which irritated her, and she wondered if his night's activities had proved more soothing than sleep. She tried to look at him with cool detachment, but succeeded only in blushing.

The rest of the day followed the same pattern. Alec was in a rare good mood, brimming with witty conversation. Caro would watch him, remembering the humiliating tears she had shed the night before over the sound of a woman's voice in his room, and her heart would harden with bitterness. But then he would speak to her, his voice dry with laughter, or he would grasp her arm with his warm, strong fingers, and Caro's heart would melt again.

They spent nearly the entire day together, during which Caro found herself unable to start a quarrel. Alec took her out walking after breakfast, answering all her questions about New York City.

"I know it looks quite hopeless now, but I would be willing to wager any amount that New York will snap back from this magnificently. I don't doubt that everyone will be living the good life in the extreme now that the war is over, and New York will just sit here and absorb all the benefits. I have a feeling that this city will be larger and more bustling than ever in a very short space of time."

As they strolled along, Caro was acutely conscious of the admiring stares she was receiving from every man they passed. The new hat was perched saucily atop her glossy honey-colored curls, its wide brim accentuating her delicate face and expressive golden-brown eyes. The gauzy layers of her gown clung tantalizingly to the ripe curves of her body, and Caro felt as if she were wrapped and floating in gossamer.

The weather was almost too perfect to be real in October, for the sun was shining in a dazzling blue sky, and the air was mild and sweet.

Alec watched Caro's smiling face as she looked curiously around while they walked. He could see how the men were all looking at her, and she would blush adorably whenever someone stared too boldly. She was so obviously enjoying her newfound elegance that he didn't have the heart to cut their walk short, although all his instincts shouted for him to shield her from those insolent, daring eyes. Only the realization that he had been looking at her just as openly all day long kept him in check, and he managed to keep up a casual flow of conversation, as if he were blind.

Meanwhile, Caro was worried about Alec's inattention and lack of concern over the attention she was attracting. She could hardly credit that he was the same man who had raged at her about Colonel Kosciuszko only two nights before. She thought again of what she had heard while in bed the night before, feeling unaccountably depressed at the realization that he simply didn't appear to care enough to get mad anymore. Wondering again who the girl had been, the idea occurred to her that perhaps Alec was in love. If that were the case, it would account for his altered behavior, but this new possible solution did nothing to lift her spirits.

Madame Vontaine was waiting in Caro's chamber when they arrived back at the inn. She had spread out over the bed the three more new dresses, and beamed in anticipation of Alec's praise.

The gowns, each in a different style, were lovely. The first was a polonaise, fashioned of expensive pale-gold silk and trimmed with ivory. The second gown was more traditional, ankle-length with a long boned bodice, deeply scooped ruffled neckline, and a modest bustle. The material was white muslin with narrow yellow and pale-green stripes over a snowy lace-edged petticoat. The last gown took Caro's breath away. It was designed in the same style as the dress she wore, in candlelight ivory overlaid with fragile layers of peach-colored gauze. The bustle at the back was softly drawn up in airy gauze, and the sleeves were long and transparent.

Caro looked and behaved like a little girl as she held each gown up against her body, dancing around the room to stop in front of the long mirror in the corner. Alec and Colette Vontaine both watched her with indulgent smiles, the latter pointing out the round boxes against the wall which contained matching reticules, chemises, shoes, hats, and stockings.

"I tried to bring one dress for every occasion—the stripe is for morning wear, the green and peach dresses are for public daytime wear, and the gold is for evening. Of course, the gauze dresses would be

115

perfectly acceptable for evening—particularly the peach. I chose it just for you, *chérie*, and it should make you look quite grown up!"

Caro looked over her shoulder with shining eyes. "Madame Vontaine, you are like a fairy godmother from a storybook! I can never thank you enough!"

"My dear," Alec commented drily, "you may rest assured that you will eventually possess dozens of gowns as lovely as these. Your dressmaker in Philadelphia will have plenty of time to create a perfect wardrobe for you."

Madame Vontaine narrowed her green eyes at Alec. "Do you mean to suggest that my gowns are substandard? I'll have you know, Alexandre Beauvisage, that I would not do such a favor as this for any other man! Do you have any idea of the long hours I spent . . ."

Alec put an arm around her shoulders as he led her out of the room and across the hall. He was smiling at her most winningly, and as the door to his room closed behind them, Caro heard him say:

"Please, Colette, spare me your recriminations. I am duly grateful for your efforts, and I intend to prove it to you!"

Caro stood in front of her mirror, limply holding the gold silk gown, all the joy gone from her eyes. Her depression soon lifted, however, for less than five minutes later Alec's door opened again and they both emerged, Colette Vontaine stuffing a wad of bills into her open reticule. Caro observed with pleasure that not a hair of Madame's elaborate white wig had been disturbed, and Alec's cravat was still securely tied. After seeing her to her carriage, he returned to Caro's room, carrying something over his arm.

"Well, infant, it appears that Colette was saving her biggest surprise for last."

It was impossible to disguise the twinkle in his eyes as he held up a remarkable pelisse for her inspection.

It was floor-length, with wide sleeves, in a warm shade of cinnamon. The cuffs and hood were trimmed in luxurious, fluffy red fox, so beautiful that Caro was afraid to touch it.

"Colette tells me she designed this for herself," Alec smiled. "She had always had a flair for the unusual. When she saw you she said she knew you would be perfect for this cloak, so she has sacrificed it. Not without being properly reimbursed, of course!"

Caro took the pelisse in her arms, caressing the soft fur as Alec continued: "Well, it is growing late, and I suppose I should leave you to dress for dinner. I had planned to dine at a friend's house tonight, but Pierre protested so loudly at the idea of my leaving you alone again that I have decided to bring you along. There will be just three of us, which is not terribly proper, but Alexander is a respectable married man, so I expect that helps a little. Will an hour be enough time for you to dress?"

"Oh! Oh, yes! I'll be ready, Alec!"

"Good. Wear the peach."

The evening air was chilly enough for Caro to wear her new pelisse in good conscience. The fur framed her face in a way that made her eyes look large and lovelier than ever, and the general effect was quite irresistible. It took a great effort on Alec's part to remain politely detached in his compliments as he escorted her to the carriage. He was unusually silent during the short ride to Wall Street, so Caro contented herself with looking out the window as they traveled.

Her face was profiled exquisitely in the darkness, haloed by its wreath of fur, and once she turned to find Alec staring at her in a way that made her flesh prickle deliciously. His face was cast in shadow, his mouth and jaw set in hard lines, his cheekbones pronounced, and his turquoise eyes piercing even in the darkness. Caro looked back at him, certain that he could hear her thudding heart as she waited for him to speak. There was something electric in the air, and Caro felt that Alec was touching her even though he hadn't moved. Suddenly the carriage drew to a stop and Maurice was helping her down.

Alec came around beside her to take her elbow, then led her up a short stairway before a plain building, one of many in a long, connected row. Before Alec could pull the bell, a face appeared at the window, flashing a grin at them that reminded Caro of Alec. The door opened to reveal a slender man with reddish-brown hair, fine features, and an air of graceful self-assurance. As he reached out to grip Alec's hand warmly, it was apparent that the two men were old friends. When Caro was introduced, Alexander Hamilton gazed at her levelly, greeting her with easy charm.

Inside the house, Hamilton took her pelisse and momentarily left the room. Alec looked at Caro's appealingly creamy shoulders against the soft peach gauze. She glanced at him in apprehension, hoping for some word of approval. Although he said nothing, his eyes told her everything she wanted to know before he abruptly looked away.

Hamilton's home was small and cozy, and as he led them into the drawing room he commented: "You must excuse the appearance of this house, Miss Bergman. Alec may have told you that I have just acquired it and have not actually moved in permanently yet. I am wary about living in New York while the British still occupy the city, and it is impossible to think of bringing my family here yet."

"Where is your wife now, Mr. Hamilton?"

"We have been residing in Albany with her parents, the Schuylers, since leaving Philadelphia during the summer."

"We shall miss you there, Alexander," said Alec. "I shall be hard put for a good political discussion!"

"That is one problem I won't be encountering!" Hamilton laughed. "There are already seven other lawyers that I know of who are locating nearby. Few of us share the same views, as you might guess! As a matter of fact, Burr will be right around the corner."

Caro listened as the two men discussed their shared memories of the war, Alec's meeting with Kosciuszko, and the latest news of General Washington. She had no idea who Hamilton was, but she gathered from the conversation that he had been closely associated with Washington during the war years. Caro watched him as they talked, deciding that he must be around Alec's age; certainly no older. There was a similarity in their manner, for both were men of intelligence, confidence, and natural charm. The likeness ended there, however, for it was obvious that they were very different in other respects. Physically, Hamilton was Alec's opposite. His Scotch ancestry was borne out in his reddish hair and fair skin, and he was dressed all in light brown. Alec's black hair shone in the lamplight, and his bronzed skin contrasted attractively with the white lace at his throat and his pewter-gray suit.

Caro could see that they were different spiritually as well. Hamilton had the air of an aristocrat with his urbane charm and ambitious intelligence. It was obvious to Caro that he had already accomplished a great deal in his short life and she felt he would not stop until he had left his mark on the emerging nation.

Alec, on the other hand, had an aura of vital energy which was constantly masked by his caustic wit and reckless charm. He moves in the circles of great, famous men, she thought, And he could be one, too. He could have been a well-known hero in the war but he would rather take the excitement and leave the glory for others. And he'll never change. His cynical voice interrupted her thoughts: "After all, my father was no gentleman. Seems to be a family trait!" Caro looked at him, feeling unaccountably tearful. Alec

119

was reclining in his chair, white teeth showing as he laughed, and he seemed to have forgotten she was even there.

A plump woman with powdered hair under a mob-cap appeared in the doorway to announce dinner. They went into the long, narrow dining room, where Hamilton sat at the head of the table with his guests flanking him. After asking Caro a few polite questions and commenting soberly that he had known and respected her father, he turned back to Alec. Inwardly, she breathed a sigh of relief and Alec's eyes met hers momentarily, flickering with amusement. Her fear that Alexander Hamilton would ask her something specific about her origins was bad enough, but when he mentioned her "father" she literally panicked as she tried to search her mind for a memory of what her family had been like and could recall nothing.

Dinner was singularly boring for Caro. The meal was plain, Hamilton apologizing that he had no opportunity to set in many foodstuffs, and supplies were difficult to come by in the ravaged city.

The two men spent the entire meal discussing the Wallingham family and the general problem of Tory persecution.

"The problem your friends encountered was by no means unique, Alec," Hamilton declared irritably. "Already I have been besieged by would-be loyalist clients here in New York. The people who left the city during the occupation are prepared to bring charges against those who stayed here and lived in their houses —behind enemy lines."

"I've heard about that so-called Trespass Act! How can it be justified under the Peace Treaty? The end of the war was supposed to have guaranteed everyone a clean slate, and it is beyond me how men can be so small-minded!"

"You needn't attempt to convince me, Beauvisage, for I am long won over to your cause. The time I have spent in New York has made me angrier than ever before. This city is in a deplorable state, as I trust you have noticed!—and in desperate need of respectable citizens with capital to return it to its former state. And yet we see these foolish Americans with whom I am ashamed to be associated, trying to expel their fellow citizens, untried and unheard. I tell you, it is a mockery of everything this war was fought to attain. This land of freedom-lovers has made a mockery of the principles we are supposedly living by. This, when the Treaty itself is barely dry and the British haven't even left our shores!"

"What is worrying me, Hamilton, is the effect this will have on our image in the eyes of the rest of the world," Alec replied. "As a new country badly in need of trade, we can hardly afford to be seen blatantly ignoring the promises of our Peace Treaty!"

Caro tried to stay alert as they continued their animated conversation, but her lack of sleep the night before was beginning to catch up with her. Alec broke off in mid-sentence when he noticed that Caro's long lashes were sweeping against her cheeks as she struggled to keep her eyes open.

"My dear," he called in an amused voice, "if you can just endeavor to remain with us a few moments longer, I shall take you home. I told Pierre I was sure you would have had a better time with him!"

Caro's sleepy smile was adorable. "I'm so sorry, Mr. Hamilton. I'm sure this is very ill-bred of me. Every time I eat at a formal dinner with Alec I seem to fail in one way or another!"

Alec shot her a withering look that she was too drowsy to notice, but Hamilton merely smiled in well-concealed surprise.

"Miss Bergman, I do hope you haven't felt that this meal was formal. I realize that it probably was not very interesting for a young lady, but I certainly did not intend that you should feel formal."

Caro laughed lightly. "Mr. Hamilton, after eating quail over an open fire in the woods, this meal seems to me to be very elegant in comparison!"

Hamilton raised his eyebrows and looked at Alec, who was glowering at Caro. She, in turn, merely smiled drowsily at both men. Alec managed to toss off the remainder of his brandy so quickly as to appear almost rude, and minutes later they had said goodnight to Alexander Hamilton and were inside the carriage. After preparing himself for a heated quarrel with Caro, Alec was quite disconcerted when she snuggled up against his shoulder, wearing an angelic smile, and proceeded to go to sleep. He held her tightly against him and wondered why he hadn't left this impossible minx where he found her.

Chapter Eleven

THE JOURNEY FROM NEW YORK TO PHILADELPHIA took them two long days, but Pierre informed Caro that they had made remarkably good time. Alec's carriage was lightweight and well-sprung, and Caro, riding inside, scarcely felt the bumps. Alec rode Ivan most of the way, and Caro found herself watching them through the window. She couldn't help admiring the picture they made—two graceful, strong, elegantly arrogant creatures. Alec's hair was as black and glossy as Ivan's coat, and Caro could see much similarity between their proud, handsome heads and long, muscular legs.

The morning they left New York, Alec had appeared at breakfast with several books for Caro to read on the journey. For her own part, she had procured a pack of cards from Pierre to keep in her reticule, hoping for many enjoyable games along the way. She tried to act pleased and grateful when Alec presented her with the books, but the knowledge that he would not be sharing the carriage with her after all was a bitter disappointment. Caro had hoped that the long hours of enforced togetherness would serve to bring out the old Alec. His constant air of impersonal, friendly courtesy was making her feel frustrated, unhappy, and lonely, for it seemed that he had gone away from her somehow. She actually found herself praying that he would shout at her, but his manner remained coolly unruffled and there was no way that Caro could have guessed the effort he was exerting to retain his poise.

During the carriage ride the night before, Alec had stared at her sleeping face and determined to sever all the strange emotional bonds that had formed between them. He was certain that it would serve the best interests of them both, a conviction that he sometimes felt he was reminding himself of every damned minute. En route to the inn, he had come frighteningly close to tipping up her tiny chin and kissing her while she slept. Alec was unaccustomed to feeling disturbed by his feelings for a woman, and his relationship with Caro had been fraught from the beginning with a frustration that he decided he could gladly live without.

It was late afternoon when they ferried across the Delaware River, somewhat upstream from Philadelphia. The process was slow, and Alec decided that Caro was deserving of some company.

He found her looking surprisingly fresh after the tedious two-day journey, wearing the striped dress that Madame Vontaine had made. The boned bodice could not conceal the shapely curves of Caro's breasts, which showed appealingly above the stiff ruching trim at the neckline. As Alec settled himself in the seat across from her in the carriage, Caro was aware of his eyes insolently undressing her and she felt her cheeks grow hot with color. However, when he met her eyes, his were opaque; and when he spoke his voice was coolly courteous.

"Well, Caro, we're almost home now. Actually, we're almost to *my* home. It is later than I had planned, so I have decided that we shall go directly to my house while there is still daylight. After a bath and some supper, I will take you down to Philadelphia to my parents' home."

"Why do you say 'down to Philadelphia'?" she inquired in puzzlement.

"I suppose that I should have explained to you that I live away from the actual city," Alec smiled. "I have only recently acquired my home in Germantown, through the misfortune of the original owner. Germantown is more of a village, located out in the country, and six years ago this month it was the scene of one of the war's major battles. The owner of my house was killed accidentally, and after his family fled, the house was occupied by various British officers. After Yorktown I was heading north, and just happened to be there at the right time to get the house."

"So you live in the country—and your parents live in the city?" Caro asked apprehensively.

"A splendid deduction, *chérie,*" he replied mockingly. "I suppose you cannot see me as a country squire, and indeed the role may not suit me at all. However, I have maintained a small house in town ever since I came of age and I found myself too readily accessible. My ardent hope is that by removing myself from the nucleus of society I may be more discriminating about the functions I attend and the people I associate with. Also, Belle Maison is an incredibly lovely place with a fabulous library. There is a great deal of land, so that I can keep a large stable, and the garden was a showplace in the past. It needs a lot of work, but I'm rather looking forward to it." He laughed then, as though he didn't believe his own words, and Caro ventured a smile.

"Do you call it Belle Maison, then?"

"Yes—that was Natalya's idea. By the way, did I mention to you that my grandmother lives on my property?"

"I believe you said she had come to Philadelphia lately and had her own house."

"Yes, well, that house is located behind mine. We are even connected by an underground tunnel, and she

125

takes a devilish pleasure in surprising me at the oddest moments!"

Caro giggled, her dimples showing. "She sounds like an unusual grandmother! I believe I shall like her!"

"That is part of the reason I intend to get you away from my house—Grandmère is almost more unpredictable than you are, and I shudder to think what would happen if I had both of you to contend with at once!" Alec smiled and reached out to touch her chin reflectively. "Of course, Natalya is a little hellcat as well, and no doubt you two will be stirring up all manner of mischief. However, that will be Maman and Father's problem, not mine. Thank God!"

He leaned forward then, looking outside to watch as they reached shore. Caro had little opportunity to ponder Alec's words after that, for the next half-hour was well filled by the ride to Belle Maison. The countryside was lovely as they journeyed northwest from the Delaware River. Caro occasionally spotted a large house set back in the trees, but somehow she recognized Belle Maison even before Alec brought Ivan alongside the carriage and called to her:

"There it is, *chérie,* my humble abode!"

In the deepening twilight the house was bathed in a rosy glow that made it even more beautiful in Caro's eyes. Built of red brick, it was solid and imposing in its simplicity. To Caro, there was an aura of confidence and strength about the house which instinctively reminded her of Alec. There were fourteen many-paned windows across the front, all with pure-white casements, beautifully plain against the red-brick background. When Alec jumped from Ivan's back to help Caro down she found herself standing on a wide brick pathway that led to the white front door. Alec raised an eyebrow, looking down at her face to glean her reaction, and she gazed back at him with shining brown eyes full of pleasure.

Just as she was about to speak, the front door flew open and a figure clad all in blue appeared.

"Sacha! You are home at last! I declare I thought you would never arrive!"

The girl came running down the walk, throwing herself into Alec's open arms. For one horrified moment Caro believed she must be his wife. He was smiling indulgently as she hugged him repeatedly, finally managing to disentangle himself from her grasp.

"Natalya, you little chicken, will you kindly curb this display of sisterly affection? You are growing far too ardent for my taste. Please unhand me and then have the decency to tell me what in God's name you are doing here?"

When she moved back a fraction from Alec's chest, Caro got her first clear look at Natalya. She was quite tall, appearing willowy, with the same fine bone structure as her brother. Her lustrous black curls were pinned up on her head, revealing a long, graceful white neck. She had brilliant sapphire-blue eyes, as clear in their color as Alec's were. Her face was proud, yet beautiful and full of humor, and there was much in her expression that reminded Caro of Alec.

"Sacha, you shall never know how I've missed you —life has been exceedingly dreary. However, I have confidence that matters are going to improve rapidly, for Maman and Papa have left for France and I am to stay here with you! Grandmère has been in wonderful spirits and I know that we three shall have a marvelous time!"

Suddenly she seemed to see Caro for the first time, and her eyes were filled with friendly curiosity.

"Sacha—"

"I thought you would never ask, chicken. Don't panic, for I've not married, and remain your same sane brother. This young lady is Caroline Bergman, my ward. She is the daughter of the man whose farm I now own in Connecticut. Caro, this is Natalya, my—uh—sister."

Natalya doubled her fist and poked at Alec's arm. "You needn't say it as though you wish I weren't!" She leaned toward Caro then, whispering loudly, "Actually, he's mad about me, but just refuses to admit it."

Alec rolled his eyes heavenward, but a smile played at the corners of his mouth and Caro found herself laughing.

"Hello, Natalya! I have heard a lot about you, and I—"

"Girls, I hate to interrupt this meeting of the minds, but it has grown dark here before my eyes and I am at a loss for a reason why I should stand in the walk all evening when there is a perfectly good house only a few yards away."

He grasped Caro's arm with one hand and Natalya's with the other and led them through the front door. Caro spent the next few minutes looking around the first floor of Belle Maison, and falling in love with it.

The entrance hall was laid with English brick running in a diagonal pattern, and all the walls were beautifully paneled to the ceiling. There was a graceful arch with double doors which led to the stair hall, two lovely parlors opening on either side of the hall.

Caro found that though these rooms were rather sparsely furnished, each piece was perfect. Her favorite room in the house was the north parlor, which was exquisite in its very simplicity. The furniture was all beautifully carved Queen Anne, principally a graceful wing chair embroidered with green, yellow, and brown crewelwork and a lovely settee upholstered in rich yellow damask. The paneled walls were painted white, and there were no curtains, for the recessed windows had interior shutters, and to Caro's delight, window seats.

Alec and Natalya finally persuaded her to visit her

new bedchamber and freshen up before continuing the tour. Natalya led her up the wide, curving stairway and down the carpeted hall, seeming to open a door at random. Caro stood on the threshold of her new bedroom and drew in her breath. The room was dominated by a large Sheraton field bed with an ivory net canopy and a spotless white spread. To Caro, it looked as though the canopy were fashioned of a million tiny snowflakes. The furniture was lovely, upholstered in a soft moss green, and even the white china pitcher and bowl were sprigged with delicate green flowers.

"This room used to belong to the wife of the man who built Belle Maison," explained Natalya. "He planned and furnished it for her while they were still betrothed, so I suppose that is why there is such an aura of love here."

"But no one sleeps here now?"

"I imagine I would, but I like my own chamber farther from Sacha's, and everything in it is blue. That is my favorite color."

Caro smiled. "It suits you!"

"Thank you!" Natalya spread her skirts and sat up on the high bed, slender ankles showing. "You must know that I am consumed by curiosity! But before I start asking questions, I thought you might like to know that my brother told me you will be staying here permanently—or at least until my parents return, and that won't be for months! While we were downstairs I asked him what his plans were. Of course, it's terribly improper for you to be here in the house with Sacha, but there seems to be no alternative. Isn't it exciting? We shall have such fun!"

Caro bit her lip, uncomfortably conscious of the immense wave of euphoric relief she had felt at the news that she would not be parted from Alec.

"I imagine your brother is quite put out. You can't

know how anxious he was to deposit me at your parents'. I have been a terrible trouble to him."

"Really? How lovely! It is such fun to bother him, for he has a marvelous temper. Sacha is always so cool, always so witty and ready with a set-down that it becomes a challenge to try to unnerve him. Of course he is on to me and Grandmère after all these years, so we are often unsuccessful."

Natalya's beaming face was so open and friendly that Caro felt instinctively drawn to her.

"He has told me that you are a mischief-maker," she smiled. "However, I could hardly credit that the things he said of your grandmother were true!"

"I'm certain that they were. She is such fun—I would have adored knowing her in her youth. Of course, Papa was a rakehell himself in his younger days, and I suppose such things are inherited. Sacha and Nicholai certainly fit the family mold!"

"I heard about your parents; how they met and all." Caro paused, laughing in remembrance. "As a matter of fact, I was afraid that Alec was a pirate himself when we first met. I even asked him, and he found that terribly amusing."

Natalya clapped her hands together, laughing with delight. "Oh! I wish I could have seen that! Did you truly imagine that Sacha was a pirate?"

"Well, yes. It is easy for you to see the humor in it, but to a person who does not know Alec he appears terribly dark and lawless. I wasn't really afraid of him, but he just seemed to fit the part. I can still see him—bearded, his shirt open—so hard and handsome . . ."

Caro was looking past Natalya, speaking in a low voice that seemed to forget it was in conversation. Natalya slid off the bed and crossed the room, touching Caro's shoulder.

"Say, you aren't in love with Sacha, are you?" she asked in a tone that managed to sound frank and gentle all at once. Caro started at her words, then laughed nervously, unable to meet Natalya's level blue gaze.

"Goodness, no! Believe me, nothing could be farther from the truth! I am far too intelligent to commit emotional suicide over a—a—scoundrel! I have nothing but sympathy for any woman who falls in love with Alec!" she cried in an unnaturally loud voice.

Natalya eyed her shrewdly before replying, "I certainly meant no offense. It's just that I like you so much, and what you said just now is God's truth. Sacha breaks girls' hearts like pieces of fine china, and yet the silly fools return for more. He has lost respect for females over the years, and now he only uses them for his pleasure. He will never marry, and it is just as well, for he could never love any woman for more than a week." She paused, watching Caro's eyes cloud. "I didn't mean to offend you. I simply was terrified at the thought of you losing your heart to him, for it would be hopeless—a tragedy! Especially a girl as pretty as you are; there must be dozens of men at your beck and call, Caro. I can feel that you will be a huge success!"

Caro attempted an unconvincing smile.

"Yes, that's what Alec keeps telling me."

"Well, he is right. Now, let us speak of other matters. Where are your gowns?"

"I didn't bring very many. I believe that Alec intends that I should have some new ones made here."

"Really? That's awfully thoughtful of him. A lucky thing, too, for fashion is altering quite rapidly. I believe that we are finally getting caught up with all the changes that took place in Europe during our war. Skirts have risen to the ankle, you know, and everyone is bringing down their hair from those great heights. Frizzing is the vogue now, but it takes some getting used to!"

At that moment, there was a tapping on the wall, and Caro looked across the room in surprise. Before

131

she could speak, an entire panel slid back and a tiny old woman appeared.

"Bonjour, mes filles!" she called in a cheerful, charmingly accented voice. "Sacha has asked me to request your presence downstairs for dinner, *maintenant*. I thought that I would give you a surprise!"

Natalya laughed in delight as she went to help her grandmother.

"Thank goodness Sacha and I warned Caro about you, Grandmère. You could have frightened her badly!"

Alec's grandmother looked remarkably well for her age. Caro could see that she was very wrinkled and had thin white hair, but she exuded an aura of vitality and happiness that made her seem young. Her hair was tucked beneath a lace cap, and her petite, agile form was clad in a lovely gown of aqua watered silk. Diamonds sparkled at her throat and wrists, but her brilliant blue eyes seemed to shine even more as she smiled at Caro.

"Bonjour to you, little Caroline. My grandson has told me a great deal about you, and I have a confidence that we are friends. Would you consent to call me Grandmère?"

Caro grasped her outstretched hands in impetuous affection.

"I would be most honored—Grandmère."

The old woman turned her sharp eyes on Natalya then, declaring, "Sacha spoke at some length about our Caroline. She has made an unusual impression on him!"

Blushing furiously, Caro blurted, "He found me to be quite a tiresome irritation, if that is what you mean. I believe I nearly drove him to distraction these past few days."

"Oui, and I imagine that he found one easily enough," murmured Grandmère as she cocked an eyebrow in a gesture that Caro found all too familiar.

"Grandmère," Natalya ventured, "Caro has yet to have a moment's peace since she walked into Belle Maison. Why don't we let her freshen up before supper?"

"Bien sûr! We must not tire her out with our chatter. Let's go back through the passageway. We shall send Sacha up to fetch Caro. Would a quarter of an hour be long enough, *ma chère?"*

"That would be fine. Thank you."

After the panel had clicked shut behind Natalya and Grandmère, Caro went over to the basin. Picking up a bar of scented soap, she put both hands into the warm water. She stood there then, merely moving her fingers idly, Natalya's question ringing urgently in her mind:

"Say, you aren't in love with Sacha, are you?"

Her new friend had given voice to the strange, conflicting turmoil of emotions that she had been half afraid to analyze. Her forehead puckered in a frown and she whispered aloud, "No! It cannot be that! I will not allow it to be!"

She could hear Natalya's voice again and her heart ached warningly.

"It would be hopeless," she had declared. "A tragedy!"

Chapter Twelve

⌒つ

ALEC'S FAMILIAR KNOCK SOUNDED AT THE DOOR AS
Caro was putting the finishing touches on her hair.
Having changed into the new cream-and-green gauze
gown that had attracted so many admiring looks in
New York, she felt her spirit lighten somewhat. When
she opened the door to admit Alec, she saw his eyes
darken in the silent compliment she had come to recognize. Humiliatingly, she felt herself blush and instinctively put her hands up to her hot cheeks. Alec
smiled ironically.

"Are you warm, *chérie?*"

"No—yes—that is . . . "

"Your conversation is unusually stimulating this
evening, my dear! Do you mind if I come in?"

"But—"

"I assure you, neither my sister nor my grandmother
will spread any tales to soil your reputation. Luckily,
they do not suspect that even I would stoop to child
molesting," he said caustically.

Caro watched him enter the room, closing the door
behind himself. His lean brown face was unusually
tense, and his voice more cynical than ever. He was
looking exceedingly handsome, however, clad in a
burgundy velvet coat over a dark waistcoat and frilled
white shirt, all of which fit without a wrinkle on his
perfect physique. When he walked slowly over to Caro

she caught a breath of his familiar, appealing masculine scent and suddenly felt faint.

"Caro," he commented more gently, "you seem unusually quiet and unanimated tonight. I hope no one has upset you."

"No, no—on the contrary, your sister and grandmother have been extremely kind to me. They have both made me feel very comfortable."

"Then perhaps I do not?" he inquired, raising a black brow.

"Why do you say such a thing?" she asked tensely.

"Because I sense that you are ill at ease in my presence. I had come to believe that you were a female not given to either stammering or coyness."

"When have I ever been coy to you?" she queried hotly.

Alec's eyes sparkled in approval. "That's better, infant." He reached out then and tipped her chin up so that he might look into her brown eyes. "How does the idea of living here lie with you?"

"I should be asking you that question, Alec! You were so elated at the prospect of being rid of me, and now here I am like a great millstone hanging around your neck!"

Alec laughed suddenly and his hand moved down to curve around her warm neck.

"I can think of worse millstones, *ma petite*. Although I'll admit frankly that this whole situation is damned awkward."

Caro could scarcely breathe beneath the touch of his hand.

"Yes," she heard herself reply, "I suppose that I shall put a damper on your love life—being in the way in your bachelor household and all."

Alec raised both brows in uncharacteristic surprise, for he could have sworn there was a note of jealousy in Caro's voice.

"On the contrary," he answered. "It is I who will

135

be putting a damper on your love life. My parents' house in town would have provided a much more advantageous spot from which to make your debut in the social world. My own reputation is less than chaste, and this location is, at best, remote. . . ." He paused, puzzling at the sudden light in her warm eyes. "However, I am certain that with all your attributes you shall have no problem attracting suitors."

The light dimmed. Alec stood there then, looking down at her silently, fighting an impulse to kiss her delicious-looking lips. Caro saw a muscle tighten in his jaw, and when he spoke again, his voice was more caustic than ever.

"Let me offer you my arm, *chérie,* and let us hasten to the supper table. I fear that the wine will have grown warm in my absence."

For Caro, dinner was a meal that alternated between great gaiety and extreme awkwardness. All of them, Grandmère included, consumed no small amount of wine, and neither Natalya nor Caro was capable of handling it gracefully.

"This is one of the things I adore about staying with Sacha," Natalya exclaimed. "He never tells me I must drink no more than two glasses of wine!"

"I am beginning to regret my leniency," Alec said drily, watching Natalya and Caro giggle over some obscure joke. Caro's cheeks were rosy, the dimples appearing in them almost constantly, particularly when Alec spoke to her. She was delighted by the bantering conversation going on around her, for the three Beauvisages were at their wittiest that evening. At one point they began to speak of card games, and Alec recalled the afternoon Caro had beaten him four times at piquet. His laughter was infectious to her, and she chimed in, her eyes and cheeks glowing. Suddenly, she realized that both Grandmère and Natalya were watching them thoughtfully and she felt naked.

They know, she thought, remembering the night at Wallingham's farm that she had tried so hard to block out of her mind. She realized that they could not know Alec had made love to her, and couldn't believe they would ever guess it. "Perhaps they can see something that even I have refused to admit."

After they had all retired to the parlor and Grandmère had taken up her needlework, Alec asked suddenly: "How long do Maman and Father intend to stay away? Did you say they were in France? I assume it is something to do with the vineyards—there's no problem, is there?"

"Gracious, no!" exclaimed Natalya, still feeling the heady effects of her four glasses of wine. "I'm certain that they will tour our vineyards while they are there, for I know Papa has been mentioning that they were overdue for an inspection, but the deciding factor in their journey was a letter from Dr. Franklin! He wrote to them from Passy, telling of the great passion for ballooning that currently exists. After telling them of an experiment that he was planning to journey to Paris next month to view, he invited Maman and Papa and Katya to join him. As you know, there is no joke too outrageous to appeal to Maman, and Papa is ever ready to embark on a new adventure. And, of course, the Jays are there, as well as the Adamses. So, off they went!"

Caro was listening in wide-eyed astonishment, but Alec merely lit a cheroot and smiled sardonically.

"Just when I needed them most!"

"*Tant mieux!*" retorted Grandmère. "You are a grown man and it is time that you commence to be responsible for someone other than yourself. We all know that Jean-Philippe and Antonia would love and welcome Caroline as a daughter. But, in truth, she belongs here, *n'est-ce pas?*"

She looked unflinchingly over her spectacles into Alec's narrowed eyes. Caro realized full well that

Grandmère's innocent words held quite another meaning, and she squirmed uncomfortably. At that moment, the front door burst open and a loud voice proclaimed from the entry hall:

"Welcome, oh prodigal brother! I have—"

A young man appeared on the parlor threshold, an elegant cape lined with red satin flung back over one shoulder. He stopped short, staring at Caro with disbelieving emerald eyes.

"Have I died? Am I in heaven?" he exclaimed at last, and Caro smiled slightly, remembering Kosciuszko's greeting on the night they met.

Alec got to his feet instantly, white teeth showing in a grin that held a tinge of cynicism. Crossing the room, he placed his cheroot between his teeth and grasped his brother's hand with both of his own.

"Nicholai, it is good to see you! It appears that the wild existence of a society bachelor has not done its worst to you yet!"

"You have taught me well, brother!" The younger man shook the proffered hand in open affection.

Caro was surprised to see that Nicholai Beauvisage had rich chestnut hair in contrast to Alec and Natalya's black locks. He was not quite as tall or powerfully built as his brother, but there was an undeniable grace in his movements. His features were clearcut and handsome, and his green eyes twinkled in constant good humor. Faced with a smile of such dazzling charm, Caro found it impossible not to like him.

Alec was eyeing his brother skeptically as he introduced Caro. "Nicky, I have the honor of presenting to you my ward, Miss Caroline Bergman. Caro, this is my brother—I believe you may have heard me speak of him."

Caro dimpled. "Of course, Alec! Mr. Beauvisage, it is a pleasure to meet you at last."

He bowed deeply, raising her hand to his lips in an improperly long kiss.

"Miss Bergman, I am humbled in the presence of such rare beauty." He gazed at her with twinkling emerald eyes. "I would deem it a great honor if you could call me by my Christian name of Nicholai. I would not suggest it, but I noticed that you addressed my brother as Alec, and—"

"Why, of course—Nicholai! I should like it above all things to dispense with all unnecessary formality with everyone in Alec's family."

Alec cleared his throat loudly and Caro turned her head to see that he was scowling.

"I'm sure that you must be fatigued, my dear. The hour is late, and I don't doubt that Natalya has planned a full day for you in town on the morrow. So—"

"Wait, Sacha!" Natalya broke in. "Before you pack us off to bed, I am most anxious to ask you something."

"I'm listening," he replied, exhaling a stream of smoke.

"I am throwing myself on your mercy to beg for a ball on Caro's behalf! Oh, please, Sacha! It would be just the thing now that that nasty war is finally over! There have been so few parties as yet, and this would be a perfect way to establish Caro in all the right social circles. I beseech you—"

"Please do not—I have heard too much already." Alec's mouth was twisted with sarcastic amusement. "Grandmère, what do you think of this wild scheme? I fear that I shall have to leave these social matters to your discretion."

Grandmère smiled impishly. "Sacha, it sounds like much fun to me. Also, I believe it would be a fitting debut for such a remarkable *jeune fille* as our Caroline."

"I'll second that!" offered Nicholai cheerfully. His brother frowned at him.

"When I desire your opinion, I will ask for it.

As for your plan, Natalya, I promise to consider it overnight. I imagine that you have thought of the fact that there is no ballroom in this house?"

"Of course, Sacha! What sort of silly goose do you take me for? We can use Maman and Papa's drawing room. Besides, their home is much more conveniently located."

"Do not expect me to make daily excursions into Philadelphia while you are arranging this affair, little sister!"

"Are you saying that we can have the ball?"

"I said that I will consider it. Now, kindly cease this tedious chatter and run along upstairs, Natalya. I shall see Caro to her room." Alec turned to Nicholai, only to find that his brother was gazing at Caro in awe. "Nicholai, kindly endeavor to moderate your worship of my ward. If you will wait in the library for me, I will join you there in a few minutes and we can talk."

Natalya bid everyone goodnight and sped upstairs to her room. Taking Caro's arm, Alec led her out into the entry hall. Her cheeks were rosy, her golden-brown eyes glowing with contentment.

"I simply adore your family, Alec," she declared.

"That's all very well, but I did not notice such deep affection on your part before Nicky arrived."

Caro beamed up at Alec's scowling countenance. "I like him. He makes me feel special."

"I daresay that you are not the first object of his extravagant attentions," he muttered darkly.

Remembering the quarrel that they had had at Van DerPat Manor, Caro decided not to provoke him further. She felt his arm encircle her waist as they mounted the stairs and knew he was not really angry with her.

"I have promised you not to be so high-handed, haven't I," he allowed.

"Yes, Alec," she breathed softly.

140

"Well, then, I suppose I had better get in practice for all those young swains who will be dancing attendance on you. I can't have you calling me a tiresome toad now that I am in my own home, can I?"

"I shan't, Alec!"

They were outside her bedroom door, and Caro decided to take advantage of his rare mellowness toward her.

"May I speak with you alone for a moment?"

"Certainly." He followed her into the room, closing the door, then settled into a chair near the fire and stretched his long legs. "Have you a problem, *chérie?*"

Caro was pacing near the bed, but at his words she turned and stopped next to his chair.

"I know you will think this is vastly foolish of me, and I suppose I shall regret my outspokenness later, but I simply must tell you what is on my mind."

"I would appreciate it—I think." Alec smiled tentatively. Suddenly Caro sank down on her knees beside him, clasping his hand with both of her small ones.

"Could you—that is, would it be possible for you to try to like me a little? I may be mistaken, but I came to believe at one time that we were becoming friends. I'll admit I do not understand exactly what the nature of our relationship was, but you did treat me as though you enjoyed my company—most of the time." Alec's eyes were clearer and more sharply turquoise than she had ever seen them as he listened in astonishment. He would have spoken, but Caro rushed on, "What I mean—I suppose—is that in spite of all that occurred, I felt close to you and now I realize that it all meant more to me than I thought. When I've been with you . . . I've scarcely thought about the fact that my entire past is unknown to me—I haven't even cared! Then, ever since those men, and the barn, and all—you have treated me so coldly. All I can think is that you no longer like me—and I miss the way it used to be—

and," her voice began to quaver, tears glistening on her long lashes. Alec reached over and gathered her onto his lap, letting her cry against his white shirtfront.

"Egad, Caro, this is the greatest pack of foolishness I have heard yet from a female. I should never have come in here with you, I can see that. And God knows I should have limited the wine you and Natalya were gulping! Don't you realize that the things you have said to me would be better left unspoken?"

His arms cradled her securely, and though his voice was gentle, it held a note of bitterness. "But then, ours must be a special case, for which I take complete blame. If I had never bedded you that night, none of these complications would have arisen."

Caro stiffened in his arms, but he was not to be silenced.

"If it is the truth you crave, *chérie,* then I suppose it is best that you have it. My attitude toward you has nothing to do with my regard for you. I like you immensely. In fact, I often surprise myself in that respect. However, I also desire you strongly, as a man desires a woman, and it has come to run in my blood." His eyes blazed into and seared the depths of her soul. "I am never free from wanting you, Caro, and that is why I must build barriers between us. I would not hurt you again—and it is not because of my gentlemanly ethics, for I have none. It is because I do— ah, care for you. In my own way." He paused, scowling into the fire. "Jesus, I have always maintained that virgins are nothing but trouble!"

Caro's tears had ceased, and she was listening to him in horrified fascination. The words that came to her lips were involuntary, seeming to push up from some inner, lost recess of her mind:

"Are you saying that what you feel for me is actually *lust?*" she whispered at last.

Alec's jaw tightened and with one quick movement

he grasped her arms, one hand carelessly grazing her breast, and set her on her feet and stood up.

"A very apt expression, my dear." He smiled ironically at Caro's ill-disguised desire and strode to the door. Looking back over his shoulder, he cruelly added, "But then I must not forget that you are well acquainted with lust!"

Chapter Thirteen

NICHOLAI WAS WAITING FOR HIS BROTHER IN THE magnificent second-floor library that spanned the width of the house. The walls were paneled in rich dark mahogany, their built-in bookshelves filled with over two thousand volumes. There were window seats on all sides, so that a reader might choose the one with the best sunlight at any time of the day. All the furniture was new, finely carved Chippendale, and Alec's pigeonholed, fall-front desk dominated the room.

Nicholai poured brandy from a half-full crystal decanter and helped himself to one of Alec's cigars. It was almost gone when his brother finally strode into the room.

Looking up with a cheerfully innocent grin, Nicholai exclaimed, "Sacha, here you are at last! I have been waiting most impatiently to ask for the lovely hand of your ward in marriage."

"Shut up, Nicky. I am in no mood for your stupid jokes, particularly if they concern Caro. God, I need a drink!"

After pouring himself a generous amount of brandy, he sank into a chair and loosened his cravat.

Undaunted, Nicholai spoke up genially, "I hate to say this, dear brother, but you have been a trifle testy ever since I arrived tonight. I am beginning to believe that you have lost all brotherly affection for me!"

"I'll admit that you did put me off with that nauseating drama over Caro, but she is the real cause of my ill-temper. I haven't had a moment's peace since I got tangled up with the vixen, and I am sorely afraid that matters will not be improving soon. How could Maman and Father leave the country at a time like this?"

"I dare say they would be overjoyed to hear that you have need of them after all these years, Sacha! Maman is forever despairing of the fact that you are such a stranger in their house!" Nicholai laughed lightly.

"That is beside the point," Alec muttered illogically.

Nicholai scratched his head, then endeavored to turn the conversation.

"How did you fare on your trip to Connecticut? Are your new lands to your liking?"

"That is another sore subject. Damn, it seems that my life has been hopelessly complicated ever since I left Philadelphia last month. And I believed all my problems were ended with the war!"

"Sacha, kindly cease this ranting and explain what you mean. All this cursing and complaining is quite out of character for you!"

This produced a small quirk at the corner of Alec's hard mouth.

"I daresay you're right. I mustn't let that child get the better of me."

"How did she get back into this?" Nicholai exclaimed. "And anyway, you're right there. I've never known you to bother yourself over *any* female!"

"That's what has me so damned mad!"

"Surely you aren't letting this guardian role go to your head?" he inquired.

"On the contrary, Nicky," Alec replied with a sardonic twist to his lips. "At any rate, I suppose I might

145

as well tell you all, beginning with my journey to Connecticut. I confess that I feel a need to discuss this with someone."

"You have my wholehearted attention."

"Well, you'll recall that I won that property from a man named Josef Bergman. It was in a card game."

"Vaguely."

"He was an officer and a fine man, and I really had no intention of holding him to it, but I decided to leave matters as they were until the war's end. He was an honorable man, and I felt he would want to stand by his debt, particularly in view of the others in the company.

"At any rate, he told me that he had some papers to give me, but I put him off, telling him it could wait. Shortly after that he was wounded, and I saw him before he died. He told me, 'You must take care of it all—all, Beauvisage. Do you promise?' And, of course, I did. He said that there was a key to his strongbox in his waistcoat pocket, and that I would find papers explaining everything. He died then, even as he spoke, and I was called back to the battlefield before I had any chance to see to his effects. I returned to his body before they removed it, but there was no key. Stranger yet, when I investigated his belongings I found no strongbox at all. Needless to say, I thought it all quite peculiar, but I assumed that the key had somehow been misplaced or stolen. I imagined that there were valuables in the box, and some devil had just made off with it.

"Well, Cornwallis surrendered the next day, and Bergman's farm was pushed to the back of my thoughts. Fortunately, on the night of the poker game he had drawn me a rough map showing the location of the place, and I found I still had it. You know that I had no opportunity to go up there until this fall, and all the way I really worried little about those papers of his, for I assumed that they must have detailed his property. I had no interest in those facts, for I had the feeling that he had family, and I fully intended to just cancel the debt and leave the entire property with them."

Alec paused, leaning over to pick up an ash that had fallen from Nicholai's cigar onto the Persian rug.

"At any rate, I found a singularly strange state of affairs awaiting me in Connecticut. Bergman's farm was quite handsome, and it had the look of habitation —and since two years had passed since his death, my conviction that he had a family living there was reinforced. No one answered my knocks, however, so I entered through a window. There were dishes and food left out, completely convincing me that I was right. There were three good-sized bedchambers on an upper level, and I found one wardrobe full of Bergman's clothes, and in another room there were female things all around. All through the house there were things overturned—even a broken vase in the girl's room."

"Mighty queer, if you ask me!" Nicholai broke in.

"A sound deduction, brother," replied Alec, raising one eyebrow mockingly. "I set out to the nearest neighbor's house, which was less than a quarter-mile away. I felt sure that someone so nearby would be able to help me fit the pieces of that cursed puzzle together. Well, you can imagine my surprise when I knocked at the door and immediately heard it being bolted from within! A man's face appeared at the window, and he began yelling at me to be gone. I called back, telling him who I was and I am certain he took my meaning. Yet it did no good; if anything, he grew more angry. In fact, I could have sworn the fellow was afraid. I met the same response at the two other neighboring farms, both of which were at least two miles away!"

"God's name, Sacha! What was going on?"

"I never did find out. Perhaps they all feared I was

a redcoat or a Hessian, but it still seems highly unnatural. I didn't even stay the night, for I felt damned uneasy. I left a letter of explanation on the table at Bergman's house, asking to be contacted. I suppose I'll have to return if I don't hear any word, but I'll admit that this whole affair has become cursed inconvenient. Also, I've been beset with worry over that strongbox of Bergman's. Somehow I feel that there was more to its disappearance than I thought at the time." Alec rose to pour himself another glass of brandy. "Can I get you some more, Nicky?"

"Yes, certainly. But Sacha, I am doubly perplexed! When did you discover Caro? Can she have arrived here before you to explain this mystery?"

Alec looked at his brother in total incomprehension. Suddenly he realized the mistake and threw back his head in laughter.

"Sacha," Nicholai burst out, "I am missing the joke here! Kindly stop laughing and enlighten me!"

"I suppose I must, though by all rights I should consult Caro first. Ah well, too bad. I expect you'd better have another drink before you hear the rest of this incredible tale!"

Nicholai took an obedient gulp, then leaned forward in his chair expectantly. "Do stop looking so confounded amused and nonchalant and get on with it!"

"As you wish, Nicky. I don't doubt that you'll find this whole story a trifle unbelievable and confusing, for that is my own feeling, and I was there through it all! You see, Caro is no relation to Josef Bergman. I found her in the backwoods of Connecticut on my way to Wallingham's farm and brought her with me because she had nowhere else to go."

Nicholai's forehead was puckered in an expression of total bafflement. He leaned back in his chair, scratching his auburn head.

"Sacha, I am lost."

His brother began to laugh again, seeming to enjoy the situation.

"I am telling you that Caro is a stray waif—actually a runaway, I fear. I took that back route across the woods to the Hudson. Ivan and I were riding along at least ten miles past the Post Road when I saw a piece of green silk fabric in the leaves. I stopped to investigate and saw Caro lying unconscious between the trees."

"God's life, Sacha! Are you roasting me?" Nicholai's best friend was an English refugee from whom he had learned many British expressions. He used them constantly, enjoying the attention they attracted.

"I would not consider it, Nicky," Alec smiled. "The oddest thing was that she was totally garbed in male clothing; even her hair was stuffed beneath a tricorn hat. At first glance, I thought that she was a boy, but it did not take long for me to see the truth."

"I don't doubt that!" Nicholai laughed.

"Well, to make a long story short, she woke up and had no idea of her identity. I could only surmise that her horse had run off and the fall had occasioned a blow to her head causing the memory loss. The green bundle I had found contained some personal effects, including a dress. She had no money, though, and everything pointed to the conclusion that she was running away. I have no idea how she could have believed she would survive alone in those woods, but obviously the risk was outweighed by her fear of being found on the main road."

"She still does not know who she is?"

"Hasn't a clue. I can tell you this much, though— she's well-bred and educated. She speaks French, is well-read, plays chess among other difficult games, and has flawless manners. Of course—she's damned outspoken and impetuous . . ."

"Blister it, Sacha, now I know why you were glowering at me so ferociously downstairs tonight! The girl is yours, isn't she?"

"Absolutely not! She'll not be yours either, though, Nicky, so just forget it. Caro will meet a man who will treat her properly."

"She's quite an unusual female, isn't she? Egad, I can just imagine some of the young ingénues we know clad in breeches in the middle of the Connecticut woods alone. You know, Sacha, in spite of what you've said, I'd lay odds that she'd have made it somehow. The girl's got a quality . . ."

"Yes, I know. She's unique among all the women I have ever known. She has guts, too. You wouldn't believe . . ."

"Hmm?"

"Never mind. It's a long story."

"Say, brother, am I to understand that you two were traveling alone together through the wilderness?"

Alec's face was inscrutable.

"That's it."

"Well?" Nicholai leered, his emerald eyes sparkling.

"Shut up, you imbecile. And I never want to hear you discuss Caro in that tone of voice again. Do I make myself clear?"

"Why—of course," he stammered, eyes wide, confused by his brother's reaction.

Alec's jaw was set in a hard line as he stood up and shrugged off his coat.

"It is very late. I would suggest that you spend the night here. We can have breakfast tomorrow and you can fill me in on your activities."

"That sounds fine to me, Sacha," Nicholai replied cautiously. "Thank you. And—may I ask just one more question?"

"Of course."

"You really intend to tell everyone that Caro is your ward? Aren't you worried that someone might have known Josef Bergman and will expose you both?"

"That is a chance we will have to take, I suppose. I highly doubt that anyone will notice her last name enough to inquire into her parentage. You aren't to tell anyone the truth about this, Nicky. The story about Caro and me spending those nights alone together in the woods would spell instant social ruin for her."

"Haven't you considered marriage yourself? The girl has been hopelessly compromised, you know. Even if nothing did happen."

Alec shot Nicholai a withering look, for his brother's sarcastic tone was not lost on him.

"I suggest that you mind your own damn business. Caro and I both knew what we were about. There will be no marriage of honor between us—we would not suit, and it would be a mistake for us both. Let us dismiss this subject now, Nicholai. You have heard far too much already."

He untied his cravat with one hand, tipping his brandy snifter up with the other to drain it. Then, picking up his coat, he turned back to his brother.

"I bid you good night. I would recommend the bedroom east of Natalya's."

"Good night, Sacha," Nicholai murmured as he watched Alec walk out of the room. His keen emerald eyes were perplexed as he sank back into his chair to finish his brandy.

"Somehow," he mused aloud, "the pieces do not quite fit together. And Sacha is not himself—definitely not himself . . ."

Caro was unable to sleep, even though her large bed was deliciously comfortable. There was a very low fire burning in the fireplace and she finally got out of bed and lit a candle. Carrying along a plush quilt, she settled herself in a chair near the window. There was a crystallized pattern of frost edging the windowpanes and the night was clear and bright with starlight and moonlight.

Caro folded her legs up against her breasts, clasping her hands around them and resting her little chin on her knees. There were more thoughts spinning through her mind than she could manage to sort out. Nor was she certain that she wanted to understand what was happening inside her heart.

Perhaps, she thought, if I knew who I were, or what my past has been, it would help me to direct my emotions. I feel so odd and unattached—as though I am not truly a person . . .

Her frequent confrontations with Alec had a way of leaving her ever confused, no matter what their outcome. She had turned to him tonight in an effort to force him into a commitment of his friendship, for he had been the only secure and dependable part of her life so far. In spite of everything, Caro had always felt that he understood her. Now she was unsure of everything. Alec was acting more impersonal toward her every day, and his blunt confession that evening had left her uneasy in quite a different way. Although she was sure she could count Natalya, Grandmère, Nicholai, and Pierre as friends, somehow it was not the same.

Feeling acutely melancholy, Caro drew a deep breath and turned her cheek against her knees. Her thoughts were pulled back to the Wallinghams' barn and she found herself straining to keep in focus a mental picture of those reptilian yellow eyes, hoping that she could remember why they seemed so uncomfortably familiar to her. Even if the memories were bad . . . at least it would be better than living in this empty limbo!

Across the room, a movement caught her eyes as a door she had never noticed opened. Caro's head came up with a swiftness born of instant panic.

Alec stood in the doorway, holding a pewter candlestick. Shadows played on his lean brown face, and she was shocked to see that he was naked to the waist. In the leaping flicker of the candlelight, his chest seemed broader and darker than ever, and Caro noticed the hard, muscled ridges creasing his stomach. White teeth flashed in a sudden grin as he walked nearer.

"My dear, you look as if you've seen a ghost. I am not the bogeyman you know, for all my lustful inclinations."

She laughed nervously, pulling the quilt over her breasts, which were poorly concealed beneath her thin muslin bedgown.

"You certainly startled me! I confess that I had not even realized the existence of the door! Where does it lead?"

Alec's grin deepened, grooves forming on either side of his mouth. In the eerie half-light of the room he looked to Caro like the devil himself.

"To my bedchamber, *chérie*. Didn't Natalya tell you whose room you occupy?"

"Why, she said it belonged to the wife of the man who built Belle Maison . . ." Her voice trailed off weakly as sudden realization dawned. Alec raised one black brow in taunting amusement, looking as though he were enjoying himself immensely.

"I thought you would feel safer knowing I am nearby; you may rest easy in the knowledge that my own bed is but a few short yards away, my dear." His mocking tone echoed in the quiet room.

Caro's face was lovely in the melting candlelight as she apprehensively turned her large brown eyes up to him. She saw a muscle tighten at the base of Alec's throat, and his hard stomach seemed to knot.

"Please do not alarm yourself, *chérie*. I did not come in here with rape on my mind. Although," he chuckled softly, "the thought has crossed my mind since then! I was merely undressing when I saw the

153

unusually strong light beneath your door. The hour is quite late, you know—could you not sleep?"

She relaxed visibly at his words, warming to the gentler tone of his voice.

"No, I could not. I suppose it is the strangeness of the new room—and the knowledge that I am embarking on a new life without even knowing what my old one was like . . ."

"I trust that our earlier conversation did not upset you? I should not like to cause you a sleepless night."

"Do not overestimate your impact, sir," Caro replied in what she hoped was a cool voice. His sudden amused smile was not the reaction she looked for.

"Touché, ma petite." He bent over her then, running one brown finger up her creamy neck to tip her chin back. "Do not worry that I shall creep into your bed while you sleep, for I hope I have not reached such depths of depravity yet. However, if you like, I will see that the door is sealed. Or you may move—"

"No!—That is, I do trust you, Alec. And . . . I really will feel safer knowing you are near."

He bent over her, so close that she inhaled the aroma of cigar smoke and brandy, and his hand cupped her tiny chin securely.

"Perhaps," he whispered huskily, "the thought of finding me in your bed is not as repugnant as you would have me believe?"

Caro could not see Alec's face clearly in the shadows, but she faintly perceived a glittering turquoise spark before he closed the distance between them. His mouth brushed her own so lightly that she felt faint with hunger. Their lips clung and Alec traced the outline of one of Caro's breasts with his free hand. Her breath was coming in little gasps that betrayed her desire, but she was powerless to control it, for the soft touch of Alec's mouth tantalized her beyond belief. Her entire being waited for his kiss to deepen and his strong arms to encircle her. Alec's tongue brushed her

154

lower lip as he ran his forefinger over her nipple, then he drew back.

Caro's breasts were rising and falling with unnatural rapidity as she stared up at him. Alec straightened completely, running a hand through his raven hair as he smiled ruefully.

"That was unkind of me, wasn't it? I suppose I needed to prove something to both of us, but God knows I'd have been better off leaving it alone. It is a crime for a woman to look like you do, Caro—too bad you're not made of ice, because it is what's inside of you that ultimately draws me on." He paused, looking down ruefully at her tear-filled eyes. "Scares you, doesn't it? Believe me, sweetheart, it scares me too."

Chapter Fourteen

SITTING IN HER WINDOW SEAT SIPPING HOT TEA, CARO viewed the outbuildings and gardens behind Belle Maison appreciatively. It was a clear, colorful morning, and the early sun's warmth lightened her mood. Watching the servants hurrying over the raised brick footpaths between the kitchen and the house, Caro felt that their energy was infectious. Then an all-too-familiar pair of shoulders came into view below her window and she watched as Alec bent to absently pick a late-blooming purple aster. He seemed to survey the garden, which consisted chiefly of boxwood-edged flower beds which were divided up by the brick walkways. Few blooms were now left in October, but Caro felt that the garden held great promise for springtime, and wondered what flowers would appear.

A manservant stopped to converse with Alec, who appeared to Caro to be singularly stern. The servant nodded repeatedly, bowed twice, then hurried into the house. Alec strode on past all of the outbuildings, and Caro noticed that he wore riding boots and soft buckskin breeches. The last building had the appearance of a stable, and he entered it. She waited, sipping her tea, until he appeared again, leading Ivan. Mounting gracefully, Alec put a heel into the giant black stallion's flank and they galloped off into the field beyond. Alec's dark head was held proudly, arrogantly high,

156

and Caro's face burned when she recalled how he had caressed her the night before.

At the same moment that horse and rider disappeared from view there was a soft tapping at her door and Natalya's pert face appeared.

"Good morning! I see that you are out of bed, which is certainly a good sign! May I come in?"

Caro laughed nervously, pressing her hands against her hot cheeks. "Please do! Am I being very slow this morning?"

"Goodness no, for it is barely nine o'clock. I am an incurable early riser, except after the nights I have been to parties. I felt certain that you would still be asleep, but Rose told me you had already rung for your tea, so I decided to burst right in!"

Natalya was wearing a stunning gown of strawberry satin edged with stiff white ruching. Her black hair seemed shot with blue lights in the morning sunshine, and her cheeks were in rosy harmony with her gown. Caro regarded her with open admiration.

"I truly wish that I had your coloring, Natalya. You can wear the loveliest colors, and your complexion is so perfectly white!"

The other girl laughed charmingly as she perched on the edge of the bed. "Don't be a goose, Caro. You have far too much beauty of your own to waste energy envying mine. Wait until you hear my news! Sacha has instructed me to take you into Philadelphia today and see that you are fitted for a full wardrobe. New chemises and stockings and hats and everything! He said that price is no object! Isn't that fabulous?"

"But—I couldn't accept—"

"Don't be silly! Besides, I should think you would have learned by now that it is foolish to argue with Sacha. Now, hurry and get dressed and we can breakfast together downstairs." Hopping to her feet, Natalya ran over to hug Caro. "It will be such fun!" she exclaimed before slipping out the door.

157

Less than two hours later, Caro had her first view of Philadelphia. The city itself was almost exclusively concentrated within one square mile, bordered by Vine Street to the north, the Delaware River to the east, Lombard Street to the south, and Seventh Street to the west.

Caro fell in love immediately with the "greene, countrie towne" which was barely one hundred years old. All the streets were a spacious sixty feet wide, and were arranged in a gridiron pattern: straight streets intersecting at right angles with others. The houses were all impressively neat; generally Georgian in design, built of brick and two or three narrow stories high. The raised brick footpaths which bordered the streets were shaded by elegant poplar trees, and the general atmosphere was one of pleasing, harmonious prosperity.

"Of course, William Penn planned it all," explained Natalya, who observed Caro's interest in her surroundings. "All the streets are named for things that grow in the country. Should you like to take a short tour before we go shopping?"

"Oh, yes—that would be marvelous!"

At Alec's request, Pierre was driving their small, lightweight carriage, and he smiled at Natalya's idea. Staying on Third Street, they passed row after row of connected, elegant homes.

"Pierre," called Natalya, "why don't we turn around at Pine Street?"

As they paused to accomplish this, she pointed to a building on the northeast corner.

"Do you see the house there next to St. Peter's Church? Kosci lived there a few years ago when he came here to plan Philadelphia's fortification against attack. My parents' house is just a few blocks away, so we all saw a great deal of him. I understand that you met him at the Van DerPats'?"

"Yes! He is a fascinating man."

"I agree," Natalya smiled saucily. "I'll admit to a small infatuation with him—I was little more than twelve at the time and he seemed to be the most exciting man in the world."

"That's quite a compliment, considering who your brothers are."

"Do you find them exciting?" Natalya inquired with a sidelong glance at her companion. "I shouldn't have thought you'd have formed an opinion of Nicholai after such a brief acquaintance."

"Well, if he is at all like Alec—" Caro replied, stopping in mid-sentence as she realized her admission. "All right, then, I will concede that I believe Alec is an exciting man! It would be impossible to think otherwise, I should say!"

"I was only wondering if you have some evidence to back up your claim," Natalya returned boldly, watching as Caro blushed to the roots of her honey-colored hair.

In front of them, Pierre cleared his throat meaningfully, then said, "We have arrived at the Beauvisage residence, mesdemoiselles. Do you wish to go in?"

The carriage drew up before a magnificent Georgian mansion built of red brick with large white-shuttered windows. It was three stories tall, and considerably wider than most of the other houses Caro had seen. Natalya smiled proudly, then asked: "Do you like it? I am immensely fond of it, myself. It is a much different type of house than Belle Maison, of course, but its charm is undeniable. There's a lovely garden in back —one of the nicest in town, I believe." She leaned forward, addressing herself to Pierre. "We shan't stop. I fear that I would chatter on and on and we would never get away."

They drove on, jogging over on Chestnut Street to detour onto the tiny court which boasted Benjamin Franklin's home.

"Of course," Natalya said, "he hasn't lived there

much since it was built, but you can believe that it has his touch—even if he had to give the directions at a distance!"

"Has he been in France a long time?" she asked tentatively. Natalya wrinkled her forehead in surprise.

"Actually, he has not been in France for more than about seven years, I believe. Of course, that is a long time to us, but he was in England for many years before that. Longer there, I think, than he has been in France. Papa and Maman have known him very well, and I was able to visit him several times while I was at school in France. He is a most extraordinary man! I have often thought that he and Grandmère would have suited very well, but Dr. Franklin has scores of younger lady friends in Passy. For a man of his age, he has tremendous energy!"

Caro listened attentively to everything Natalya said all that day. In fact, she was so busy listening and looking that she was sure Natalya found her quite dull.

Once they reached High Street, located immediately north of Franklin's home, the girls abandoned the carriage and set out on foot. Pierre followed them at a polite distance.

It was past noon by this time, and the marketplace was bustling. To the east, Caro could see the clean brick-pillared stalls of the outdoor market, but she was not to shop there that day. Natalya took her to the exclusive dress shops, where instructions from Alec had mysteriously preceded them. The seamstresses viewed Caro with frank curiosity until Natalya brazenly informed them that she was only Alec's ward and *not* his mistress.

Caro was turned this way and that, measured and fitted for what seemed to be an eternity. After the fittings for her gowns and the orders for underclothes and accessories, they continued on to the millinery shops on Second Street. The two girls were like children as they tried on lovely wide-brimmed hats with frothy ostrich plumes in every color imaginable. Caro was astounded to hear Natalya order an unbelievable quantity of hats, pushing her out the door before she could protest too loudly.

"I know you're scandalized, but this is what Sacha wants, Caro, and you may as well relax and enjoy it. I would give anything to be in your place today!"

"All I know is that I am exhausted. Can't we go home now?"

"One more stop," Natalya sang out gaily as she linked arms with Caro. "You wouldn't want to go barefoot, would you?"

"No," she sighed. "I suppose not."

"To be honest," laughed Natalya, "if I did not know better I should swear we were assembling a trousseau!"

Back on High Street, they reached the shop owned by John Wallace, which dealt exclusively in women's shoes. Most of his stock was imported and there was everything to delight the feminine eye; shoes fashioned in elegant worsted, satin, and brocade of every color.

Finally the afternoon's work was done and the girls left the shop to find Pierre and the carriage waiting outside. Caro sank gratefully into the upholstered seat, momentarily shutting her eyes.

"I never knew that shopping could be so exhausting," she murmured.

"You'll find that it is an accomplishment which is readily acquired," laughed Natalya.

It was nearly sunset when they reached Belle Maison. Neither Alec nor Nicholai was there, and the three women ate a quiet evening meal alone. Caro felt strangely melancholy as the night wore on, and finally pleaded a headache and went up to bed early. Although she fell asleep almost immediately, part of her mind was alert all night long, listening and hoping for the nearby door to open.

Chapter Fifteen

THREE INCREDIBLY LONG DAYS PASSED BEFORE CARO
and Alec again met face to face. Each morning she
jumped out of bed with the sunrise to station herself in
the window seat. Alec appeared without fail at the first
pink glimmer of light, then stopped at each of the
outbuildings. He always looked rested and alert,
wearing casual riding clothes and boots that somehow
assumed an unquestionable elegance on his lean body.
She would watch as he conversed at length with the
gardener, pausing to greet each serving person who
hurried from the kitchen to the main house. The fresh-
faced young maids turned radiant smiles up at him,
and Caro wondered how many were secretly in love
with their master.

Alec would stop in the orangerie, emerging with a
large, perfect piece of fruit, then continue on to the
stables. By the time he and Ivan appeared back in the
sunlight, the orange would be gone, and moments later
Alec would mount the stallion and disappear into the
trees. That would be her last view of him for the entire day. She had no idea where he went or how he
spent his time, and was uncomfortable asking Natalya
or Grandmère questions about Alec.

For her own part, there was enough right at Belle
Maison to occupy her days. Natalya gave her a
detailed tour of the house the morning after their Phil-

adelphia excursion, even revealing the secret passage-
ways that wound behind the walls. When they followed
the tunnel that ran under the garden to Grandmère's
little cottage, Caro got her first view of that house.
The rooms were small, well organized, and yet warmly
inviting. When Grandmère asked the girls to join her
for tea, Natalya declined and returned to the main
house, but Caro stayed behind. She found Grandmère
to have a curiously relaxing effect on her, for all her
witty outspokenness. Caro was certain that the old
woman truly liked her, and she seemed to have no
doubts about the promise of her future.

"You are made of fine fiber, Caroline," she told her
confidently. "Do not doubt that Sacha knows it too,
or he would not have brought you to his home. He is
a stubborn, proud man, and it will take him some
time to realize the truth."

Grandmère would never come directly to the point
when she spoke of Alec and his relationship to Caro,
but she seemed to have definite ideas about it—at
which she chose only to hint. Caro could not bring herself to question the old woman further, any more than
she could bear to explore her own emotions privately.

Grandmère spent the bulk of her days in her cottage
or outside in its tiny private garden. She usually appeared in the main residence for tea and meals, but
if she was not present no one worried.

"I must have a life of my own," she explained to
Caro. "Sacha has the same streak of independence
running through him, so we understand one another.
He sees to it that I am left alone, and consequently I
feel free to visit with him more often. I cannot abide
pressure."

Needlework appeared to be her greatest pleasure,
for her house was filled with the fruits of her labor.
There were seat covers, pillows, quilts, and samplers
of every description. Caro learned that she also enjoyed painting and was amazingly skilled at it. On

163

the walls hung several views of the garden in bloom, as well as some remarkable portraits of family members. Caro got her first glimpse of Alec's parents on Grandmère's sitting-room wall, and was not surprised to see that they were unusually good-looking people.

After her first visit to Grandmère's cottage, Caro found an excuse to return each afternoon, until it became an unspoken habit.

One cold twilight found Caro seated on Grandmère's richly carpeted parlor floor, not far from a blazing fire. The older woman was perched in a huge wing chair, embroidering a linen tablecloth. Caro took a comforting sip of her hot tea, laced liberally with honey, and looked back over her shoulder.

"Grandmère . . . would you tell me about your youth? What was it like in France when you were my age?"

The old woman peeked over her spectacles with a smile, continuing to work as she began:

"I was raised as any young girl of noble birth—*une enfance ennuyeuse.*" She made a face. "I had a governess, then tutors, and *enfin,* a rather *drôle* dancing master. This was in Paris, where these things were *très important—tu sais, l'art* to sit, to stand, to walk." Light, gay laughter filled the cozy room. "I was taught Latin, and how to sing and play the harpsichord. *Ensuite,* I went away to *le couvent* to finish my education like other girls my age."

"A convent?" A shower of sparks scattered through Caro's head, but the memory disappeared as quickly as it had come, like a comet on a summer night.

"*Oui.* It was the custom to keep girls locked away until a marriage could be arranged. *Mon père* did this to me, but I was not so willing. I was *soupe-au-lait, sais-tu?* Hot-headed! They took me home for this wedding—"

"How old were you?"

"*Quinze ans.*"

"Fifteen!" Caro gasped.

"*Chérie,* many other girls were married at younger ages. Betrothals were made for mere children of seven! *Mon père* was very pleased, *pour* he had found for me *un grand homme—le marquis!* Étienne's parents had died with *le* smallpox and he was in need of a dowry to restore his château in Touraine—on the Loire River. He was not quite so young, *peut-être . . .* twenty-one. *Si,* the day that he came to *le maison de ma famille* to meet me, I decided to escape. On the grounds, I encountered a stranger—*très beau et charmant!*" Her blue eyes sparkled in memory. "I thought him to be a new stableboy, or some such, and begged him to help me escape from the ogre who would marry me. He laughed, and I fell in love in that instant—*une aventure merveilleuse, n'est-ce pas?*"

"Yes!" Caro agreed, growing used to Grandmère's odd bilingual speech. One never knew when a word would be spoken in English or French. "Did he help you run away?"

"*Oui.* Gladly. All the way to his château in Touraine!"

"Oh, Grandmère—it was Étienne?"

"*Naturellement! Mais,* two days passed before he confessed to me that *he* was *l'ogre*—and by then I was lost. *Et ma virginité, aussi!*" She chuckled and Caro blushed under her keen eyes. "Ah, he was such a man! A man to produce a son such as Jean-Philippe and grandsons *comme* Sacha *et* Nicholai."

"Tell me the rest, won't you?"

Grandmère laughed softly, delighted by Caro's interest.

"*Bien . . .* we lived a long and happy life together. Étienne died but ten years past. Our château is splendid . . . it belongs to us still; Antonia *et* Jean-Philippe may be there even now. Ah . . . when he was *un enfant,* those were happy times. I had three—Jean-Philippe, Camille, *et* Brigitte. Camille lives *maintenant* à Cherbourg, *mais* Brigitte . . . died many years ago."

"Oh—I'm so sorry."

"Non, chérie—this is part of life. I have had much happiness. Étienne was *un amant*—my lover—more than fifty years. We used to keep a lovely house in Paris where we would go for weeks on end to enjoy the excitement of the lovely city. There was opera, ballet, concerts, carriage rides in *le Jardin du Roi* . . . and our life in Touraine was rich with joy. The country there is so lovely: lush, and rolling, with the Loire twisting throughout. You must have Sacha take you there to see our grand château one day! There are splendid horses—Étienne's passion—and our vineyards give delicious wines. For the most part, Voudrays, *mais aussi* a natural sparkling wine called mousseaux. It is much like champagne . . ."

Natalya suddenly burst through the door to call them to dinner. That conversation was ended, but it would be repeated in countless variations as the relationship between Caro and Grandmère warmed and mellowed. The old woman was extremely discreet about questioning Caro, however, though she did not appear to know the truth of her past—or lack of it.

Pierre remained at Belle Maison most of the time, and he and Caro began to play cards to pass the long evening hours. Sometimes they were successful in persuading Natalya and Grandmère to join them in a game of Lanterloo. The old woman protested her ignorance loudly, then invariably scored a resounding victory, blue eyes sparkling with mischief.

On the night of Caro's first day left to her own devices at Belle Maison she retired quite late, finally deciding that Alec would not be making an appearance at all. Before she fell asleep, though, she heard movement in the room next to hers, followed by the sound of Alec's deep voice in muffled conversation with Pierre. She was surprised at the tide of happy relief and contentment that swept over her at the knowledge that he was nearby. Before she could think anymore, she fell into a deep, dreamless sleep that enveloped her like a warm embrace.

The second night was much different, for she lay awake for what seemed like hours, listening in anticipation. But the next morning Alec was in the garden as usual, so she assumed he must have been in his room at some point during the night.

That afternoon, Caro returned from her visit with Grandmère earlier than usual. She lay on her high, deep bed and tried to rest, but found her mind too full of thoughts. The prospect of another long, uneventful night filled her with dread, for not even Natalya planned to be at home. She had an engagement to dine at the house of one of her many beaux, and Caro had urged her to go. She knew that Natalya had turned down several invitations to keep her company and realized that their friendship would soon sour if Natalya constantly felt restricted. Besides, Caro thought angrily, it is not her responsibility to amuse me. It is Alec who should be giving up social engagements to be with me!

Impulsively, she decided that a distraction was in order—in the form of literature. The prospect of escaping reality for the evening through a book was immensely appealing.

Caro hopped off her bed and went to the wardrobe to find a dress she could easily slip into. Several of her new gowns had already arrived, and she hastily withdrew one. Fashioned of simple white muslin with no overskirt, it boasted a wide rose-colored sash at the waist, and the neckline was cut low to reveal a large portion of her sweet young breasts. Caro cared little for her appearance, however, as she slipped out of her room in her stockinged feet and scampered down the hall to the library.

The Persian rug was soft beneath her feet as she pe-

167

rused the great built-in bookcases. Familiar names and titles leaped at her from the fine leather bindings: Voltaire, Locke, Milton, Cicero, Bacon, and Johnson. Eagerly, Caro gathered up several of these volumes, along with copies of Richardson's novel *Pamela* and John Trumbull's popular *Progress of Dullness*. Shafts of bright sunshine broke through the trees on the west side of the house, illuminating the cushioned window seat in that corner of the library. Caro settled herself there, tucking her feet beneath her skirt, and began poring over the books. She had already finished two chapters of the seductive *Pamela* when a deep voice broke her reverie.

"I am so pleased to see you are making yourself at home, Caro!"

She looked up, startled, to see Alec standing by his desk, his mouth quirked in an ironic smile.

"I did not even hear you come in!" she exclaimed, suddenly conscious of her feet tucked beneath the crumpled white skirt and her breasts nearly spilling out of her bodice as she leaned forward over the book. Alec watched with devilish amusement as Caro tried unsuccessfully to straighten herself out. When she untangled her legs, tiny white-clad feet peeped out, and her attempt at getting her breasts farther inside her neckline brought an open grin to his dark face.

"Please, Caro, do not move anymore! I am only human, you know. Perhaps not even that!"

She flushed, wishing she could pull the nearby curtain around her body. Alec was, as ever, maddeningly cool as he perched on the corner of his desk, eying her with enjoyment. He was clad in an open-necked white linen shirt with lace at the wrists. The muscles in his thighs showed beneath buff-colored breeches, which contrasted perfectly with the folded-down earth-brown jockey boots he wore. His clothes, though well made, would be unremarkable on any other man, Caro mused as she watched him. He would look dashing in monk's robes!

Alec's eyes were boldly fixed on her bosom as he asked, "Am I to understand that this is one of your new gowns?"

"Yes," Caro replied miserably, trying to shrink back farther into the corner. Alec bit the corner of his mouth in an effort to repress another grin.

"If this is a sample of the best of your new wardrobe, then I must give my hearty approval!"

"I cannot help but believe that this dress is your doing, sir. Pray do not look so innocently surprised at the sight of it!"

Alec threw back his head, laughing with sheer joy —a gesture that Caro had nearly forgotten.

"To be frank, *chérie,* it is not the sight of the dress itself that holds my interest!"

Caro turned her head away to conceal the hot blush that was creeping up her cheeks, searching all the while for a scathing retort. Unable to think of one, she looked back at Alec, wrinkled her nose, and promptly put out her tongue. His response was less than satisfactory, for he laughed harder than ever, exclaiming in mock horror: "Ah, Caro, I am truly crushed! You have delivered the ultimate insult!"

She was seething with frustration until he walked over to her and grasped her tiny wrist. At the touch of his hand, Caro went weak and tingling. Coherent thought was difficult, anger impossible as she gazed helplessly into his keen turquoise eyes.

"Tell me the truth," Alec said in a more serious tone. "Are you happy with your gowns? I trust that the others are not so—ah, attractively revealing. I should not like the rest of the men in Philadelphia to enjoy the beauty upon which I gaze now. They are not so deserving as I, *n'est-ce pas?*"

"Alec," Caro said stupidly, "don't be foolish! And so far this is the only gown which is made like this."

Her heart stopped as he lightly trailed one brown finger over the firm curve of her breast.

"That is a relief," he grinned. "You may save this little fashion for me alone."

A voice inside Caro cried out that she should slap his hand away and coldly sweep from the room. However, she neither moved nor spoke. Alec touched her cheek softly.

"Well, the hour grows late and I had better have a bath before dinner. I'll see you downstairs, Caro."

He had almost reached the door when Caro regained her composure and scrambled to her feet, calling, "Alec, please wait!"

He paused, looking back at her expectantly.

"I must thank you for the gowns! You must not think that I am ungrateful, for in fact I am quite overwhelmed by your extravagance! You truly shouldn't have—"

"But I wanted to. You deserve beautiful things, Caro, and it is a rare delight to see a female who does not turn into a preening, vain peacock when clad in an elegant gown." He smiled at her with uncommon sincerity. "I shall never forget the day we walked in New York and you wore that new green and ivory gown . . ." Alec's voice died away when he caught sight of Caro's radiant face. "I'll see you at dinner, then."

Caro had a long bath before the evening meal, soaking in a brass tub filled with steaming jasmine-scented water. The prospect of an evening with Alec lifted her spirits immeasurably, and Natalya was surprised to find her humming cheerfully when she popped into the room.

Caro was sitting on a low chair, clad only in her chemise and petticoats while her lady's maid dressed her shining honey-colored hair. Pulling up a chair next to her, Natalya declared gloomily:

"You will not retain that good mood long when you hear my news."

170

"We'll see!" laughed Caro.

"Well, to be honest, any other night I would prefer to dine at home, for Sacha is much better company than Stanley or Robert—or any of these other stiff-necked suitors I am plagued with!" Caro gave her a slightly quizzical look, but Natalya was rushing on. "Tonight, though, I bless Robert and his stuffy parents for inviting me, because Sacha's current mistress is dining here and she is a detestable creature who unfailingly sets my teeth on edge."

She paused, her clear sapphire eyes searching Caro's face, which had suddenly gone pale. "Are you all right? You look as though you've seen a ghost!"

"Why, I'm fine. But Natalya, how do you know she is his mistress? Has he told you so?"

The other girl stood up, smiling bitterly. "Sacha does not need to tell me. For one thing, he does not waste his time on light flirtations—or on women who value their moral standards. I am not implying that he has ever stooped to the cheap sort, because I've never known him to be rebuffed by any woman. He chooses the sophisticated ones, though—the women who will not be hurt at the end. He has a definite dislike for emotional entanglements—probably because they are always one-sided!"

"Yes, I know," Caro replied in a low voice.

"Do not let Madeleine get under your skin," advised Natalya. "She is a cunning woman, very sharp-witted, but it all becomes more bearable when one realizes that she is playing a losing game. She fully plans to marry Sacha, but it will never occur."

"How can you be so certain?"

"Because he will never marry—have we not both told you so already? Besides, Sacha's interest in Madeleine Chamberlain is strictly categorical."

"But why does he bring her here to eat with his family?"

"I really couldn't say. I would guess that she

171

coaxed him into it and he gave in to silence her—probably after one too many brandies. Caro, cheer up! You look like a rejected wife and just moments ago you had the glow of a new bride."

Grandmère appeared at the secret passageway in Caro's wall right after Natalya left for the evening, and the two allies went down to dinner together. Caro wore her favorite gown of peach-colored gauze along with a stunning emerald choker that Natalya insisted on lending her. Her hair was swept up in shining curls that charmingly framed her winsome face.

"That gown is perfect for evening," Grandmère pronounced. "The color goes beautifully with the candlelight and your skin. Sacha will be proud of your appearance."

Caro wanted to reply that she was sure Alec would not care how she looked, but instead heard herself saying, "Will you tell me about Alec's . . . guest?"

Grandmère curled her lips in evident distaste.

"You must mean Madeleine Chamberlain. She is a new war widow, but her mourning was remarkably short-lived. The moment that Sacha bought this house in the spring, she devised ways to see him. My grandson has always been appreciative of beauty—especially when it is being offered to him to enjoy at will. That is all the story there is at this time, but I feel certain that Madame Chamberlain has a plot of her own worked out." She paused, squeezing Caro's hand. "Let us descend, *petite chérie*. I am confident that you will not let her get the best of you—or of Sacha, for that matter!"

Alec was standing at the foot of the stairs waiting for them. Caro felt her heart flutter at the sight of him, for he was looking extremely handsome in an indigo-blue coat over a gold brocade waistcoat and cream-colored shirt. His face, brown against his expertly tied

172

cravat, registered amused surprise at the sight of his grandmother.

"Grandmère, can you never enter a house in the normal fashion? I thought you were still at home dressing!"

She accepted his arm, observing him with bright dark eyes. "I thought that I should accompany Caroline to protect her from our—ah, esteemed dinner guest."

"I'll wager that Caro can take care of herself," Alec responded sharply, his face hardening in annoyance. "And I will thank you to hold your tongue, Grandmère. I will not tolerate any little scenes tonight. Madeleine is a guest in this house and I expect you to treat her accordingly."

Grandmère arched an eyebrow rebelliously, but kept silent. As they entered the parlor, Caro's gaze was instantly drawn to the stunning woman who stood before the delft tile fireplace. She had hair the color of the flames that flickered behind her, and her skin was milky white in contrast. Tall and slender, Madeleine Chamberlain had a face that was both elegant and sensuous with its winged eyebrows, thin nose, and pouting mouth. As they drew nearer, Caro was astonished to see that the woman's eyes were a vivid shade of violet, and that they assessed her with naked cunning.

"Well, well, so this is little Caroline! I have heard a great deal about you, child!"

Nicholai, who stood beside Madeleine, rolled his eyes.

Repressing an impulse to giggle, Caro replied, "That is very flattering, Mrs. Chamberlain. I am sorry to admit that Alec has neglected to tell me a thing about you!"

Madeleine's eyes narrowed a fraction as she looked over Caro's head to Alec. "Alexandre, darling," she purred, "I had no idea that your little ward was so mature—or shall we say, presentable!"

"Presentable!" Nicholai interjected. "The girl is a raving beauty!"

Madeleine eyed him coldly as Alec declared, "I believe I am ready for another glass of wine. Can I get one for you and Caro, Grandmère?"

"Really, Alexandre, are you sure the child should be drinking spirits?" Madeleine called after him as he went to procure the glasses. Caro found herself staring irresistibly at the other woman, and hating herself for her fascination. Madeleine's dress was a work of art and Caro felt suddenly dull and short beside her. It was fashioned of exquisite lavender silk, cut daringly low to reveal a voluptuous bosom, and tucked into an elaborate bustle in back. Clear, dazzling amethysts sparkled at her neck and in her ears, and Caro was conscious of a painful envy burning inside herself.

During dinner, she watched Madeleine talk to Alec, her sensuous mouth alternately petulant and radiant. He looked at her with smoldering eyes, and Caro tried to imagine them naked together, Alec kissing Madeleine's long neck. Feeling ill, she barely touched her ham, despite Nicholai's cheerful conversation. She watched thankfully as the *pots au crème* were being served and Madeleine's cool voice rose above the others:

"Alexandre, now that I realize your ward is an older girl, I would be delighted to arrange for her to meet some boys her own age." Her eyes met Caro's. "Wouldn't you like that, dear? After all, I'm sure that a nice girl like you would not wish to impose on Mr. Beauvisage's hospitality any longer than necessary."

Caro lifted her chin and spat out, "I am here at my guardian's invitation, Mrs. Chamberlain. I am totally subservient to his wishes."

One of Alec's mobile eyebrows flew up in amusement and Caro had the satisfaction of seeing Madeleine's smug smile tighten with anger. Nicholai squeezed Caro's hand under the table. When she stole a sidelong glance at him she saw that he had his knuckles pressed against his mouth to conceal an irrepressible grin.

Later, when the party had adjourned to the north parlor, Alec slipped away from Madeleine momentarily. Caro felt his hand touch the nape of her neck, and turned around a trifle too quickly.

"Alec, do not tell me that you are alone!"

"Try not to provoke me, infant," he replied with a reckless grin. "I am feeling warmer toward you after that marvelous remark you made about being subservient to my wishes. That was classic! I confess I was on the verge of laughing out loud!"

"I have a feeling that your—ah, friend would not have appreciated that!" Caro replied impulsively. She was relieved to see that he continued to smile at her. "What are you looking so pleased about, sir? I suppose that you think after what I said you have me where you want me!"

Alec's eyes were gleaming as he leaned down closer to her ear, inhaling the fragrance of jasmine.

"I wish that I did, *chérie*," he murmured in a low voice underlaid with laughter. Caro felt her face grow warm under his bold gaze, but she looked up challengingly.

"Touché, monsieur! You have—" her voice broke off as she met Madeleine's venomous eyes across the room. Grandmère had engaged her in an impressively polite conversation, but it was obvious where her attention lay. Caro bit her lip. "Alec, I think Mrs. Chamberlain is growing lonely. I do not want to impose on your hospitality, you know, so I had better retire now."

The look of regret that flickered in his turquoise eyes left a glow inside her that lasted a full hour. It was only when she was perched on her window seat, clad in a warm bedgown, that her heart turned cold. She had planned to look at the stars and bask in her small glow of contentment, but instead she found herself watching Alec and Madeleine strolling on the garden footpaths. They were bathed in silver moonlight, and he had one arm around her shoulders in a way that looked possessively affectionate. Caro sat transfixed, watching as they paused and Alec slipped the hood of Madeleine's cloak back from her face. They kissed then, so long that Caro felt near to vomiting at the end. However, the worst part came a moment later, when Alec looked up and clearly recognized Caro's white-clad figure staring out of her window.

Chapter Sixteen

AS THEY BREAKFASTED IN THE UPSTAIRS SITTING ROOM the next morning, Natalya told Caro that her brother had given his permission for the ball.

"Before Christmas, he said. We have tentatively settled on the sixth, so that gives us little more than a month to set our plans. Won't it be exciting?"

Caro managed a strained smile, wondering why Alec was suddenly so anxious for her to make her social debut.

"It is very kind of you to go to all this trouble for me," she replied in a rather flat voice.

"Fiddle-faddle!" Natalya exclaimed. "I am your friend, am I not? Besides, I shall doubtless enjoy it all as much as you! I've been thinking though, Caro . . ."

"About what?"

Natalya spread blueberry preserves generously over her warm bun.

"Well, about you. May I be frank?"

Caro felt an instinctive panic, for she had no wish to be frank even with herself. "I suppose so," she allowed.

"Please, Caro, do not retreat from me," Natalya pleaded as she reached out to press her hand. "I am convinced that you are in desperate need of a friend; someone your own age. I know that you talk to Grandmère, but she has told me you never discuss yourself. I would not press you on this, but I can see your soul in your eyes whenever Sacha is near!"

Caro almost spilled tea down the front of her green-and-white-striped muslin dress before she managed to return the cup to the saucer.

"Please hear me out," cried Natalya, "for your own sake! Perhaps you will not face the facts, but I can tell readily enough what they are. I knew it the first day, but I let you persuade me that black was white. You are in love with Sacha. Yes! I will not listen to your arguments, for I know what is true. I am desperately afraid that your affliction may be incurable, for I have never known a woman to make a full recovery after losing her heart to my brother. I have seen them come and go for a dozen years, and it is pitiful! Even the cool, hardened ones are not immune; the only difference is that they have few illusions. They do not really expect Sacha to fall in love with them, so their disappointment is not so great at the end. That is why he steers away from young girls like you, Caro. What a tangle this is! I cannot think why your father knowingly set you in this snare, unless he tendered some dream that Sacha would marry you. I do not mean to sound cruel, but I must speak the truth before it is too late!"

Caro sat totally speechless, her eggs cold on the plate before her. Natalya leaned closer, her blue eyes soft with sympathy.

"Do you imagine that I cannot understand? I am a female too, and even I have suffered some infatuation with Sacha. When I was younger I thought he was the most exciting, vital person in the world, and he would treat me like I was beautiful and special. There is something magic about him—I know it, too! An aura that draws people to him like moths to a flame. In the war, he could go anywhere, on any mission, and he always succeeded. People do his bidding unfailingly—he could even captivate enemy camps! He is either loved intensely by those who cannot help themselves, or he is hated by those who envy him. And I do love him, make no mistake about it. Why do you think I stay here rather than with my sister Danielle while my parents are away? Usually Sacha is at home more, for he loves Belle Maison. He gives me pieces of his time and I devour them shamelessly. To be with Sacha is to know excitement and happiness so intense that one almost hurts!"

"I agree," Caro murmured in a low voice.

"So you will admit to me that you love him? If you can face it, that will be the first step. I hope!"

Caro nodded miserably and Natalya took her cue, pondering only briefly whether or not to divulge her family secret.

"There is something about Sacha that I have not told you—a tragic mystery, if you will. Perhaps if you know this you will understand that he has truly lost his vulnerability to love." With wondering dread, Caro waited for her to continue. "Even I do not know the entire story—I have pieced it together over the last few years from different people. Apparently, Sacha met someone during the war, a lady of independence. Her parents were Tories and left the country, but she stayed behind, pledging loyalty to the patriot cause. You may know that Sacha was a spy of sorts through much of the war, and it seems that this girl—Emily, as I recall—traveled around with him part of the time when he was on the road alone. His love for her made him trusting, and of course she had no parents to restrict her. The war was a time when few rules of any sort were followed; people simply lived for the moment.

"At any rate, to make a long story short, Kosci told me that it was discovered that she was a spy for the British all along. He hinted that Sacha may have even been the one who found her out. Can you imagine what that must have done to him? Their love affair was still young when she was caught, but you see she was spying on *him,* canceling out everything he did! I heard from different people that she was imprisoned or died; Nicky swears that he overheard Maman and Papa talking about her and they said she had been hanged! Mary Armstrong, a friend of ours, heard a rumor that Sacha was there at the time—forced to watch her die. It was after this whole incident that he gave up spying for a time and joined Papa at sea aboard their privateer. He couldn't have lived out the rest of the war more recklessly than he did; it is a miracle he wasn't killed.

"Now, I couldn't say how much of this is true, for Sacha himself has never spoken a word about Emily to me. The mere thought of asking him strikes terror into my soul!" She laughed shakily. "So, you can see, that though Sacha has always been something of a skeptic when it comes to true love, *now* his heart is hardened completely against seemingly innocent women."

Caro looked stricken as she tried to assimilate all that Natalya had said. The thought of Alec deeply involved with another girl—traveling alone with her! —was almost too much to be borne. In her mind, she could not get past that to the tragic ending of the story.

"But, Natalya, no matter what this Emily did, she must have loved Alec. It would have been impossible for her not to have loved him!"

Natalya nodded matter-of-factly. "Of course she did. That's what makes it so sad."

"Well, I'm glad you told me," Caro lied huskily. "I only wish I had known earlier—perhaps it would have helped me resist him . . . but I doubt it." She groaned, pulling at the glossy curl until it hurt, and Natalya saw a gold spark flash momentarily in her brown eyes. "I swore to anyone who would listen that I would not give up my heart to him. He warned me the first day we met that he was no gentleman and I realized even then that loving him would be hopeless."

"Yet you couldn't help it. One can rarely control the heart with the mind, you know," Natalya told her wisely.

"I hate him for doing this to me!" Caro declared, tears spilling onto her cheeks. She felt as if flood gates had been opened inside her. "I cannot even control my own emotions anymore. I blush constantly, I lose my voice, or worse, stammer like a schoolgirl. And he laughs at me!"

Impulsively, Natalya moved next to Caro and hugged her.

"It is good for you to talk about it, but not for long. We must fight this devil that possesses you, Caro! I know so many fine young men and we cannot let you sit about pining for Sacha. I intend to take you out to meet all my friends—we cannot afford to wait until your ball. With any luck, you will be able to ease your pain in activity. And, who knows—you may just meet the man who will make you forget my brother."

"I suppose you're right," Caro replied sadly. "I know that that is Alec's wish."

Later, as she and Molly galloped through the dry fields on their morning ride, Caro thought back to the days when she and Alec had been all alone in the woods.

Each day takes us farther and farther away from those happy times, she thought. The memory of the two of them riding together through the trees, laughing and teasing, seemed as unreal as a dream. She thought how stupidly naïve she had been, innocently lying against him at night. And yet, there was a strange feeling in her heart that insisted it had all been real—and right. Perhaps if we had never left Wallingham's farm our ending might have been different, she mused sadly.

The next month passed swiftly, and Caro found herself propelled by Natalya through a maze of activity. They went into Philadelphia nearly every day, visiting friends and planning Caro's ball. The entire staff at the Beauvisage house threw themselves into the arrangements, for with the family away they had little else to do. Caro was astounded by the number of details preparing for a party encompassed.

It was in early November that Danielle Engelman appeared for the first time. Natalya and Caro were sitting in the huge white kitchen, discussing the supper arrangements with Mrs. Reeves, the cook. It was a chilly, overcast day, and Caro felt uncommonly content as she sipped tea near the great blazing hearth. Suddenly the kitchen door swung open and a tall, striking woman with stylishly frizzed hair under a wide-brimmed green hat swept into the room.

"Whatever are you doing back here?" she inquired in a voice of authority. Caro cast a glance at Natalya, who was looking decidedly unenthusiastic over the newcomer.

"For your information, Danielle, we are making arrangements for a ball that Sacha is giving next month."

"A ball! Whatever for? Particularly with Maman and Papa away!"

"It is for his ward, whom you see beside me. Caroline Bergman, may I present my married sister, Danielle Engelman."

It appeared that Danielle had heard nothing of the new developments in her brother's life. Immediately taking charge, she ordered Mrs. Reeves to have tea brought to them in the small parlor. Natalya and Caro followed in her wake as she glided from the kitchen, declaring that she wanted to hear "everything." Caro watched her, in her mind hearing Alec's voice saying, "Danielle is the only sane person in the family." She recalled the tone he had used, and decided he had not meant it as a compliment. It struck her as being rather odd that she had been at Belle Maison all this time and had never met this older sister.

The teatime conversation lasted over an hour, and Caro could not dislike Danielle. She was obviously pushy and snobbish, but Caro sensed that she was hiding behind this façade. There was something rather sad in the way Danielle asked casually for news, trying to appear unconcerned at her exclusion from the goings-on at Belle Maison. She spoke animatedly of her husband and their two children, but it was obvious to Caro that she longed to be part of that bright magic circle formed by the rest of her family.

When at last she stood to put on her pelisse, Danielle looked hopefully at Natalya. "I insist that you let me help you girls plan this ball!" she said. "Maman would want it, you know. After all, I have much more experience in these things than you do, Natalya."

Natalya bristled under her sister's condescending tone, but before she could respond, Caro spoke up:

"I think that would be wonderful, Danielle. We should be grateful for any time you can spare."

Danielle's face was wreathed in smiles as she bid them good-bye. The two girls stood in the doorway, watching as she was assisted into an expensive-looking coach.

"Whatever possessed you, Caro?" Natalya burst out. "Do you want that stick-in-the-mud hanging about every day?"

"But she's your sister!"

"I sometimes find that hard to believe. Maman says that Danielle has been different from the start—that she somehow assumed the personality of her governess while she was a child. She always looks down her nose at Sacha and Nicky and me, so we just leave her alone with her horrid husband. He is more of a snob than she! Sacha has tried to be nice to her, but then she begins pointing out all his vices and he loses his temper all over again—"

"I feel sorry for her," Caro said quietly. "Perhaps it takes an outsider to see how desperately she wants to be one of you. Somehow she missed getting all that Beauvisage charm, wit, and spirit of adventure. Can't you see how it must have been for her growing up with all of you? She had to do something to salvage her pride, so she pretends to everyone that she is better than the rest of you. I think it is awfully sad!"

Natalya was listening to Caro's speech in stunned silence. "Do you really believe," she asked, "that is the way it was with Danielle?"

"I'm certain of it. I cannot believe that none of you could see it. Especially Alec. He has always seemed unusually perceptive to me. . . ."

"Well, then, you see you were all wrong about him! He is terribly cold and unfeeling!"

"Stop trying to influence my feelings. You cannot push me out of love, Natalya. If you don't mind, I believe I shall go out for a walk."

"Not alone!"

"Yes!" Caro turned sharply, color flooding her face. "I am tired of being fussed and worried over. I feel smothered—and I miss Alec! Now, please leave me alone!"

She hurriedly donned her lovely fox-trimmed pelisse and ran out of the house. Natalya looked as if she was about to follow, but thought better of it and reluctantly closed the door. Caro folded her arms across her breasts, putting her face down against the cold November wind. As she stopped on the corner of Spruce and Third streets, waiting to cross, a familiar blue and black phaeton came into view. Alec held the reins expertly and next to him sat a chilled-looking Madeleine Chamberlain, her hands thrust deep into an ermine muff. She wore a vivid crimson pelisse, which was also edged in ermine, and would have looked stunning if not for the sour expression she wore.

Caro stood immobile, wanting to duck out of sight but unable to move her feet. Alec was laughing over at Madeleine, in an apparent effort to coax her out of her temper. Her frown vanished quickly enough, however, when she spotted Caro standing on the footpath.

"Alexandre!" she cried maliciously. "There is your little ward! Do stop."

Alec's eyebrows drew together at the sight of Caro alone in the middle of Philadelphia. Reining in his team of perfectly matched grays, he leaned over Madeleine to shout:

"What in God's name are you doing out here all by yourself? Where is Natalya, or that maid of yours? Have you lost your mind?"

It was the first time he had spoken more than two words to her in a week, and Caro felt her head spin in reaction. Bright patches of cold and emotion stood out on her cheeks as she cried:

"No, I have not lost my mind, but I expect to momentarily if I do not get some peace from you Beauvisages! Kindly confine your attentions to Mrs. Chamberlain and leave me alone!"

Her voice was quavering with barely suppressed tears as she turned and fled, her hood falling back as her honey-colored hair cascaded down her back. Alec was shouting, but she could only hear Madeleine's words as she called:

"So nice to see you, my dear!" in a poisonously sweet voice.

It was not to be the first time that Caro would see them together, although after that they were always inside a closed carriage. She had no trouble spotting Madeleine's flaming hair; in fact, she came to be able to see it on a busy street filled with vehicles.

185

Caro's own personal relationship with Alec was rapidly deteriorating as November wore on. Occasionally, they met in the hallway, or he dined at home, but there were no more private conversations between them and he took great care never to touch her. Caro even gave up watching him in the mornings after he turned around one day in the middle of a conversation with the housekeeper and looked straight up at her window and into her eyes. She was convinced then that he had known she had been observing him all along.

Even though she was always busy, Caro's misery seemed to grow like an unnatural thing. She still went frequently to Grandmère's for tea, but the old woman did not appear ready to offer her any solutions. She did, however, continue to drop hints that Caro found unsettling. Sometimes she would comment with studied casualness:

"I feel that you are not happy here, Caroline. Perhaps you are going about things incorrectly?"

Then she would close her eyes in a way that told Caro the subject was not to be pursued.

To make matters worse, she was meeting many young men through Natalya. One of them, an earnest young Scotsman, was showing all the signs of hopeless love. His name was Everett MacGowan, and he was rapidly rising in the business world as a protégé of the financial wizard Robert Morris. He was intelligent, sincere, ambitious, and full of awed respect for Caro. Natalya declared him the ideal suitor, but Caro was alarmed by her own total lack of emotion toward Everett. In fact, she was becoming apathetic about everything and everyone except for Alec, and her most consistent emotion where he was concerned was a dull, aching sadness.

By the end of November, all the arrangements had been made for Caro's ball, which would be held December 6. On the afternoon of the winter's first snowfall, Natalya persuaded Caro to venture forth to shop for their new ball gowns. They were in the process of dashing through the dense snowfall from their carriage to the door of a prominent dress shop when Caro collided forcefully with a tall man crossing the brick footpath. Losing her balance, she sat down hard in the snow. Immediately, she felt two familiar arms lifting her up, holding her around the waist in a grip that made her tingle.

Looking up, Caro saw Alec's sharp turquoise eyes burning into her own. His black hair glistened with snowflakes.

Neither of them spoke, and then a soft voice broke the silence: "Sacha, do let go of the young lady! What's come over you?" Caro saw a tiny blond girl at his side, reaching for one of his arms that held her own waist. Alec seemed to focus on the outside world for the first time, but he did not let go of her.

"It's all right, Mary. This girl is my ward." He looked back at Caro then. "You aren't hurt, are you? Where were you going in such a damned hurry?"

A glimmer of laughter touched his eyes, and Caro could feel Natalya pulling her away from him almost frantically.

"Mary is right, Sacha! Let go of Caro!"

His hands released her and she tottered back against Natalya, murmuring, "Of course, I'm fine. That was terribly discourteous of me. I am sorry."

"I accept your apology, *chérie*," Alec replied with a mocking grin. The little blond girl called Mary suggested that they take shelter inside the shop.

"Sacha is so silly about running out in all sorts of weather. Every day is like an adventure with him!" she giggled.

Caro's heart went cold, but she heard herself say in a strained voice, "Alec—I hope you do not mind— I was on my way to be fitted for a new ball gown.

Natalya insisted that you would want to buy one for me, so—"

Alec was frowning. "She is absolutely correct. The fact is, I have already purchased it. It will be ready for you in time for the ball, Caro."

All three girls stared at him in amazement as he turned toward the door.

"Coming, Mary?"

He bowed slightly to Caro and Natalya, then he and the tiny blond disappeared into the swirling snow.

Chapter Seventeen

CARO'S PRIVATE LIFE REACHED ITS INEVITABLE CLI-
max one day during the first week in December. It
began in a most ordinary manner, with Caro break-
fasting in the sunny downstairs dining room with Natalya. There was still a thin layer of snow outside, but
it was melting rapidly.

Caro had her first hint that the day was not going to
be routine when the front door slammed and the head
butler went scurrying down the brick entry hall. There
was a general commotion, and Caro felt her heart begin to race at the sound of a deep, familiar voice. Moments later, Alec appeared in the doorway, clad all
in tawny brown over a pale yellow waistcoat. His
black hair glistened with droplets from the melting
snow on the trees, and his color was high after the
ride on horseback from Philadelphia.

"Good morning, fair blossoms of beauty. I believe I
shall indulge in a cup of coffee and your company."

His mood seemed unusually light to Caro, who had
grown used to a coolness in his manner toward her.

"Dear brother," Natalya said, "you have become a
stranger in your own house! We should be honored by
your presence."

Alec arched one black brow at the sarcasm in her
voice, but made no reply. After shrugging off his

brown coat, he seated himself across from Caro and smiled at her.

"How have you been, *chérie?* I must say that you are growing more beautiful each time I see you—if that is possible. Your active social life must be agreeing with you."

Natalya glanced at her brother suspiciously, then noted with alarm the attractive rosy flush in Caro's cheeks. She was indeed looking especially lovely that day. Her hair was freshly washed and swept up in loose, glossy curls that shone in the bright sunlight. Her topaz velvet dress complimented her coloring, and the bodice, edged in creamy French lace, artfully hugged her breasts. Natalya could see the way Caro's golden-brown eyes melted under Alec's reckless gaze and knew that she had to do something. Before the other girl could answer Alec's compliment, Natalya spoke up:

"You would be very pleased by all the suitors Caro has acquired, Sacha! They are all fine young men— particularly Everett MacGowan. He is so handsome and sincere, and I strongly suspect that he has fallen in love with your little ward!"

A serving girl appeared to set a cup of coffee down before Alec, and he sipped at it thoughtfully. Contrary to Natalya's prediction, he did not look the least bit pleased at her news.

"In love, eh? I seem to recall meeting him last summer at the Willing Counting House. I suppose I'd better speak to him—that is if Caro returns his—ah— regard."

He was watching her with an alertness well concealed by his nonchalant attitude. "What do you say, Caro? I've never seen you so silent!"

"Why—I don't know what to say, Alec! I really hardly know Mr. MacGowan. He's certainly very courteous and—"

"Respectful? That's a necessity, you know!"

Alec's eyes had gone hard, and there was no mistaking the caustic note in his voice. Hearing it, Caro lifted her chin at him.

"Let me remind you, sir, that you were the one right from the first who set such store by that virtue! I have never been given any opportunity to decide for myself what qualities I desired in a man!"

"You foolish child, I have only been acting with your best interests in mind! You know nothing of the world—"

"Please, you two," Natalya broke in frantically, "do stop this silly quarreling! Have you come back from town today just to start an argument, Sacha?"

His square jaw was set as he scowled darkly at both girls.

"No, as a matter of fact, I have some good news. Our parents are home."

"Home!" cried Natalya. "How can that be? They did not plan to return until March or April!"

"It seems that Dr. Franklin is not well. He is suffering greatly from gallstones. Maman had no wish to burden him with a long visit or to go back to the Loire, so they decided to return now before winter set in for good." His keen eyes were on Caro. "I have arranged for you to move into town tomorrow. Maman is anxious to meet you—and I imagine you will be pleased to be nearer MacGowan and your other friends." He rose then, raking a hand through his raven hair. "I believe I'll go deliver these glad tidings to Grandmère. I bid you ladies good morning."

All through the remainder of the morning, Caro was obsessed with Alec's news. Natalya told her frankly that it would be all for the best to get out of his house, reminding her that she would be moving along with her. Caro was only conscious of the fact that she and Alec were growing farther and farther apart.

The girls and their maids spent two hours packing

191

in their rooms before luncheon. Natalya waited until then to tell Caro they were having guests for the meal.

"Stanley begged me to allow him a visit, so I suggested that you might enjoy Everett's company. Both of them will be arriving shortly."

"Oh, Natalya," moaned Caro, "I am in no mood to make polite conversation with Everett MacGowan. Couldn't you make some excuse . . . ?"

"Nonsense!" Natalya declared as she brushed a piece of dust from Caro's arm. "This is exactly the sort of diversion you need right now. Now, do try to freshen up before they arrive."

When Caro left her room a few minutes later to join Natalya in the parlor, she found Everett MacGowan already waiting in the entry hall. The butler was taking his and Stanley Redmond's coats, while Natalya stood between them, chattering animatedly. Caro paused, unobserved, at the top of the stairs, to contemplate the red-headed young man below. He was of medium height, but well built. His features were even and unremarkable, but when he turned his hazel eyes on Caro, they burned with an emotion that transformed his entire face.

From their first meeting, Everett had been unable to stop staring at the winsome girl who seemed to be made of honey and cream. Caro sensed that beneath his unfailingly courteous manner there beat a heart filled with passion, and this knowledge made her feel extremely uneasy whenever they were together. Even now, she could not bring herself to take the first step down the stairway until Stanley turned and spotted her.

"Ah! Here is our golden dove! Do come down, Miss Bergman!"

Everett immediately turned shining eyes up to her, staring rapturously as Caro descended. He was there at the bottom step to clasp her hand, startling Caro with the unnatural heat of his skin.

"Miss Bergman, permit me to compliment you once again on your great good looks. I have been anticipating our luncheon together with much eagerness!"

He was beaming at her, his fair skin flushed with happiness.

They went in to luncheon, but Caro found she had no appetite. Everett MacGowan seemed to be unusually nervous, for the color never left his face and he scarcely took his eyes from her during the entire meal. His manner made her uneasy, even vaguely nauseous, and she began thinking of excuses to retire to her room. Natalya seemed to be bored herself, paying a minimal amount of attention to the ardent Stanley Redmond.

The plates had been cleared away and cups of warm maple custard were being served when Alec appeared. Caro, whose nerves were already worn thin, felt giddy at the sight of his dark, cynical face, and Natalya was suddenly animated. Alec had shed his coat and vest, and was looking very cool in his ruffled muslin shirt and tawny breeches.

"Well, well," he drawled, narrowing his eyes as he drew in smoke from a thin cheroot. "What a charming scene this is! Caro, you did not tell me you were expecting Mr.—ah—MacGowan, isn't it? An unfortunate oversight on your part, infant! I'm certain you heard me say I wanted to speak to him." Alec strolled over behind Caro's chair and casually rested his brown hands on her bare shoulders. Feeling her stiffen, then quiver beneath his touch, he smiled almost maliciously. *"Ma petite,* you must not be nervous! I will not bite your young man!"

His eyes went to Everett's: icy, mocking turquoise meeting nervous, shining hazel.

"I understand that you have developed a deep regard for my ward, Mr. MacGowan. I certainly cannot blame you, for she is a lovely girl. We are very close —isn't that so, Caro?" Casually he lifted a hand to pat her cheek in what appeared to Everett to be a fatherly gesture.

"Caro!" Alec exclaimed in mock concern. "You are feeling very warm! I do hope you are not ill."

"As a matter of fact, I do feel rather . . . unwell," she murmured in a strained voice. Before she could continue, Everett jumped to his feet and grasped her hand.

"Miss Bergman, I beg you for a moment of your time! Please do not refuse me, for I have something of the utmost import to say to you."

He looked up at Alec then, his courage building.

"Mr. Beauvisage, could I persuade you to allow me a private interview with your ward? I assure you that I have always treated her with the greatest respect and propriety."

Alec lifted a lazy brow, but his eyes glittered dangerously at Everett's words. Caro could feel the pressure of his hands on her shoulders increase painfully as he replied:

"Mr. MacGowan, I am confident that you are a true gentleman. If Caro feels well enough, then far be it from me to place any obstacles in the path of true love."

Everett appeared oblivious to the bitter note in Alec's voice. "That is exceedingly kind of you, sir. Miss Bergman, perhaps we might walk alone in the garden?"

Caro longed to refuse, but could see no graceful avenue of escape. As Everett helped her to her feet, she glanced back momentarily at Alec, and his penetrating gaze sent a tremor through her. A servant appeared with Everett's and her wraps, and moments later they were out in the garden. Most of the snow had melted, and the sun was bright in the clear blue sky. Caro, however, could not appreciate the weather as they walked over the wet footpaths in silence. Everett's nervousness was a tangible thing, yet she had no desire to ease his discomfort with a friendly word. Finally he stopped short, gathering his courage, and blurted:

"Miss Bergman, I must tell you of my feelings for you or burst from the pain of keeping them inside of me. I realize fully that our acquaintance has been brief, but I believe that I fell in love with you the instant we met." Caro was regarding him with a mixture of amazement and panic. "You must not look at me so, my dear! I cannot credit that my confession comes as a surprise to you, for you must have read my feelings in my manner. You are the most wonderful girl in the world—so sweet and gay and lovely! You always have a kind word for everyone, and never act as though you are anyone's better. No man could help but love you, and I know that I am not alone even now. That is why I must declare myself before some other man can claim you!"

His face was blotched with color, and covered with a thin film of perspiration. Caro could feel his hot hands grow moist as they held hers, and momentarily feared that she might be sick right there. Everett saw the awful expression on her face and plunged on in an even louder voice than before.

"Do not reject me, I beseech you! I am humbly begging for your hand in marriage, Miss Bergman! I know that I do not deserve you, but my love knows no bounds. I shall spend the rest of my life taking care of you and loving you. My position in life is very respectable and my future is bright. Someday I shall achieve the status of Robert Morris himself in the financial world! You will never regret marrying me, I promise you."

Caro's normally clear head had returned to her rapidly during Everett's impassioned speech. Her expression of panic softened to one of compassion as she regarded the young man before her.

"Please, Mr. MacGowan, do not go on. I am deeply sensible of the honor you have done me in asking me to marry you. Any girl would be proud to be your wife and I am moved and flattered by your words of love. I must refuse, however."

"No! No! Please do not! I know that you cannot live here forever; Beauvisage is not your father, God knows, and you cannot feel any family attachment. Why do you refuse yourself—and me—marriage?"

"My reasons are personal. I wish that I could share them with you, but I cannot. You are right about my staying here at Belle Maison, however. It is not a . . . fair situation. Natalya's parents have just returned from France today and we will both be moving to their home in Philadelphia tomorrow. Mr. MacGowan, I have seen very little of the world as yet, and I would not trust myself to make a decision regarding anything so important as marriage. Not at this time. I fear that I would make you very unhappy if we were to marry, for I am not the paragon you take me for. My faults are numerous, I assure you!"

She smiled up at him with bittersweet affection and saw that his eyes were shining with tears.

"I cannot accept that, Miss Bergman," he choked. "You are the loveliest, purest—"

"Indeed not," she returned firmly. "Please promise me that we may remain friends, Mr. MacGowan. And someday when you are married to a woman who deserves your love you will remember this day and be grateful to me for my frankness."

After he had left her alone, Caro sat down on one of the low garden benches and rested her head against a nearby oak tree. A heavy feeling of melancholy closed around her as the wind came up and blew golden curls against her cheeks. Suddenly it seemed very cold to her, and she was conscious of a great

196

fatigue. After a long time, Natalya came out of the house, treading so softly that Caro was not conscious of her presence until she was sitting down beside her.

"Dear Caro, are you all right? You have been sitting here for over an hour! Everett would not tell Stanley or me what had happened, and Sacha forbade me to come to you until now. You are positively white! Please tell me what is wrong!"

Caro let the taller girl put her arms around her and rested her forehead against Natalya's shoulder with a sigh.

"I simply don't know what's going to become of me. Poor Everett asked me to marry him and his emotion was pitiful. I felt so sorry for him—and for me, too. I seem to be accumulating a large amount of self-pity these days."

Natalya's arms stiffened as she said in a strained voice, "But, Caro, surely you don't mean to say that you refused him!"

Caro's head came up in surprise. "Of course I did! How could I accept? I have no love for the man!"

"What does that signify? As long as you are in love with Sacha, you are an emotional disaster when it comes to any other man. But, Caro, can't you see that if you continue this way you will wither and die! Your only hope is to marry someone who loves you and pray that his love will heal your heart. I am certain that in time you would come to love Everett—he is a fine man with a promising future! What sort of a life do you think awaits you as Sacha's ward?"

Caro moved away and looked off toward the house.

"I do not share your sentiments, Natalya, and I cannot accept your advice. It is easy for you to direct me to enter into a loveless marriage when you have no such prospects yourself. I know better than anyone what a romantic you are. You will never marry until you are blind with love!"

"Yes, but my case is different! Your situation is desperate, Caro—"

"Not so desperate that I would cheat Everett by marrying him without a glimmer of love for him. He is a nice man and deserves someone who can make him happy."

"But, Caro!"

She stood up then, averting her eyes.

"I believe I shall drop in on Grandmère. I have not spoken with her since we learned we will be leaving Belle Maison tomorrow. I should like to tell her good-bye privately."

"Rose has finished packing your trunks," Natalya said flatly. "You needn't worry about that. Sacha shows no signs of leaving the house tonight, so it will probably be easier for you to pass some of the time with Grandmère."

Caro smiled weakly at her, then glanced again toward the house. Natalya thought she perceived a flickering golden spark in her friend's brown eyes, but then she turned away and proceeded across the garden. Twilight was gathering swiftly, and the shadows soon swallowed her up. With a resigned shrug, Natalya got to her feet and pulled the hood of her nithsdale closer about her face to ward off the sharp evening chill, then she too left the garden to head for the welcoming lights of the main house.

Grandmère did not seem surprised to find Caro on her doorstep so near to dinner. In fact, Caro had a feeling that she was expecting her. The cozy candlelit parlor with its paintings and crewelwork beckoned to her like an old friend. Grandmère did not join her immediately, but said conversationally from the doorway:

"*D'abord,* why don't I get a glass of wine for you, *ma chère?* I have some excellent Chablis here that I brought from France. It will relax you."

Without waiting for an answer, she left the room and

returned with two crystal goblets and a matching decanter of wine on a silver tray. Seating herself next to Caro on the narrow settee, she poured the wine with tiny, steady hands.

"Do you like my tray?" Grandmère inquired pleasantly. "Sacha gave it to me for my seventy-fifth birthday. A silversmith called Paul Revere made it. I understand his work is quite well known."

Since she appeared to be waiting for a reply, Caro offered, "Oh, yes. I have heard of him."

When she looked up into the old woman's bright dark eyes, they seemed to look into her very soul and know all her secrets. The knot of tension inside her relaxed as she regarded her friend and sipped the light, fruity wine. A part of her wanted to reveal the truth about her past and her relationship with Alec, but somehow she could sense that Grandmère knew everything already.

"Well, *ma chère,* my grandson tells me you will be leaving us tomorrow. I do not need to express to you how much I shall miss your company. My fondness for you is truly genuine."

Caro felt hot tears welling up in her eyes at the exquisite tenderness in Grandmère's voice. The old woman took one of her hands lightly, and Caro found her warm, dry touch oddly comforting.

"My concern for you is genuine, *aussi,*" Grandmère continued gently. "I deplore meddling in any form, but it is my affection for you—and my grandchildren—that has brought me to this point."

At these words, hope flooded through Caro and she burst out: "Oh, Grandmère, I should be so grateful for any advice you could give me. My life is in such a muddled mess!"

"You would not need advice from me if you had followed your own instincts from the first, Caroline. You are a bright, clever girl, and you have a goodness within you that would have led you on the right course.

Your only mistake has been allowing your humility to make you so insecure that you have listened to other people's advice."

"I do not understand . . ."

"Mais oui, ma petite. Je crois que tu fais. Excusez-moi—but then, Sacha tells me you know French?"

"Yes . . ."

"That is good. You will need to know other languages. But, I digress. All I really wish to say to you, Caroline, is that you should not listen to Natalya. Because she is Sacha's sister, that does not mean that she is all-wise. In fact, her views are immature and very biased. Her image of Sacha is still founded in the hero worship of a *jeune fille* and a sister, for she has not seen enough of him to alter it much. *Certainement,* she knows him quite well, but only the part of his personality that is a brother. I would almost venture to say that you have probably come to know my grandson as well as anyone; that is to say, his true nature."

Caro was looking at her in disbelief, but somehow could feel her usual buoyancy creeping back into her heart.

"You cannot credit that what I say is true?" Grandmère smiled. "I have no proof, but Sacha and I are quite good friends. He has never had to fear a parent's censure from me, and I have endeavored never to judge him or advise him. He is an elusive man, and it takes special qualities in a person to hold him near." She paused, watching Caro shrewdly. "I understand that you two became quite close during your days alone in Connecticut?" she asked innocently.

Caro blushed in the shadows, but couldn't resist a small smile. "I thought that we did, Grandmère. But Alec is a confusing man, and I was quite confused myself. . . ."

"Of course, I can understand that. But you were doing your best then, before you had outside influence.

Tell me, who else besides my granddaughter has been talking to you about Sacha?"

"Well, Mrs. Van DerPat—and Pierre—and, then Alec told me himself at the start that he was a scoundrel, and—"

"Oui. I know what he is. His father and his grandfather were the same." Grandmère's wrinkled face looked almost young for an instant as she smiled reminiscently. "My husband, Étienne, was the best sort of rake. Ah, I can still see that devilish gleam in his eye that made me go weak with love. There are only a few such men born, *ma chère*—men with indescribable charisma. Women swarm around them like bees to honey, but it is only natural that no ordinary female could hold their interest. An extraordinary man needs a special woman, and *quelquefois,* it takes years before he finds her. And then, he cannot see that there is a change; you see how it is?"

Caro nodded, and Grandmère paused to pour some more wine, giving her a moment to consider what she had heard.

"I must explain also about Natalya," she continued at length, her brow puckering like dry parchment. "I have a theory, which, *naturellement,* may be completely wrong—*sais-tu?* But, as much as I love my granddaughter, I can still see clearly enough to recognize the flaws in *toute ma famille.* Natalya is young; headstrong and sure of herself like all the Beauvisages. She is very convincing, *non?* All her life she has passionately adored Sacha, and he has been good to her in return, unwittingly feeding her worship by not letting her down. *Bien sûr,* he has an effect on all women— even I am not immune to the spell he casts! But Natalya, in her youth, has basked in the special place she sees herself as holding in his heart. As long as Danielle remains aloof from her brother, and he continues to carry on only the most casual of love affairs, she imagines that she is closer to him than any other female. You see, Antonia and I are too old to really count!" She laughed softly. "You are a very real threat to her! Understand, though, that my granddaughter has never realized all of this clearly. She is a kind, good girl and loves you fiercely. She has convinced herself that no woman can win Sacha's heart, and this is the premise that she works from. Any envy she feels for you is deeply hidden—even from herself. She believes that she is working for your best interests —*comprends-tu?*"

Caro's cheeks were rosy from the wine, her brown eyes liquid with contemplation. "Someday Natalya will meet the right man," she murmured, "and then she will have no more time to think of Alec. All the young men she sees now are far too wishy-washy!"

"Like Mr. MacGowan?" Grandmère inquired innocently.

"You knew about him?" Caro exclaimed. "But of course you would. He proposed to me today with great fervor."

"And you turned him down?"

"I do not love him."

The two women sat in the dusky candleglow, smiling at each other with unspoken understanding. At length, Grandmère reached over to smooth Caro's windblown curls. "It is dinnertime and everyone will wonder what has become of you," she prodded gently.

"Won't you come, too?"

"Non, I have had a tiring day. I believe I shall retire early."

Impulsively, Caro leaned over and hugged the old woman so hard she was afraid she had hurt her.

"Thank you, thank you, Grandmère. You have truly opened my eyes."

"D'accord. You must promise me something, Caroline," she replied, drawing back to look at her determinedly. "Never doubt your own instincts, for you probably know more of the truth than those who have

known Sacha all of their lives. Do not seek anyone's counsel! And do not hesitate to reach out with both hands to grasp what you want. Life will pass you by if you wait and wonder and worry. You will find that the grandest rewards are those you must take the risks to win! 'Follow your heart' is a well-worn cliché, but it is still viable. Do you understand?"

She arched a pale brow in the Beauvisage way, and Caro beamed back at her gaily. Getting to her feet, she gave Grandmère's tiny hands a final squeeze and declared:

"Win or lose, I shall gamble tonight! Wish me luck!"

Chapter Eighteen

CARO FELT A STRONG NEED TO BE ALONE FOR A WHILE
to collect her thoughts. Strolling back across the moonlit garden, she could see that the downstairs windows
were ablaze with light and guessed that dinner was
getting underway. On an impulse, she entered through
the servants' door and followed the dark winding back
staircase up to the second floor. Rose, her maid, was in
her bedchamber, packing away a last batch of freshly
washed underclothes. She contrived to look disinter-
ested when her mistress appeared, cheeks flushed and
hair windblown.

"Rose," Caro said excitedly, "could you take care of
a couple of things for me?"

"Certainly, ma'am."

"I should appreciate it if you would tell them downstairs that I shall not be dining tonight. Simply say
that I am tired and wish to retire early."

"Yes, ma'am."

"Then, I would be so grateful if you could arrange
a true bath for me. In the brass tub—here in my
room. Could that be accomplished?"

"Why, yes, I suppose so, ma'am. Will there be anything else?"

Caro grinned. "Yes—I'm famished! Is there anything to eat downstairs that could be brought to my
room?"

Rose's gray eyes widened somewhat.

"Why, to be sure, ma'am. I'll bring you a tray."

"Thank you, Rose! You are a great help to me!"

The maid almost ran into the door as she backed out of the room, and Caro pressed a hand to her mouth to suppress a giggle.

Once alone, she hopped up onto the spotless white spread covering her bed and lay back to gaze up through the fragile pattern of white net. The candles which burned around the room threw long shadows across the ceiling above her, and little by little Caro could feel her confidence ebb with the afterglow of the wine. Closing her eyes, she forced herself to concentrate on Grandmère's encouraging advice. In her mind, she could see Alec clearly, his eyes penetrating even in her memory.

I have to try, she told herself firmly. I shall never know if I do not try. And God knows, my situation cannot grow any worse.

Refusing to dwell on the possibility of rejection and its consequent humiliation, Caro got up to inspect the trunks which stood against the far wall. They were all new and elegant, filled to the brim with beautiful clothes. One of the smaller ones held her underthings and bedgowns, which Caro sorted through carefully. Finally she drew out an unusual gown that might have been made of the most delicate gossamer. Pale lemon in color, it was fashioned of two transparent layers of the finest batiste, and the neckline was cut low to leave little to the imagination. Slender ivory ribbons were woven in to form a high waistline, while expensive French lace edged the shallow bodice and hemline. Caro held the bedgown up against herself, looking in the full-length mirror and wondering why Alec would choose such a garment. She had never seen anything like it, for the prevailing fashion for bedwear dictated a loose, warm white gown with a high, sensibly buttoned neck.

"This bedgown," Caro mused aloud with a faint blush, "is obviously not meant for sleeping!"

At that moment, there was a quick tap at the door, and she swiftly stuffed the gown into the nearby bureau before calling, "Come in!"

Rose appeared, bearing a tray loaded with heavenly smelling food and a small decanter of red wine.

"There's roast beef here, ma'am, and fresh muffins, besides the rest. Perhaps you could eat while I arrange your bath?"

Caro was beaming.

"Thank you, Rose! You are a gem! Let me help you with that!"

She took the tray from her and set it on the table near the window. After Rose left the room, Caro retrieved the crumpled gown and hung it up in the empty wardrobe. Then she turned her attention to the meal awaiting her, eating with more enjoyment than she had felt in days. Her first glass of wine doused the nervousness which had been creeping up on her, and she was beginning a second glass when Rose and another maid came in carrying the bathtub. In a matter of minutes, they had filled it with steaming water, and Rose added a sachet of jasmine and clover.

"Thank you again," Caro said affectionately. "You have been a wonderful maid to me since the first day I arrived at Belle Maison. I only wish you could come with me tomorrow."

Rose flushed at the warmth in her mistress's voice, then said, "It has been a joy to serve you, ma'am, for you've always treated me splendidly. You have never put on airs or ordered me about, so I've come to enjoy doing special things for you. You're a rare person, Mistress Caroline, and I truly wish you luck and happiness in your new life. I've been to the elder Beauvisage house before and it is a grand place and so are the people there. I know they will be good to you."

Impulsively, Caro hugged Rose before sending her on her way with, "I really shan't need any more help tonight, Rose. You go along now—you've been working hard doing all this packing and you deserve a rest."

"But—your hair—and the bathtub . . ."

"I shall dry my own hair—if only to prove to myself that I still can! And I will ring for whomever is about when I am finished with the bathtub. Are you satisfied?"

Rose looked doubtful, but finally Caro was alone, and she speedily shed the topaz velvet dress and peeled off her underclothes. The water was blissfully hot and soothing. She leaned back and rested her head against the high back. Then, while leisurely sipping the wine left in her glass, Caro resolved to formulate a plan for the rest of the evening.

But she found it impossible even to think of attempting to seduce Alec, knowing that she would be playing with fire. At last, she decided not to plan anything, for all she was really sure of was her need to see and talk to Alec. She could not leave things the way they were.

The bathtub was sitting in front of the fireplace, and Caro soon began to feel very warm and flushed. Suddenly, the connecting door behind her opened, and Caro looked back over her shoulder and was surprised to see Alec standing on the threshold.

"Egad, Caro, life with you is full of pleasant surprises! I heard that you were dining in your room, so I decided to see if you were ill. I take it you are not . . . ?"

Caro, already uncomfortably warm, felt her face flame before his bold gaze. She had no way of knowing how lovely she looked, as Alec appreciatively took in her burnished gold curls and her pink, delicious-looking wet skin. All but the very tips of her breasts was revealed above the water, rosy and swelling as

207

they quivered with emotion. Her eyes met his, and Alec was surprised at the unconcealed warmth in their golden-brown depths, which even her disconcertion could not mask. Something in her expression made the blood pulse in his loins, and it took all the self-control he could muster to comment nonchalantly:

"I have a strong feeling that it is not at all proper for me to be standing here now. Our Mr. MacGowan would be horrified at my lack of respect."

His amused expression showed no sign of penitence, and he made no move to leave, but leaned against the door frame and crossed his arms over his chest.

"Alec," Caro exclaimed in a shaky voice, "how can I bathe with you standing there? Would you have my water grow cold?"

He laughed at this, white teeth gleaming in the shadows.

"I cry pardon, *chérie*. I would not be accused of such a crime against womanhood!"

Still laughing, he turned and disappeared, closing the door behind him. Caro was trembling so much that she could barely finish her bath, and the skin that had been so warm moments before was now reduced to gooseflesh.

At last she emerged from the water and towel-dried herself energetically before the fire until her body tingled. Removing the cloudy yellow gown from the wardrobe, Caro hesitantly slipped it over her head, tying the ivory ribbons below her breasts. It clung to every curve of her body, even revealing the pink tautness of her nipples as they strained against the bodice. Her skin glowed golden in the warm candlelight as she sat down in her favorite chair to pull the pins from her damp curls. Her hair shone like honey as she brushed it dry before the fire, trying to decide what she would do. A full half hour passed before she summoned up all her nerve and stood up. After tying her lustrous curls back with a thin ribbon, Caro wound some creamy lace around her throat, having decided it was the perfect finishing touch.

Her heart pounded suffocatingly as she went to the door and listened. There was no sound, and she wondered what she would do if he were not in his room. Then she wondered with a qualm why she had imagined he would be, for the evening was not far advanced. Opening the door a fraction, she peered into darkness and found that a small dressing room connected her bedchamber to Alec's.

As her eyes grew accustomed to the dim light, she saw the tawny brown coat he had worn that day slung across the back of a chair. A large, imposing wardrobe was opened on one side to reveal dozens of flawlessly tailored garments, and Caro inhaled deeply of the intoxicating aroma of Alec that clung to his clothes. Then she looked to the next door and saw the bright light that shone beneath it. At that moment, the door opened, firelight from the room beyond framing Alec's tall, shadowy figure. Caro felt faint with fear, shock, and mortification. Shrinking back against the door to her own room, she could see the orange glow of his cigar in the darkness, then the familiar flashing white of his grin.

"Caro, do not tell me that you are lost! Did you forget which door led to the hallway?"

The mocking laughter in his voice brought a rush of hot blood to her face. Before she could speak, Alec ground out his cigar in a pewter dish and closed the distance between them.

"It really is you!" he declared as he scrutinized her face in the dim light. "I thought perhaps I was having a vision—that God might have sent an angel down to convince me to mend my evil ways!" One brown hand closed around her soft upper arm and he gave a low whistle of surprise. "What's this, fair angel? Bare flesh?"

He lost no time in pulling her out of the darkness

and into his own large bedchamber. Caro saw his eyebrows shoot up, then come together over his sparkling turquoise orbs as he held her at arm's length. Her breasts were heaving and Alec feared that momentarily they might escape their tenuous restraint.

"Jesus, Caro, what have you got on?"

Her eyes flashed at the tone of his voice. "You should know, sir! Didn't you personally order all my clothes?"

"Let me rephrase my question, then. *Why* have you got it on? If you were planning a rendezvous with young MacGowan, you certainly chose the wrong avenue of escape!"

He was laughing softly, and his eyes gleamed as he looked at her in a new way. Caro felt totally naked, and now wished she had never found the gown. There must have been another way to break those barriers of his down! she thought wildly. I am prostituting myself!

Alec caught her shoulders, pulling her against him with a roughness that caught her off guard. When she looked up into his face in surprise, she found his eyes had deepened to the stormy sea-blue that she had seen the day he came upon her attackers in the barn. His hands gripped her shoulders with a strength that made escape unthinkable, and when he spoke, there was a note in his voice that Caro had never heard before.

"Of course, my dear, there is always a possibility that you were not looking for the hall door, for why would I show yourself in that? And, I must rule out the theory about MacGowan, because I know that you sent him packing this afternoon. So, it seems I am left with only one conclusion." Lifting a black brow ironically, he smiled with one side of his mouth as his arms slid from Caro's shoulders to encircle her back. Her eyes were wide and unblinking with naked fear, but he ignored them and her rigid body as his mouth

210

closed over hers. His kiss was almost brutal and went on for so long that Caro felt she would choke. When at last she managed to struggle free, she gasped:

"Alec! You hurt me!" as she tried to blink back the tears that sprang to her eyes. His own face was totally void of sympathy, however, and his left arm pinned her against him like a band of steel as he tipped up her tiny chin with his thumb and forefinger.

"Caro," he said in a low, hard voice, "I have long been weary of these schoolboy games I have been forced to play with you. I am not accustomed to the role of the respectful callow youth and I find it does not agree with me. As long as you kept your distance, you were relatively safe, but now you leave me no choice. I have warned you of my rules repeatedly, and you have flouted them this night. The game is ended, *chérie*—I will play no more."

Caro watched in stunned silence as Alec put out the candles by snuffing the flames between his thumb and forefinger. She saw now that he was clad only in his breeches and linen shirt, its ruffled cuffs falling across the backs of his brown hands. He wore no cravat, and the shirt was open halfway to his waist, revealing his massive chest covered with crisp black hair. He paused at the desk which stood in one corner of the spacious room, gathering up some papers he had evidently been working on when he heard her in the dressing room. His movements were unhurried, and Caro realized vaguely that she could run away if she wanted to. When the candles on the desk were extinguished, Alec observed her momentarily before walking back to her. In the warm glow of the fire, Caro's flushed pink skin looked as soft as a ripe peach. She appeared strangely composed as she met his gaze with large and unreadable eyes.

As he drew closer, he saw a softness in their brown depths that surprised him. Staring at her with his penetrating turquoise eyes, he encircled her tiny waist with his hands, then slowly moved them upward. Caro did not flinch when he pulled the ribbon that held her bodice secure, and slid the straps from her shoulders. Her sweet, young breasts were revealed, as the gown fell around her feet in a lemon-colored pool. Alec's eyes smoldered as they raked over her, and then his hands went out to touch her. As he caressed her, his fingers exploring softly, Caro could feel herself begin to quiver, beset by the inevitable giddiness that accompanied his touch.

"Ah, *chérie*," he murmured with a trace of a smile, "at the risk of sounding tedious, your body is magnificent!"

His tanned fingers traced a leisurely, burning trail up her slender thighs, over the curve of her hips, then paused to caress her breasts with teasing lightness. When they reached her neck, untying the lace that encircled it with one deft movement, he bent his head to press his lips against its fragrant softness. Caro dropped her head back, and Alec told her softly, "I had to take that damned ribbon off, my dear, because I don't intend to be deprived of one square inch of your body."

There was humor in his voice and Caro surprised them both by looking up and smiling irrepressibly. Her eyes twinkled and the barest suspicion of a dimple showed next to her mouth. Alec, while caressing her satin-smooth back, raised an eyebrow in mock horror.

"Caro, is it possible that you actually smiled at me at a moment like this? Can you really be so free of inhibitions?"

Her lips curved even more, and Alec felt her relax against him.

"I have been drinking some wine," she whispered loudly.

"How much?" he inquired, smiling as he pulled the ribbon from her hair.

"About four glasses. Not all at once, though!

212

Grandmère gave me some of it quite a while ago." Caro felt quite pleased with herself.

"Ah—well, four glasses of wine should not be enough to severely impair your judgment. I do not intend to feel guilty this time because you are intoxicated!" Her breasts were pressing petulantly against his bare chest. "You do know what you're doing, don't you, Caro?" he inquired gruffly.

Her voice was clear as she answered, "Yes, Alec, I'm afraid I shall have to admit it to us both. I know exactly what I'm doing—or I will, as soon as you tell me what it's called!"

He had never before seen a woman's eyes shine with an equal measure of desire and innocence. As he lifted her easily in his arms, his voice came huskily in her ear:

"I don't plan to tell you another damned thing, Caro. I am finished with conversation—at least for tonight!"

The moon was high in the clear, starry sky when Caro awoke with a start. Silvery, luminous beams of light arched through the tall windows, bathing the room in pools of moonlight. At first she felt confused, but then she felt Alec's muscled shoulder beneath her cheek, the hair on his chest faintly tickling her. Gingerly, she attempted to sit up, but found that he was lying on top of the bulk of her hair. She was barely able to move enough to see Alec, who lay with one arm curved over his head, the other encircling Caro. His jawline was square, but he slept with a faint smile on his lips and the sound of his even breathing and steady heartbeat warmed her as she lay with him.

The bed they slept in was enormous. A Hepplewhite four-poster with fretted testers, it was luxuriously comfortable. Caro could scarcely refrain from moving against the soft sheets, and in Alec's hold under the goose-down comforter, she felt cozy and warm even though naked.

She wondered if Alec had really intended for her to spend the entire night in his bed. After what had seemed like hours of lovemaking, they had lain together in this same position, Alec softly teasing her breasts with the hand which now rested near her elbow. At the time, she had not thought she could ever sleep, but apparently they had.

Memories of what had gone before crowded her mind in a kaleidoscope of pleasure. Alec had told her to help him undress, but she could only manage the shirt. She had huddled beneath the covers, watching him peel off his breeches, slim-hipped and well muscled in the firelight. The pressure of his hard naked body had caused her to gasp aloud, and even now she remembered Alec's soft chuckle. After that, they had both been beyond coherent thought or speech, and Alec's lovemaking had aroused feelings within her that she had never imagined existed.

At first, he had gone so slowly, tantalizing her with his hands and mouth until she began to moan softly and move against him. Instinctively, she had opened her mouth with eagerness when he kissed her. She had shuddered with desire, her fingers playing in his glossy hair, when his lips and tongue skillfully teased her taut breasts. She had lain helplessly trembling with pleasure as his hands touched and caressed her, awakening every hidden sensuous nerve.

When at last he had moved above her, parting her thighs, Caro felt that she could stand no more. A tremendous, delicious pressure had built up inside her, increasing with Alec's every touch or kiss. Looking up, she saw him smiling down at her, then he covered her mouth with his at the same moment of his penetration. Caro felt a painful shock that soon grew into an almost unbearable pleasure as Alec moved rhythmically within her. Her body arched to meet his again and again while she grasped at his back, searching for something to hold onto and finding only hard, moving muscles. All at once, the pressure within her loins seemed to explode, dissolving into a delicious, tingling heat that spread up from between her thighs and reached and seared her heart and her very soul.

She remembered now that she had panted unashamedly, and Alec had laughed affectionately as he moved off her. After that he had smoked a cheroot, letting her try it when she asked. He had walked across the room to pour two snifters of brandy, barely coating the bottom of her glass. Caro had watched with enjoyment the way his lean, sinewy buttocks moved, surprising herself again. While they sat in bed sipping the brandy little was said, but Alec had idly twisted a strand of her hair around his finger, and their bare legs touched intimately beneath the covers.

Caro would never have imagined that there could be more, but there was. After the brandy was gone, Alec cradled her in his arms and kissed her so avidly that she felt faint. This time, it took little encouragement from him for Caro to begin to return Alec's caresses. The warm feel of his body and the play of his muscles beneath her fingers were incredibly enjoyable for her. Her heart would pound with excitement when he guided her hand to a different place, and finally he began to groan as she hesitantly caressed him. In the end, his mouth had devoured her again as the pulsing built within her, and they had coupled once more, urgently. Their bodies found ecstatic release at the same moment and Caro knew nothing would ever be the same. . . .

Now, lying against his still body, Caro wondered why she felt no shame or embarrassment. She remembered her first wave of panic when Alec had dragged her into his room, realizing now that she had wanted this all along. Her need for him had been eating away at her insides, robbing her of her natural joy in living. Now, as she rubbed her chin against his chest, Caro felt totally satisfied and contented.

In answer to her snuggling caress, Alec's hand suddenly slid over her arm to cup a warm breast. With one graceful movement, he was on top of her, turquoise eyes twinkling sleepily in the moonlight.

"Never have enough, eh?" he teased, and Caro smiled saucily up at him.

"I confess that lust seems to have overcome me. . . ."

"It always does," he murmured, kissing her leisurely as she clasped her hands around his neck. "It always does."

Caro reluctantly opened her eyes to the shadowed warmth of the covers which were pulled up to her forehead. Sunlight filtered in through the opening above her eyes, and drowsily she recognized the sound of distant, short splashes. Slowly, she adjusted her knees against the bed, nudging her way up until her head emerged from its cozy cocoon.

"Ah—awake at last. My little flower of virtue greets the light of day!"

Alec's voice, rich with amusement, revived Caro like a cold splash in the face. Immediately, she propped herself on an elbow to search him out. He was standing in front of his bureau mirror, shaving. To Caro, no man could have appeared more attractive, and she found a remarkable fascination in his movements. Bare-chested and brown in the sunlight, he stood smiling at her, his lower face covered with white cream. Caro could only beam back at him, feeling that old familiar flush creeping into her cheeks. Alec walked over to the bed, admonishing:

"Jesus, Caro, how can you blush at me now? I had hoped we had left those charming but revealing expressions behind us!"

Then, before she could speak, he ran his finger across his cheek, then leaned forward and topped her nearest breast with a dab of soap. Forgetting her nakedness, Caro hopped to her knees to retaliate.

"Alec, you are incorrigible! I—"

She broke off at the sound of knocking at the door. Alec appeared coolly imperturbed in spite of Caro's instant panic.

"Oh, dear!" she whispered as Pierre called:

"Monsieur, I have your coffee."

Alec was poorly suppressing laughter as he answered, "That's fine, Pierre. Ah—why don't you just set it outside."

There was a bewildered pause.

"Mais, monsieur, what about your shaving?"

"I'm doing it myself today."

"Yourself, monsieur?" The increasingly confused tone of Pierre's voice delighted his master. Caro, meanwhile, had taken refuge under the covers, certain that the valet was going to open the door. "But what about your dressing?" he called again.

"I can manage, thank you."

"Mais, monsieur, I must prepare your clothes!"

By now he was clearly agitated, and Alec laughed out loud. "Pierre, you are getting excessively maternal in your old age! I assure you that I am perfectly capable of handling these tasks alone."

"As you wish, monsieur," he conceded in an offended tone.

Caro listened for the sound of retreating footsteps before cautiously peeking out. Alec was back at the basin, shaving with clean, quick strokes of the long razor.

"What a coward you are, infant!" he laughed. "It is fortunate that women do not have to go to war— you would be digging a hole in the ground at the first sign of an unfamiliar face!"

"That's not so!" she returned heatedly. "I had good reason to hide. What would happen if Pierre had found me here?"

Alec bent to rinse his face, then rubbed it with a towel as he crossed over to the bed.

"You wouldn't be ashamed of what you've done, would you?" he inquired in a light tone which was countered by his piercing turquoise eyes. "I had the distinct impression last night that you were acting with a clear head and were happy afterward."

"Oh, no!" she exclaimed, sitting up. "I really am not ashamed, Alec. Although—I suppose I ought to be . . ."

One of his black brows arched, but his face remained serious as he ordered, "Get up, Caro, and come over here."

She hesitated for only a moment before obeying him. As she moved to stand in front of him, she felt the sun's warmth on her bare skin as well as Alec's appreciative gaze. Her inhibitions all melted away, however, when he put his arms around her, his hard chest with its crisp black hair pressing against her breasts. She turned large questioning eyes up to him and he kissed her with a lazy warmth that left her weak and hungry.

His lips were tracing a fiery pattern over her neck and shoulders as he murmured, "Caro, you have done nothing wrong here with me. You are a good girl— that is something in your heart that can never change and it transforms everything you do into an act of virtue and beauty." Alec paused, tipping her chin up and smiling down at her. "It took me a while to figure it out. None of the old rules apply to you, because you've created a whole new set of standards. Maybe it's because you have no memory and can't remember all those rules. Or maybe it's just *you.*" He kissed her again, and Caro wrapped her arms around his neck, feeling him grow hard against her stomach.

"Jesus," he moaned with a pained smile. "You know, it's that body of yours that always throws me off the track. No good girl has ever been made like you are;

that's how I finally realized they must have broken the mold with Caro!"

There was another knock at the door.

"Sacha!" Natalya called. "What's this cold coffee doing outside your room?"

"Oh, God," replied Alec, "I forgot about that!"

With amazing speed, he reached for the shirt he had worn the previous night and helped Caro put it on.

"She's probably on her way to your room. Get moving!" he commanded softly, adding a slap on her bottom as she scurried toward the door to the dressing room.

"Are you all right?" Natalya inquired curiously. "Shall I bring it in for you?"

"Don't bother," Alec replied as he opened the door. Over his sister's shoulder, he could see Pierre hurrying down the hallway, an envelope in his hand.

Chapter Nineteen

PIERRE HAD BEEN SUSPICIOUS FROM THE BEGINNING, and the feeling increased when he went into his master's bed-chamber and watched him read General Washington's communication. A light fragrance of jasmine assailed Pierre's nostrils when he glanced at the huge bed which was in a state of total disarray. Unwillingly, he associated the scent with Caro, and suddenly felt afraid.

Alec tossed down the paper and said curtly, "Prepare my uniform. I'll be leaving immediately on horseback for New York."

"New York! *Mais,* monsieur—"

"General Washington is arriving there tomorrow and will be meeting with his officers for the last time. He'll be bound for Mount Vernon then, and I'll wager he hopes never to see any of us again!" Alec laughed. "I must reach the city by tomorrow evening, so I cannot afford not to go by horseback. Just pack me the bare essentials."

As Alec reached for his coffee, Pierre walked toward the dressing room, his glance falling on a frothy pile of lemon bedgown near the fireplace. Afraid to investigate further, he continued on to get his master's clothing from the wardrobe. When he re-entered the room, the spot where he had seen the mysterious yellow garment was bare, and Alec stood across the room unbuttoning his breeches.

Pierre helped him dress and assembled his extra clothing and necessities for travel. Alec was checking his appearance in the mirror while his valet gathered the previous day's clothes for the laundry.

"Monsieur, where is your shirt? I cannot seem to locate it," Pierre said in a puzzled voice. With a sharp glance, Alec retorted:

"You begin to wear on my nerves with your ceaseless questions, Pierre. It is not my province to keep track of my clothing, so I suggest that you tend to your duties and endeavor to refrain from bothering me."

Caro was shocked to learn that it was past nine o'clock when she returned to her own bedroom. Barely managing to change from Alec's shirt into a high-necked bedgown before Natalya's knock, her nervousness increased at the sight of the brass bathtub full of cold water which sat before the fireplace. She was positive that Natalya, and later, Rose, could both easily read the lie in her face as she explained:

"I finished my bath so late that I fell asleep before I could ring for someone to remove it."

"Did you just wake up?" inquired Natalya with studied casualness. "Rather odd for you, Caro—especially since you went to bed so early last night. Why weren't you at dinner? We were all quite worried!"

Caro's face went blank as she sat down at her dressing table to brush her hair. Before she could frame a reply, Natalya exclaimed:

"But how silly of me. I suppose you couldn't bear to sit with Sacha all evening, knowing that today we're leaving Belle Maison. That was awfully sensible of you." She paused, frowning. "Don't tell me you fell asleep without braiding your hair? It's in a terrible snarl!"

Caro tried to duck her head to hide the telltale blush that stained her skin.

"Yes! Actually, I did. I was exhausted last night. Grandmère gave me two glasses of wine, and they must have combined with that hot bath to truly sedate me."

"Two glasses of wine? Whatever for? Why, it was barely five o'clock when you went over to her cottage!"

Caro brushed her hair agitatedly. "Really, Natalya, I can't see what it matters! I really should be getting dressed for breakfast. Perhaps you could call Rose for me—"

"Certainly! My, you are as jumpy as Sacha this morning!"

Caro's spirits were high by the time she left her room for breakfast. She had even declined her usual cup of tea in her room in her anxiety to see Alec again, and as she hurried down the stairway, the whole world seemed to have taken on a rosy glow. The plans for her move into Philadelphia that day seemed obsolete in her mind, for she instinctively felt that Alec would change them. Even though he had never actually pledged his love to her or made any verbal commitment, his last words that morning had left her brimming with new hope.

Pierre stood near the dining-room door, waiting.

"Mademoiselle—"

Caro smiled shyly as she met his eyes, sensing that somehow he knew.

"Good morning, Pierre! Isn't it a beautiful day? I am famished—"

"Mademoiselle, I have been asked to speak with you. M. Alexandre wished me to tell you that he has gone to New York."

"New York?" Caro's face fell and Pierre's heart swelled with pity.

"Yes, mademoiselle. General Washington is journeying home to Mount Vernon and he wishes to meet with his officers in New York tomorrow night. It is to be a last farewell, I think."

"But—how long will Alec be gone? Did he know about this before—that is—"

"The general's message was only delivered this morning, mademoiselle. As for the duration of Monsieur's absence—I really cannot guess. Four days would be the smallest time."

Caro looked crushed, and indeed, she felt that way. As she thanked Pierre and walked woodenly into the dining room to sit down, she realized that her despair was much deeper than that of the past month. Alec had left her, which meant that today she would move into Philadelphia with the senior Beauvisage family to await her first society ball, to be held in four short nights.

The plate of buckwheat cakes with maple syrup that sat before Caro was long cold when Jean-Philippe and Antonia Beauvisage arrived. Natalya forgot her worry over her friend's downcast appearance at the first sight of the smart, polished carriage speeding up the drive.

"Maman and Papa and Katya are here!" she exclaimed, tossing her napkin up and scrambling to her feet. As Natalya dashed out the front door and down the brick walkway to meet her family as they emerged from the carriage, Caro was reminded of her own arrival. Caro stood in the door watching, somehow stirred by the appearance of Alec's mother and father.

Antonia Beauvisage was exquisitely petite, built much like Caro herself. She was darker, however, with gleaming russet-brown hair and sparkling emerald eyes like Nicholai's. Her dress was a delectable pistachio green trimmed in palest rose, and atop her auburn curls was perched a lovely matching hat, exactly the right shape for her face. Even as she embraced her daughter, Antonia looked up to meet Caro's eyes, smiling at her as though pleasantly surprised.

223

Jean-Philippe Beauvisage was arrestingly attractive, a man of ageless charm and great magnetism. Tall and broad-shouldered like his eldest son, his hair was white with gleaming blue highlights. He was tanned, his handsome face etched with deep lines that somehow seemed to add to his appeal. As they came up the footpath, Jean-Philippe lifted an eyebrow and flashed a white smile at Caro that so reminded her of Alec that it instantly melted her heart.

It was late afternoon by the time they left Belle Maison. Caro felt perilously close to tears as she looked around her bedroom for the last time. All traces of her occupancy had disappeared; the bed was so flawlessly made up that it appeared never to have been slept in.

Carefully, she withdrew Alec's shirt from a corner of her trunk and crossed over to enter his dressing room. She pulled open the door to his wardrobe and hung up the shirt, then reached inside to touch a familiar coat, rubbing the sleeve against her cheek and pressing it to her nose. Her heart ached, for somehow she felt that by leaving Alec's house she was severing the bond that had grown between them and cutting off her last chance to win his . . . love.

Seeing that the door to his room was ajar, Caro peeked inside apprehensively. A maid she had never seen before was dusting, her back to the dressing room. The bed that she had become a real woman in—a woman who could match the passions her man had awakened—was neatly made up, all the chaotic wrinkles they had made smoothed.

Suddenly, as Caro tried to remember, the entire night took on a dreamlike quality of unreality that chilled her. There was a cold, dead pressure on her heart that would linger through all the days of cheerful festivity ahead.

Antonia Beauvisage was, in Caro's eyes, a paragon of womanhood. Naturally charming and candid, it was impossible not to like her, and in Caro's case she inspired instant affection and trust. Even the self-assured, independent Natalya seemed to soften and relax in the presence of her parents.

In Jean-Philippe Beauvisage Caro was so struck by the many similarities between father and son that she felt uncomfortable whenever he smiled at her.

The one thing about the sophisticated Beauvisages that fascinated her was the highly charged atmosphere whenever the husband and wife were together. Caro was immediately aware of the strong sexual currents that ran between them, an amazing fact in light of their thirty-four-year marriage. Neither of them appeared to be fifty years old, and Caro guessed from what Alec had told her that Jean-Philippe must have been nearer sixty. Antonia was still beautiul, the only signs of her age being the gently etched lines around her eyes and mouth and the silvery strands that laced her auburn hair.

By the time the half-hour-long carriage ride from Belle Maison to Philadelphia was over, Caro had decided that the key to their youthfulness lay in their love for each other and their vital spirits. Though Antonia's voice could hold that certain warm, maternal tone, for the most part she conversed in the manner of a young girl. As for Jean-Philippe, Caro was astounded by the same wit and flair she had seen in his sons. His eyebrows arched and his sapphire eyes twinkled with all the charm of a spirited young man, making it easy for Caro to imagine him as the dashing captain of a pirate ship. She could also picture a young Antonia captivated by him.

As the gleaming black carriage drew up outside the Beauvisage house on South Third Street, identically attired servants materialized to handle all the girls' baggage. Natalya and Katya walked up the steps with their mother, while Caro found herself guided by the strong brown hand of Alec's father. The housekeeper appeared in the doorway, attended by two immaculately garbed maids who took their wraps.

"Caroline," said Antonia with a warm smile, "this is Mrs. Forbes, our housekeeper. Did you meet her while we were away?"

"Yes, Mrs. Beauvisage. Actually, Natalya and I stopped by here several times."

"Oh yes! The plans for the ball! Well, I certainly hope that all the arrangements are made. Isn't it set for the sixth?"

"Don't worry, Maman," Natalya broke in. "We have seen to everything. Mrs. Forbes and Mrs. Reeves, and, believe it or not, Danielle have all helped tremendously."

Antonia's finely drawn brows lifted momentarily. "Danielle? Have you seen much of her, then?"

"As a matter of fact, yes!" Natalya's voice rose a pitch. "Caro somehow took a fancy to her, and now they are the best of friends. Caro claims to have uncovered all the motives for Danielle's insufferable behavior and actually feels sorry for her!"

They were walking toward the front parlor. Antonia's jewel-like eyes were watchful as she turned to Caro to say, "Well, this is all very interesting. We shall have to talk about this later on, Caroline—alone."

Jean-Philippe left them to retire to his library, and after Mrs. Forbes arranged for a meeting with Antonia to discuss the ball, the three women were alone. The rich green and ivory brocade of the settee made a striking background for Antonia's understated beauty, and Caro found it hard to keep from staring at her.

"Well, my dears," she said with a girlish grin, "what mischief have you been doing? I imagine it was great fun for you at Belle Maison!"

Natalya cast a meaningful glance at Caro before saying, "Actually, Maman, Caro has not been feeling very mischievous. I have contrived to throw her together with my friends, who are quite gay as you know, but without much success. Can you believe that she refused a marriage proposal from Everett Mac-Gowan?"

"Who? Do you mean the young man with the unruly red hair? Goodness, Natalya, isn't it rather early for proposals?"

"I thought so!" Caro burst out. "Besides, I did not love the man in the smallest way."

"I see," Antonia nodded. "Natalya, I cannot imagine why you are acting so belligerent about Caroline's decision. I thought you were a great believer in true love!"

"Perhaps, but in this case, Caro's love is ill spent on the wrong man. She will pine for him until it kills her, when she might have a chance for some happiness with a more worthy man!"

"Natalya!" Caro's eyes were wide with outrage.

"That is enough, I think," Antonia told her daughter sternly, noting Caro's dismay. "I believe that Caroline has been wrong to trust you with her confidences. Kindly refrain from revealing any more to me or to anyone else."

Bright spots of color flamed on the cheeks of both young girls, each for different reasons. At that moment, tea and cakes arrived to provide a welcome distraction, and though Caro found the hot liquid soothing, she could not eat.

After tea, Antonia led the girls upstairs to their rooms. Natalya's was the same one she had occupied for seventeen years, charmingly decorated in periwinkle blue, with white lace trimmings.

Farther on down the hall was the spacious bedchamber Antonia had chosen for Caro. The large canopy bed was hung with rich drapes embroidered with rose stitching on a satiny white background. Roses were worked subtly into the white and gold carpet, while the tall windows had curtains of the same fabric that graced the bed. All the furniture was highly polished cherry, each piece unique.

"Oh," Caro breathed, "this room is too beautiful for me—"

"Nonsense!" Antonia exclaimed with a soft laugh. "Do not underrate your importance, Caroline! Besides, if you are to make your home here with us you must be comfortable."

An icy hand squeezed Caro's heart.

"Yes . . ." she murmured, "you are so very kind to take me in. Alec told me how wonderful you both were, but I never imagined . . ."

Antonia's eyes flickered as she heard the statement she had been waiting for.

"I like you very much, Caroline," she said simply. "I am sure that in time I will come to love you dearly, so it is no inconvenience to have you here. Tell me, how do you like Sacha? He has been fair to you as a guardian? I would not like to think he had shirked his responsibilities even though I must admit it is not a role I would have cast him in! I cannot describe the surprise I felt when Nicholai told us the news!"

Antonia was laughing softly, and Caro felt herself relax after the initial shock of her question. She could not prevent the flush that crept into her face, however, and it was impossible to meet the older woman's eyes.

"Why, he has been—he is, that is, I would not say he has shirked his responsibilities. Of course, he is very busy. But, he has been kind to me—and I am most grateful to him. . . ." She trailed off lamely.

"Oh, dear! That sounded horribly artificial! I fear that you must detest the man to find a compliment such an effort!" Antonia declared.

"Oh no!" exclaimed Caro, her heart in her eyes as she looked up defensively. "That is, I have no cause to detest him. Actually, we have been rather good friends. . . ."

Antonia smoothed back a loose curl that swept across Caro's temple. "Let us speak no more of Sacha, for I can see I have made you uncomfortable. Why don't I leave you for a while—I'm certain that you are tired and would like to rest before dinner."

Antonia's smile was irresistibly warm, and Caro felt the coldness in her breast thaw a little. She sighed and looked around her lovely room, remembering the nights the stars and trees had been her canopy, soft leaves had been her bed. Those days were gone and Caro tried to believe she would be happy in her new home. She hoped Antonia would help her.

Chapter Twenty

THE NEXT FOUR DAYS WERE THE BUSIEST CARO HAD ever known, or at least could remember. Antonia was always in the thick of things, and smiling gaily, seemed to thrive on the happy activity. Jean-Philippe was seldom at home during the day, but one morning Caro saw him arrive shortly before luncheon. She had gone to her room to freshen up before joining the others in the dining room, and had just reached the middle landing on the staircase when he came through the front door. He strode to the doorway to the parlor, where he slipped his arm around Antonia's slender waist. Giggling softly, she let him lead her into the room, her eyes dancing with happiness. There was something poignantly familiar in Jean-Philippe's movements as he caught her in his arms, his eyes sparkling with laughter before bringing his mouth down to cover hers in a kiss so passionate that it took Caro's breath away. Antonia wrapped her arms about her husband's neck, pressing herself closer as color mounted in her cheeks.

Caro crept quietly back up the stairs to wait until she heard their voices float up to her. When she descended again, the entryway was empty, and she wished it had been she and Alec embracing so lovingly.

Inside the dining room, Jean-Philippe leaned back

in his chair, an eyebrow raised at his wife in cool amusement, holding a glass of wine in one hand and clasping Antonia's hand with the other. She looked up, rosy-cheeked with happiness, as Caro entered the room.

"Ah, Caroline! I imagine you are ready for a good lunch. Come and sit down. The others will be right along."

Katya appeared momentarily, grinning broadly at the three adults. Charmed by her guileless, precocious personality, Caro had liked her immediately. Her hair was braided down her back in a lustrous ebony plait, and her azure eyes shone with energetic good spirits. She was proud of her intellectual prowess, showing off at every opportunity, but Caro found it impossible to be irritated with her, for her manner was not the least bit obnoxious.

She seated herself next to Caro, chattering gaily about her lesson in Latin that morning. Her father was quizzing her when Nicholai appeared, the young blond girl from the snowstorm on his arm. Caro's surprise was evident, increasing with the cheerful greeting accorded Mary by the other Beauvisages.

"Caro," Nicholai said with a smile, "I must introduce you to Mary Armstrong. Mary, this is Caroline Bergman, Sacha's ward."

Mary beamed at Caro, then said, "We have met, Nicky. How are you today, Miss Bergman?"

Antonia leaned over in Caro's direction. "Mary is like one of the family—she has grown up with Nicky and Natalya, and is close to all of us."

"I—I know," said Caro in confusion.

After lunch, Mary sought her out, asking for a moment alone. They slipped away to the library and sat side by side in a window seat.

"I know you must think this is all very odd," Mary giggled. "I could tell that first day that you imagined me to be one of Sacha's lighto'loves, so to speak. Would that I were! I would cut off my hair if either

231

of those Beauvisage men would give me a second look that wasn't brotherly! I wouldn't have you think I was playing both sides of the fence with them, though. Besides, I got the impression that you might have a feeling of your own for Sacha . . . ?"

Caro was embarrassed, both by this newest revelation and Mary's frank question. She felt flustered and confused by the other girl's open friendliness, after having believed her to be out to trap Alec.

"I know! It's none of my business," Mary supplied cheerfully. "Anyhow, you needn't worry that I am any competition. Sacha enjoys my company because I don't pressure him or breathe down his neck in mad pursuit, but I've yet to have him bestow on me one of those burning looks that Madeleine Chamberlain is always receiving. What a witch she is!"

"You don't like her?" Caro asked, warming to the topic and her new friend.

"Ugh!" Mary declared with feeling, tossing her blond curls. "I happen to know that Sacha doesn't like her either."

"He doesn't?"

"No—but he adores her body. Isn't that revolting? I imagine she is terribly abandoned—like some wild animal. Men like that sort of thing."

Caro colored, remembering her own night of abandon, and Mary wrinkled her nose knowingly.

"Ha!" Mary exclaimed suddenly. "Of course, we both know that we would secretly love to have Sacha adore our bodies!" She paused, her eyes dancing mischievously. "Actually, there was rather a gleam in his eye the day we met you in the snowstorm. I confess to feeling a trifle jealous. But, I like you all the same, for I have resigned myself to the fact that I haven't a chance with Sacha. I would much rather see you get him than Madeleine, but I fear that he will always remain an elusive bachelor. He's just a born heartbreaker."

"I'm afraid you're right," Caro replied, adding, "I really do appreciate your kindness, Mary. It is obvious why this family thinks so much of you!"

"I truly love all of them. And I can see why they love you, Caro. May I call you that? And while I'm winning awards for honesty, I may as well add one more thing . . ."

"What's that?"

"Well, from what Sacha said to you the other day, I have an idea that I may have been the model for your new ball gown!"

"What?" exclaimed Caro.

"The day we saw you, as well as the morning before, I spent with him in the company of Philadelphia's most exclusive dressmaker. He kept holding material up to my hair, and while the woman pinned things onto me, Sacha had the nerve to say, 'Add another two inches in the bust, and cut in one at the waist'!"

Caro almost hopped off the seat in excitement.

"Oh, Mary—what did it look like?"

The other girl watched her shrewdly.

"I mustn't tell you. I know you'll be happier in the end if it is a surprise, and besides, Sacha would horsewhip me if he thought I'd betrayed him." She smiled then, impishly. "It's outrageously beautiful—but, knowing Sacha, the dress may not be for you at all!"

The passage of each day and night of Caro's separation from Alec found her feeling more melancholy and unsettled. Apart from him, she brooded more on her lost past, and finally, the night before the ball, she had a dream.

It had taken her more than two hours to fall asleep, and when she did, her slumber was fitful. Her mind whirled with the confusion of her many problems and as sleep deepened, Caro found herself in a classroom. Books were opened across a writing table and she was working with quill and ink on a long sheet of parchment. Someone put an arm about her shoulders and she looked up into the kind face of a nun, who spoke to her in melodious French. Caro answered and turned back to her work, then the pressure around her back increased to the point of pain. She found that the sister had been replaced by the hazy form of a man with glowing pale-yellow eyes—all she could see were those horrid eyes as his grip tightened like a vise and his face came closer and closer. . . .

Caro fled from the room through a labyrinth of dark stone passages, footsteps echoing behind her, until she came out into a courtyard. Her eyes picked Alec out in a crowd and she rushed toward him, only to be held at arm's length by a girl dressed in an elaborate ball gown.

"The dress is mine!" she announced, and Alec glanced coolly over at Caro before taking the girl's arm and leading her up the steps of a scaffold. He put a noose around her neck, then returned to the ground, where Caro once more sought his protection.

Suddenly Madeleine, Natalya, Gretchen, and Mary burst from the crowd, surrounding Alec so that she could not reach him.

"He's mine, he's mine!" each girl cried, joined by the voice of the woman on the scaffold. Alec's face was blocked from Caro's view, replaced then by pale-yellow eyes and hands like claws that pulled her farther and farther away.

The day of Caro's ball dawned mild and clear, Antonia exclaiming that it was difficult to believe it was December. The day was spent in a flurry of happy activity as the second-floor drawing room received its last polishing. All sorts of tantalizing aromas wafted through the house from the kitchen, and Caro was told that Mrs. Reeves had forbidden anyone to cross her threshold.

234

Danielle arrived early, spending the day with the three women, for Jean-Philippe had disappeared, and Nicholai failed to make his usual appearance. There was such festiveness in the air that everyone seemed to be infected with high spirits—except Caro.

Although she smiled and laughed along with the others, her nerves were taut after the ordeal of her restless, nightmare-filled night. In the light of day, it all seemed less menacing, but she was tense now as she listened hopefully for Alec's step outside or the sound of his voice. However, there was no sign of him, and to make matters worse, no gown had arrived. By the time afternoon tea was served, even Antonia was beginning to look worried.

"You girls are certain that Sacha said he had taken care of it? That is odd in itself, but if it is true, then the gown should be here. He is not one to give his word lightly. Could it be that you told him the wrong day?"

"No, Maman," Natalya replied emphatically while pouring cream into her tea. "In fact, Sacha even came to my room before he left Belle Maison Monday, specifically to confirm the date of the ball."

"Good!" Antonia smiled with relief. "It sounds as if he plans to return in time, then. Even though the reason for his absence would be easily explained, it does rather seem that as Caroline's guardian he should be present."

Caro felt a relieved bubble of pure joy swelling up in her breast, almost dispelling the heavy coldness that lurked there.

"Well, you certainly looked pleased by the likelihood of Sacha's presence!" Antonia told her. "I suppose that all those strangers will be easier to face with your guardian at your side."

Before Caro could reply, Danielle spoke up dreamily: "Oh, Maman, remember all the lovely balls we had here before the war? It hardly seems possible that

235

Sacha and I were ever so young." She paused, laughing in memory. "Do you recall the night that Sacha and Miss Meadows both disappeared and Mr. Powel discovered them in the—"

Antonia cleared her throat loudly, her twinkling eyes belying the sternness of her voice as she said: "Danielle, I'm sure that we all remember that occasion only too well. I fear I shall never be able to forget it! And, as for Caroline, we mustn't corrupt her with such sordid tales. Now—who would like another cake? I imagine it will be some time before we eat again. . . ."

By five o'clock, Danielle had returned to her home to prepare for the ball and Antonia was trying not to appear overly frantic as she made a cursory inventory of her own gowns to see if she had anything that might be suitable for Caro. Although her clothes were far from matronly, they were more tailored than those of a young girl, and of course, Natalya's gowns were far too long. By five-thirty she had sent a maid over to the Armstrong home to see if Mary had anything suitable for Caro to borrow.

For her own part, Caro felt worse than miserable. She was convinced that not only would there be no gown, but also that Alec would not be coming home.

He probably never wants to see me again, she thought dejectedly as she watched Antonia pace frantically over the rose-patterned carpeting. He probably feels trapped. Perhaps he'll just stay in New York until I'm safely married off to someone else!

Her study in self-pity was interrupted by the appearance of Mrs. Forbes, who was looking surprisingly animated. "It's here!" she exclaimed, standing aside to admit two young serving girls. One carried the dress, while the other was laden with various little boxes.

"Oh, Caroline!" Antonia cried, pulling her to her feet. Natalya, hearing the commotion, ran down from her room to investigate. Crackling tissue was peeled away to reveal a gown so beautiful that Caro was

236

certain she was dreaming. Everyone's mouth opened simultaneously to form silent O's and Caro could feel her eyes stinging with tears of shock.

The gown was perfect. Fashioned of oyster satin, the bodice and overskirt were exquisitely embroidered with glittering gold flowers. Sparkling petals curved around the low neckline to form a shallow bodice, while all the other flowers were studded with perfect, dazzling diamonds. The petticoat that showed beneath the artfully draped overskirt was edged with rows of gold ruching. Reverently, Antonia took the gown from Mrs. Forbes and held it against Caro.

"My dear, it is simply fabulous! I couldn't be prouder of Sacha or more pleased for you. Look, Natalya, the color blends with her complexion perfectly! I can hardly believe that Sacha was capable of this—for without Caroline present, the dressmaker could not have helped him plan it at all!" Her eyes took in the deep flush that spread over Caro's cheeks, along with the obvious ecstasy of her expression. "Well, little one, you shall be a princess tonight. Perhaps you will meet your prince?"

"Perhaps . . ." she agreed hesitantly, looking to Natalya. Her friend raised her eyebrows, but her smile lacked enthusiasm.

Danielle arrived early in the evening, her husband in tow. Caro found it difficult to muster the same sympathy and understanding for Thaddeus Engelman that had drawn her to Danielle, for he was clearly a conceited snob. Caro had witnessed a marvelous change take place in Danielle over the past month. All her condescending airs had disappeared and now her only fault was an enthusiastic eagerness that occasionally grew irritating. She even appeared to be a trifle embarrassed by her husband's actions that evening, and Caro felt sorry for her.

All the women looked beautiful as, one by one,

they congregated in the large drawing room with its imported crystal chandeliers. Danielle wore rose silk, Natalya was resplendent in her usual sapphire blue, while Antonia looked stunning in rich emerald velvet. Caro, however, drew a chorus of sighs when she appeared in the doorway. The dress fit her to perfection, artfully displaying every soft curve. Among the accessories which Alec had chosen was a small velvet box which contained a choker of topaz and diamonds so beautiful that Caro was rendered speechless when they had opened it. It encircled her neck now, gleaming in the candlelight. Her dress stood out from her hips on wide hoops, every golden flower seeming to shoot off sparks, and her honey-colored curls were softly swept up, with three or four falling over one shoulder. Alec had also sent a box of pale-yellow rosebuds and Caro had woven them into her curls, sensing that this was his intention.

Nicholai was the first person to reach Caro's side, and she couldn't help admiring his handsome appearance. Lifting her hand to his lips in a warm kiss, he declared:

"Caro, you are a dream come true. I cannot believe that such beauty can be real."

She laughed happily, aware that she looked wonderful.

"Thank you, sir! And, I am very real, let me assure you of that!"

After the guests began arriving, it was not long before the ballroom was comfortably crowded. Caro was frankly awed by the splendor that met her eyes everywhere she turned. The men were richly garbed in velvets with fine lace at their necks and wrists, and jewels sparkling at every available spot. She soon felt her own beauty diminishing as she saw other women wearing gowns so extravagant she found herself openly staring.

There was dancing, along with a constant supply of wine and food. Antonia had seen to it that no detail had been overlooked by the girls, for there were delicacies of every description including sweetmeats, cheeses, floating islands, trifles, and over a dozen varieties of tarts.

Caro felt momentarily uneasy when Jean-Philippe led her out onto the polished dance floor for the first time. As always, she felt flustered in his presence, and her discomfort doubled when he took her in his arms. She was totally unsure of her dancing ability, but once the music began her feet moved gracefully of their own accord. There was a cluster of musicians against one wall, playing violins, cellos, flutes, and a harpsichord. The total effect was liltingly melodious to Caro's ears, and she relaxed in Jean-Philippe's arms, smiling up into his twinkling sapphire eyes and bantering as easily with him as she did with Alec.

After that, there was no rest for her. She danced so much that she occasionally neglected to watch for Alec, and she even began to forget that Madeleine Chamberlain was there, watching her constantly. Caro had felt sick when she first saw her, looking exquisite in richly decorated yellow silk. Her violet eyes had met Caro's soft brown ones, staring at her with open hatred, and Caro had unconsciously shrunk back against the young man next to her.

However, there were a great many charming people present who helped her to ignore Madeleine's presence. Natalya whispered to her that all the cream of Philadelphia society was present, and Caro believed it. Early arrivals were Samuel and Elizabeth Powel, who lived next door. She learned that Powel was the mayor of the city, and had held that office earlier under English rule before the Revolution. Mrs. Powel was middle-aged, but interesting in appearance, possessing great charm and a talent for coquetry that Caro found unsettling. Also present was another neighbor, Fran-

239

cisco Rondón, the smoothly charming diplomatic representative to the United States from Spain.

Caro met Gouverneur Morris early on and liked him immediately. One of Philadelphia's leading and more colorful citizens, he was imposingly tall with a deep, commanding voice. She had already heard the story of the leg he had lost in a supposed fall from his high-perch phaeton. Natalya had confided to her that the common belief was that he had jumped from a lady's window to escape a husband who had returned early. Gouverneur was suavely charming and outspoken, but Caro liked him because he appeared simply to enjoy himself. They became fast friends, and she even gave up a dance to stand and talk to him.

Another new friend was Mary Morris, whose husband Robert was the well-known financial wizard and current partner of the unrelated Gouverneur. She came up to Caro early in the evening, a soft-spoken, friendly woman in her thirties, and introduced herself. Her good wishes were so sincere that Caro felt drawn to her as she had been to Antonia. She soon found herself promising to have tea with Mary soon at the Morris house on Front Street.

"My two sons have just left for school in France," she explained, "and I find I am rather lonely. I should so enjoy your company!"

"I would love to come," Caro replied enthusiastically. "I am very eager to make friends."

"You shall have no trouble in that respect! I am only sorry that Sally Jay is with John in Paris. She is nearly your age, and a marvelous person."

By midnight, Alec had still not appeared, and Nicholai took Caro down to supper. There was a change in his manner that vaguely unnerved her, but she could not pinpoint it and finally decided that she was imagining things.

In fact, Nicholai had been doing a lot of thinking that night and all of it was about Caro. In Nicholai's eyes, she had never looked more beautiful, and Alec's warning had never seemed so distant and unimportant.

Dinner was a long succession of courses—celery soup, cream of Quahog soup, warm rolls of every description, fish soufflé, chicken smothered in oysters, roast beef, herbed spinach, Harvard beets, baked squash, chocolate mousse, and Williamsburg orange cake. Caro found that Alec's face danced in her mind whenever she looked at her plate, and her uneasiness was increased by Nicholai's watchful eyes.

In the candlelight, Caro's burnished curls and peach-gold complexion were set off to their best advantage. Nicholai decided that he had never seen her eyes more richly golden brown, her mouth sweeter, or her cheeks more attractively rosy. The more he looked at her, the farther Alec's command receded in his mind.

After dinner there was a lull in the activity, for everyone felt too full to dance. Many people remained at the table, talking and drinking, while others mingled upstairs in the spacious ballroom. Once Nicholai and Caro had gotten up from the table, he gently led her into the entry hall and stopped.

"Caro," he said in a low voice, his green eyes unusually serious, "would you like to stroll for a moment in the garden? It's a beautiful starlit night and I feel sure that the fresh air would do us both good."

She paused, considering, then answered, "Well, I suppose it would be all right. I confess that I should adore a brief respite. I guess I am not accustomed to the hectic pace of society."

Moments later he was protectively draping her shoulders with the fox-trimmed pelisse, and they walked unhurriedly into the moonlit garden. The air had grown cooler with the darkness, but still felt pleasantly mild. The garden behind the Beauvisage house was part of a large enclave shared by several mansions. The walks were paved with flagstone and statuary lined the stone walls, indistinctly outlined in the shadows. Caro held back when Nicholai attempted to lead her very far from the house, instinctively feeling that something was amiss.

"I think we had better go back," she told him firmly. He stopped then, grasping her hands with his, which were warm and strong, unlike Everett's. She didn't want a repeat of that scene.

"Wait, Caro! I must speak with you. There are some things I feel I must say!" He looked earnestly into her eyes.

"Nicholai, perhaps you have had too much wine—"

His emerald eyes flashed down at her, and even in the darkness she could see the emotion in his handsome face.

"Damn it, it is not the wine! It is you! If I am intoxicated, you are the cause! I—"

A deep voice, bitterly cynical, came from the direction of the house.

"Dear brother, I would suggest that you go somewhere and sober up. Don't run away, though, for I crave a bit of private conversation with you later."

Caro's heart beat high in her throat, and suddenly she was overcome with a feverish heat. Her eyes, though, were riveted on Alec, and she barely heard Nicholai speak.

"Deuce take it, Sacha! You're not God, you know. You cannot run her life for her, or mine either. I am losing my regard for you pretty quickly these days!"

"I am desolated," Alec replied coolly. "Now, kindly cease this mindless prattle and leave us. Anything that you wish to say to me I shall endeavor to suffer through later." He paused, ominously. "Then it will be my turn."

Nicholai was flushed and breathing hard in the cool night air.

"Caro, I don't know if I should," he began, turning to her, but broke off in mid-sentence at the sight of her face as she gazed at his brother. Wordlessly, he turned and left the garden.

Alec's handsome physique was outlined against the glowing house, and when he strolled toward her, Caro could see that he wore his uniform. He looked so magnificent that she could hardly breathe as she watched him approach her with that leisurely, panther-like stride she had always admired.

It was evident that Alec had worn the uniform all day, for he smelled of horses and fresh air. His deep-blue coat with long buff lapels and countless gold buttons fit him perfectly, while biscuit-colored breeches skimmed his muscular thighs, meeting turned-down black boots at his knees. He wore a gold-buttoned vest of the same buff shade, above which fell a simple lace jabot, and gold epaulets gleamed against his broad shoulders.

To Caro, however, his tanned face looked worn, his cheekbones more prominent than ever. Most alarming was the dark iciness of his eyes as they coolly appraised her appearance.

"Well, I see the duckling is a swan at last. I can see why you have become the belle of this ball, *chérie.*"

The sarcasm in his voice stung her, but she put up her chin and replied, "I can't thank you enough for the dress, Alec. It's really too lovely—"

"That is apparent!" he laughed bitterly. Caro felt him grip her arms, his fingers biting into her flesh. "Sorry I'm late, but then I suppose one brother is as good as another, eh? I'm certainly glad to see that the social world agrees with you—I guess that I have done my part now, *n'est-ce pas?*"

His arms went around her then, and Caro thought she would suffocate from the sheer strength of his grip. One hand came up to grasp the loose curls that fell over her shoulder, pulling them back until Caro was staring into his face. The look in his eyes terrified her, for they burned with rage and passion, and when he kissed her, his lips seemed to sear hers. His tongue plundered the softness of her mouth and then he was kissing her ear and blazing a fiery trail down her delicate neck. Her breasts rose and fell with emotion as Alec's lips found them, all the gentle teasing gone from his seduction.

He released her then, as suddenly as he had grasped her, his eyes opaque in the silver moonlight and his jaw set in a hard line. Caro stumbled backward, pressing trembling hands up to her burning cheeks, her breath coming in loud gasps that seemed to echo in the vast walled garden.

"I hope you don't mind, *chérie*," Alec said with a caustic smile, "but I should be very frustrated if I made that long ride home for nothing."

He turned then, disappearing into the brightly lit house.

Somehow, Caro found a stone bench and dropped onto it. Most of her hair had come down, tangled with pins and bruised rosebuds, and her face and neck throbbed from Alec's kisses. She was beyond coherent thought as bitter tears welled up in her eyes and trickled down her face. The feverish feeling of minutes before had given way to an icy chill that made her tremble as she wept.

It was a long time later that Caro managed to pull her hood up over her tangled curls and make her way back to the house. One of the maids saw her and ran over, alarmed at her appearance.

"Miss Bergman! Are you all right?"

Caro forced a wan smile. "As a matter of fact, Hannah, I don't feel very well. Just tired, I think, but I do believe I'll go on to bed. Would you explain to Mrs. Beauvisage for me?"

The next morning Natalya sat on Caro's bed, sipping tea and sharing her impressions of the evening.

"I had an absolutely fabulous time! Philip Freneau

244

is a wonderful dancer! How could you have gotten tired so early? I'll confess that I was having my suspicions about you and Nicky before Hannah came up to explain your absence. The odd part is that he never appeared again—not even to tell Maman or Mary goodnight."

Caro's eyes flickered as she looked up over her teacup.

"I—I think he may have left."

"How odd! Nicky is usually the one we have to force out the door at the end of a party—and he's never gone to his home without saying good-bye!"

"Perhaps he just felt too tired to face the crowd."

Natalya frowned, then shrugged her white shoulders, dismissing the subject.

"You know, Caro, Sacha arrived after you disappeared. He was looking for you, but I don't suppose you saw him. Anyway, he was still dressed from riding, but you can believe that Madeleine didn't care. He could have been covered with skunk spray and she would still have clung to him. Ugh!"

"Alec stayed then?" Caro asked huskily.

"Yes—I suppose you're sorry you missed him. Well, you shouldn't be, because it would have ruined your whole evening to see him with Madeleine. He drank too much, too, and seemed awfully grouchy."

"Oh . . ." she breathed.

"Let's talk happy, Caro! You were a queen with a court last night and have no good reason for looking so downcast. Do you know that some of the men were wondering if you might be like Cinderella, from the fairy tale, who vanished at twelve o'clock?" Caro failed to smile at this, and Natalya grew more persistent. "Didn't you have a wonderful time? Don't deny it, you goose, because it was written all over your face!"

Caro mustered up all her strength as she attempted to brighten. "Of course, I had a wonderful time, and I

245

truly appreciate all the work you and your mother and everyone else did on my behalf. You are all angels."

Natalya laughed with pleasure.

"Tell me, did you meet your prince last night?"

"In a way, I suppose I did . . . but it wasn't a scene from a fairy tale, I'm afraid."

Chapter Twenty-one

AFTER NIBBLING AT BREAKFAST, CARO MADE AN EX-
cuse to escape from the house and all the curious, concerned eyes that watched her. Donning her new
crimson Nithsdale, she set out on foot alone, hoping
to clear her head and summon her inner resources.

As she made her way briskly up Third Street, passing Willings Alley, Caro mentally reviewed her meeting with Alec. The more she thought about it, the
angrier she became. So unjust! she seethed. To con-
demn me without even asking for an explanation!
Nicholai is right—Alec takes too much upon himself!
Crossing Walnut Street, still relatively deserted before
noon, she continued on toward the High Street Market,
determined now to find a way to Belle Maison.

"I must confront him," she decided. "I was so weak-
kneed last night—letting him say those things to me
and then melting in his arms like a spineless schoolgirl!"

By now, her little feet were almost running as she
passed Chestnut Street, approaching the Work House
and Gaol. Her mind was busily composing the heated
speech she should deliver to Alec when suddenly she
felt a hand grip her arm through the folds of her cloak.
Startled, she nearly stumbled as she turned around.

The face of the man who held her arm seemed to
cause a small explosion of light and pain in Caro's

mind; her nightmare was reality. Instinctively, she recoiled from him, knowing him, but frustratingly unsure of his exact identity. For a long moment he did not speak, but narrowed his pale-yellow eyes and smiled at her with chilling cruelty.

A tiny, wiry man of surprising strength, he was dressed in the height of fashion in an elaborate royal-blue velvet suit which did little to offset the incredible grotesqueness of his face. His small tight mouth, long nose, and light, sunken eyes were ugly in themselves, but the effect was made horrifying by skin that was pock marked and covered with scarlet blotches that appeared to be the result of burns. Caro tried to back away, but his grip on her arm only tightened over the bruises left by Alec.

"Well," he said at length, in a voice that made her flesh crawl, "I see I have found you at last. It has been a long ordeal, but I believe it was worth it."

"Who are you?" Caro cried, fear born of recognition flaming in her eyes.

"You needn't be coy with me, my sweet. I have come to take you with me. We will be married tonight, and this time nothing can thwart my plans."

He pulled her closer and the nearness of his face filled her with revulsion. Forcing herself to think clearly, Caro relaxed in his grip as he eyed her with a mixture of suspicion and pleasure.

"Perhaps you've missed me, then? You've reconsidered?" he inquired in a whining tone, and Caro attempted a shy smile.

When he brought his reptilian eyes level with hers, she could sense his guard lowering and in one quick movement she jerked her arm away, pushing him down on to the pavement. Without a backward glance, she lifted her gown and Nithsdale with both hands and ran toward High Street and the marketplace. Merchants were setting up their wares in the brick-pillared stalls as Caro darted inside. When she found a sheltered corner, she paused, hastily unfastening and shedding the crimson cloak. Then she was off again, speeding out the other side of the market and into an adjoining alley. Zigzagging between the buildings, she followed near the perimeter of Arch Street, emerging on Fourth, next to the Quaker Burying Ground. By now, her breath burned in her dry throat each time she inhaled, and her feet hurt in her tiny slippers. Pausing to clutch at the wrought-iron fence which bordered the cemetery, she spied a carriage waiting in front of the Academy building across the street. The driver had a kindly look, and Caro felt so desperate she decided to take the risk. After one furtive glance down Fourth Street, she darted across to the carriage and gazed beseechingly up at the driver.

"Sir, are you acquainted with Alexandre Beauvisage?"

"Why, I know who he is of course, madame," he replied in surprise.

"I am his ward. I am in trouble, terrible trouble, for a horrid man is chasing me and means to abduct me. I must get to my guardian. Can you take me?"

The driver might have refused if she had looked less beautiful and helpless. Hesitantly he muttered, "Well, my employer isn't due out of there until after luncheon, so . . . I suppose I could help you."

Leaning over, the man helped Caro onto the seat beside him, and though she glanced longingly at the closed coach behind them, she decided not to press her luck. As the horses trotted around to start up the street, the man told Caro in a voice that lacked his desired sternness:

"This had better be on the level, young lady! You'll be in a lot of trouble if you've been ribbing me!"

Caro closed her eyes, relief flooding her with an intensity bordering on pain.

"No," she sighed, "I'm not ribbing you, sir. And I'll

see that you are well paid for the help you've given me. Just hurry, please!"

Alec stretched his long, sinewy limbs lazily in the sunlight as he forced himself to come awake. His thick, sooty lashes flickered briefly as he blinked against the bright light that poured into the bedroom, and with a groan he rolled away from it, burying his face in the pillow.

Vaguely, he was conscious of a commotion in the hallway which seemed to be nearing his door, and winced when it burst open.

"What the hell?" he complained, lifting his head just enough to see the doorway. Caro stood there, Pierre behind her, and they were both suddenly speechless. Irritably, Alec propped himself on an elbow, demanding, "What is going on here? Kindly explain yourselves so I can go back to sleep!"

Pierre backed away, pulling the door closed while Caro came to life, scrambling up on the bed. If Alec was startled by her ridiculously disheveled appearance, he did not show it, merely dropping back against the deep pillows as he eyed her with a mixture of irritation and amusement.

"Oh, Alec," Caro exclaimed, "the most awful thing has happened to me!"

"Worse than that ball last night?" he inquired blandly.

"Be silent!" she cried. "This is important! I was accosted on the street this morning by the most horrid lizard of a man. He said he was going to take me with him and marry me!"

"Caro, you can't be serious—" Alec's brows drew together darkly.

"I am! I am!" she nearly screamed, and he reached out to take her fluttering hands. "The worst part is that he *knows* me, Alec—from before. And—and, I know *him*."

"What? Are you saying that your memory is back?"

"Not much—but I recognized him immediately—he was horribly familiar. Do you remember my saying that the man at Wallingham's barn reminded me of someone? It is this hideous person! His eyes . . . !" She shuddered. "He was in a nightmare I had . . . and today, I knew what his voice was going to sound like before he even spoke! What is so frustrating is that I cannot remember more than that. I do not know his name, or who he is, or what my past connection with him was. I simply *knew* him, the way I did Molly that day we found her in the woods—but this was more intense. Maybe because I was so terribly frightened."

"You say he was trying to abduct you?"

"Yes! He held on to me with a grip that felt like a steel trap. He said that this time nothing would thwart his plans."

Alec's eyes sharpened, as he said, "I must say, that sounds rather ominous. But, how in God's name did you get away from him? And how did you get here? And what were you doing out alone to begin with, infant?"

"Stop treating me like a child!" Caro cried passionately, trying unsuccessfully to wrench her hands away. "I am an adult and can come and go as I please!"

"Certainly!" he shot back. "At the risk of getting kidnapped by the first man that you meet! Use your head, Caro."

"I did! I got away, didn't I? And I'm here now, aren't I? I let him think I was weakening under his irresistible charm and then I pulled away and pushed him down really hard. I never knew I was so strong! You should have seen me run, Alec! I'll vow that everyone thought I had lost my senses—"

"A suspicion I have fostered for quite some time,"

he muttered sardonically. Caro ignored him and continued:

"Luckily, I found a carriage with a driver who consented to bring me to Belle Maison, so here I am. And now, you must help me, Alec!"

He swung his long brown legs over the side of the bed and Caro blushed, averting her eyes at the sight of his naked body in the sunlight. Pulling on the breeches from his uniform, Alec began to shave and Caro could tell from his expression that he was thinking.

"I'll tell you what," he conceded at last, "you may remain here and breakfast with me. We can discuss this matter then. Now, run along and tell Pierre to get his ass in here. I don't wish to attempt any more of this hysterical conversation until I get some coffee."

Pierre was waiting discreetly at the end of the hall, and after speaking to him, Caro proceeded downstairs. Even though it was nearly noon, hot breakfast dishes were being assembled on the dining-room table, their fragrant aromas stimulating Caro's appetite. Being back at Belle Maison in Alec's protection had an amazingly relaxing effect on her, and, in spite of everything, she felt an irrepressible glow of happiness deep inside. Sitting down at the table in the spacious sunny dining room, she began to lift the covers off the dishes, helping herself to a few samples while she waited. A maid beamed at her while setting down a cup of steaming coffee, which Caro sipped gratefully.

Far off down the drive a speck appeared, surrounded by a cloud of dust. Caro was soon able to distinguish a horse and rider, and felt immediate panic at the splotch of royal blue showing beneath the man's billowing cape. Backing away from the table, she stood still until she could make out his face, then she ran on watery legs up the stairs to Alec's room. Throwing open the door, she ignored Pierre's startled expression and sped into Alec's arms.

"What now?" he inquired a trifle incredulously, patting her head. "Were you attacked by an egg?"

"He's here! He's here! He just rode up outside!"

"Who? You surely can't mean your lizard friend—"

"Yes!" She was pulling frantically at his neatly pressed coat sleeves.

"Lizard?" Pierre asked irresistibly.

Alec smiled at him over Caro's head. "That's right," he said cheerfully. "And just for the record, I have long been classified as a toad. A tiresome toad, at that!"

"Alec!" Caro cried, "this is no time for jokes! The man is an evil, gruesome creature and I am afraid!"

His arms briefly tightened around her.

"There is no reason for hysteria, my dear. I suggest that you compose yourself and put a little trust in me. Come along now, and I shall take care of everything."

Alec put a supporting arm around her waist as they walked down the hall. In low tones of amusement he admonished her, "Really, Caro, I never thought to see you quake so with terror before a mere man! After all my attempts to intimidate you failed so dismally I was convinced that you possessed unnatural courage and fortitude. Where is all that hellfire that you used to attack me with at every opportunity?"

His light chiding strengthened her, and she felt a surprisingly powerful desire to make him proud of her. The butler met them at the foot of the stairs, informing Alec that a Mr. Pilquebinder was waiting in the rear parlor. As they passed a mirror, Caro saw her reflection and stopped in horror.

"Alec," she hissed, "I look terrible!"

He grinned. "At the risk of appearing rude, I fear I must agree."

The worst part was her hair, which tumbled over her head in every direction, windblown and snarled. Her muslin dress was bedraggled and soiled from her run through Philadelphia and the open-air drive to Belle Maison.

"Perhaps he won't want you now," Alec teased, and Caro laughed in spite of herself. Her smile died, however, when a shadow fell across the hallway and Mr. Pilquebinder appeared. Alec's face remained impassive as he regarded the grotesque little man who stood before them.

"How do you do? Why don't we go inside?"

Caro was amazed at the courteous tone of Alec's voice, but Pilquebinder did not return his smile. In fact, when he looked at Alec his eyes glowed with live hatred.

"I have a few things to say to you," he began, but as Alec led Caro past him, the man had no choice but to follow them into the parlor. Alec and Caro sat down on a green velvet settee, leaving a wingback chair vacant for Pilquebinder. Caro was pleasantly surprised to feel Alec drape a protective arm around her shoulders as he leaned back with studied casualness.

"May I ask who you are, sir, and the nature of your business here?"

The other man, who was squirming nervously, jumped to his feet and began to pace.

"My name is Ezra Pilquebinder, Mr. Beauvisage, and I have come to claim my betrothed. I must request that you relinquish her into my care immediately!"

Caro opened her mouth in horror, but Alec merely smiled coolly as he replied, "I am afraid that is quite out of the question, Mr. Pilquebinder, for the woman you appear to refer to is my wife."

Luckily, Caro was already looking shocked, so her reaction to Alec's words was not apparent to Mr. Pilquebinder. He, however, turned bright red, and his pale eyes glittered eerily.

"Your wife!" He paused, attempting to compose himself. "I do not believe that. No, it is impossible."

"Hardly," Alec returned blandly, while caressing Caro's shoulder with idle intimacy.

"I demand proof!" Pilquebinder exclaimed in a tone of whining frustration.

"Certainly, sir. I do hope you won't mind waiting while I send a man into town to procure the necessary documents from my attorney. If you will excuse us, my wife and I would like to indulge in some long-overdue breakfast. Make yourself comfortable."

Pilquebinder was spluttering with rage as Alec helped Caro up and escorted her out of the room. When they were out of hearing range, she looked up at him incredulously.

"Why did you say that?" she whispered shrilly. *"What* are you going to do?"

Before Alec could answer, they both looked toward the front parlor. A high-pitched hissing came from inside, and when they looked around the threshold, they beheld Grandmère peering out from the confines of a closet.

"What in God's name are you up to now?" Alec demanded.

"Come over here, you two," she replied with an enigmatic smile. "I have the answer to your problem."

"Eavesdropping? God, I had almost forgotten that that whispering closet existed!"

"Oh, it's here, all right, and it extends into the wall of the south parlor as well. It's fortunate for you that I am so curious!"

"Sneaky would be a more apt description," Alec replied drily.

"Pas du tout! I was simply coming through the passage from my house when I heard all the commotion. Can you blame me for taking an interest in my grandson's welfare?"

"Will you kindly get on with it? What is this master plan of yours?"

Grandmère let him help her out of the whispering

closet, but did not move any farther. Beckoning to them to come closer, she whispered:

"*Eh bien*. You can pretend to be sending a message to your attorney, *mais vraiment* it will be addressed to the nearest cleric. You can come with me through the passage, meet him in my house, and be married before that odious man is any wiser. Do you not agree that it is the only course, Sacha?"

He paused, eyes twinkling as he pretended to consider her words. Caro's heart constricted with nervous apprehension and disbelief as she watched him.

A small half-smile played at his lips when he finally replied, "I fear that I am caught at last. You two go ahead while I give the letter to Pierre."

Caro's thoughts were frantically jumbled as she followed Grandmère down into the musty tunnel that connected the two dwellings.

"This is not right!" she whispered at length. "He does not want to marry me! He will hate me!"

"Nonsense, *ma petite*. It is what he wants, even if he is too stubborn to face the fact head-on. Do you think I would be a part of this if I were not certain it was destined? Our M. Pilquebinder may be more of a friend than you realize, for he has become the perfect catalyst to bring Alec to this inevitable event. Ah—here is the door. *C'est tout droit.*"

Caro still looked worried, and as Grandmère opened the panel that shielded the tunnel from her sitting room, she reached out to clasp her hand.

"Do not worry. Trust me."

"But—" Caro blurted, "I understood that there was another woman in Alec's past—during the war—and . . ."

"Pooh!" Grandmère spat the word, declaring, "*Je t'en prie—l'oublies!*" Instantly, the subject was dropped and she was crisply cheerful. "*Maintenant,* we must endeavor to transform you into a bride!"

The memory of her reflection in the hall mirror brought an expression of horror to Caro's face.

"Grandmère, I am a fright! What shall we do?"

The old woman took over competently, leading Caro into her bedchamber and going to work. In minutes the wilted dress was off and Caro was washing with steaming, scented water. Grandmère took the pins out of her tangled hair, brushing it until it curled lustrously down her back. There was a noise in the parlor, followed by Alec's voice assuring them that it was he. Caro sat on the bed, clad only in her thin chemise, while Grandmère excused herself mysteriously. She viewed herself in the mirror, her golden-brown eyes alive with excitement and anxiety, her cheeks flushed becomingly, and her skin looking soft and clean. "Well," she mused, ruefully regarding the soiled dress which lay nearby, "I couldn't have picked a worse day to ride up front with the driver!" At that moment, Grandmère reappeared, wreathed in smiles as she held up a gown for Caro's inspection. Fashioned of rich white satin, now warmed with age into a candlelight hue, the dress was of the outdated Watteau style of 1725. Beautiful pearls and diamonds were encrusted around the petticoat and up the edges of the loose overdress. The neckline plunged low, ending in a profusion of jewels which were intended to draw attention away from the wearer's décolletage. Caro drew in her breath.

"Grandmère, it is beautiful! But where . . . ?"

"It was my own wedding dress," the old woman replied happily. "I cannot express the pleasure it would give me to see you married in it, *ma chère.*"

She helped her dress then, and pinned up her hair with considerable skill into soft curls that framed Caro's radiant face. The gown was exactly her size, and Grandmère saucily opened the overdress to reveal the rosy breasts that showed behind.

"You are a bride *ravissante,*" she declared. *"Et*

257

maintenant, dépêchons-nous. I have heard the minister arrive."

Alec stood impatiently with Parson Brown and Pierre in the sitting room, irreverently drinking brandy. He turned when he heard the door open, his turquoise eyes sweeping Caro approvingly. For her own part, the sight of Alec, incredibly attractive in black with a silver-and-wine-colored waistcoat topped by a snowy lace cravat, took her breath away. Blood pulsed in her face, and when he came forward to take her hand an unsettling tingle ran through her body. Alec's eyes rested boldly on her bosom, white teeth gleaming against his tanned face as he whispered, "You are looking exceedingly lovely, *chérie.*"

The marriage ceremony was performed speedily by the somber-faced Parson Brown, and afterward Caro could recall it only vaguely. She kept expecting Pilquebinder to interrupt the ceremony, or that Alec would change his mind . . . or that perhaps this was just a dream. At the end of the ceremony, however, she was completely alert when the parson declared, "You may kiss the bride."

Caro demurely turned her cheek to Alec, who grinned at her recklessly and caught her in his arms. His mouth came down over hers, kissing her with leisurely expertise until she forgot the parson and wrapped her arms around his neck, molding her body to his. When he let her go, embarrassment set in and she blushed hotly at the sight of Parson Brown's scandalized expression.

Alec was smiling as he whispered to her, "It's all right, you know. We're married now."

Caro looked up into his mocking eyes and found herself laughing. Grandmère appeared from the background to hug them both warmly. Her eyes were misty as she scolded Alec, *"Maintenant, vas-y doucement, mon fils.* I expect you to start behaving decently. This is a serious step you have taken."

Alec smiled ruefully. "I know, Grandmère! And I promise to try to swallow my medicine without making too much of a face. Anyhow, I'm used to the idea —I've seen this coming for a long time, and I had a feeling it was as inevitable as death."

He laughed, and Caro tried not to think about the content of that statement.

Grandmère produced two bottles of excellent Chablis blanc, and the four conspirators toasted while Parson Brown looked on. The wine tasted delicious to Caro, and Alec watched her in amusement as she held out her glass for more. Her face was glowing with an open joy that even his jocular attitude toward the wedding could not diminish. To feel Alec's hand at her waist and know that he was her husband, whatever the circumstances, were enough to make Caro feel incredibly ebullient.

Pierre returned to the house through the passageway to deliver the marriage certificate to Ezra Pilquebinder. Minutes later, however, he was back.

"Monsieur, he insists that he must speak with you personally. I confess that his manner is quite threatening."

Alec's face darkened dangerously as he removed his arm from Caro's shoulders and rose to his feet.

"Damn that man!" he said angrily, ignoring Parson Brown. "He shall have his conversation with me, and I'll wager he'll wish that he hadn't tried my patience so sorely this day!"

Tossing off the wine that remained in his glass, Alec ground out his cigar and disappeared into the aperture in the wall. Some minutes later he returned, frowning in a way that discouraged any questions Caro had wanted to ask. Parson Brown left soon after, and Grandmère began to complain of acute hunger. Caro was relieved to see Alec grin again in response to the old woman's broad hints.

"Are you trying to hurry us onto our honeymoon? Shall we set sail for France this afternoon?"

"I wish that you might," she retorted, wrinkling her forehead in concern.

"I can take care of my wife, Grandmère. If need be, I will do the rest of the world a favor and eliminate that disgusting excuse for a person."

"Is he gone?" Caro asked tentatively.

"Yes. And if the man has any regard for his own safety he'll never let me see him again."

"Alec, please tell me what he said!"

"Oh, very little of any importance. He shouted a great many idle threats that failed to frighten me in the least. It seems he has a difficult time accepting defeat in the matter, but he won't back up his claims to you with any evidence." He paused, narrowing his turquoise eyes thoughtfully. "One thing that did seem odd—I would swear that he holds some sort of grudge against me personally, beyond what I have done to him this day."

"Did he say so?" Caro asked anxiously.

"Not in words, but he kept staring at me in the most maniacal way, and there was something in his manner . . ."

"Oh, Alec!"

"Enough of this," he declared abruptly, helping Caro to her feet. "I want the two of you to stop looking so worried; all is well now. Grandmère, thank you, and we shall see you later." Alec grinned over his shoulder as he and Caro stepped through the door opening onto the garden. "Much later."

Outside, all the trees were gray and bare against the blue sky, but to Caro the garden couldn't have appeared more beautiful if it had been the first day of spring.

"At the risk of underplaying my appetite for you, *chérie,* I plan to order us a disgustingly large lunch which I intend to devour before I do anything else,"

Alec told her casually as they strolled toward the house.

"I confess I am ravenous!" Caro exclaimed.

"Well, I am pleased to hear that. Maman was telling me last night that you seemed to have completely lost your appetite. She was worried for your health, infant." His eyebrow lifted and Caro knew he was teasing her.

"I seem to be feeling much better!" she laughed frankly. "And now that I am your wife, I would appreciate it if you would stop using that loathsome name for me! I am not an infant!"

Alec glanced at her breasts, his mouth quirking in a half-smile.

"I suppose I really must concede that point."

When they entered the house, all the servants, alerted by an excited Pierre, rushed forward to express their congratulations. Caro smiled until her face hurt, and even Alec appeared rather pleased.

"This is your mistress now," he told them. "See to it that you all obey her unfailingly." He turned to the cook. "Elsa, I am exceedingly hungry. Could you contrive to prepare a meal that would do justice to this occasion? We will eat in my chamber."

Caro flushed happily as she ascended the stairs on Alec's arm. The euphoria that filled her entire being was almost more than she could contain. A small voice in the back of her mind warned that the best strategy would be for her to match Alec's coolness, but it was impossible to conceal her feelings. When they reached the master bedroom, Caro slipped off her shoes and darted into the dressing room to peek into her old bedchamber.

"I thought I would never see these rooms again," she confessed as Alec came up behind her, encircling her waist with his arms.

"I gather you were not pleased by that prospect."

"I was miserable the day I left," she answered

frankly, turning in his arms to meet his eyes. "Oh, Alec, how could you have left me that day the way you did? I have never felt so wretched in my life!"

"I could not waste time on explanations—I was lucky to make it to New York in time as it was." His voice softened slightly under her wide-eyed regard. "Besides, I felt that it was probably the best solution in the long run."

Golden sparks kindled in her eyes.

"The best solution! You made love to me all night long—and the best solution at the end was simply to discard me like some plaything that you'd grown bored with? Don't you have any feelings or scruples? And what about me? How could you use me so cold-bloodedly? You knew that I was no common slut! You knew—"

Alec silenced her tirade with a kiss that melted all rage, even as she struggled against him. In the end, her heart was pounding in a different way and she was shamelessly kissing him back. When he released her, his turquoise eyes were cool.

"Spare me your outrage, Caro. I have never lied to you since the day we met—certainly not by promising you anything that I did not intend to deliver. If anything, I belittled my feelings for you—to both of us. You did not get anything the other night that you did not ask for, and now you have me where you want me, and you have the nerve to bitch at me already! I won't stand for any more of it, Caro, or you'll be back in Philadelphia. Mr. Pilquebinder would be only too happy to take you off my hands. Do I make myself clear?"

Caro gulped and nodded as there came a soft tapping at the door to the master suite. Alec opened it to admit a serving girl who pushed a teacart laden with a dozen covered dishes. Pierre appeared behind her with another chilled bottle of wine and two glasses, and seeing Caro looking forlorn, he went across the room to her.

"Madame Beauvisage, I want to offer you my most heartfelt congratulations." He lowered his voice then to a whisper. "He would not have done this for anyone else but you. In Monsieur's case, that counts for a lot."

Caro smiled then, realizing the truth in his words. After Pierre had left, she watched Alec shed his coat and vest, loosening the frilled cravat with one quick pull. He is like a magnificent wild animal, she thought. It is what makes him so special. I would not want to tame him and he will hate me if I try.

Alec opened the wine and poured, then held a glass out to her. Caro smiled, her heart in her eyes as she hurried over to him.

"I am sorry, Alec, for the things I said. Truly!"

He lightly touched her cheek with one brown finger.

"Forget it. Perhaps we both needed to say those things—but now it is done. It was wrong of me to threaten you with Pilquebinder, for I would probably die before I would see him touch you. Now, let us eat. We shall both need our strength this afternoon!" He grinned wickedly as Caro blushed with shameful delight.

Chapter Twenty-two

LOOKING BACK, IT SEEMED TO CARO THAT THEY MADE love unceasingly during the first twenty-four hours of their marriage. After lunch, Alec had undressed her unhurriedly, admiring and caressing her body in the bright daylight.

"I might as well warn you, *chérie,* that I plan to shamelessly abuse my privileges as your husband," he told her in a tone of casual amusement. "If I must be married, then I intend to make the best of it." Caro beamed happily as he pulled the pins from her hair, and Alec's own smile widened. "I am so glad you approve, dear wife."

When they were in bed together, Caro told herself that Alec was expressing physically the emotions that he would not put into words. He was gentle and demanding by turns, as she responded ardently, as always. More than once she had to stop herself from crying out her love for him, but she forced herself to hold back, sensing that someday her chance would come.

The sunlight was dimming into a warm glow when Alec left their bed at last. While pouring more wine for them, he looked back at Caro, lying against the pillows. Her skin was peachy-pink in the gathering twilight, her large brown eyes liquid with deep contentment, and her hair spilling across her breasts like pure honey.

Alec grinned. "You look like a cat who has just consumed a quart of cream."

Caro smiled drowsily, stretching her arms over her head with artless grace.

"You have hit on the perfect description," she murmured.

Carrying the glasses of wine, Alec crossed the room and rejoined her in bed. Caro immediately slipped inside the circle of his arm, molding her soft warm body to his, and Alec was soon setting down his glass. As his brown hands began to touch her again in ways that made her nerves tingle, Caro somehow managed to find her voice.

"Please wait," she whispered, without conviction. "I want to talk to you." Alec ignored her, lifting up her golden curls to kiss her shoulder. Caro gasped, biting her lip. "It's about Nicholai."

His head came up as he regarded her coldly. "I had hoped you would have enough good sense to allow me to forget that matter."

He reached over to pick up his glass again, but Caro tugged at his bare arm insistently.

"Don't you see how unreasonable you're being? You have condemned me most unjustly and I demand the right to clear my name!"

"I wasn't aware that we were in court," he replied caustically.

"I cannot allow you to think that I would betray you with Nicholai! I could never have let him touch me! I—"

"I suppose you were forcing yourself to endure him in the garden. Perhaps you felt sorry for him? Or perhaps he dragged you there by force? Unfortunately, my dear, I know how easy it is to 'rape' you!"

His words stung her with the force of a physical

265

blow, and she was horribly conscious of the tears that welled up in her eyes.

"You are insufferable!" she choked. "How can you be so unfair? So cruel? Why will you not trust me or believe me?"

Alec's keen turquoise eyes watched her closely, and he thought for a moment that she would hit him in her angry frustration. When he reached out to pull her against him, she struggled in his arms like a fighting cat, but his grip was unbreakable. Alec turned her over on her back, pressing her into the pillows and rolling on top of her to pin her down. Salty tears ran from the corners of her eyes down across her temples and into her hair as she squirmed beneath him.

"That's enough, you little hellion," he told her with a soft laugh. "You are either telling the truth, or you're a damned good actress—so I'll take a chance and believe you this time."

Gently, he kissed away her tears and her body grew still. When his lips grazed hers, she hungrily sought them in a kiss that left her weak with desire. Alec could feel her body arching against his and for a moment he paused, his face dark and finely chiseled as he gazed down at her. White teeth flashed in the shadows as he murmured:

"Perhaps this marriage will not be such a bad arrangement after all."

Noon had come and gone the next day when Caro finally woke up. One of Alec's warm brown arms was draped across her hip, his face touching her breasts. For a moment, she laid her cheek against his shining raven hair in utter contentment.

"Alec," she whispered, "wake up."

When he stirred, muscles moved down the length of his lean, tanned body.

"Christ," he muttered, narrowing his eyes against the sunlight that flooded the room. "It must be late."

After raising his head to kiss her lingeringly, he got up and stretched.

"I could use a bath," he declared, running a hand through his hair. "How about you?"

Caro blushed ridiculously and Alec threw back his head and laughed.

"You can contradict yourself in the most humorous ways, *chérie!*"

Shrugging into a dark blue robe, Alec stuck his head out the door and unceremoniously yelled for Pierre. Minutes later, a hot bath was waiting for them in Caro's room and Alec lifted her into it, raising a mocking black brow at her shy smile when he joined her.

Afterward, he chose for her a simple gown of damask rose velvet that highlighted her glowing complexion. Caro watched him shave as she drank her tea, and after donning a slate-gray suit with a gray-and-black brocade waistcoat and a pure-white ruffled shirt, he escorted her downstairs. The servants watched them with discreet curiosity as they breakfasted at nearly two o'clock. Caro found herself bantering with Alec with all the ease and enjoyment of their early acquaintance. He watched her consume an enormous amount of food, commenting drily:

"My dear, I hope that your appetite will not remain at this level permanently! I have no wish for an obese wife—in fact, I believe that would be just cause for divorce in this house!"

"Oh, do be quiet," Caro laughed. "If I am not allowed to nag, then neither should you!" She smiled saucily at him between bites of her warm blueberry muffin, and Alec could not repress an exasperated grin.

"I can see you will be quite unmanageable."

"Alec, if the day ever comes when you cannot manage me it will be a tremendous shock to me!" she replied honestly.

Pierre appeared in the doorway to announce, "Madame et monsieur, your carriage is waiting."

Alec looked at his wife, eyes twinkling. "You'd better gobble down that muffin, my dear. I fear I must wrench you from the table."

"You are abominably rude, sir!" Caro laughed as he pulled out her chair. Turning to Pierre, she inquired, "Why don't you endeavor to teach this brute some manners, Pierre?"

He smiled cheerfully, then joked, "I'm afraid that is your task now, madame."

Alec threw back his handsome head and laughed with delight.

"Touché!"

At Alec's request, Parson Brown had visited the Beauvisage house after the wedding to explain Caro's absence. It happened that Nicholai had arrived there for luncheon, sporting a dark bruise on his left cheekbone. The parson delivered his message with great courtesy, but declined to elaborate.

"Major Beauvisage asked that I inform you that he and his wife will call here tomorrow. I believe that they wish to be alone today."

Natalya was frantic with curiosity, while Nicholai, strained and pale, insisted on going to Belle Maison. Jean-Philippe took his arm to restrain him, Antonia watching her son with concern. Katya seemed to be the only person who felt like celebrating the news, declaring that she was delighted to have Caro as a sister.

The next day, Nicholai arrived at the house on Third Street before breakfast and the whole family settled down to wait nervously for the newlyweds' arrival. Only Jean-Philippe appeared unaffected by all the excitement, though he did remain at home all day.

Everyone was understandably overwrought by mid-afternoon, and when Alec's carriage was sighted on the street at close to three o'clock Natalya nearly screamed the alert. With an effort, Antonia and Jean-Philippe persuaded their children to sit down in the parlor and refrain from making a scene. The parents went to the door to welcome Alec and Caro.

Antonia had been confused by Parson Brown's startling news, but somehow not surprised. In the back of her mind she had sensed that Caro was in love with Alec, but it had been a worry to her, for she knew her son and his past only too well. She was seeing them together now for the first time, and Caro's radiance was apparent even from a distance as she smiled up at Alec. Antonia was heartened by the affectionate expression on his face and the way he kept a protective arm around his bride's waist. Somehow she had sensed that Caro's early disappearance from the ball was linked to Alec's bad temper and Nicholai's bruise, and now with this newest development she was more certain than ever.

As Caro ran up the steps to hug her, Antonia felt she was seeing an entirely different girl. Where before she had seemed sad, with suffering in her large eyes, her beauty was now comparable to a perfect rose in full bloom. Her skin glowed, her eyes sparkled, her lips looked soft and well kissed, and even her hair seemed more lustrous. Antonia embraced her with sincere affection.

"I couldn't be happier, Caroline."

"Nor could I, Antonia," she exclaimed exuberantly.

To Caro, Jean-Philippe appeared altered. Where previously all the qualities he shared with Alec had been painful reminders, they now served to make him an extremely special person in her eyes. He seemed pleasantly startled by her friendly smile and warm embrace, but lost no time in hugging her back and offering his best wishes.

Alec remained his usual debonair self, his turquoise eyes careless yet watchful as they followed Caro.

From the beginning he coolly dismissed the suddenness of their marriage, smilingly explaining that he had been overcome by the realization of true love. Antonia did not believe it any more than Natalya or Nicholai did, but she did sense the strong currents of emotion that flowed between her son and his new wife.

He plays at nonchalance, she thought, but he cannot take his eyes off her.

Nicholai seemed a changed person as he stared coldly across the room at Alec and Caro. All the gaiety and sparkle were gone from his green eyes, and yet even now his wounds were beginning to heal. Watching him, Antonia knew that it was not part of the Beauvisage makeup to remain unhappy for long, and Nicholai had always been the most light-hearted and fun-loving of all her children.

"He will make a fast recovery," she whispered to Jean-Philippe. "Perhaps I should ask Mary Armstrong to dinner . . ."

Natalya, for her part, was having an inner conflict between her feelings of betrayal and her curiosity. At last, inquisitiveness got the better of her and she began to bombard Caro with questions which Alec neatly parried.

"There is really nothing to tell, dear sister," he said carelessly. "I simply decided that I wanted to marry Caro and, once the decision was made, we were overcome by impatience."

"That's right," Caro added firmly, suppressing a bubble of laughter that rose in her throat.

"But Caro was here eating breakfast yesterday morning!" Natalya argued. "She only went out for a walk! How could—"

"Do not pry so," Antonia admonished, winning a broad smile from Alec. "You surely can leave them a few lover's secrets!"

"Honestly, Caro," Natalya declared in annoyance, "I wouldn't be surprised if Sacha has known all this time that you loved him. You two were probably carrying on secretly when all the while I thought your heart was breaking!"

Caro flushed hotly. "Do be quiet!"

"On the contrary," grinned Alec, squeezing his wife's hand. "I find this new turn in the conversation quite enlightening!"

Caro pushed at him playfully and he laughed out loud at her embarrassment.

"Surely you want me to know everything about you, dear wife? I believe that a lengthy *tête-à-tête* with my sweet sister would be quite educational!"

At that moment tea and cakes were served, and to Caro's great relief the subject was changed. Jean-Philippe began to discuss the shipping trade with his sons while Caro sipped her tea, happy merely to feel the hard pressure of Alec's arm against hers.

After a few minutes, Antonia exclaimed, "Sacha, through all of this excitement we have neglected to ask about your meeting with General Washington! Do tell us about it!"

"Mon Dieu!" echoed Jean-Philippe. "How could we have forgotten that?"

Alec laughed. "I am not sure it was worth the ride, considering I had less than a dozen hours' sleep in four nights. I do not suppose that Washington would have been pleased with my absence, however, and it was a good opportunity to say a last farewell to many close friends."

"Everyone was there, then?" inquired his father, leaning forward in his chair.

"Every officer who was close to him, except Lafayette. I suppose it was worth a great deal to me just to see them all at once, for it was a damned sad occasion. We all met at Fraunces Tavern and drank together a last time. Washington had no speech prepared, but his words were eloquent all the same, and I'll confess that many of us wept by the time we joined in that final toast. The general bade each of us come and take him by the hand—Henry Knox went first and they threw their arms about each other . . .”

“You and your comrades shared a great deal,” offered Antonia in a low voice.

“Yes,” Alec agreed, his tone bittersweet. “More than men should be expected to endure, I suppose. Perhaps that’s the reason for the strength of the bonds we formed during those years.”

“What did General Washington say to you?” Katya asked.

“Nothing. I believe we were all past words. But his eyes were filled with tears—a most affecting sight, let me assure you.”

“Has Washington departed for Mount Vernon?”

“No. In fact, I believe he is en route to Philadelphia even now. He mentioned that Annapolis is his eventual destination—he must return his commission, you know. As a matter of fact, he is worried that he may even have to forego Christmas at home, for he cannot leave Annapolis until the twenty-third or twenty-fourth.”

Jean-Philippe raised an eyebrow. “I cannot conceive of the general not reaching Mount Vernon by Christmas day if that is his wish.”

“I suppose you are right,” Alec grinned.

As tantalizing aromas began to drift out from Mrs. Reeves’ kitchen, Antonia eyed Caro and Alec hopefully. “You must stay for dinner. We still have so much to talk about!”

Alec looked at Caro, his eyes resting on the sweet curve of her neck.

“Alas, Maman, we have already made our plans for the evening. I beg your indulgence.”

Natalya and Katya voiced their disappointment emphatically, but Nicholai looked relieved as his brother rose.

Dusk was gathering as they said their good-byes and

departed for Belle Maison. Caro loved the cozy interior of the carriage, her heart quickening as Alec settled himself beside her and encircled her with one arm, drawing her near to him. As they set off, however, his eyes were on the buildings that they passed, sharply alert as though he were looking for something Caro was not quite brave enough yet to try and gain his attention, so she merely rested her head against his shoulder and waited for him to speak.

They were passing a small dark alley between Arch and Race streets when Alec suddenly thrust her away from him, calling to Maurice to stop immediately. Leaping lightly to the street, he disappeared into the shadows, and Caro could faintly discern the form of another man running ahead of Alec. Panic and fear consumed her as she began to descend to the ground and follow her husband. Maurice was at her side immediately, warning her in agitated French that she must not take another step. After pushing her back inside the coach, he also broke into a run, following his master.

Only a minute passed before Maurice returned, opening the door to speak to Caro. "It is all right, madame," he said in slow English, a faint smile playing at his mouth. "Le monsieur is quite able to look after himself! I believe he only sought to speak to the man we saw, for he bade me return to watch over you."

Even as Maurice finished speaking, Alec appeared in the distance, sprinting easily toward the carriage. The driver opened the door for him, and he dusted off his coat sleeves as he sat down beside her. A muscle twitched angrily in his cheek before he spoke.

"As you may have guessed, that was our friend Pilquebinder. I had warned him yesterday to make haste in his departure from Philadelphia, yet he has blatantly defied me. The man is too strange to be human, and I'll frankly admit that he worries me."

The carriage continued on its way to Germantown in what was now total darkness. Caro tried to read the expression on Alec's face, but could only perceive the hard line of his jaw as he stared out into the night, deep in thought. She was chilled by his words and instinctively huddled against him for warmth and reassurance. As if he could sense her feelings, Alec put his arms around her so that she could rest her face against his broad chest.

"I fear that there's only one answer for this," he told her. "Until I can see that man dead you shall not leave my sight. I don't think he will stop at anything to get you and I do not plan to take any chances with your life. I will appreciate your cooperation in this matter, my dear—you shall have to be prepared to go everywhere with me from now on and give up all your privacy. I fear it will not be a very serene existence."

Caro's heart soared as she smiled to herself against the silver buttons of his waistcoat.

"I shall try to adjust, sir. After all, you know I am totally subservient to your wishes!"

Alec laughed out loud at that, tilting up her chin to look into her eyes.

"You are the most impertinent minx—" His words broke off as Caro boldly pulled his head toward hers.

Chapter Twenty-three

IN THE WEEKS THAT FOLLOWED, CARO WAS HAPPIER than she had ever believed possible. Alec let his business slide with his new marriage and Christmas provided a double excuse. Occasionally, men would come out to Belle Maison to speak with him, and before any of these conferences, Alec always arranged for Caro to be in the company of Pierre and usually Grandmère as well. She was never left alone, but the advantages of this situation outweighed the inconveniences since she spent nearly every waking minute with Alec.

They rode together every morning, even in the snow, and gradually Caro came to know nearly every corner of the five-hundred-acre estate. Many hours were spent in the library, where Caro would perch in a window seat and read while Alec worked at his desk. She was to learn that he read a great deal himself, at a speed which astounded her, often completing an entire book in a few hours. During the afternoons, they visited Grandmère together, the old woman watching them with shrewd satisfaction as they bantered good-naturedly back and forth.

Even though she could sense that a strong bond had formed between them, Caro knew that her marriage was far from ideal. Alec never mentioned the word love or even spoke of their future together, and at times, she felt that he longed to be free of her completely. The circumstances of their marriage worried her, until she began to have nightmares in which Alec would invariably leave her alone in the woods. They always ended with her running through a maze of trees, screaming his name uselessly. When she woke, he would be holding her in the darkness, asking her to tell him what she had dreamed.

"Was it anything that might give us a clue to your past?"

"No," she would murmur dismally. "Far from it."

Most of the time he would cradle her in his arms until she was calm again, helping her to relax with a few drowsy kisses. By the time his warm, hard body moved over her in the darkness the horror of her dream would be swallowed up in the splendor of their union. It was at those times that Caro was convinced that he loved her as she loved him, and afterward she would fall asleep in his arms, contented and unafraid again.

By mid-December, preparations were well underway for Christmas, for Caro had persuaded Alec that they should have a full celebration in their house. At her urging, he invited his family to spend the holiday with them and Antonia agreed immediately.

"It will be the first time in thirty-five years that my parents will not have been in their own home on Christmas," Alec told Caro a trifle sadly.

"She is pleased—she told me so! They can still have a celebration there, too, Alec. Don't worry."

After two weeks of marriage, Caro had nearly forgotten about Ezra Pilquebinder, but Alec had not. One afternoon she had left the bedroom while he dozed on the bed, and stood examining a bookshelf in the library when Alec suddenly appeared in the doorway. His eyes were stormy with rage as he gripped her arm so hard she gasped.

"What the hell do you think you're doing? Are you

trying to scare me to death? How many times do you have to be told that you are not to be alone—not under any circumstances!"

Tears of anger and pain sprang up in her eyes as she tried to wrench free from his bruising hold.

"You are being ridiculous!" she choked. "Would you have me be a prisoner in my own house?"

He regarded her in silence for a long minute, and when he spoke his voice was dangerously low.

"If you continue to defy me, you will find yourself a prisoner of someone very different, and this house you value so highly will be lost to you. Perhaps you would prefer to share your bed with Ezra Pilque-binder? Do not doubt what I say, Caro—you cannot be sure of safety even here at Belle Maison." Dropping her arm, he crossed the room to his desk, then gazed back at her coldly. "You would do well to make Mr. Pilquebinder the subject of your nightmares, for I cannot but believe that I have been unfairly cast."

That night, a sudden snowstorm provided an excuse for Caro to break the silence that had continued stubbornly between them since their confrontation in the library.

After an unbearable evening meal, during which Alec drank too much wine, Caro and Pierre began a game of chess in the parlor. Alec sat in his favorite wing chair appearing to read, but Caro's practiced eye easily detected his lack of concentration, for he was staring at each page as though it had insulted him.

Pierre beat Caro easily two games in a row, and finally she got up restlessly to look out the window. The trees that lined the long drive were outlined in black against the deep indigo-blue sky, and even as she watched, the first snowflakes began to drift out of it. Multiplying rapidly, they fluttered gracefully to the ground, each one unusually large and well defined against the dark background.

277

The beauty of it brought out Caro's impulsive gaiety and before she could remember their quarrel, she had thrown herself on her knees beside Alec's chair, pushing his book away as she smiled up into his face.

"It is snowing! Please say that we may walk in the garden! New snow at night is one of my favorite things—"

His eyes softened and Caro thought for a moment that he might smile. Before he could refuse her, she jumped up, pulled him to his feet, and led him, muttering gruffly under his breath, past a grinning Pierre. Moments later they stepped into the garden, and even Alec was impressed by the unique beauty of the night. Caro, her face framed by the fox hood, pirouetted in the snow, catching a delicate flake on her tongue and laughing in delight. Alec watched her, trying halfheartedly to resist her charm, but smiling at her in the end when she came dancing back to him.

"Isn't it lovely?" she asked, her cheeks pink in the cold. When he reached out silently to take her face between his two hands, Caro's expression sobered. Grasping the lapels of his coat, she stared up at him gravely.

"I'm so sorry, Alec," she apologized. "I did it again! My foolish tongue has caused me such problems with you since the first day we met, and I never seem to learn!" Two large tears ran down her cheeks, melting the snowflakes that had lingered there. "One day you will tell me I have done it once too often, and then I will be turned out for good. And I'll deserve it! It was completely my fault again, and—"

"Will you shut up!" interrupted Alec in tones of exasperated amusement. He brought his face down to hers, tasting the saltiness of her tears and then the familiar sweetness of her lips. Caro's arms slipped around his back as she rose on her toes to fit her body nearer to his.

"You're right about one thing," Alec murmured against her hair. "You talk entirely too much."

By morning there was a thick blanket of snow covering the grounds of Belle Maison, sparkling beneath the bright sun. Downstairs, Alec and Caro ate a large breakfast, Caro declaring that her appetite had been stimulated by the excitement of the snow. After finishing her second cup of coffee she rose to pace before the dining-room window, gazing longingly at the shimmering white carpet outside.

"How I long to romp in it like a child," she sighed, turning to find Alec grinning at her.

"I can't imagine why you hesitate," he commented drily, tapping the ash from his cheroot. He regarded her slowly, taking in the childlike sparkle in her brown eyes and the irrepressible smile that played at her mouth.

"Come over here," he commanded, gesturing for her to sit on his lap. Caro did so with pleasure, and Alec put his free arm around her waist.

"At the risk of spoiling you," he began, "I may have a solution for your problem. How would you like to go ice skating today?"

Sparks of pure gold lit up her eyes as she stared at him in disbelief.

"Do you mean it? Honestly?" A small frown appeared. "But what if I cannot ice skate?"

Alec threw back his head with laughter.

"Then I shall have even more fun teaching you how! It will be a rare delight to watch you taking pratfalls on the Delaware River!"

There was not even one footprint to mar the crystalline perfection of the snow that stretched across the grounds of Belle Maison when they set out for Philadelphia in the sleigh. Christmas bells had been attached to Ivan's harness and he pranced along in the winter sunshine, playing his role to the hilt. Caro was bundled up in her fox cloak with a cozy blanket tucked around her legs. One arm was linked through Alec's while her hands were clasped together inside her thick fox muff, and her face glowed with chilled excitement.

Alec seemed unusually relaxed, particularly compared to his bitter rage of the day before. From time to time he would smile at her affectionately and Caro thought he looked magnificent in his heavy navy blue coat with its gold buttons. He seemed to thrive in the cold weather, for their daily rides on Ivan and Molly always left him more vigorous and vibrant than ever.

The lightweight sleigh skimmed along over the road to Philadelphia under trees flocked with fresh snow. The time flew by for Caro, as it always did when she was enjoying herself with Alec. He tooled the sleigh himself, handling it deftly in Philadelphia as they sped down Third Street toward the Beauvisage house. Caro was conscious of the admiring, sometimes envious glances of the pedestrians, who turned to watch as they whizzed by, Ivan's bells jingling gaily.

They arrived unannounced to find Alec's family decorating the entry hall of the house with sprays of evergreen and holly. Natalya and Katya immediately accepted their invitation to join the ice-skating party and soon they were on their way to the banks of the Delaware.

The river was already crowded with skaters, most of whom were men.

"It's really not considered particularly elegant for women to be seen here," Alec confided to Caro with a smile, but she raised her chin rebelliously.

"I do not care! I intend to have fun today and proper society can go hang!"

He helped the three girls fasten their black, curled-up ice skates and Natalya and Katya set out immediately, laughing with delight as they skidded shakily over the ice. Caro held onto Alec's arm, watching them wide-eyed as they gained confidence and speed. Looking up at her husband, she saw him lift a dark eyebrow as he inquired lightly:

"Well, m'lady, are you ready to venture forth?"

Smiling gamely, she replied, "Of course—but do not let go of me!"

Arm in arm they slowly slid forward on the glassy river, drawing grins from the men who glided past them, calling greetings to Alec. Caro was surprised to realize that her feet were steady, and she felt sure of her balance. Alec seemed to sense her confidence, gradually building up speed and drawing her into wide turns.

"I believe you have played me false, *chérie*," he told her with a laugh. "You were probably born with ice skates on and should be leading me right now!"

His praise brought a pleased glow into her cheeks and she slid her arm down merely to hold onto his hand. As they glided deftly over the sparkling ice, Caro felt a wave of pure pleasure sweep through her body, for they were skating together with perfect symmetry.

Alec let go of her hand then, drifting back toward the bank to join the others who had stopped to watch. With an incandescent smile and an artless, fluid grace, Caro forgot everything except Alec's reckless smile as she skimmed effortlessly across the ice, etching a delicate pattern of turns and figure eights in its frosty surface.

When she pirouetted swiftly and finally slowed to a stop, embarrassment set in at the sight of so many watchful eyes. Katya was mesmerized by what she had seen, while Natalya swallowed her envy to tell Caro how beautifully she had skated. Alec merely squeezed her mittened hand, regarding her with a pride that Caro could sense was flavored with his usual light mockery. He guided her over to lean against the hull of a small boat which sat on the ice, hugging the river bank. A fire burned nearby and Caro turned her face in its direction, grateful for its warmth. Hundreds of chimneys peeked at her from the snowy rooftops of Philadelphia, each one expelling pale-gray wisps of smoke.

"Well," commented Alec, "we have exposed another of your many accomplishments! What shall it be next—painting perhaps?"

"I imagine I could do tolerably well on the side of this old boat," she giggled, basking in the comfort of his arm about her. Natalya skated up to them then, and at the same moment one of Alec's friends gestured to him. Alec excused himself and skated over to greet his friend. Thus, Caro was left alone with her new sister-in-law for the first time since the morning of her marriage. Natalya watched her shrewdly.

"I have been dying for an opportunity to speak to you in private, Caro. Honestly, Sacha hovers about you like a hawk—I never would have thought he would make such a protective husband. Even now he is watching you! Does he expect some bogeyman to come and snatch you away?"

"Of course not!" Caro exclaimed hotly.

"You know, this is all *very* queer. Was I right the other day about you two carrying on all along behind my back? I cannot conceive of you practicing such a deception, but at the same time, there doesn't seem to be any other answer! Sacha couldn't have fallen in love and decided to marry you in an hour's time! I know that he would give a step like marriage a great deal more thought—especially since he has avoided it so diligently all these years!"

"Natalya, really—I do not know what to say to you. Alec has already explained—"

"We are friends! You can be frank with me, can't you? Everything that Sacha said to us was so pat as to be almost ridiculous. It would be so out of character—"

"Ah!" a deep, sarcastic voice broke in from behind

282

them. "But surely, Natalya, as a romantic female you could be transformed under the spell of true love!" Alec's face was serious behind the mocking smile. "Do not be so inquisitive, little sister. You really must learn to mind your own business."

Caro's heart pounded with relief while Natalya blushed under Alec's cool regard, stammering an apology.

"It is all right," Caro told her before Alec could speak. "I understand your curiosity, but there is really no mystery to solve. Alec and I are married now and we are very happy, but that is no reason for *our* friendship to cease. You and I should be closer than ever now that we are related!"

Natalya's crestfallen face brightened somewhat and Alec reached out to pat her cheek, adding, "All is forgiven, chicken, as long as you confine your inquisitiveness to someone else's affairs. No more questions—is that clear?" Natalya nodded and Alec drew Caro closer to him.

As the final preparations were made for Christmas, Caro's days were busy and blissful. Alec followed the German custom of bringing a tree into the house and set up a plump Scotch pine in the rear parlor. That evening, they strung corn and berries to wind through the branches while Pierre carved little wooden ornaments which Grandmère painted. Alec told them he had learned about Christmas trees during the war, when he had crossed the Delaware with Washington to surprise the Hessian troops at Trenton. They had been so deep in their festive celebrations that an attack had been the last thing they expected.

Candles were set in every available spot, filling the windows with a cheerful welcoming light and spreading a warm golden glow over the rest of the house. Caro placed garlands of pine and holly on the front door, then hung them liberally through the hallway and over all the mantels. On Christmas Eve Alec produced a spray of mistletoe which he fastened on the arch dividing the entry hall. He was delighted to be able to initiate Caro into the English custom attached to the plant.

"What is that?" she inquired suspiciously. "Those berries look quite evil. Are you trying to poison me?"

Alec suppressed a grin, though his turquoise eyes were twinkling as he coaxed, "Why don't you come over here and take a closer look? The leaves have a very interesting shape."

She raised her finely drawn eyebrows as if to say, "Who cares?" but approached cautiously. Alec surveyed the outline of her figure beneath the rich green velvet dress she wore and his lips twitched with irrepressible amusement.

"Have you hidden some insect in there?" Caro inquired with playful distrust. Alec drew her under the mistletoe. "Actually," he smiled, "I do have an ulterior motive and there is more to this little plant than meets the eye."

Caro glanced up warily at the oval leaves and clusters of waxy red and white berries. Alec's arms slid around her waist, caressing the velvet that covered her back. "There is a rather charming custom that is always practiced beneath the mistletoe, so pay attention and learn it well. You must take care never to find yourself under it with any man but me or I shall be forced to take drastic measures!"

"What are you talking about?" she exclaimed in bewilderment.

"Talking is not the right word, my dear. Allow me to demonstrate."

There were devils dancing in his eyes as he tilted her chin back with a tanned forefinger until she was gazing up at the mistletoe. His other arm drew her closer until her breasts pressed against his chest, then he kissed her slowly, tasting the sweetness of her pliant mouth and the honeyed softness inside. Something warm and vital passed between them; Caro could feel it tingle through her veins like a tangible thing. When Alec lifted his head, his lips clung to hers momentarily and she could read the desire in his eyes, briefly accompanied by something else that she could not name. If Grandmère had not appeared, Caro felt that he would have spoken, or taken her up to bed.

The memory of his eyes and the elusive magic of the mistletoe kiss played at the edges of her mind all that afternoon and evening. It reawakened the issue that had become her greatest puzzle—the question of Alec's true feelings. She knew that he loved her body and that he hungered for her in a physical way that never ceased to excite her. There were times, however, when she felt that he was trying to convey a deeper message to her, but after the moment passed, she would decide that her imagination was overactive. Hovering in the back of her mind, along with the memory of the tragic Emily, were some miserably haunting words of Natalya's:

"Sacha breaks girls' hearts like pieces of fine china, and yet the silly fools return for more. He has lost respect for females over the years, and now he only uses them for his pleasure. He will never marry, and it is just as well, for Sacha could never love any woman for more than a week."

Caro wondered how long the man she married would want her, for she couldn't quite believe he loved her.

Chapter Twenty-four

GRANDMÈRE JOINED THEM FOR DINNER THAT NIGHT, the first meal she had shared with them in several days. Caro knew that she had been purposely leaving them alone, and appreciated the gesture. The two women had not spoken at length privately since the night she had gone into Alec's room, but Grandmère's affection, support, and approval shone in her bright blue eyes each time she looked at Caro.

Their Christmas Eve dinner was simple, for the cook was already deep into her preparations for the next day's feast. The entire house was aglow with burnished candlelight, providing a perfect background for Caro's radiant golden beauty, while outside snow flurries swirled through the winter sky. At Grandmère's urging, Alec had prepared a scaled-down wassail bowl of whipped syllabub made with white wine, cream, and grated lemon with a dollop of frothy beaten egg white on top. Caro loved it, and found that it served to enhance her holiday mood even more.

After dinner, Alec transferred the wassail bowl to the parlor and the three of them sat talking before the fire. Grandmère told Caro of her Christmases as a child in the French countryside, when she would put out her sabots on the hearth for Père Noël to fill with candy and toys.

"Every year we made a *crèche* with more *santons*—

small clay figures coming to see the Christ child. We would keep the *santons* year after year, adding new ones to the old. As a child, I loved that more than any other Christmas custom, and I saw to it that Jean-Philippe and Antonia continued it in their home."

Alec smiled, remembering. "I broke one of the little peasant figures one year—it was one of the oldest, made by Maman before I was born. I was terrified, but although Danielle was urging me to destroy the evidence, I could not bring myself to go skulking around."

"I recall that!" Grandmère exclaimed. "Jean-Philippe was so proud and impressed when you came to him and showed him the broken *santon*. You said, 'Papa, I did this, but I will not accept a punishment because it was an accident and I am very sorry about it.' When they wrote to me about it, I knew *les choses* of which you were made."

Alec laughed and lifted the candle from the table next to him to light a cheroot. As it flared briefly, he noticed Caro, staring into the delft tile fireplace with faraway brown eyes. Leaning back in his chair, he smoked in silence, watching her, while Grandmère bent busily over her crewelwork. At last he reached out to touch her hand and she started, blinking to refocus her eyes.

"Are you feeling all right?" Alec inquired with unusual gentleness.

"Yes," she breathed, frowning slightly as though bewildered. "I think I was just remembering something, but of course, I can't be sure if it was real or merely a dream. . . ."

"Tell me," he said quietly, and Caro met his clear eyes.

"It was awfully strange; I imagine you'll laugh at me! But I could see in my mind the door to the house —not Belle Maison, but another house—fly open and a mysterious man throwing in a present. Throwing it at me, then disappearing immediately. I'm sure that I

287

was very young—a little child. I remember unwrapping it and finding layer upon layer of paper—so many that I believed there was no present inside at all."

She paused and Alec prompted, "Go on!"

"I can't remember any more. That's all."

His eyes were sparkling and he squeezed her little hand tightly.

"That is a fantastic clue, Caro, though I can't imagine that we shall make anything more of it. I know what it means though—you must be Swedish, for you were describing the Christmas custom of the *Julklapp*—that crazy, multi-wrapped gift brought by an elusive, unrecognizable person. Does that help you remember any more?"

"No . . . but it's wonderful just to know that little bit about myself. Do you suppose I grew up in Sweden?"

"I doubt it. You have no accent whatever—and the fact is that all Americans were foreigners a short while ago. Everyone brought their particular customs with them across the sea—like Grandmère's *crèche* with the *santons*."

Caro smiled at him, dimples showing in the firelight. Grandmère spoke up then, from her chair:

"Sacha, I will stay to watch you light the Yule log, but then I must go. I suddenly am very tired."

She waited until Alec had turned away, then winked broadly at Caro. He got up to call to Pierre, tossing off another cup of syllabub while he waited. Then they disappeared outside and Caro waited in ignorant anticipation to see what would happen next. When they came noisily back down the hall, they were carrying a huge log which they took into the south parlor by the decorated tree, where the fireplace was cold. Grandmère's wrinkled face was lit up with a childlike smile as she took Caro by the hand and they followed Alec and Pierre.

"Bring me some pine boughs, sweetheart," Alec

called, and Caro ran to fetch them, beaming at the term of endearment.

The evergreens were spread across the log as Pierre summoned all the available servants to come and watch. Alec took Caro's hand to pull her nearer the fireplace as he poured a generous amount of fine wine over the giant log. Then, a charred piece of wood was produced which Alec held up to a nearby candle.

"Tradition," he told her in confidential tones. "This is part of the Yule log that burned at Father and Maman's house last year."

Then he held the burning piece of wood down to the decorated log, and as it burst into glorious flames, everyone cheered. Caro clapped too, looking up at Alec's proud, handsome profile outlined against the orange glow. Suddenly, he turned, catching her in his arms, and kissed her soundly while the cheering and clapping grew louder in their ears. Caro was blushing happily when he let her go, regarding her with eyes that danced with devilish laughter. He grasped her elbow and they went forward to wish everyone a Merry Christmas, Alec offering whipped syllabub to all.

In a few minutes, the servants had disappeared discreetly, taking their wassail with them, and Grandmère began to yawn extravagantly. After she had kissed them and left via the whispering closet, Caro suddenly felt unaccountably shy. She went over to the fireplace and looked at the blazing log with serious interest. Alec came up behind her, folding his hands around her waist, and Caro found it difficult to breathe.

"So! You say this log is supposed to burn the full twelve days of Christmas!" she exclaimed in a voice that sounded unusually high and faraway to her. Alec's lips grazed her neck and she flinched as if he had burned her.

"That is what we hope for," he answered lightly, pressing a warm kiss where her shoulder curved into her neck. Caro's skin crawled pleasurably, and Alec could feel her shiver. "I'm not making you uncomfortable, am I?" he inquired with cool amusement. "Actually, my purpose is quite the opposite."

Gently he rotated her body until they were face to face, or rather chest to face. In the leaping firelight, he looked exactly like Satan to Caro, all black and bronzed with flashes of white as he smiled recklessly down at her. Her senses swam as he bent nearer until she inhaled the intoxicating aroma that was part of him.

"Why so flustered, *chérie?* Can this be the same brave girl who unhesitatingly slapped my cheek—more than once, as I recall!"

She could not think clearly enough to make a proper retort, and her long lashes swept across her cheeks as she looked away from his penetrating turquoise eyes. Immediately he took her chin between one brown thumb and forefinger, lifting her face. She saw him quirk a black brow, and one side of his mouth went up in a half-smile.

"Do not try to hide from me, Caro," he said in a low voice as his hard fingers moved to trace the outline of her cheek. Her chin began to tremble and Alec's gaze sharpened as he met her melted-caramel eyes.

"Surely you are not afraid?" he inquired more tenderly, cupping her chin to still it. Then, gently, he lowered his head and closed his eyes as their lips met. Something stirred deep inside Alec and when he opened his eyes he saw a tear glistening on Caro's cheek.

"What is this?" he asked, kissing it away. "Why should you cry?"

She spoke at last, with an effort:

"I don't know! I do, but then—oh, never mind!"

"Ah!" he laughed, and the rich sound of it filled the empty room. "I see! Madame, you are a paragon of wisdom. The female mind is a wondrous thing!"

Caro's cheeks flamed. "You may jest, but I cannot! Will you never be serious?"

The laughter died out in his eyes then, replaced by something that made her heart constrict. Releasing her, he walked away, his lean physique growing muted as the shadows closed around him. Caro could not move or breathe as she waited by the fire. When he strode back, Alec did not touch her, but merely stood at a short distance, eyes narrowed and jaw set as he seemed to concentrate.

"Damn!" he exclaimed suddenly. "This is cursed difficult. I swear I would rather do battle with the British than endure this torture again!"

Caro's eyes widened, but she did not speak. Reaching out, Alec pulled her roughly to him, his expression softening somewhat at the touch of her body against his.

"This is all your fault, you know!" he told her in a dangerous voice. "You have tampered with me in ways that should be outlawed! I vow that I would have done myself a favor if I had left you beneath that tree, you vixen! My entire existence has been totally disrupted right from the beginning and I can see now that I'd have been wise to follow my instincts then! You were casting your spell on me from the first and do not think I wasn't aware of it. I am no fool, madame! I knew you were dangerous stuff, but by then it was too late!"

Caro's irritation at this tirade was growing by the minute, and finally she pushed herself away from him and raised a warning finger.

"That is quite enough, sir! I refuse to stand here and be slandered by the likes of you! You rogue! You are a fine one to talk of spell-casting, for you surely must be expert in the art! Now tell me, what is the point of this insulting attack upon me?"

Alec's eyes were blazing back at her, but she met them unflinchingly, her chin raised in hostile defiance.

"Come here, you hellcat," he commanded in a menacingly low tone. Caro took a rebellious step backward and with one swift movement he caught her and imprisoned her in his arms.

"Bitch," he whispered, but his voice caressed the word and Caro shivered. "You ask me to come to the point, and I can see it is too late to pray for deliverance from my fate. I am up to my ears in this, and God knows it's probably been a lost cause from the moment I pulled that hat from your head in the woods of Connecticut."

Caro was holding her breath, afraid to exhale for fear of breaking the spell that held them. Alec stared at her before speaking again, and Caro could see his soul revealed in his incredible turquoise eyes.

"Damn you, Caro, you've got me. I'm out of my mind with love for you."

His mouth seared into hers with an intensity that left Caro breathless and shaking. He kissed her again and again, crushing her ribs with arms that felt like bands of steel, his lips possessive and reverent, merciless and tender by turns as he tasted every inch of her sweet flesh. Blood was pounding in Caro's head and her breasts pulsed warmly beneath Alec's deft fingers as he undid the hooks down the front of her gown. Her nipples stood out in little peaks against her thin chemise and he swiftly tore it away from her, his mouth burning her breasts while evoking a hungry, shameless response in her. Without wasting a movement, Alec undressed her. Caro's fingers reached out to fumble with his buttons until he came to her aid, and as she pulled his garments away from his hard, well-muscled body he was surprised to feel her hands touching him eagerly. Caro kissed the lean ridges of his stomach and caressed his muscular buttocks, then she heard him groan softly and suddenly he bent to lift her effortlessly in his arms. In a shadowed corner of the parlor, he laid her down on the Oriental rug and they made love with an urgent ecstasy that imprinted itself permanently on both their hearts.

Afterward, Caro was sure that it was all a dream; even while she moved and spoke and touched, she was not convinced that she was dealing with reality.

They did not sleep at all that night. Alec pulled his fine linen shirt over Caro's head and, wearing only his breeches, led her upstairs to their bedroom. Before joining her in the big bed, he went to the dressing room and returned carrying a small velvet box. Caro's eyes shone with excitement as she looked at it, afraid to hope.

"Little one, this is your Christmas and wedding present both. Enjoy it—God knows it has been justly earned!"

There was a tiny button on the front of the box that released the catch, and when it flew open Caro beheld the most perfect ring she had ever seen. Bringing it near the candle which burned at the bedside, she saw that it consisted of a dazzling circular diamond surrounded by smaller emeralds so that it resembled a flower. The band was of rich gold, and the inscription inside read:

"C—I love you—A 1783."

She closed her eyes in an effort to still the tumult in her heart, and felt Alec take her hand, sliding the cool ring down her finger. He kissed her palm tenderly, declaring, "Our marriage is real now, truly consummated this night. I cannot play at love anymore, Caro."

Something snapped inside her, and she threw her arms about his neck, crying, "Alec, I cannot believe this is happening. I never thought I would have the opportunity to tell you that—I love you. Oh, how I love you."

He grinned in the old way she adored.

"I know—you have told me already."

A puzzled frown puckered her brow. "I do not understand—"

"I fear that I have long held the advantage over you, *chérie,* for I inadvertently learned of your true feelings early on. I had my suspicions anyway, but you confirmed them while we were at Van DerPat Manor."

"What do you mean?"

"Just this. Do you recall the first day that you regained consciousness—the day I came into your room and found you out of bed?"

"Yes . . ." she allowed hesitantly.

"I take it then that you have not forgotten the quarrel we had on that occasion? I believe it came about as a result of your introduction to Gretchen."

Caro's eyes narrowed at the name. "Please come to the point!" she demanded.

Alec laughed, obviously enjoying himself, then said, "Don't rush me, infant." Pausing, he rubbed his cheek in mock forgetfulness. "Oh, yes! I believe that Katrina paid you a long-winded visit after I left, during which I amused myself, finally deciding that due to your weakened condition an apology from me was really in order. So, I went back to your room, opening the door to find you asleep. I went to your bedside and took your hand, thinking to rouse you. However, you grasped at it quite eagerly, never opening your eyes, and said in a clear voice, 'Oh, Alec—I love you!' "

"Do not say it!" Caro gasped in horror. "You are making this up!"

"It is God's truth! Do you take me for a liar as well as a rogue?"

"Oh, dear," Caro moaned, color flooding her cheeks. "What did you do?"

"Needless to say, I got away from there with all possible speed. I was terrified for the first time in my life —quaking with fright before a silly, impetuous little minx. Let me tell you, I was mad at myself as well as you."

"I remember you that night when I came down to the library. You were horrid."

"Believe me, sweetheart, I felt horrid. I suppose I continued to feel that way until our friend Pilque-binder conveniently took matters out of my hands. I don't know if I could have ever brought myself to face the truth otherwise."

"Please, Alec, do not behave as though you have been so badly beaten. You have the attitude of a wild horse broken against its will! I have no wish to tame you or take away the magnificent spirit that sets you apart from all other men. It is your very wildness that I love most! If you will only let me be your friend and share your life I will be the happiest woman in the world."

His eyes sparkled with humor as he put a dark hand against her cheek.

"Do not deceive yourself, Caro. You are, in your way, as spirited as I am, so stop acting so meek. I appreciate your offer to just blend into my woodwork, but I expect a great deal more from you than that. Never stop giving me hell and a good time, or I will lose interest in you. I am unversed in the ways of true love—for all I know, in my case, it may be only temporary. I have every confidence in your abilities, however, so don't give me that forlorn look." Idly, he ran a finger over her shoulder. "This conversation grows tiresome. Why don't you put out that candle and let us explore some of the finer points of wedded bliss." Caro blew out the candle and turned eagerly to embrace her husband.

Chapter Twenty-five

THE DINING-ROOM TABLE FAIRLY GROANED BENEATH its sumptuous burden, displaying an array of dishes filled with everything to delight the senses. A large golden-brown turkey dominated the feast, accompanied by a roast goose and a huge Christmas pie which contained large quantities of different birds. There were vegetables of every sort and three types of fragrant biscuits and muffins, plus a variety of imported wines which were disappearing with amazing speed.

Antonia sat near the center of the table, flanked by Nicholai and Katya. She found that she had little appetite, for her mind was preoccupied by Caro and Alec. Her son had insisted that Grandmère occupy the hostess's chair at the opposite end of the table, placing Caro next to him. As if that wasn't odd enough, they were behaving as if they were completely alone in the crowded room. Alec seldom released her hand, and they whispered and laughed together like the most ardent young lovers.

Antonia was naturally pleased by what she saw, but nevertheless, quite perplexed. Caro and Alec had been a baffling riddle from the very beginning, and each time she saw them her confusion deepened. Although her rakish son, with his cool mockery for life itself, had always been rather an enigma to her, she was totally beyond comprehension of him this time.

If only we had not been in France when he first brought her to Philadelphia, she thought in frustration. Unlike Natalya, she was not inquisitive by nature, and she knew that her lack of maternal meddling had kept Alec closer to her. Often, after a brandy or two, he would let down his defenses and confide a little in her. This time, however, it was obvious that he was keeping his own counsel.

I should not be so curious, she admonished herself. As long as they are happy, that is all that matters. It is none of my affair after all.

Dessert was served then, everyone exclaiming at the sight of the plum pudding in a blaze of blue, brandy-fed flames. There was mince pie, too, and Katya solemnly told Caro that if she did not eat a piece on each of the twelve days of Christmas, she would not be happy during the twelve months to come. Alec laughingly warned her to make them small, declaring that he would not tolerate a fat wife, no matter how happy she might be.

After dinner, everyone repaired to the south parlor which was warm and cozy with its evergreen trimming, the decorated tree, and the steadily burning Yule log. The entire house was fragrant with pine and the aromas of delicious food. However, the spirit of Christmas was most evident in the eyes of Alec and Caro.

Pierre appeared in the doorway bearing a huge silver wassail bowl. Today it was brimming with hot lambswool, which Caro learned was a mixture of ale, sugar, spices, eggs, and roasted apples to which thick cream had been added, with sippets of French bread. Everyone raised their cups to toast Christmas, exchanging an embrace with whomever stood nearest. Alec bent to hug his mother and lightly lifted her off the floor.

"Why don't you and I go out and look at the mistle-

297

toe?" he inquired, turquoise eyes dancing. Antonia smiled up at him and raised her eyebrows.

"I should like that very much!"

Laughing, he leaned over to whisper to Caro, then took his mother's arm and strolled from the room. They passed under the arch dividing the entryway, the mistletoe forgotten. Alec leaned against the door frame of the north parlor, still holding her hand thoughtfully.

"Dear Maman, I suppose you are wildly curious to know what is going on with Caro and me!" he said frankly. Antonia flushed.

"Why, Sacha, that is a terrible thing to say! How could you accuse me—"

"I see you do not deny it!" he laughed, leading her inside to sit on the yellow damask settee. "Actually, I feel rather guilty for not speaking to you earlier about this. I will not pretend to tell you the entire story, but there are some facts which Caro and I both feel you have a right to know."

"Sacha, you must not feel obligated—"

"No, it will help to clear matters up among us. Caro loves my family and is very devoted to you in particular, so I have every hope that you two will form a strong bond as time goes by. She is a poor liar and it distresses her to deceive anyone—particularly those people she is fond of. So, this is as much for her as for you, Maman."

"Well, since you put it that way," she twinkled, "I have been wondering . . ."

Alec's mouth quirked as he lounged back against the settee and crossed his long legs.

"I suppose the most important thing—and the hardest to believe—is that I am actually in love with that little girl. She probably is a witch, but whatever the reason, I find I am totally captivated. The reason that you have witnessed such extremes in our relationship is that I was fighting against that persistent emotion

298

with all the violent futility of a moth caught in a spider's web. Looking back at all the ludicrous things I said and did, I can see that I was lost right from the beginning."

"I suppose that the thought of defeat at such delicate hands was a hard dose for you to swallow!" Antonia commented with a knowing smile.

"Well said, Maman. During the weeks since Caro and I met, I have quite frequently behaved abominably. Of course that is nothing new for me, but the circumstances seemed to alter when Caro was affected. Anyway, since our marriage I have gradually come to face the truth, and now I feel enormously relieved."

Deciding not to inquire into the reason for their strange, hasty wedding, Antonia replied, "She is a rare girl, Sacha. I cannot describe the pleasure one derives from seeing Caro look so radiant."

"You need not make an attempt, for I have been basking in her glow these last eighteen hours. I am delighted to realize that I have been able to give her the happiness she deserves."

Antonia stood up, reaching out to touch his shining black hair.

"It has been years since I heard you use the word 'delight' unless it was in sarcasm. That is enough to make this Christmas memorable for me."

Christmas was not formally over until the sixth of January. On the Twelfth Night, Alec bundled Caro and Grandmère into the sleigh and they rode into Philadelphia to help the family dismantle all their Christmas decorations. They drank hot buttered rum, and when they were done, Jean-Philippe tossed the accumulation of dry pine boughs in to burn with the barely glowing remnants of their Yule log.

Grandmère had brought along a carefully wrapped Twelfth-cake, which Caro learned she had baked herself every year since her marriage. It was a splendid confection, dark with spices and fruit, heavily iced, and decorated with gold and silver stars, brightly colored flowers and crowns, and miniature figures of the Three Kings.

Mary Armstrong had dropped by to lend a friendly hand, and Caro found her company distinctly pleasing. Not only did she enjoy talking to her, but the sight of Nicholai laughing heartily at Mary's witticisms brought her profound relief. His emerald eyes twinkled with familiar gaiety, and when he spoke to Caro, she could see that the angry pain had gone from them, fading away with the bruise on his cheekbone.

The crowning moment came with the cutting of the Twelfth-cake. Jean-Philippe placed a generous slice on Caro's plate, explaining, "My mother has baked a bean and a pea into this cake. Whoever finds the bean becomes the Twelfth Night King and the girl with the pea will be the Queen."

"But what happens if they find the wrong ones?" she asked.

"If that is the case, then the finders may choose a partner and we will have two sets of 'royalty,' " laughed Jean-Philippe.

Everyone fell silent as they ate their cake, while the suspense built. Katya impatiently broke her portion up with her fork, suddenly exclaiming:

"Look, look! *Regardez-moi!* I have found the bean!"

Grandmère beamed at the little girl.

"Alors, Queen Katya, you must choose a king."

Without a moment's hesitation, she scrambled off her chair, black braid flying, and ran into Alec's arms. He embraced her lovingly, hoisting her onto his lap with a gallant smile.

"I am honored, your highness," he declared with mock gravity.

Across the table, Nicholai produced the pea and Caro's heart began to pound with apprehension. She knew, however, that the last of her worries were over when he turned to Mary and grinned. Her china-blue eyes went wide with surprised delight as Nicholai transferred her onto his lap and proceeded to kiss her until Jean-Philippe cleared his throat.

Caro couldn't recall ever feeling such bubbling contentment, and it showed in the smile that she turned on Alec and Katya.

"This is a wonderful tradition," she declared, then leaned forward to speak confidentially to her little sister-in-law.

"Tell me, is there a reason why those two pieces of cake were set aside? I thought perhaps I could take them home to Pierre and Rose."

"No!" cried Katya. "Those were cut for God and Our Lady! We must keep them here for the first poor person who comes to our house. If Pierre is very poor, I suppose he might qualify, but he must come here to get them!" She paused, considering. "It seems very odd that you do not know about the pieces for God and Our Lady. Didn't you have a Twelfth-cake at your house before you married Sacha?"

Caro raised panicky eyes to Alec, who interceded coolly. "Listen, your highness, don't you know that it's only in France that portions are kept for God and Our Lady? Probably everyone else in Philadelphia who is having Twelfth-cake tonight is eating the *whole* thing!"

"Really?" Katya answered, while Caro breathed a sigh of relief.

"Yes," he replied, adding smoothly: "Besides, Caro is Swedish, and in Sweden they do not have Twelfth-cakes at all."

"Not at all?" she echoed in horrified tones. Caro smiled thankfully at her husband over Katya's head, and he winked back.

301

Chapter Twenty-six

WITH CHRISTMAS BEHIND THEM, CARO SAW MANY changes begin in her life with Alec. Now that his personal life was in order, Alec began to devote more time to his business interests. Caro knew also that he had men watching for Ezra Pilquebinder, but he still refused to let down his guard, and that was fine with her.

By mid-January, there was a tremendous thaw which brought with it springlike temperatures. Alec began making daily trips into Philadelphia, and Caro was his constant companion, whom he treated with the same lighthearted comradeship that he accorded his male acquaintances. She preened when he spoke to her about his business dealings, even in the presence of his friends. With great patience, Alec set out to acquaint her with the ships he owned, the newspaper he helped to publish, and the overall administration of the five-hundred-acre estate on which Belle Maison stood. On several occasions, he brought her along to Bradford's London Coffee House, where merchants gathered to discuss all the latest news concerning ships, prices, and politics. Alec was proud of his lovely young wife and his acquaintances beamed with approval at the happy couple.

Caro learned quickly, and before long was able to converse easily with him and his acquaintances on almost any subject, including politics. Alec's friends, among whom were Gouverneur Morris and the electrifying writer, Philip Freneau, began to visit their home with growing frequency. Alec invariably invited Caro to join them, and none of the men seemed to mind her charming presence or her interested participation in their conversations.

Gradually, Alec began to relate to her some of his experiences during the war. Although he glossed casually over his own risks and the dangers involved, Caro could sense from his generalities that his exploits had been seasoned with his usual reckless flair.

Her own impressions of the war were vague, so when Alec mentioned battles and names Caro was in total ignorance. Slowly, she began to piece together the story of his part in the Revolution, frequently turning to Pierre for help. At night, when she lay in Alec's arms after lovemaking, he would smoke while she gently questioned him. This was Caro's favorite time of day, for they were both mellow with satisfaction and love for each other, and Alec's voice would caress her lazily in the darkness.

She learned that he had actually spent much of the war in the company of the army, being present when Washington had crossed the Delaware River at the end of 1776 to surprise the Hessians at Trenton and win the first great victory of the war. Later, in the fall of the next year, he had accompanied his friend Kosciuszko up the Hudson River to Bemis Heights. Caro heard of Kosci's talent in laying the American defenses before a battle.

"As an engineer, his genius and inventiveness were unsurpassed," Alec told her frankly. "And his devotion to the cause of liberty—all over the world—is single-minded."

He described in sketchy terms his roaming life as an American spy, never mentioning the ill-fated love affair with Emily, and Caro could see no trace of pain

—or regret—in his eyes when he spoke of those days. However, he never explained the reason why he had suddenly changed his wartime role, joining his father on board a privateer which had been converted just before the British began their occupancy of Philadelphia. The American Navy had been sadly wanting, so many of the more prosperous shipowners had outfitted their own crafts to attack and take enemy vessels. Originally Jean-Philippe had built the few smaller, sleek boats to outmaneuver and outsail England's restrictive trade acts, but now, with the war, they served a different purpose. Father and son captained the two main crafts which had black hulls bisected by a yellow stripe between the wales, while the four smaller boats were painted in contrasting colors. Alec remained with his ship, until 1779, when eighteen-year-old Nicholai had replaced his brother, who had left to join Francis Marion's guerrilla band in South Carolina.

Graphically, Alec recounted their adventures on board the privateer, and Caro listened with high interest. One night he told her about their friend Philip Freneau's war experience aboard a privateer, a story which made her more thankful than ever for Alec's constant luck in eluding the enemy.

"Jesus," he declared, "Freneau had the fates against him. I was with Marion during the time when Philip built and captained the *Aurora,* but I was regaled from people on the coast with tales of his daring command. I always felt that if you forgot the danger in an exploit, you would be secure, and strangely enough, it always worked for me. Somehow, the more I laughed, the safer I became. Sad to say, our friend was not so lucky. He managed a few narrow escapes in his colorful career aboard his privateer, but in the end he was captured and finished the war aboard a prison ship. Fortunately, Cornwallis' surrender followed shortly and he was released." Alec laughed. "I

304

get the definite feeling, however, that he has lost his taste for adventure."

"You should not make fun of him," Caro teased, "since, after all, your own wild youth is behind you."

As soon as it was out, she regretted the jibe, and when Alec pushed her playfully back against the pillows, she could not have been more surprised.

"Do not say so, madame," he admonished her, white teeth gleaming in the darkness. "As long as you share my bed, my life will never be tame."

Caro awoke one morning early in February to find Alec already out of bed and shaving. A lacy pattern of fluttering snowflakes met her eyes when she sat up to look out the window, and she sprang out of bed like a child to press her face against the glass.

"Snow!" she cried. "It's snowing again at last! I was beginning to believe that winter was only a joke!"

Alec set down his razor and joined her at the window, wrapping his arms around her body, clad in its thin lawn bedgown.

"Either it's an evil omen or a good one," he murmured, inhaling the sweet fragrance of her hair. "With snow, it's hard to tell."

Caro laughed and led him firmly back to the basin, standing on her toes to finish shaving him.

"I'll have you trained yet, my dear," he said, while carrying her back to the bed. Caro's dimples quivered beneath his smoldering gaze, but he surprised her by only smoothing back her honey-colored curls.

"I have something to tell you. I meant to give you the news last night, but I was mysteriously distracted." He smiled recalling the passion—ever growing—they had shared. "The truth is that I have received word that our friend Pilquebinder has left Philadelphia at last. He was bound for Boston at last sighting, and I shall be duly informed if he should chance to reappear in our vicinity."

"Well! That's wonderful news!"

"I was sure you would be pleased," he replied, sitting up to wipe a stray spot of soap left on his cheek. "This will mean a great deal more time alone for you, *chérie*. You will not need to accompany me everywhere from now on."

Caro's face fell, but Alec, sitting on the edge of the bed, did not see her reaction.

"Oh," she said blankly.

"I have already made provisions in town for accounts for you in all the best shops. I give you a free hand to choose whatever you like for the house; I have heard that there have been numerous shipments from France of late, and I'm sure that Maman or Molly Morris would be happy to give you any help you may desire."

In the midst of buttoning his shirt, he glanced back at her over his shoulder. Caro sat in the middle of the spacious Hepplewhite bed looking very forlorn.

"Listen, sweetheart," he told her firmly, "I expect you to stand on your own two feet. Stop looking as if you have been deserted, for that is not my wish or intention. You must not become too dependent on me, though—isn't that clear to you?"

She gulped loudly and nodded. Relenting, Alec smiled and went to her, and Caro told him softly, "I only like to be with you!"

"And I like to be with you, *chérie*. Do not worry— you shall never be neglected as long as you are my wife."

As he bent to kiss her, Caro found the buttons of his shirt and unfastened them with a newly acquired proficiency. "Vixen," he murmured as she pulled him back onto the bed.

Alec was firm in his conviction regarding their need for separate interests, and as spring approached Caro's horizons were rapidly expanding. She made many new friends, for people appeared to like her on sight, and her new sense of self-worth enriched the quality of her marriage to Alec.

During February, she followed his suggestion, enlisting Molly Morris and Antonia to help her add her own touch to the decoration of Belle Maison. Her mother-in-law expounded with enthusiasm on the new wallpaper being stocked by William Poyntell in his recently expanded South Second Street shop.

"Since we just redecorated this house shortly before the war broke out, it is out of the question for me to indulge in such extravagances," she told Caro. "But, it will be almost as much fun to share your shopping trips and I will truly enjoy answering any questions you may have. I am particularly anxious to visit Poyntell's, for he is blatantly advertising paper hangings 'of the most modern and tastey . . . patterns, suitable for every part of a house,'" she quoted blithely.

Caro found that most of these "modern and tastey patterns" reflected the new Chinese influence. Trade was opening up with the Orient, while Europe had already begun to produce their own interpretations of Chinese design in everything from furniture to pottery. The wallpaper patterns were uniquely appealing, and Caro decided to use two of them at Belle Maison. The upstairs sitting room in which she and Alec frequently had afternoon tea was done over with an arborescent design in varying shades of blue. It was a huge success, and Caro went ahead with confident enthusiasm to have one of the extra bedrooms papered with a delicate pattern of tree peonies and cherry blossoms against a pale-gray background.

To celebrate her good taste and accomplishment, Alec had a new desk delivered to Caro, along with all the proper pens, ledgers, and other tools necessary for keeping household accounts. A room on the second floor adjoining the library was converted into a small, feminine study for her, and Caro was fully cognizant of the compliment intended. From that day on, she was in complete charge of the household, and Alec never questioned her judgment. She planned the meals, oversaw the help, inspected the housekeeping, and balanced the books. An unlimited supply of money was put at her disposal, but Caro was scrupulously careful not to abuse her husband's generosity and trust. In fact, it soon reached the point where he enlisted Caro's friends as informers to keep him posted on the things she dreamed idly about having. Then, when Caro thought he was making an inspection of a new ship, Alec would pay a visit to William Savery, the cabinetmaker, or the currently fashionable dressmaker. More than once, Caro looked up from her eggs at breakfast to see a new highboy or perhaps a dozen elegant gowns being brought up the front steps. Alec would lower his newspaper enough to raise one dark eyebrow in his reckless way, and Caro would fall in love all over again.

In early March they made a joint decision to redecorate the north and south parlors, and Alec took time out from his business life to accompany Caro on her shopping excursions. She was determined to have his taste incorporated into those two important rooms, and he found it impossible to say no to her pleading brown eyes. Besides, it gave him an excuse to spend extra time with her, and that was a luxury they both enjoyed to the fullest.

The two rooms ended up as eloquent expressions of the happy Beauvisage marriage. The north parlor was decorated in shades of emerald green, with tapering damask-covered Chippendale furniture and a highly colored English rug patterned with flowers. The walls were painted a delicate pale green, a task which Caro decided she would execute herself. It took nearly a week, even with Grandmère, Pierre, Natalya, and Alec lending their help, and by the time it was done, Caro had abandoned any plans for the painting of the other rooms. The day the furniture arrived a surprise gift from Jean-Philippe was delivered—a fabulous glass and ormolu chandelier. Pictures and fresh flowers were added to complete the effect, and from then on, no one ever entered Belle Maison without effusively complimenting the room.

The south parlor was not as striking, but no less lovely when finished. Cream walls and furniture upholstered in a mellow shade of gold combined for a rich, relaxing effect. A beautiful Kuba rug woven in a pattern of ochre, gold, and sea blue added a bright touch, and when the afternoon sun poured into the room it was Caro's favorite spot in the house.

When the bills began to arrive, Caro went out to Alec's little office behind the greenhouse to show them to him. She was horrified at the amounts, but he merely laughed and pulled her down on his lap.

"I adore that concerned little frown of yours, sweetheart," he murmured while nuzzling the soft hollow at the base of her throat. With one careless gesture he removed the lawn modesty piece which Rose had placed inside the low-cut neckline of her gown.

"If you have any more of these, throw them away."

As his lips found her breasts, Caro's heart began to beat with such force that she could scarcely think.

"Alec. Alec! You must not—"

"Indeed?" he replied coolly, arching an eyebrow. "I suppose that you propose to stop me?"

"I believe you must be mad!"

"Mad for you, m'lady." He smiled while unfastening the first three hooks on her bodice. "Ah, but your skin is sweet."

His lips burned the hidden places that were so tenderly susceptible to his touch. The nerves that ran down to her thighs tingled warningly, but somehow Caro found her voice:

"I meant that you must be mad to have allowed

me to make such extravagant purchases! Have you seen these bills?"

With a superhuman effort, she pulled the top of her bodice closed and crossed her legs in an attempt to put out the fire that was smoldering there. Alec leaned back in his chair and reached for the cheroot that lay smoking in the pewter dish, his lips quivering faintly as he regarded his wife.

"Am I to take this as a rejection, my love? Have my kisses lost their appeal for you so soon?"

Caro ignored the sparkle in his eyes as she thrust the pile of bills at him.

"I did not come over here to be seduced in broad daylight where someone could walk in at any moment!"

"Pity." He looked sad, then brightened suddenly. "Would you like me to lock the door?"

"No!" Her face was flushed in a combination of anger and embarrassment. "Stop laughing at me, Alexandre Beauvisage. You should not make fun of me when I am trying to be serious!"

"I cry pardon, dear wife. Pray continue."

Caro fumbled with the hooks on her gown and Alec grinned, placing the cheroot between his teeth as he deftly came to her aid.

"I only wish to know if you realized how much you have spent on our redecoration of Belle Maison!" she cried at last in desperation.

"Am I to understand that you are doubting my ability to meet these bills?" he asked in amusement.

"Well, not exactly, but these figures—"

"Yes, prices have become quite prohibitive these days. Just sign the bills, Caro, and do not worry so. Haven't you learned yet to trust me?"

"Of course, but—"

"Your penchant for contradiction is growing quite annoying, sweetheart. Can't you get it through that pretty head of yours that we are wealthy?"

"We are?" she echoed, wide-eyed.

"Definitely. Actually, wealth and prosperity are running rampant in Philadelphia these days. I fear it's a natural reaction to that long war. The collapse will come before long, but you may rest assured that we will not be greatly affected."

"You are certain?"

"Trust me," he repeated, and Caro found that she did. Relaxing, she leaned against his chest and let him kiss her.

"Alec," she said as he reached over the desk to put out his cheroot. "How is it that you can be rich when you are so young? It is particularly difficult to understand since you were fighting in the war these last years."

He laughed, but his eyes were serious as he said, "My father has a favorite quotation by Edward Young that he emphasized to me early in life. It is: 'Youth is not rich in time: it may be poor. Part with it as with money, sparing—.' I never forgot that and it has always been my feeling that my youth was the best and most productive time of my life—I was determined not to waste it. So, I sought adventure, but I also made certain that I would never have to worry about a living. Money is not much on my mind, but that is because I know that I have an unlimited supply. I know how to make it with a minimum of effort, so you must never trouble yourself with the size of our bills. There will always be plenty of funds to cover them, my love."

Caro's eyes twinkled. "I am glad to hear that. And now that I have no more cause for worry . . ." Her voice trailed off as she snuggled against him, but Alec's mobile eyebrow flew up in mock horror.

"Madame, you cannot be suggesting that I seduce you here—in broad daylight—where someone could burst in at any moment!"

"Well," she allowed, "perhaps you ought to lock the door."

Chapter Twenty-seven

TULIPS AND DAFFODILS BEGAN TO PEEK THROUGH THE dark earth as spring came in late March. Alec and Caro were soon stopping on their way to the stables each morning to check the progress in the garden. Little by little it began to bloom, the end result more beautiful than Caro had ever imagined, and Alec was well pleased. Purple wisteria cascaded lusciously down the arbor wall, while bright pansies, bearded iris, azaleas, and sweet william crowded the boxwood-edged beds in brilliant profusion. They both agreed that the garden was a bit wild and riotous as a result of its neglect during the war, further deciding that they liked it that way. Grandmère was delighted, and as the air grew fresh and sweet, she began to venture outside to paint each afternoon.

The meadows behind the estate where each day they rode Ivan and Molly grew lush and green, dotted with wild flowers. Alec began wearing his finely cut jackets less and less, appearing most often in only an open-weave muslin shirt, fawn-colored breeches, and jockey boots. Caro's wardrobe was altered as well, at Alec's insistence. They went into Philadelphia in early April to visit the dressmaker, who fitted her for dozens of new spring gowns. Most were of the finest soft muslin, in delicate sprig patterns or light stripes. The hemlines were at the ankle now, a fashion that Alec heartily endorsed. He also insisted on buying her several pretty parasols to match her dresses. Caro pleaded for some chip straw bonnets which framed her face appealingly; each tied under her chin with a ribbon of a different color. Alec also arranged to have seven new riding habits made for her—one for each day of the week.

They stopped briefly at the house on Third Street before returning home, and found Eliza Powel there having tea with Antonia. It was she who hinted broadly that the newly married Beauvisage couple should be considering the idea of giving a party. On the drive home, Alec told Caro why.

"Her motives are ridiculously transparent," he said cynically. "The run on the Bank of North America has brought a sudden halt to the gay social life here in Philadelphia. Did I tell you that sixty thousand pounds worth of Robert Morris's bills have gone to protest? I would not be surprised if Eliza Powel should simply wither up and die without her customary rounds of parties!"

Behind his sardonic laughter, Caro could sense that he was thinking. He looked out across the woodlands as they drove along, and she watched him, noticing that his face was tanner than ever, his turquoise eyes even more startling in contrast.

"Well," he said at last, "I hate like hell to accommodate Eliza, but perhaps her idea has some merit. You deserve a party to show off what you've done with Belle Maison and I have been incredibly bemused not to have realized it myself."

"Alec, I do not need a party! As long as I have you, my social life is busy enough."

"No, I really think it's a good idea. People have probably been wondering and gossiping about you and I shall enjoy setting them straight."

Caro wrinkled her nose with a mischievous smile as she said, "Now that you mention it, I wouldn't mind

313

gloating at the jealous expressions on the faces of the former women in your life!"

In the end, they compromised with a small-scale garden party. Caro sent out handwritten invitations to a dozen of Alec's contemporaries and a dozen of the older, more established families. Everyone accepted eagerly, and as the date for the party approached, her own excitement increased surprisingly. Grandmère assured her that she was perfectly justified in her pride at being Alec's wife.

"You have every right to want to show him off," she said firmly. *"Sans doute,* you would be impossibly smug and self-satisfied if you had been *autour d'ici* to see the shameless way that all the women of Philadelphia pursued him these past ten years or more."

The day of the party was warm, even for April, with white puffs of clouds floating in the clear azure sky. Caro bustled around the house all morning with several of the serving girls at her side, while Alec retreated to his office outside.

"Flowing bowls" of port and rum punch were prepared for Alec's approval, with a dozen varieties of tea cakes and cookies. Caro had decided to leave the front and rear doors open, so that the guests could mingle wherever they chose.

Crabapple, magnolia, and dogwood trees were in full bloom across the velvety lawn in front of Belle Maison, and the air was filled with their sweet fragrance. It was as beautiful and inviting there as in the garden.

Alec returned to share a light luncheon with his wife, then accompanied her upstairs to dress. Caro went into her adjoining bedchamber where Rose was waiting to assist her, while Pierre was on hand to help Alec, a task that he seldom performed now that his master was married.

Rose arranged Caro's hair so that it fell in a cluster

of soft ringlets, intertwined with narrow yellow ribbons and magnolia blossoms. Honey-colored tendrils curled against her cheeks, accentuating her fresh beauty. The gown she wore was a light muslin, sprigged in yellow, that made her look as lovely as any spring flower in the garden. Rose fastened a lace-edged yellow ribbon around her neck, and the only jewelry she wore was the stunning emerald-and-diamond ring. After a sparing application of Alec's favorite jasmine-scented perfume, Caro stood back to regard herself critically in the mirror. Rose clasped her hands with a rapturous sigh.

"Madame, if I may say so, you look truly beautiful! You have always had rare good looks, but there is something in your eyes now—"

"Love," Caro replied with a wide smile. She paused at the faint sound of laughter outside and ran to the window. A carriage stood outside that she immediately recognized as belonging to Gouverneur Morris.

"The guests are beginning to arrive!" she exclaimed, and was running to the door when Alec's voice drifted up the stairs. "Alec has gone down without me!"

Since Gouverneur was such a good friend, Caro felt no need to stand on ceremony and decided to join them without waiting for Alec to return to escort her. Lifting her skirts, she scampered down the hall to the top of the stairs, but froze there as the smile died on her lips. Madeleine Chamberlain stood in the middle of the sun-drenched entry hall, her red hair gleaming as she gazed up at Alec. Caro took in the white hand that she laid on his arm, as well as the spark that flared in Alec's eyes. In the back of her mind, she could hear Mary Armstrong laughing, "I've yet to have him bestow on me one of those burning looks that Madeleine Chamberlain is always receiving . . . he adores her body."

As she began to wonder if she might be sick right there, Gouverneur glanced up and spotted her.

"Ah! So here is our little buttercup! Madeleine, doesn't Caro look lovely?"

Madeleine leveled poisonous violet eyes at Caro and purred, "She does look rather sweet, Gouverneur. So charmingly childlike."

His eyes danced with humor as he replied, "Do try to keep your claws concealed, my dear. Next you'll be hissing aloud."

Alec laughed as he went to the stairway to meet Caro.

"You look enchanting, my love," he told her. "Like a ray of sunshine straight from heaven."

The two women came face to face, Madeleine's eyes filled with such hatred and jealousy that Caro instinctively drew nearer to Alec.

"I'm so sorry I did not make those arrangements sooner to introduce you to some young men. It seems that you had to settle for the first thing that came along," Madeleine said venomously.

"Egad!" Alec exclaimed dramatically. "I think I have just been wounded!"

Caro ignored him. "Perhaps I am an excellent judge of quality," she replied smoothly. "After meeting Alec, I realized that to look farther afield would be a waste of precious time."

"And of course you were placed in such a convenient position, living here under the guise of being his ward."

"It did rather help to fan the flame," she admitted with a frankness that left Madeleine at a loss.

Alec was watching this exchange in utter amusement, finally deciding that enough polite insults had been traded.

"This is all very entertaining, ladies, but I must call halt. I see the Shippens alighting from their carriage."

Gouverneur tactfully drew Madeleine into the parlor for a glass of rum punch while Alec grasped his wife's arm as she started out to greet the new arrivals.

"I'll not be judged guilty yet, m'lady. Madeleine's presence here is purely Gouverneur's doing—I had no knowledge of his plans."

Caro turned blazing eyes up to him and whispered, "That hussy! How dare she set foot in my house and act as if I am the intruder! I would like to—"

"Yes, I can well imagine, my little hellcat! For right now, you shall have to settle for bestowing your most charming smile on the Shippens."

Caro turned to find their guests already in the doorway and blushed hotly as Alec led her over to them. Mr. and Mrs. Edward Shippen were the parents of Peggy, who was now in exile with her husband Benedict Arnold. Mount Pleasant, the magnificent home that Arnold had obtained for his new wife, was located not far from Belle Maison. Ironically, Peggy was destined never to live there.

While Alec and Caro exchanged greetings with the Shippens, two more carriages drew up in the drive, and the party became lively. Within an hour, elegantly garbed figures with powdered hair were strolling through the house and garden, carrying on polished conversations as they imbibed freely of the punch. Caro found herself constantly separated from Alec, and she could not refrain from watching for his broad shoulders and raven hair every time the crowd shifted. All the guests seemed to want to talk to her, but she knew that she would have enjoyed herself more if not for the nagging worry of Madeleine Chamberlain's presence. More than once, she saw her with Alec, chatting brightly, and Caro's heart constricted painfully at the sight of them together. The fact that they made a strikingly attractive couple did not help. Madeleine was clad in sultry plum silk that clung to her alluringly, while large, brilliant sapphires gleamed against her creamy skin. Alec could have dressed with the intent of coordinating with her, for his handsome gray suit and Prussian blue waistcoat seemed to be made to go with Madeleine's gown.

It was evident that there was no romance brewing between Gouverneur and Madeleine, which made Caro wonder all the more what could have possessed him to bring her to Belle Maison. He was off in a deep conversation with Natalya or Mary Vining most of the afternoon, seldom even giving notice to Madeleine. She, in turn, only had eyes for Alec, and as the hours passed, Caro's imagination worked overtime as she watched her husband's reactions to his old flame.

By the time dusk began to cloak the garden, she gave up her hope that the guests would leave by evening. Alec went back to speak to the cook, and before long, hot food began to appear on the tables to replace the little teacakes. The men were now freely indulging in brandy as they ranged through the parlors, smoking cigars and long-stemmed pipes and discussing the latest financial crisis.

Antonia came to Caro's aid, seeming to sense that her thoughts were elsewhere. Candles were lit, and couples were seen sitting close together on the garden benches. It was a marvelous, starry night, perfect for love, Caro thought dismally.

She tried to console herself with the fact that her first party was an obvious success and everyone seemed charmed by the new mistress of Belle Maison. Also, Nicholai was constantly at the side of little Mary Armstrong, and Natalya was unusually ebullient under the attention paid her by three or four handsome men. Even Grandmère was in high spirits as she won game after game of whist from John Dunlap, who was the successful publisher of the *Pennsylvania Packet*. He remained cheerful in the face of defeat, and they laughed together through the evening.

Alec was not altogether inattentive. Caro found that this was particularly true whenever he noticed her in the company of another man. One after another they engaged her in conversation, staring at her golden beauty with open admiration. If Alec was in sight, he would suddenly loom up behind her, encircling her with a possessive arm, while giving the gentleman in question a pointed look. Then, just as Caro found herself cheering up, someone would appear to lure him away and Madeleine was usually lying in wait nearby.

It was almost eight o'clock when Nicholai interrupted her conversation with Philip Freneau to tell her that he and Mary were about to leave. Several guests had already departed, and Caro was immensely relieved to see the party coming to an end. Alec was nowhere to be seen, so she went to search him out so that he might bid his brother good-bye. After passing through the south parlor without spying his dark head, Caro realized with a qualm that she had not seen Madeleine lately, either. The garden appeared deserted at first, but a voice from the furthest shadows reached her ears and she backed up against the arbor wall, listening against her own will. As her eyes became accustomed to the darkness, she made out the figures of Alec and Madeleine standing close together on the footpath farthest away. She strained to make out their words, but could only recognize the teasing caress of Madeleine's voice. Then, as Caro's heart rose to catch in her throat, Alec grasped Madeleine's arm and they disappeared into the greenhouse.

Horrified, painful shock overcame her as she leaned against the cool stones, fragrant wisteria brushing her cheek. Through eyes blurred with tears, Caro saw Nicholai's handsome face swimming above her.

"Caro!" he exclaimed in alarm. "What is wrong? Are you ill?"

Alec watched Madeleine through narrowed eyes, wondering how a woman so coldly conniving could have ever managed to warm his bed so effectively. He thought of Caro's sweet, responsive body and guileless smile, and his annoyance grew. Madeleine was clutching at the lapels of his coat, cooing:

"Alexandre, darling, I have been positively *ill* these last months. All I could think of was you, *married,* and I have been existing only on the hope of seeing you alone. Why did you not call on me? I thought that everything was fine between us—particularly that night at your parents' after that ball—" Her voice broke dramatically as she squeezed out a small tear. Alec's lip curled in an expression far from sympathetic. "I know that that child must have trapped you somehow —there could be no other explanation. But that does not mean that it must end between us! I cannot see why you should be trapped in a marriage with someone so ill-suited, so unsophisticated—"

His fingers closed around her arms as he thrust her away in disgust.

"Please spare me the rest of this performance. I do not think my stomach can tolerate another sentence.

"Madeleine, I only brought you here to avoid making a scene outside where someone might hear me. I have something to say to you that has been on my mind all afternoon."

"Of course, darling . . ." she faltered, trying to ignore the painful grip of his lean brown hands.

"It is this: I want you to get out of my life for good and if I never see you again it will be a relief. You've insulted Caro from the beginning, and since I've known her I've grown increasingly revolted with myself for ever having treated you so tenderly. I must have been mad."

Her violet eyes darkened with fury and disbelief.

"I don't believe you!" she shouted. "This is impossible! I refuse to take this from you, you bastard—or from her! That baby-faced, simpering—"

Alec was on the verge of striking her when Nicholai burst through the doorway. His fists were clenched with rage and veins stood out on his neck

as he strode up to his brother, ignoring the whining
Madeleine. Over Nicholai's shoulder, Alec perceived
Caro, ethereal in her white dress, coming toward the
greenhouse through the darkness. He did not even see
Nicholai's first punch, which caught him squarely on
the chin. Momentarily, he staggered into a bank of
orchids, but regained his balance. Raising a hand to
rub his jaw, he regarded his brother in irritated perplexity.

"What the hell is going on here? Has the whole
world gone mad?"

Nicholai advanced toward him, fists raised warningly.

"I have been wanting to do that for a long time.
You may have caught me at a bad moment that night
last December, but this time it will be a fair fight!"

"Are you suggesting that Caro should serve as the
prize again? You never learn, do you? I'll be damned
if I can figure this out—"

He ducked neatly as Nicholai swung at him again,
then brought one hard fist up into his chin, sending
him reeling back against the wall. Nicholai's eyes
blazed while a thin stream of blood trickled from the
side of his mouth.

"You are the worst sort of scoundrel, Sacha," he
said in a choked voice.

"And you are the worst sort of fool," Alec replied
coldly, raising a black brow. "Do not force me to
humiliate you any further."

At that, an enraged Nicholai jumped out and began to circle around his brother. When he made his
move this time, Alec dodged him easily and brought
his fist in hard to his stomach. Nicholai crumpled on
the dirt floor, groaning aloud, while Alec turned
away to find Caro standing in the doorway, her face
paper-white. Madeleine had disappeared. His eyes
were stormy as he walked over to her, leaving Nicholai where he had fallen.

"What do you know about this? Have you been leading him on again?"

Caro could barely comprehend his words, but as they began to sink in she felt all her hurt and anger explode. Without a moment's hesitation, she raised her little hand and slapped him with all the strength she could summon. For Alec, it was the last straw. With one sweeping movement, he caught both her wrists, briefly contemplating crushing the bones.

"What in the name of God is going on here?" he shouted, his eyes two blue flames. Caro saw the muscle in his cheek move warningly.

"You should know! You are the one carrying on clandestine trysts with Madeleine Chamberlain in the greenery while I keep our guests entertained! And *you*—you devil!—you have the audacity to accuse me—" As words failed her, she stamped her foot for emphasis, adding a frustrated "ooh!"

Alec was thinking hard, and as usual found it difficult to stay mad under the energetic fury of her attack.

"I have been called a lot of uncomplimentary names this evening!" he commented. Nicholai was struggling to his feet, and Alec went back to steady him. In a low voice, he inquired, "Am I to understand that you were defending Caro's honor here tonight?"

"That's right. Someone has to," he replied through clenched teeth.

"To be sure, dear brother," Alec smiled ironically. "Unfortunately, you needn't have bothered, for Caro has not been wronged. I was merely in here telling Madeleine all the reasons why I can't endure the sight of her."

Nicholai's eyes widened as an embarrassed flush crept into his face.

"I suppose I ought to mind my own business," he muttered.

"It would be a wise course. I really don't appreciate

322

your interference in my marriage, Nicky." He paused for a moment, considering. "One more thing—did Caro send you on this heroic mission?"

"No. It was all my doing. I found her crying against the arbor wall and she said she'd seen you taking Madeleine in here. I was furious, I can tell you. The thought of you hurting Caro again was more than I could bear. It opened up a lot of old wounds."

Alec nodded, glancing back over his shoulder to find that Caro was gone.

"Nicky, let us call a truce and get out of here. I have a lot of awfully complicated untangling to do tonight."

He handed him a handkerchief to clean the blood off his chin, and together the brothers walked back toward the house.

Mary met them at the edge of the garden, impulsively throwing her arms around Nicholai.

"Where have you been? Nicky, are you hurt? Your face! And what is wrong with Caro? She came running through here a few moments ago looking like she'd seen a ghost!"

Alec did not bother saying goodnight as he strode through the south parlor and took the stairs three at a time. When he reached their bedroom, he flung the door open to find the chamber empty. Wheeling around, he started down the hall, only to notice that the door leading to Caro's former bedroom was closed and a light shone under it. Knocking loudly, he shouted:

"Caro! Are you in there?"

The door opened just enough to allow Rose's long nose to peer out.

"Master Beauvisage, Mrs. Beauvisage is indisposed," she quavered. Alec towered above her like the devil incarnate.

"The hell she is! Open that door and get out of the way," he ground out in a dangerously even tone. Rose cast one sorry look back at Caro and did as she was told.

Alec slammed the door behind her retreating figure and turned to find Caro in her old Sheraton field bed, wearing a high-necked bedgown, with the covers pulled primly up to her throat. Although she strove for an icy expression, the wide brown eyes and flushed cheeks gave her away. Alec casually extracted a dark cheroot from a case in his vest pocket and walked over to light it with the candle on her nightstand. He stood there smoking, regarding her with cool turquoise eyes, as unreadable as they had been in the old days. Caro shifted uneasily and then mustered her nerve and raised her chin.

"You had no right to send Rose out or to force your way in here," she said in what she hoped was a haughty tone.

"You think not?" he returned blandly.

"No!" Caro faltered. "After all, I must have some rights—some privacy—"

"I beg to differ with you, madame. The day that you came into my room in that yellow gown, or more to the point, the day that you accepted my protection in the woods of Connecticut—you gave up all rights as far as I am concerned. And now, as long as you remain my wife you shall share my bed—willingly or not."

Imperceptibly, he narrowed his eyes, while lifting a black brow in a questioning arch.

Caro was feeling a pleasant sort of alarm, which heightened when Alec asked, "Whatever inspired you to put on that bedgown? It is a gesture I cannot appreciate." He stopped, and Caro saw a spark flare in his eyes. "You will swelter on a warm night like this with all those bedclothes, *chérie.*"

With a snap of his wrist he pulled the covers away from her.

"Alec!" Caro cried, excitement and outrage mixing in her voice. "I cannot allow you to—"

"It is not necessary that you give your permission, my dear," he broke in mildly. "You'll find that it really doesn't matter much one way or the other."

He leaned forward, grasping the neck of her gown, and ripped it cleanly down the front with one easy movement. Caro saw something flicker in his eyes that she could not read and, to her alarm, she felt herself shiver with an emotion quite unlike the outraged panic she knew she should have been feeling.

"Alec, how dare you?" The memory of Madeleine and him disappearing into the greenhouse flashed painfully into her mind, and her anger returned. "Are you so cold-blooded that you can be unfaithful with one woman and still turn back to your wife that same night?"

He came as close to striking her then as he ever had. Instead, he clenched his fists so hard that his flat nails bit into the palms and drew blood. Caro shrank back at the sight of his hand coming toward her, but he only grabbed her hair, twisting it around his wrist with a violence that brought her up on her knees. Her gown fell open, revealing swelling breasts and a smooth, flat stomach.

"You will regret those words, Caro, and the lack of trust you have shown me," he said in a tone of voice that chilled her heart. She fell back against the pillows when he released her, leaving her room the way he had come in. Caro cringed as the door closed with a resounding, final slam.

Chapter Twenty-eight

IT WAS A LONG, EMPTY NIGHT FOR ALEC AND CARO. Each expected the other to make the first move toward a reconciliation, but pride stood in both their ways.

Up at six o'clock, Alec dressed quickly in russet breeches, a roughly woven muslin shirt, and his softest boots. Without bothering to shave or button his shirt, he strode down the hall. Pierre was approaching from the opposite direction, but Alec did not slow his pace.

"I'm going riding," he growled.

"Mais, monsieur—" he began, but Alec was already on his way downstairs. Reaching the entry hall, he turned toward the door leading outside. At that moment, Caro rounded the corner of the dining room and they collided head-on, Alec's arms grasping her waist automatically to steady her. At the sight of the new cinnamon riding habit she wore, his eyes widened.

"Am I mistaken, or is it only six o'clock?"

"It is," Caro replied stiffly.

With that, he gripped her elbow and she half ran along beside him all the way to the stable. Silently, they mounted their horses and turned toward the meadow, Alec riding aggressively, raven hair ruffling in the fresh dawn air. At first, Caro lagged behind in an effort to ignore him, but soon realized that it would be impossible. Before long, Molly caught up to Ivan and they rode on and on at a pace that soon jolted Caro into forgetfulness.

The horses were growing winded when Alec reluctantly reined Ivan in near a lush thicket. Springing to the ground, he led the stallion toward the trees, and Caro followed suit. It was an incredibly beautiful spot, assailing the senses with all the best qualities of spring. The rich, soft grass was spattered with clusters of pink clover, the heady fragrance of which filled the air. The trees which grew close together in a circle were luxuriantly verdant; in fact the leaves were so dense that only a small amount of sunlight could penetrate into the copse. A clear stream ran along the perimeter, which Ivan and Molly found immediately, bending their handsome heads to drink.

Alec sauntered between the trees and dropped down to sit back on his heels in the bed of grass. Caro hesitated a few feet away, feeling uncomfortably nervous now that they were alone. The only sound was the quiet splashing from the stream where the horses were drinking, and with a pang Caro realized that Alec had not spoken a word to her since they left the house. His parting words the night before had terrified her, for she was only too well aware of the power of his temper. She had lain awake through the long hours of darkness, filled with bitter regret for the pride which had led her to that final confrontation with her husband. She had realized, too late, that he would not have come to her unless he intended to mend the trouble between them. A thousand times she berated herself for not going to their mutual bed in the first place. "I behaved like a child. Alec was right—I am his wife no matter what, and I owe him my trust. God knows that four months ago I'd have accepted him on any terms, in spite of anything he did."

Caro bit her lip, trying to decide what she should do, but before she could make up her mind, Alec's voice broke the silence.

"Come over here, infant," he said without looking back.

Eagerly she obeyed him, scrambling over to sit down as near as she dared. When he turned to meet her eyes, Caro was appalled at the exhaustion that showed on his face. Her heart melted. Wordlessly, Alec took her shoulders and eased her back into the deep grass, leaning across to kiss her with hungry passion. When his immediate need had been abated he relaxed, turning his scratchy cheek against hers, then closed his eyes and sighed deeply. Caro's arms went around his broad shoulders, straining to hold him ever closer, while hot tears of relief stung her eyelids. Finally, Alec laughed softly in her ear.

"Do you mean to break my neck?" he asked. "I was hoping to call a truce!"

"I was so afraid I'd ruined it for good last night, Alec. So afraid I'd never have you hold me again!"

His head went up and he brought his elbows around to hold himself off the ground as he gazed down at her.

"Sweetheart, I am sure we'll have other fights as serious as this one, so you mustn't be thinking I'll desert you just because I get mad."

Caro's words stumbled out: "I suppose the first one is the most frightening—especially with someone like you. I always feel like I am married to some untamed creature who must inevitably be free. It seemed that the moment had come last night! Oh, Alec, if you had only seen your face . . ."

He smiled a little and smoothed back her tousled curls.

"Yes, I've been told that I do appear rather intimidating when I'm angry. I never thought to see you cowed, though! Come to think of it, I guess you weren't at the time—seems to me you were quite courageous. And impertinent!"

Caro flushed, but a dimple winked in her cheek as she retorted, "Also stupid!"

"I'll admit that you were tempting fortune some-what, my dear! What I want to know is if you meant it. Did you really think I was making love to Madeleine last night?"

"I—well—"

"Damn!" he ejaculated, springing to his feet. Caro watched him stride a few yards, then stop, raking a hand through his black hair in aggravation. When he turned back to face her, his expression was one of barely suppressed fury.

"I really thought that you and I had built something meaningful these past months. Haven't I shown you that I love you? Have I been a fool to believe it is truly possible for unquestioning trust to exist in a relationship? Don't you know that the only reason I led such a varied love life in the past was because I simply didn't give a damn for any of them?" He moved back in front of her and hunkered down, roughly cupping her chin with a brown hand. "You really underestimate me, madame. Take my word for it now when I tell you that I can easily resist the allurements of any woman alive—with one possible exception—if I so choose."

"Who—who is the exception?" Caro quavered, her heart beating against her breastbone.

"You, for Christ's sake! And that's the last idiotic question I want to hear from you!" He paused, clenching his teeth as he sought control. When he continued, his voice was low. "Now, Caro, I believe I'll leave it at that. I had considered giving you a full explanation of what happened last night, but I don't care to waste my breath discussing this any further. If you can't stand it, you can go to Nicholai. I told him the whole story last night."

"You made up, then? I was afraid—"

"Yes," he replied briefly, then his tone lightened. "By the way, you wouldn't happen to know where

Madeleine ran off to, would you? I've never known her to retreat so quickly!"

Caro's cheeks grew pink as she guiltily looked away from Alec's sharp eyes. "Well—"

"Yes?"

"I sort of asked her to leave."

A black brow shot up.

"Asked? How, precisely?"

"I—ah—believe I told her to keep away from my husband or I'd scratch her purple eyes out," she replied in a low voice, staring at the blossoms of clover near Alec's knee. He looked at her in momentary disbelief, then slowly he began to laugh, finally tipping his head back to roar with enjoyment.

Caro watched, feeling a spark of happiness kindle and spread through her until she was laughing with him. Finally, he caught her in his arms, kissing her with smiling lips until Caro had to pull away to gasp for breath. Her quick breathing altered as Alec's fingers tore away the gold buttons on her new jacket and vest to cup her breasts through the expensive linen blouse she wore. With a few quick movements he untied her intricately fastened stock and, seconds later, Caro found herself lying half naked in the sweet grass, while the morning sunlight warmed her skin. She pulled Alec's shirt out of his pants, giggling at her efforts to unbutton them, while he speedily removed her cinnamon skirt. Caro delighted in the sensations of his hard, hairy chest on top of her, and the cool, tickling grass under her, wondering if perhaps the entire experience was a dream. Alec kissed her and caressed her until she felt weak with desire, then penetrated with a force that seemed to trigger an explosion inside her. Her nerves felt as if they were being bombarded by a million fiery sparks as she bent against Alec again and again.

Afterward, Caro lay exhausted in his arms, closing her eyes as he traced soft patterns over her face and hair with a lean finger. There was a closeness between them that defied words, and when Alec spoke at last, breaking the spell, his voice sounded regretful.

"Caro? Are you asleep?"

Her warm brown eyes opened slowly as she gave him a dimpled smile.

"No. But I'm dreaming anyway."

"I hate to intrude then, but there's a matter I want to discuss with you. We'd better get some clothes on so I can clear my head!"

After pulling on his breeches and boots, Alec helped Caro into her things. He tied the stock on her blouse, then ruefully eyed the vest and coat, both of which were totally void of buttons.

"I suppose I'll have to replace this habit," he remarked ironically. "It's a good thing I can afford it!"

"Perhaps if you were not so rich you might be forced to cultivate a little patience," Caro laughed.

"Believe me, sweetheart, money is the last thing on my mind when you are close to me! Anyhow, it was worth it. Easily."

"My attire ought to cause a few raised eyebrows when we arrive back at Belle Maison. They'll all think I ran into Ezra Pilquebinder or some equally depraved creature."

"You can tell them that you did," he replied drily, as they settled themselves against a tree. Alec put an arm around Caro and stretched out his long legs.

"I did a lot of thinking last night," he began. "I decided that you and I should get away from here for a short while. You never had a honeymoon and I think that the time alone would be beneficial to our relationship. We've been through a lot since our marriage—and before, Lord knows—I'd like to get away from all outside influences for a while. What do you think?"

Caro was beaming. "I think it's the most splendid idea I've ever heard! Where will we go?"

"I have to make a trip back up to Connecticut to

clear up the business with that farm, and I thought you could accompany me. Afterward, if you feel like it, we might sail to France." His voice was deliberately casual. "As a matter of fact, I have been considering the idea of making the journey up the coast by boat. Would you like that?"

Cheeks flushed with excitement, Caro exclaimed, "Like it? I'd love it! What sort of a boat would we go on?"

"Well, I've been engaged in a little project with Father to outfit one of the privateers as something of a luxury craft. We've put in the finest woodwork, paper hangings, furniture—every comfort of home. There are only two cabins with beds, so it lends itself to romance, and to swift travel." He stopped, rubbing his jaw. "The only drawback is the danger involved. Sea travel is not renowned for its safety—that's why hardly anyone sails. The risk is considerable, and there are numerous shipwrecks on the rocks along this coast."

"Oh, Alec, I would feel secure with you no matter where we were. I think you lead a charmed life."

White teeth gleamed as he replied, "For your sake, let us hope that is the case." Then his tone grew more serious. "Listen, Caro, there is something else I want to talk to you about. It's a subject I've been meaning to raise for weeks now, but every day has seemed too happy to be shadowed by this—"

Caro's stomach tightened apprehensively as he looked down at her before continuing.

"It's about your past. No—I don't know anything yet, but it's not for a lack of effort on my part. That's the reason we've stayed here all this time; I've been waiting for news."

"News from whom?"

"I have a few people working on this for me—up and down the coast. I'm about ready to call a halt for now, though. It seems that when the war ended, girls were running off by the dozens with men of every persuasion—colonials, redcoats, loyalists, Hessians—you name it. Until the smoke clears and more of them are located, I can't see that we'll be able to learn anything. In the meantime, perhaps you'll be able to make some discoveries on your own in Connecticut. . . . I'm sure the chances are slim that we'll be anywhere near your original home, but it's still a possibility. And it will be a damnsight better than sitting around here!"

"Alec—have you heard any more about Ezra Pilquebinder?" The image that continued to haunt her dreams flashed painfully in her mind.

"I know that he is nowhere near Philadelphia. You know—I'd be half tempted to let this whole business of your past drop if it weren't for him. But I have to get to the bottom of this one way or another. We can't have Pilquebinder hanging over our lives forever, especially when we don't know what his part in all this means. . . ."

He was looking off into the distance, his jaw set thoughtfully.

"You know," Caro said wistfully, "I used to think that I was incomplete because I didn't know what my background was. I thought that was the reason that I was so mixed up all the time and that if I could remember everything, all my problems would clear up. But now I don't really care very much. Of course, I'd like to know—but if I never find out, it will be all right. I have learned that today is what counts. I'm complete now because I have you—you've made me whole."

The concerned expression in Alec's eyes changed as he tipped her chin up and their lips met.

"Ah, sweetheart," he murmured warmly, breaking off at the sight of Ivan prancing out of the trees. He circled around restlessly, tossing his black head, and came to a stop in front of them. Alec eyed the horse in amusement.

"God, you look pleased with yourself! Molly must be too shy to face her mistress right now, eh?"

Ivan neighed, stamping one hoof against the grass, then faced them and showed his large white teeth. Caro burst out laughing.

"Look at him—he's grinning at us! If I didn't know better, I'd swear you two were related! Taking advantage of us innocent females—"

"Please!" Alec broke in. "We already feel guilty enough. The only point of consolation is the realization that you and Molly both love the hell out of it."

Ivan threw back his head and whinnied in agreement.

Chapter Twenty-nine

THE SAME GENTLE ROCKING THAT HASTENED HER sleep at night disturbed Caro's dreams in the morning, and now she came slowly awake. The privateer, which had been rechristened *Enfin Amour,* was the loveliest little boat Caro could imagine. Though considerably smaller, the cabin she and Alec shared was even more comfortably appointed than their bedchamber at Belle Maison. Decorated mainly in a rich dark red, it boasted a huge four-poster hung with velvet drapes and the most beautiful Oriental rug Caro had ever seen. There were great roomy wardrobes, plush wing chairs, and even a kneehole desk for Alec. So far, it had not been touched.

Caro snuggled down into the feather tick, enjoying the softness of the silk sheets against her naked body. Instinctively, she reached out for her husband and came fully awake when she discovered his absence. Sitting up, Caro squinted in the sunlight. It was the first time he had been out of her sight since they had boarded the *Enfin Amour* two nights before, a circumstance she now determined to correct with great haste.

Scrambling out of bed, Caro crossed naked to the wardrobe and extracted a thin satin wrapper which did little to conceal her curves. For a moment, she was swept by a feeling of giddy nausea, but after a few deep breaths it passed. It seemed that the illness had been chasing her for over two weeks, but so far she had eluded all but the most fleeting symptoms. Mind over matter, she thought proudly, heading for the door.

The only other passenger aboard the craft was Pierre, who charted their course by night, and during the day as well when he wasn't sleeping. Caro had quickly taken to the idea of the total privacy they enjoyed at sea, particularly delighting in the chance to wear little or no clothing. Now, she stepped out onto the deck in the sheer wrapper, which clung to her body like gossamer. The sun was like a globe of pale-yellow fire in the cloudless sky, but the breeze from the ocean was cool and refreshing.

Alec stood only a few feet from their cabin, adjusting one of the sails to catch the morning wind. He was shirtless, and an appreciative Caro watched the muscles ripple across his wide, brown back as he worked.

"I thought perhaps you had gone for a swim to cool off after last night," she greeted him.

Alec laughed, turning to meet her dimpled smile. His hair was like polished ebony in the sunlight and the eyes that sparkled in his tanned face were as vividly turquoise as the sea that churned nearby.

"Ah, wench, that idea is tempting." He leaped lightly down to the deck beside her, taking in her appearance with a bold gaze that brought a rush of warm blood to her cheeks. Alec laughed again. "Well, you *should* blush after your conduct last night! Such abandon!"

"Alec, you do bring out the harlot in me."

"I see that you are dressing the part," he teased, sliding lean-muscled arms around her waist. "I gather that life at sea agrees with you?"

"Supremely."

As she spoke, Alec bent to cover her open mouth with his own, and Caro's arms encircled his sun-warmed shoulders and neck. They kissed lazily at first, then more intensely, and a hungry Caro pressed her body nearer. Her breasts swelled against the thin material that separated them from Alec's broad chest until his hand slipped around to her belly to open the wrapper. She could feel his own urgency against her fiery loins and shivered when his head bent to caress her neck, then her breasts, with burning lips.

"I think it is time for breakfast," he whispered hoarsely. As though she were a child, he lifted her into his arms and carried her back to the still-warm bed.

"Heaven could not be more perfect than this," Caro murmured contentedly. Physically satiated, she lay in the shelter of Alec's arms, her face against the ticklish black hair that covered his chest.

"I am inclined to agree," he replied, smiling through the smoke of his cheroot. "In fact, I am tempted to take down the sails and drift for a few days . . . or weeks."

"Oh, let's . . . forever."

"Infant, I fear we would soon starve."

"We could catch fish!"

"That's an interesting thought. But there's the matter of water—"

"We could drink wine! There must be a lifetime supply aboard."

Alec chuckled. "I can see us now, spending the rest of our days here—constantly intoxicated."

"I am intoxicated as it is, without wine. Oh, Alec, I have never been so happy in my life!"

"Nor have I."

He felt something warm and wet drop on his chest. Setting his cheroot aside, he tipped Caro's face up and found her caramel eyes brimming with tears.

"*Chérie*, why do you cry?" He moved down from the pillow to hold her more closely.

"I don't know," she sobbed, pressing her face

against his neck. "I just suddenly felt overcome by it all."

Alec let her cry, thinking of the other impulsive bursts of tears that she had shed of late. More and more, he was convinced that she was pregnant, for he was also aware that there had been intermittent bouts of nausea which she had tried unsuccessfully to hide from him. Twice during the week before they sailed she had actually been physically sick before breakfast, though perfectly healthy in every other way. Was it possible, he wondered, that she did not suspect her condition?

Now, Caro laughed shakily and wiped her eyes on the embroidered edge of the sheet.

"You must imagine that I am becoming a silly female," she said with an embarrassed smile.

Alec grinned, running his brown hands over her silky thighs and hips.

"Female, yes, but never silly."

He slipped his fingers into her honey-colored hair to encircle her neck, drawing her near for a kiss that touched her with its warm intensity.

"Ah, Caro, how I love you."

The farm that Alec had won from Josef Bergman was located in a rather remote area north of New London. It took them nearly a full day to reach it in the heavy coach Alec had hired, and Caro was so tired by the time they arrived that most of her excitement had worn away.

Their night in New London had been less than enjoyable. Both of Alec's friends who lived there were away in Boston and they had been forced to lodge in a shabby inn. Caro almost wished that she had not insisted on sharing a room with her husband, for the bed they slept in was too narrow, its tick filled mostly with crunchy straw. Alec's feet went over the end,

338

and he tossed restlessly most of the night, keeping her awake as well. To make matters worse, they had eaten some rather gamey meat pie in the taproom that evening, and Caro's stomach was in a worse turmoil than usual. All in all, it was a far cry from the idyllic life on board the *Enfin Amour*. As they jounced endlessly over the rutted road, Caro leaned her head against Alec's shoulder and mentally relived all the blissful hours they had spent making love and talking during the voyage. It still amazed her that they had been together constantly for days and never run out of conversation. It had been paradise, but the twenty-four hours that had passed since they reached land had rapidly returned her to reality.

The coach ran over what seemed to Caro to be a boulder, and she bounced away from Alec's shoulder. Putting a hand down to rub her posterior, she remarked wryly:

"These seats leave much to be desired when it comes to long-distance traveling."

Alec flashed her a smile as he said, "We are almost there, *chérie*. Now, our only worry will be the state of the house."

During their journey, he had recalled the entire story of the Bergman farm to her, including all its more puzzling aspects. Since Alec knew there was plenty of furniture there, he had decided that they should stay long enough for him to get to the bottom of the whole mystery. Caro had shared his enthusiasm, but now, as angry gray clouds swelled in the hazy, yellow-tinged sky she felt it diminishing even more.

"You know, Alec, I somehow feel that our lives have been jinxed since we set foot off the *Enfin Amour*. I still say we should have kept on going, around and around the world . . ."

"You might have changed your mind after a few years of nothing but fish and wine," he responded a trifle sardonically. "By the way, I do hope you don't mean to imply that my life is no longer charmed?"

"Well, I hadn't thought of that, but in view of the past day . . ." she giggled as Alec rolled his eyes despairingly. "Anyhow, our immediate need for your good luck has lessened, has it not? I thought that a safe sea voyage was our only worry."

The hulking coach rumbled up an overgrown drive to stop before a two-story frame house. As Alec leaned over his wife to unlatch the door, he replied:

"Let us hope that is the case, my dear."

Hopping out, he helped her down and Caro went to get a closer look at the house while Alec dealt with the driver. He had arranged to purchase two of the horses in the team for use during their stay, and with their baggage there was also a large quantity of provisions. Remembering the cold reception he had received from the neighboring farms on his last trip, Alec was not prepared to take any chances.

Caro shivered in the sultry air, which caused her to feel strangely apprehensive. The clouds that gathered on the horizon were odd-looking, for they seemed to hang suspended, not moving but growing nevertheless. She shook herself and turned to look at the house. It was sadly in need of repair, but its good looks still shone through. The yard was overgrown, the paint peeling, yet a few tulips still managed to struggle up in the weed-ravaged flower bed that ran under the windows.

The house itself was soundly built in a combination saltbox-lean-to-style, with a woodshed connecting the barn to the main building. Caro went nearer to peek in the window when Alec came up behind her to grasp her shoulders, startling her so that her heart beat wildly.

"I cannot imagine why I am so jumpy," she exclaimed, all the color drained from her face. "There is something about this place that disquiets me." Her eyes were distant, then she managed to focus, laughing nervously. "But I am being foolish—it is probably only the weather, and the aftereffects of that depressing inn."

Alec watched her for a few seconds as she fidgeted with the ribbons of her bonnet, then decided she was probably right. Since Caro's emotions had been playing havoc with her for some time, her latest display of odd behavior did not bother him as it once might have.

Firmly taking her arm, he unlocked the door and waved her inside. The parlor in which they stood was furnished quite tastefully, with well-made pieces including a beautiful wing chair worked in crewel. A heavy braided rug lay across the planked floor, leading to the handsome fireplace with its hip-raised panels. Caro viewed the scene uneasily; her head had begun to ache. For his part, Alec strode through the rest of the rooms on the lower level and Caro managed to follow in his wake. When they came into the spacious kitchen, he threw open the cupboards. Keen turquoise eyes scanned the contents and he let out an oath, scowling.

"This is damned peculiar. I deliberately left certain things out when I departed from here last October and everything has been moved. Not only that, there is food here!" He waved an arm at the contents of the shelves. "Look at this—fresh provisions!"

Caro closed her eyes tightly in an effort to banish the pain that was cutting through her head. Her face was bleached with pain and fatigue, and Alec moved to put his arms around her.

"Sweetheart, you look terrible! You had better go upstairs and rest while I see to the rest of these details."

"No," she said weakly. "I want to see the rest of the house. I am . . . curious."

341

With every step she took and each new sight, her suffering increased. Finally, she loosened Alec's arm from her waist and sank down in the exquisitely embroidered chair. Seeing his look of concern, she tried to smile.

"I cannot understand what's come over me . . ." Nervously, she glanced around the cozy, dust-covered parlor, running her fingers over the texture of the crewelwork on the arm of her chair.

"Caro, I insist that you go up and lie down. Have a good nap." Helping her up, he held her close and untied her bonnet, letting it fall down her back. His face against her sweet-smelling hair, he reminded himself of his theory about her condition.

"You are fine, *chérie*. Don't worry." Then his eyes flickered to the window, taking in the view outside. "Listen, Caro, I've a mind to go visiting before it gets dark. I'm afraid it will rain all day tomorrow and there are some pressing matters that I'd like to get out of the way tonight. I'll go mad if I have to wait any longer for the answers to my questions!"

"But, Alec—you said that no one would talk to you last time! What makes you so sure they will now?"

"Because, God damn it, I'm going to make them! I'm out of patience and I want this matter cleared up once and for all so I can figure out what to do about this place! I have been sure all along that Bergman had family, and the way this house looks each time I arrive leads me to believe that they're around here yet. Perhaps they hide for fear that I would put them out, but if I could just find them, I would gladly *give* them the place!"

Caro's head was pounding so hard that she could barely speak.

"You don't think someone is living here *now*, do you?"

"Obviously not at the moment, considering the dust,

and probably not permanently because of the threat of me. Don't worry, before I leave you alone, I'll check the entire house—and you'll bolt the door behind me. I'm sure you'll be quite safe, though—I won't be gone long and, besides, anyone related to Bergman would have to be a good person. He was an extraordinary man."

His words echoed painfully in her ears, and by the time he had finished speaking, Caro was past listening or thinking. Alec speedily searched the house, then she locked the door behind him and gratefully climbed the narrow wooden stairway to the bedchambers. There were three, one of which was obviously a nursery. The middle room was very feminine, decorated in yellow and white. It smelled of neglect, but under the dust and sun stains, Caro could see that in the past someone had taken a great deal of trouble to make the room pretty. Oddly, her hands began to perspire as she stood in the doorway, and though her instincts told her to back out, she walked inside, almost against her will. Slowly, she moved around the room, touching things and trying to think in spite of the pain that was searing her mind. When she rounded the musty, unused canopy bed, something caught her eye that caused a momentary explosion in her brain.

A wrinkled corner of familiar bottle-green silk showed from under the counterpane. Caro's hands were trembling as she bent to pull out a dress, which was lacking the back half of the overskirt. Pictures burned in her mind of that day in October when she and Alec had investigated the green silk bundle and its contents, and she sat down heavily on the side of the bed, pressing the hem of her gown against her breastbone. She tried to think but her head hurt so much that tears of pain and confusion burned her eyelids.

"Can this mean that I come from this house?" she

wondered at last, faced with the inevitable, yet absurd conclusion.

Suddenly, a noise in the doorway startled her and she spun on the bed to meet the light, sunken eyes of Ezra Pilquebinder.

Chapter Thirty

⌒⌒

ALEC RODE ONE OF THE RATHER SWAYBACKED HORSES that had come with the coach, jogging across a fallow field toward a tree-encircled farmhouse that stood in the distance. The sky appeared almost green as the heavy clouds multiplied, and he wondered how far away the storm was.

Outside his house, Noah Willow scattered feed for a flock of eager chickens. He was anxious to finish his chores and be assured of shelter before the rain broke. So great was his preoccupation with the sultry, forbidding weather, he did not notice the horse and rider approaching the farm until they came through the trees just a few yards away.

Alec leaped to the ground, elated at having caught the man outdoors. As recognition dawned on Noah Willow, his leathery face became a mask of fear and he turned to run. However, his rawboned legs were no match for Alec's and he promptly found himself caught in a grip of steel.

"Old man," Alec said sharply, "you need not fear me. I mean you no harm!"

"You're the one!" Willow stuttered. "You're the madman! Please, let me go——"

"What absurdity is this? Who has said that I am mad?"

In a panic of self-preservation, Willow answered

345

without thinking: "Why, the new owner of the Bergman farm! He warned us that you'd come and try to 'usurp' him, but we didn't think you'd be back again—'specially after so long!"

"Have you lost your wits? *I* am the owner of the Bergman farm! I served with Josef Bergman in the war and before he died, he deeded the place to me—"

"No," Noah Willow promptly interrupted, "the other man's got the deed. He showed it to me when he came to warn us."

"The hell he did! I'd like to find this man, for those papers were stolen the night Bergman died. I must ask you to trust me and tell me all you know—it is imperative that I find out the truth."

"Well . . ." Willow frowned, and the expression seemed to lengthen his already long face. "You don't seem mad—in truth, your face seems more honest than the other's."

"Then for God's sake, tell me! Who is this other man?"

"Oh, I couldn't say what his name was. Somethin' strange, as I recall. But he came here, shortly after Yorktown, I'd say. No, wait . . . it was that spring. He said the farm was his, showed us the deed. He was mighty interested in findin' Kristy—that's Kristin, Josef's daughter. We told him that she'd been in France, in a convent school through most of the war. Josef did well on that farm, and when he went in the army, he sent her over there to keep her safe. Sweet girl . . ."

"And?" Alec prompted.

"Well, he left then. This man. Kristy come home shortly after—got back from France all on her own—and we told her about him, but she weren't afraid. Spirited girl. She lived right there for better'n a year—raised her own food and animals. Then, last autumn, this fella come back. I got the feelin' he'd been searchin' for her in France all that time! Well, he paid us another visit then. Told us Josef had asked *him* to marry Kristy and said that we should be on the lookout for this madman who was tryin' to get her *and* the farm away from him."

"That's me, I gather," Alec supplied sarcastically.

"You fit the description! Anyways, he said he was goin' to warn all the other neighbors, then goin' to take Kristy away to keep her safe from you, and that's the last I seen of them both." He paused, scratching the bald top of his head. " 'Cept, I told Ma the other day that I swore I saw him outside the house. Thought maybe he and Kristy come back to live . . ."

Alec's eyes were sharp. "Tell me, what did this man look like?"

"An ugly little fella—lots of red scars on his face. Ma's said more'n once that he reminds her o' one o' them lizards!"

From a long way off, Caro could hear a hoarse, nasal voice speaking while fingers worked at the hooks on her bodice. By sheer effort of will, she forced herself back to consciousness, opening her eyes to find Ezra Pilquebinder's horrible face only inches away from hers.

"Ah!" he whined, yellow teeth showing in a twisted smile. "You have decided to join the party, I see!"

"How did you get here?" she asked dazedly.

"Oh, I have a key, to be sure. I have been waiting for you for weeks, my dear! At last I got word that you were on your way, so I retired to the barn to wait. I must say, you certainly took your time. But now—I have dreamed of this moment for longer than you would believe, my sweet. Finding you here on your own bed was like the fulfillment of a dream—it could be autumn all over again, only this time the outcome will be different! I knew you would come back to me —even at the risk of bringing along that—that—"

The red blotches on his face darkened as he thought

347

of Alec, and Caro felt him tear open the remaining hooks on her basque. The pain in her head was gone, and now everything was pouring into her brain in a kaleidoscope of lost memories. Frantically, she tried to compose herself enough to smile stiffly up at Pilquebinder, inwardly gagging at the odor of his stale breath. His fingers stopped their groping at her chemise as he registered clear surprise.

"Yes, you're right," she choked, her heart pounding so hard it seemed on the verge of breaking. "I am so anxious to talk to you, but first I must have some water to quench my thirst. I am so dry—"

"Of course, my sweet," he exclaimed, jumping to his feet, then stopping to regard her with suspicion. "This isn't another of your tricks, is it? Well, just to be on the safe side, I'd better see to it that you can't escape me this time."

He bent over and pulled the ribbons from her hair. With swift, strong movements he tied them around her ankles so that they cut into her flesh. Then, he ripped the rest of the hem from the bottle-green silk dress and bound her wrists in front, his eyes lingering hotly on her breasts which strained against the thin chemise.

"I'll be right back, my sweet," he rasped, and ran from the room. Caro's head was too full of the past to have any room for escape plans. Closing her eyes, she remembered her childhood in that very room, and vaguely she recalled the early years spent in the nursery next door. All the pieces fit now—she knew her real name—Kristin—and she could recall completely her father, Josef. She felt a familiar throb of pain remembering the death of her beautiful mother when she was twelve. After that, there had been intermittent seasons of school away from the farm, followed by four years in a French convent school when her father left to fight for the patriots' cause.

Caro's mind skimmed over memories of her return to America and the news of her father's death as she pondered the role Ezra Pilquebinder had played in her past. She recalled now that Noah and Isabel Willow had told her shortly after her arrival at the farm that a man had been there looking for her, saying that he was the new owner of the property and her own guardian. At first, she had been perplexed and alarmed, but after a year passed with no further sign of the man, she had begun to relax.

Then, in October of 1783, he had suddenly reappeared, turning her life upside down. Pilquebinder showed her a letter in her father's hand which asked that the man in question take over his farm and, if possible, marry his daughter. It also gave a listing of Bergman's possessions that was so complete it convinced Caro of the authenticity of the letter.

"You are a remarkable man," Bergman had written, "and I pray to God that if events warrant your receipt of this missive you will carry out my plans—nay, dreams—for you and my Kristin. I know what is said of you, but I was certain from the first moment I laid eyes on you that you were the perfect man for my daughter."

Caro had been horrified by these sentiments, for she had found Pilquebinder unspeakably repulsive. Convinced that her father had been mad, and frightened to death by the perverted passion that constantly glowed in the pale eyes of her new "guardian," she had snatched the first opportunity to flee.

After consuming a huge quantity of port that first evening at the farm, Pilquebinder inadvertently fell asleep before the fire. Caro went to work. Dressing in the clothes of a former stablehand, she hastily assembled a bundle of belongings and rode away from the farm on the back of her own mare, Molly.

Now she lay back on her old bed, totally at the mercy of Ezra Pilquebinder. She had come full circle. I walked right into this trap, she thought in stunned disbelief, and Alec unknowingly led me! God, if only

I hadn't hit that tree branch, my escape would have been good and I'd have known enough never to come back here! Then she realized that she would not have met or married Alec, either, and a bittersweet pain stabbed her. She was trying to figure out how he fit into the maze of events concerning the farm and her father when the door swung open to admit Pilquebinder. He carried a glass of thick port, which Caro was forced to choke down. Afterward, he put the goblet aside and turned back to her bodice.

"You look as frightened as a cornered doe, my sweet," he sneered while stripping her clothes down to her waist. A sour taste rose in Caro's throat when he touched her breasts with clammy fingers. She gagged at the sight of his reeking mouth coming toward hers.

"Let us pass the time as we await the innocent arrival of Major Beauvisage. After I dispose of him, I anticipate a long night of much-dreamt-of pleasure with you, dear Kristin."

"D-dispose?"

"But of course—after all, you cannot become my wife until you are his widow!" he chuckled gleefully. "And, I cannot think of any man whom I could take greater pleasure in killing. Perhaps you would like to watch?"

His hands roamed over her breasts as he spoke and Caro saw his tongue dart across his lips as he prepared to kiss her.

"Please! Tell me why you should want to kill Alec! And what makes you imagine that it will be easy?"

"Easy?" he sneered. "It will be effortless. Our ill-fated major will come home to his dear wife, knocking gently on the door he so carefully instructed her to bolt. Only it will not be opened by you; I shall be the one to greet him—for the last time!" Pilquebinder's laughter was insane and Caro went ice cold at the simplicity of his plot. "Do you think that I resent the man merely because he married you?" he con-

350

tinued, pushing up her skirts to explore the rest of her body. "No, my dove, it goes back much further. I have known—and hated—the major for many years. He was always so sure of himself in the army, always the one to get the best assignments—the ones I desired. He was friends with every general, hobnobbing with Kosciuszko, and surrounded by women. There was even one who traveled with him—did you know that?"

Caro was bathed in a cold sweat of terror and her mouth seemed stuffed with cotton. Pilquebinder's hands crawled over her legs and belly until she thought she would scream from the sheer horror of it.

"Well," he went on in an oily tone, "I thought that I had my revenge when Bergman died and the major was so preoccupied that he didn't have a chance to get all those papers—until I had already confiscated them." Caro's mouth dropped open as realization dawned at last. "It was quite ironic that you two came together anyway! Too much so, if you ask me. Fortunately, I do not believe in fate, unless it is a fate that I make myself. I was always determined to get you back after you left me here, but I didn't know I would have to see Beauvisage dead until later."

At the sight of the growing bulge in Pilquebinder's breeches, Caro desperately sought to stall for time.

"What—what do you mean?"

He was ripping her clothes away completely, a thin line of saliva running from his mouth.

"Why, my brother, of course. Quintus. One of the men Beauvisage killed at that farm in New York last fall."

"Oh, no," she groaned, thinking, What madness!

He got up for a moment, untying her feet, then refastening them to the bedposts. Caro was sick with humiliation. "Quintus was living in Germany when the Hessians were hired and he decided to go along. After the war, he and a comrade deserted and I ran into them near here last October as I searched for you. They promised to keep an eye out. Quintus found you, didn't he? I reached that farm eventually, I saw the blood in the barn and my brother's own sash—and I found plenty of personal belongings inside the house that the two of you so carelessly left behind. It was not hard to trace you then. . . ."

As he spoke, he crouched over her on the bed and Caro squeezed her eyes shut, praying for unconsciousness. His putrid mouth was pressing against hers, slobbering over her breasts as something stiff probed between her spread legs.

"Dear God," Caro whispered, while Pilquebinder fumbled with the fastenings on his breeches.

Suddenly there was an ear-splitting crash accompanied by shattered bits of glass spraying in every direction, while out of the corner of her eye, Caro saw Alec's expensive boots sweeping through the window. His face was black with rage as he grabbed Pilquebinder by the hair to wrench him up in the air and off Caro. Just as fast, the smaller man drew a long, evil-looking knife from a hidden sheath, while Alec apparently had been carrying one all along.

"Prepare to die, you dog!" Alec said in a low growl.

Pilquebinder was extremely agile and wiry, and now his mouth twisted confidently as he faced his nemesis.

"Well, Major, I have been looking forward to this opportunity for a long time! You have deserved to die all along—God was on my side when he contrived to cast you as Kristin's saviour, for that has allowed me to be alone with the two people I feel most strongly about."

Alec's eyes narrowed. "I have no time for your riddles, Pilquebinder. Let us see this ended."

Clutching their knives, the two men began to circle each other warily. There was a maniacal light in Pilquebinder's odd, yellowish eyes, while Alec's own face was reckless and cool as always in the face of danger.

Caro lay on the bed, surrounded by the shreds of her clothing and trembling with fear. As she watched the two men, their bodies wary and poised for attack, she began to act without even formulating a plan in her mind. It was a struggle for her to sit up with her legs at right angles, but she managed to do so. Then, as Pilquebinder circled just one more step, his back was to her and the bed and she reached out with her bound hands, pushing at him with every ounce of strength she possessed. Alec stepped neatly aside as Ezra Pilquebinder stumbled, tripped over a footstool, and plunged forward on top of the dressing table— and his own knife.

Chapter Thirty-one

THE STORM BROKE THAT EVENING, TORRENTS OF RAIN rattling the windowpanes in the parlor. Alec had built them a blazing fire and now Caro sat beside him on her mother's settee, her head resting against the warm, muscular strength of his chest.

"I want to leave as soon as we can," she said slowly. "This house makes me feel like a ghost; it's as though I died and have come back now from another life."

"You have," Alec commented drily, lifting the brandy snifter to his mouth with his free hand. Then he tried to get a look at Caro's face. She was only now beginning to come out of the shock that had followed her near-rape and Ezra Pilquebinder's gruesome death, and Alec had been briefly afraid that she would retreat back into her amnesia. He had held her most of the time since, sensing that she really needed to collect her thoughts and sort them out. Now she was beginning to sound quite clear-headed and Alec was greatly relieved.

"I am hungry," she whispered.

"Wonderful!" he declared, setting her on her feet as he stood up. "Let us repair to the kitchen."

Back in that room, Caro was pensive while Alec clanged pots together and made a great show of cooking the meal. She was hard pressed to laugh, however, for all her emotions, thoughts, and nerves seemed to be saturated by a nonstop influx of memories. It was one thing to come to terms with and set aside her abuse at the hands of Ezra Pilquebinder, but quite another to stop the recollections of nearly twenty years which seemed to be returning to her now in full measure.

At the back of the kitchen stood a sturdy drop-leaf table, surrounded by five bow-back chairs. Caro wandered over to them, dusting the wood with a scrap of cloth she had picked up on the stairway.

"My mother used to keep five chairs here in case someone we knew—a couple, perhaps—happened to drop by during a meal. People knew that she loved company, so they did visit often."

Alec looked up from the eggs he was cooking, letting her see his interest.

"She sounds like a wonderful woman. I wish that I could have known her."

"Nothing was the same after Mama died." Caro bit her lip. "The heart went out of this house and Papa was simply lost."

"Caro, that reminds me. I know I've already repeated most of that enlightening conversation I had with Noah Willow, but I've just remembered something else. He mentioned that you were here for over a year alone—and that you came back from France by yourself! How in the hell did you manage?"

It was the closest she had come to laughing all evening. "Alec, you certainly do underestimate me! I can accomplish anything I want or need to do on my own if I decide to. I came back from France because I wanted to discover what had happened to my father; if I had stayed over there and waited, I would probably still be in the dark—and a nun by now! As to living here alone, that was easy enough. I grew my own vegetables, chopped my own wood, and forced myself to kill livestock for meat. My parents taught me well during my childhood; I simply copied all the things I had seen them do. It was lonely sometimes, but I visited the neighbors a great deal and I read constantly. A book or more a day. I was happy and learned to know myself and my own capabilities and limitations, but . . ."

"But?" Alec glanced up as he heaped food upon their plates, lifting a black brow.

"But, I'll admit that there were moments when, deep in my secret self, I dreamed of the dark, handsome rogue who would come to carry me off on his horse."

"Egad!" His turquoise eyes went wide with mock surprise. "You really do get what you set out for!"

His playful banter relaxed her and the hot food helped as well. Alec was encouraged by her appetite, watching her eat voraciously as he lit a cluster of candles to set on the table. When he sat down with his own plate, he found himself staring at Caro, watching the play of the candlelight over her loose, burnished hair. Her delicate features were etched in gold against the black backdrop of the kitchen window, but there was a troubled look in her eyes that betrayed her thoughts.

"You know," she murmured wonderingly, "it still seems so hard to believe that I was actually the girl we *said* I was—all along!"

Alec's mouth quirked. "I've been kicking myself about that these past hours. Truth to tell, I really should have thought of it before. If I'd known for certain that Bergman had a daughter your age, I'd probably have at least suspected. Now I can remember him telling me about you, but at the time I thought they were merely the delusions of a proud father. Lord knows it wouldn't have been the first time I listened to those!"

"But they weren't delusions?"

He grinned. "Actually, I'm afraid he may have underrated you, *chérie*."

"Alec, I forgot to ask you—how did you get up to that window? It looked like you were flying in mid-air, and my bedroom is on the second floor!" She paused to swallow a mouthful of bread and butter. "Also, *why* did you come that way? That creature was all prepared to kill you when you knocked at the front door."

"Well, fortunately for us, I am not quite as dull-witted as Pilquebinder liked to think. After learning what I did from Farmer Willow, I was not about to take any chances.

"As for my entrance—it is easily explained. I climbed on the woodshed, then up the slope of the roof to the top of the house. I could hear his voice in your room and from there it was merely a matter of swinging down and through the window."

Caro put a hand over her eyes. "It's a miracle you weren't killed!"

Amused, Alec replied, "That wasn't likely. I seem to be quite surefooted."

"You know, this may sound quite bloodthirsty on my part, but I am so glad that that man is dead. I am only afraid now that it's some kind of horrible mistake. Are you positive, Alec, that he is *really*—"

"Yes, Caro," he replied in a firm voice that dispelled all her fears. "As a matter of fact, when I left him in the barn he was stone cold." Reaching across the table, he put his brown hand over her smaller one and gazed at her searchingly. This was as close as they had come yet to discussing the ordeal she had suffered on the bed upstairs. *"Chérie* . . . are you sure you're all right? You wouldn't lie to me about this, thinking to spare me?"

"No. I could never live with that kind of secret." She met his eyes squarely. "What . . . happened was ghastly, but it could have been worse. The important thing is the outcome. He is dead and you are here beside me, loving me . . ."

"How true!" he smiled, lifting her tiny hand to his lips. "Have I ever told you how brave you are? And resourceful? And strong-willed?"

"Do stop! Would you have me puffed up with conceit as well?" Caro turned back to the few bites of food left on her plate to hide a blush, and as she ate, another thought occurred to her.

"Alec, I must tell you the things *he* said when we were alone. About you!" She went on to relate the story of their apparent association in the army, Pilquebinder's jealousy, and finally the identity of the yellow-eyed man in the barn.

"Damn!" Alec said in some amazement when she had finished. "I have no recollection of him before the day he came to Belle Maison. But, now I know how that Hessian weasel came to call out my name before he died. That has always puzzled me." Again he cursed in frustration. "How blind I have been! The truth has been before me all along, but I could not see it. My own dim-witted stupidity nearly cost us all we hold dear—"

"Do not blame yourself—you had no way of knowing! How could you have guessed that he should be *here* of all places, waiting for us all these weeks? I still can hardly believe it is all true!"

"Neither can I," he returned grimly, standing up. "I'll confess that it is a real weight off my mind to have all this cleared up. This has certainly proved to be an enlightening, if dangerous trip!"

They were walking arm in arm back to the parlor when Caro stopped and looked up at Alec's face.

"Do you know the part that really fascinates me? Finding out that Papa actually planned our marriage before we ever met. It makes me feel so good to learn that he knew and approved of you." She smiled ruefully. "Actually, I quite feared for his sanity when that creature showed me the letter Papa had meant for you to receive."

They were silent for a time as Caro gathered up a quantity of plush quilts in order to prepare a bed for them. They spread three comforters over the braided rug before the fire and kept two more aside for covers, adding pillows as a final touch.

Alec tenderly undressed her and tucked her in. Caro watched as he peeled off his own clothing, his lean, powerful body silhouetted by the leaping orange flames. Then, gratefully, she found the security of his embrace, pressing her ear against the brown warmth of his chest to hear the steady beat of his heart. Hard-muscled arms encircled her as he inquired gently:

"Would you like to talk? Perhaps it would help you to sort out all those new memories."

Slowly, then, Alec drew her out, and for over an hour Caro told him of the events of her life. When she finally reached the end of her story—her ride through the woods in October—she felt strangely purged. The tapestry of their life together had finally been completed and Caro was conscious of a warm peacefulness within her that spread to the depths of her soul.

When he knew that she had finished speaking, Alec kissed her forehead and moved across the quilts to stoke the dying fire. Caro thought that he looked like a classic statue cast in bronze as he leaned before the flames. When he turned back, he was momentarily surprised to see that Caro's face was lit with a radiant smile.

"Well," he commented drily, "you look quite smug and pleased—much like your usual self! May I inquire the reason for that blinding smile?"

He returned to her side, leaning against the pillows and lifting her onto his lap. As his arms encircled her tiny waist, Caro pressed her face to his gleaming black hair. She longed to be able to soak him up like a sponge.

"I am so happy, and so lucky. I feel at peace now

that all those doors have been opened and the questions in our lives have been answered."

"I'm glad, *chérie*." As he lightly caressed the nape of her neck, his eyes were distant and hard. In his mind, he knew that Caro was right about the episode with Pilquebinder, but he could not forget. Every time he remembered that first sight of them—Caro with her legs tied spread-eagle to the bedposts, her nakedness, and Pilquebinder's foul body over all, his mouth touching her sweet breasts—Alec burned with rage. The man's death had been too merciful.

Caro felt him stiffen against her and drew back to search his chiseled face before asking, "Is something wrong?"

His eyes were raw with suffering. "I wish that I could be as resilient as you are," he said softly.

"Think of the good things, Alec. Be grateful that we are together now, and free from the threat of that man."

Alec kissed her then, bending her against the long muscles of his arm as he savored her honeyed lips. Caro clung to him, relaxing, responding ardently and shivering when his mouth traveled down the soft column of her neck.

Gently, Alec caressed her taut, swelling breasts, conscious of nature's changes. In that moment, he knew what could do much to heal the wounds within him and Caro. This was the time to tell her.

Caro, however, was not in a conversational mood, for his lips had lit a fast-spreading flame inside of her. She yearned for more, ached to feel the touch of his hands and mouth—yet beyond her physical longing was an emotional need as well. When Alec eased her back into the pillows, but attempted to draw away and speak, she held fast to his neck, kissing him until his arms enfolded her to his hard chest. Caro opened her legs beneath the burning hardness at his loins. She was eager for the total ecstasy of their union, feeling somehow that the white heat of this fulfillment would burn away the last vestiges of filth and debasement that lingered on from her ordeal with Pilquebinder.

They made love with a mutual intensity bordering on savagery. Afterward, Caro lay panting and perspiring beneath him, while Alec grinned irrepressibly.

"I was going to say something a few moments ago, but you just couldn't allow me to get a word in edgewise, could you?" he chided.

Caro pretended to be ashamed. "I'm so sorry, dear. I can't imagine what possessed me. Do speak now."

"Thank you. I wanted—"

Suddenly Caro's eyes lit up and she put out a hand to cover his mouth. "Wait! I've just remembered something. Can I please talk first? Let me out—I have a surprise—"

"For God's sake!" Alec complained, trying to look upset as he moved over. Caro crawled onto the floor, then scrambled up to run to a large secretary against the far wall. She searched inside for only a moment before giving a glad cry. When she was back beside him on their makeshift bed, Alec could see that she was holding a gold-framed miniature.

"What is this?" he inquired, affectionately sarcastic. "A baby picture?"

"No, silly." She held up the miniature, staring at it with him. The picture showed a beautiful honey-haired woman with Caro's laughing brown eyes and dimpled smile.

"It's you!" Alec said, but then his dark brows drew together. "Except—"

"It is my mother. Wasn't she lovely? I seem to have neglected to mention the fact that her name was . . . Caroline."

Startled, Alec glanced up to meet her misty look. "Actually," he said with an ironic smile, "I don't suppose I should be surprised. This day seems fraught with coincidence!"

Caro beamed, tilting her face to display an exquisite profile. "Do you think that I am as pretty as she was?"

He pretended to consider the matter, scratching raven hair as he peered at her from every angle. Caro pouted.

"Alec!"

His face broke into a dazzling smile that melted her heart. Laughing, he pressed her back into the pillows and kissed the fragrant softness of her neck.

"My love, to me your beauty is matchless." Then, bracing himself on lean forearms, he looked down into her face. "May I *please* have my turn now? No interruptions?"

"I promise," Caro giggled, tracing a finger through the black hair on his chest.

"Oddly enough, it happens that my surprise also concerns the subject of mothers."

As he spoke, Alec felt his gaze being pulled toward the seemingly luminous miniature which lay beside them on the satin quilt, and he met the radiant, smiling eyes of the first Caroline. He bent his head down to his wife and their warm, loving kiss sealed the life they would share . . . happily . . . and forever.